W9-BSR-470

So empty your pockets and we'll take care of the rest. Throw out your rules, these are' ROAD RULES.

# Welcome to Road

## How to Navigate This Book

PAGE NUMBER

POINT AND DATE OF DEPARTURE

MISSION

SYNOPSIS OF EVENTS

THESE HIGHLIGHTS FROM THE SHOW CREATE A VISUAL DIARY OF THE TRIP

## KEY TO SYMBOLS

Ⓜ ...................................mission

JOB ..........................................job

🪧 ...............................welcome to

🔻 .....................................sidetrip

🏠 ..........................hometown stop

❓ ...........................................lost

💰 ..............................money trail

🛏 ..........................sleep in motel

⛺ .......................sleep at campsite

🚐 .........................sleep in Winnie

💧° .........days since last shower

〰 .....empty Winnie septic tank

😈 ...............scamming/cheating

🐰 .....................................roadkill

⚔ .....................................conflict

💀 ....................................danger

♥ ..................................romance

CUMULATIVE MILES TRAVELED ON THE TRIP

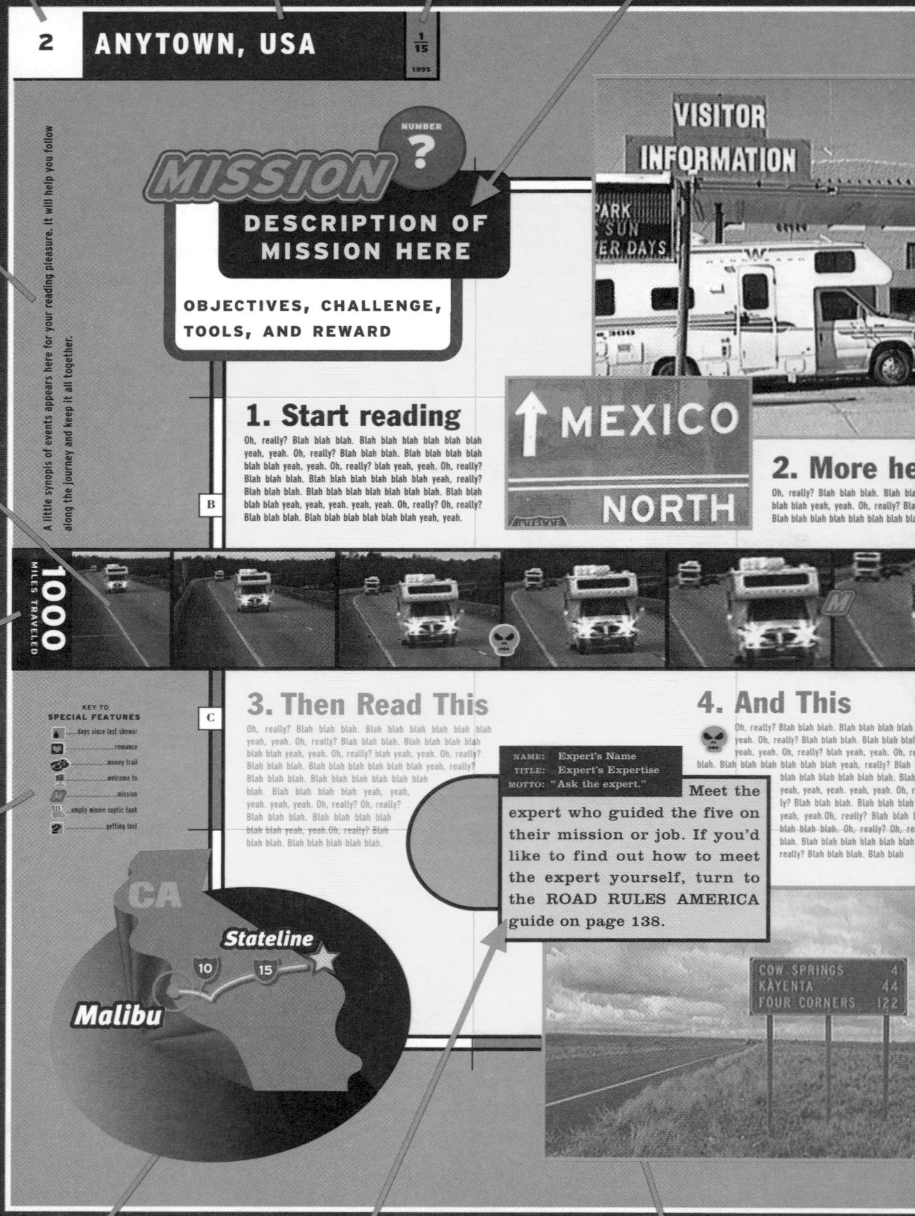

**2** ANYTOWN, USA

1/15 1999

A little synopsis of events appears here for your reading pleasure. It will help you follow along the journey and keep it all together.

**MISSION** NUMBER **?**

DESCRIPTION OF MISSION HERE

OBJECTIVES, CHALLENGE, TOOLS, AND REWARD

VISITOR INFORMATION

PARK SUN FOUR DAYS

### 1. Start reading

Oh, really? Blah blah blah. Blah blah blah blah blah blah blah blah. Oh, really? Blah blah blah. Oh, really? Blah yeah, yeah, really? Blah blah blah. Blah blah blah blah blah yeah, yeah, yeah, yeah. Oh, really? Oh, really? Blah blah blah. Blah blah blah blah blah blah blah. Blah blah blah.

⬆ MEXICO NORTH

### 2. More he

Oh, really? Blah blah blah. Bla blah blah blah yeah, yeah. Oh, re Blah blah blah blah blah blah

**1000** MILES TRAVELED

Ⓜ

### 3. Then Read This

KEY TO SPECIAL FEATURES

Oh, really? Blah blah blah. Blah blah blah blah yeah, yeah. Oh, really? Blah blah blah. Blah blah blah blah blah yeah, yeah. Oh, really? Blah yeah, yeah. Oh, really? Blah yeah, yeah, really? Blah blah blah. Blah blah blah blah blah yeah, yeah, yeah. Oh, really? Oh, really? Blah blah blah. Blah blah blah blah yeah, yeah. Oh, really? Blah blah blah blah blah.

NAME: Expert's Name
TITLE: Expert's Expertise
MOTTO: "Ask the expert."

Meet the expert who guided the five on their mission or job. If you'd like to find out how to meet the expert yourself, turn to the ROAD RULES AMERICA guide on page 138.

### 4. And This

Oh, really? Blah blah blah. Blah blah yeah. Oh, really? Blah blah blah. Blah blah blah blah blah yeah, yeah. Oh, re blah. Blah blah blah blah. Oh, really? Blah blah blah blah blah blah blah. Oh, yeah, yeah, yeah, yeah, yeah. Oh, ly? Blah blah blah. Blah blah blah blah yeah, yeah. Oh, really? Blah blah blah. Oh, really? Oh, really? Blah blah blah. really? Blah blah blah. Blah blah blah

CA

Stateline

10 — 15 ★

Malibu

COW SPRINGS 4
KAYENTA 44
FOUR CORNERS 122

EXPERT TAKE

PICTURES OF WHAT YOU DIDN'T SEE ON THE SHOW

THE ACTUAL HIGHWAYS AND INTERSTATES TRAVELED ON THESE PAGES

# Rules Road Trips

CLUE

TRAVEL PAUSED ON THIS
DATE AT THIS PLACE

THIS IS THEIR STORY,
NO HOLDS BARRED,
BELIEVE IT OR NOT

## Five strangers–

Shelly, Los, Mark, Kit, and Allison–arrive on a windy hillside in Malibu, California, remove their blindfolds, surrender their money and credit cards, and climb inside a 25-foot-long motor home. There, they find a computerized mapping system, a bounty of athletic equipment, a gasoline credit card, and a little cash. What lies ahead is a total mystery, the beginning of an awesome adventure.

Ten months later, a second set of five strangers–Devin, Emily, Timmy, Effie, and Christian–converge at the southernmost point of the US. Again, they pile into a stocked motor home and drive across the country in pursuit of daredevil missions, a sometimes-honest buck, and the always-elusive Final Destination.

Now, with this book, you can follow the very routes taken by the ROAD RULES casts, relive their most hair-raising missions, and get the inside scoop on the hottest scenes around the country. But don't take off yet, there's more: If you think you'd make an ideal Road Ruler, we have a mission designed just for you, right here in these pages. All it takes to answer the riddles we've written for you is a good sense of direction and, oh yeah, a brilliant mind. So buckle up and read on– you're about to experience the show, and the American road, at a whole new speed.

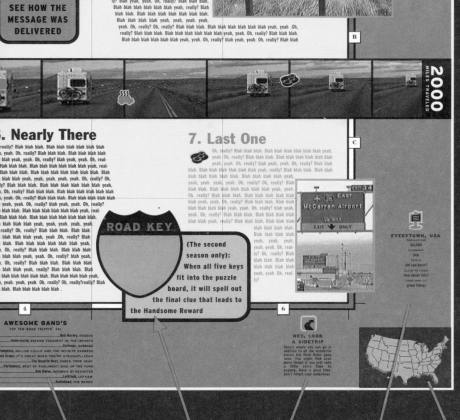

OTHER TOWN, USA  3

### CLUE

THIS LEADS OUR TRAVELERS IN THE DIRECTION OF THEIR NEXT MISSION OR DESTINATION; INSIDE THE CIRCLE YOU'LL SEE HOW THE MESSAGE WAS DELIVERED

### 5. This is Fun

Oh, really? Blah blah blah. Blah blah blah yeah, yeah. Oh, really? Blah blah blah. Blah blah blah blah blah blah yeah. Oh, really? blah yeah? blah yeah, yeah. Oh, really? Blah blah blah. Blah. Blah blah blah blah blah blah yeah, real-ly? Blah blah blah blah, yeah, yeah, yeah. Oh, really? yeah. Oh, really? Blah blah blah blah blah blah. yeah, yeah, yeah. Oh, really? Blah blah. Blah blah blah blah blah blah, real-ly? Blah yeah yeah. Oh, really? Blah blah blah. Blah blah blah blah blah yeah, really? Blah blah blah. Blah blah blah blah blah blah yeah, yeah, yeah. really? Oh, really? Oh, really? Blah blah blah blah, really? Blah blah blah. Blah blah blah yeah. Oh, really? Blah blah blah. Blah blah blah blah blah blah yeah, yeah. Oh, really? Blah blah

SUNSET CRATER
VOLCANO
1000 Feet High

2000 MILES TRAVELED

### 6. Nearly There

really? Blah blah blah. Blah blah blah yeah, yeah. Oh, really? Blah blah blah blah blah yeah, yeah. Oh, really? Blah blah blah blah, real-Blah blah blah. Blah blah blah blah blah blah. Blah blah blah blah yeah, yeah, yeah, yeah. Oh, really? Blah blah blah. Blah blah blah blah blah blah, yeah. Oh, really? Blah blah blah. Blah blah blah-yeah, yeah. Oh, really? Blah yeah, yeah. Oh, really? -Blah blah blah. Blah blah blah blah blah yeah, really? Oh, really? Blah blah blah, yeah, yeah. really? Oh, really? Blah blah blah blah, yeah. Oh, really? Blah blah blah. Blah blah blah blah. Oh, really? Blah blah blah yeah, yeah. Oh, really? blah, yeah. Oh, really? Blah blah blah. Blah h, yeah. yeah, yeah. Oh, really? Oh, really?really? h blah. Blah blah blah blah blah .

### 7. Last One

Oh, really? Blah blah blah. Blah blah blah blah yeah, yeah | Oh, really? Blah blah blah. Blah blah blah blah blah yeah, yeah. Oh, really? Blah blah blah. Blah blah blah blah blah yeah, really? Blah blah blah blah blah blah blah blah yeah, yeah, yeah. Oh, really? Oh, really? Blah blah blah blah blah blah. Oh, really? Blah blah blah. Blah blah blah yeah, yeah. Oh, really? blah blah, yeah. Oh, real-ly? Oh, really? Blah blah blah blah blah yeah. Oh, really? blah blah blah blah, yeah. Oh, really? Blah blah blah. Blah blah blah yeah, yeah. Oh, real-ly?

EAST
McCarran Airport

EVERYTOWN, USA

### ROAD KEY

(The second season only): When all five keys fit into the puzzle board, it will spell out the final clue that leads to the Handsome Reward

### AWESOME BAND'S
TOP TEN ROAD TRIPPIN' CDs

HEY, LOOK
A SIDETRIP

CLUE

ROAD KEY

A COOL PLACE TO GO
WITHIN 100 MILES OF THIS
LEG OF THE JOURNEY

THE ROAD
TRAVELED
THUS FAR

CDs (OR CASSETTES FOR THE
DIE-HARDS) THAT OUR
FAVORITE MUSICIANS WOULD
TAKE WITH THEM ON THE
ULTIMATE ROAD TRIP

INTERESTING
STUFF TO KNOW ABOUT
A PERSON, PLACE, OR
THING ON THIS PAGE

MISSION

NUMBER
0

UNCOVER THE ONE-WORD
ANSWERS TO THE EIGHT
QUESTIONS BELOW

**OBJECTIVE:** Fill in the first letter of each answer on the ROAD RULES application (page 134)

**REWARD:** Assuming you answer correctly, your savvy sleuthing will be one indication that you've got what it takes to be a Road Ruler

1. What's the only kind of Fake that Kit favors?

2. What rainy country's bridge lives in the Grand Canyon State?

3. What kind of suit is custom designed for a clown?

4. What was Los's controversial gift to himself at Four Corners?

5. What kind of shark must consume 20,600 calories a day to stay healthy?

6. What present-day cult hero, long dead, was recently photographed at a southern rib-joint?

7. What "big meal at sundown" means more than a mouthful to Effie?

8. What other Trekkers' footprints led the Road Rulers to a clue and a new boss?

**WARNING:**
Before driving your vehicle, be sure you have read the entire operator's manual.

# WELCOME

to the exciting world of motor home travel and camping. You will find it convenient and enjoyable to have all the comforts of home and still enjoy the great outdoors wherever you choose to go.

## Before Entering Your Vehicle:

➤ Be sure that the windows and mirrors are clean and unobstructed.

➤ Make sure exterior lights operate properly.

➤ Check tires for proper inflation.

➤ Look beneath the vehicle for noticeable fluid leakage.

➤ Unhook and store sewer and water supply hoses.

➤ Be sure that all of your cargo is secured in event of a sudden stop or an accident.

➤ Check around your vehicle in all directions to assure proper clearance.

## Before Driving Your Vehicle:

➤ Adjust the interior and exterior mirrors.

➤ Adjust the driver's seat for proper distance to foot pedals.

➤ Place front seats in forward-facing position.

➤ Make sure all doors are shut and locked. When doors are shut and locked, there is less chance of doors flying open in an accident.

1

2

3

5

4

17

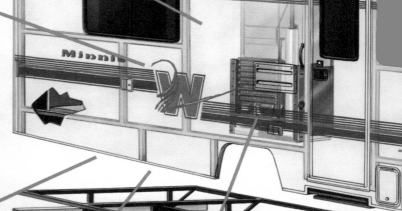

8

9

11

12

**CAUTION:**
Always remember to retract the entrance steps before traveling or moving the vehicle.

10

**WARNING:**
Do not attempt to adjust the driver's seat while the vehicle is in motion.

## Driving Precautions:

➡ Never allow passengers to stand or kneel on seats while the vehicle is in motion.

➡ Sleeping facilities are not to be used while vehicle is moving.

➡ Use care when accelerating or braking on a slippery surface. Abrupt speed changes can cause skidding and loss of control.

⑥

⑦

⑭

⑮

## Effects of Prolonged Occupancy

Your motor home was designed primarily for recreational use and short-term occupancy. Long-term occupancy may lead to premature deterioration of structure, interior finishes, carpeting, and drapes.

| ① | ROOF ACCESS LADDER |
| ② | TV ANTENNA |
| ③ | ROOF AIR CONDITIONER |
| ④ | BATHROOM |
| ⑤ | PORCH LIGHT |
| ⑥ | KITCHEN TABLE |
| ⑦ | BUNK BED |
| ⑧ | GAS TANK ACCESS |
| ⑨ | SEWAGE DRAIN LOCATION |
| ⑩ | ALL SEASON RADIAL TIRES |
| ⑪ | REFRIGERATOR ACCESS |
| ⑫ | STORAGE COMPARTMENT |
| ⑬ | SIDE VIEW MIRROR |
| ⑭ | REARVIEW MIRROR |
| ⑮ | COMPASS |
| ⑯ | FRONT GRILL |
| ⑰ | SPORTY RACING DECAL |

⑬

⑯

**WARNING:**
Never attempt to push-start this vehicle.

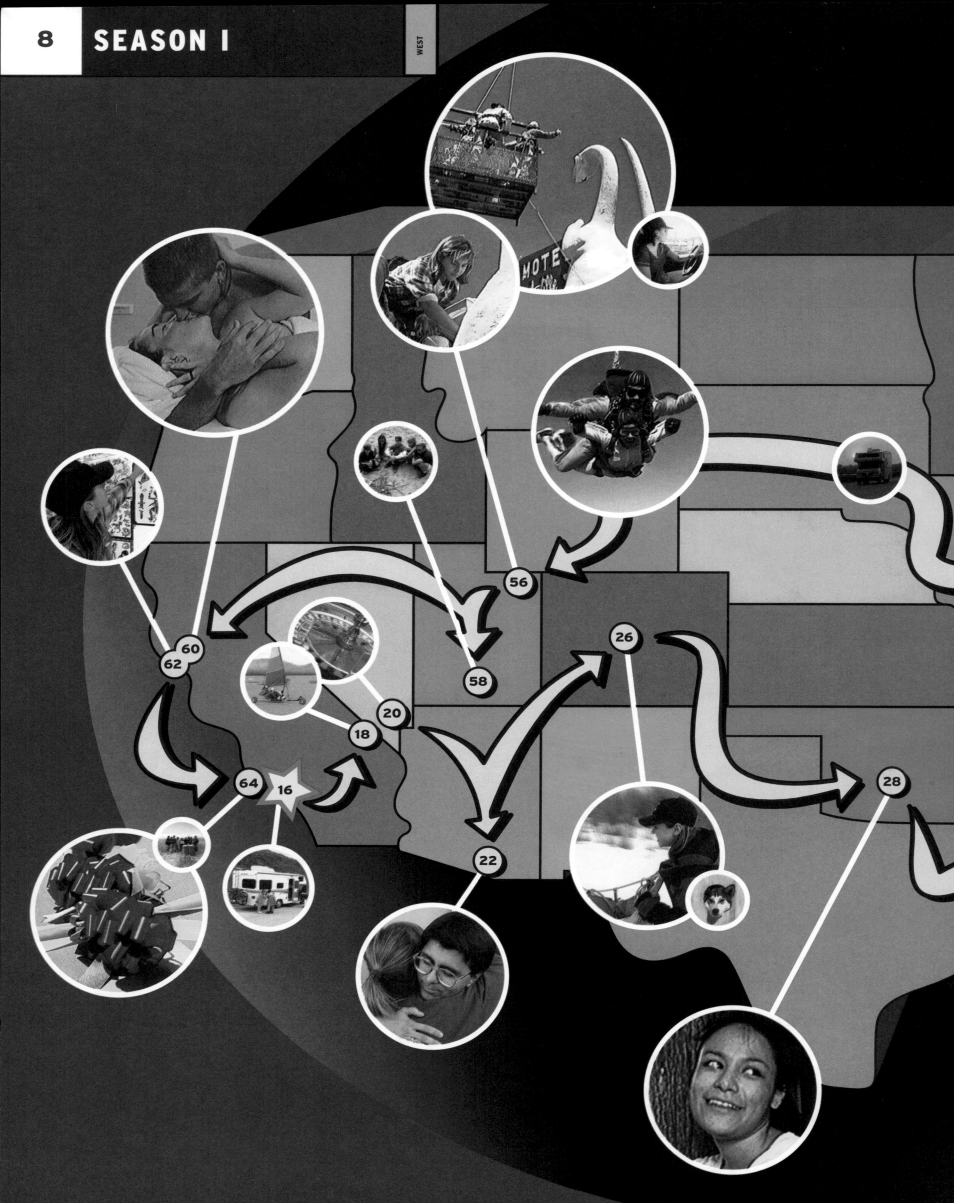

56

60
62

58

26

20

18

64 16

22

28

Guardians of the Winnie, on the dashboard

I'm Kit. I'm from Atlanta, Georgia. **I'm a very upbeat, happy person, and I'm sort of like Ferris Bueller, I fall into things.** I'm a huge fan of holidays with my family. I'm the biggest family girl you'll ever meet. My family's worse than The Cleavers. They're awesome. My brother is just the coolest cat. He calls me Junior. I get so many of my favorite lines and quotes from him, like, "Does a one-legged duck swim in circles?" Sometimes I call him and say,

"Hey, we gotta go out so I can get some new material."

I've lived in my same house my whole life. My brother and I went to Montessori elementary school and high school, less than a mile away from our house. I loved growing up here. I don't know what made it so special except for the people; the South is really warm and inviting. We had such good times.

In high school, when all the other girls were way into boys, **I was sort of a late bloomer; all I cared about was playing sports... and maybe kissing a few boys.** I used to run cross-country and track. I played soccer, tennis, softball, and basketball—any sport I could get my hands on. I'm not good at sitting still, but I do love to read.

I've read all of Grisham's stuff, even though it's sort of cheesy; I also love the old, old classics. I've reread all those books from high school because they're just so amazing, especially A SEPARATE PEACE and TO KILL A MOCKINGBIRD. Even more than reading, I love to write in my journal, especially when I'm on a road trip because there's so much to remember, and it's so easy to forget little things that mean a lot at the time.

I started road tripping when I went to college. I went to the University of North Carolina at Chapel Hill, and every summer I would live somewhere different with my friends. Freshman year it was Martha's Vineyard with about 16 other girls, and I gave tours of the islands. Sophomore year we drove cross-country and lived in Sun Valley, Idaho, which was amazing. I was a swim instructor and a lifeguard, and I wasn't certified to be either. Had eight little dudes under three years old who had never seen the water, and by the end, I'll proudly say I had them all jumping off the diving board. My junior year it was Jackson Hole, Wyoming. Then I drove cross-country one more time and lived in Aspen, Colorado, where I worked as a nanny for Barbi Benton, the PLAYBOY centerfold chick.

Since I've sort of done the States, I'd like to get one of those Humvees and go to Australia and New Zealand and just cruise around with a significant other, do a little camping out. Some of the best times are when you come upon a cool town or meet a cool local who's going to show you her favorite restaurant or let you have dinner at her house.

Maybe they picked me for ROAD RULES because I've been there, done that, and I know that what's cool for one person definitely ain't cool for the next sometimes. I'm OK with all kinds of folks—it's hard to shock me or make me uncomfortable. But once again, I fell into this. I don't think I'm an actress by any means, you're not going to see me on THE YOUNG AND THE STUPID, I mean, THE YOUNG AND THE RESTLESS, but I would love to be on TV, hosting something like ESPN. ROAD RULES is going to be good practice for me, though it's a much more personal experience than being on a show where you have a script, and everything is expected. All I know is, yesterday I was cruising along being a normal person, and tomorrow my life will be taped and then exposed. I don't expect my career to fall into place after ROAD RULES; I think being on the show will open doors for me, but it's more important to realize what I can do for myself. I've heard that some of THE REAL WORLD kids have had a hard time adjusting to life after the cameras and all the attention, but I think I'm going to be just fine.

Kit

Atlanta

GA

**STATS**

| DOB | 7/29/70 |
|---|---|
| HEIGHT | 5'1" |
| EYES | brown |
| HAIR | black |
| HOMETOWN | Atlanta, GA |
| CAR | Jeep Cherokee |

**KIT'S FAVORITE DRIVING MUSIC**

Van Morrison
Cat Stevens
Fake Fish
Cowboy Junkies
Dave Matthews Band
Anything from the '70s

**KIT'S PET PEEVE**

The smacking noise people make when they chew

PISCES

## STATS

| DOB | 2/18/75 |
| HEIGHT | 5'6" |
| EYES | brown |
| HAIR | brown |
| HOMETOWN | Oklahoma City, OK |
| CAR | Geo Storm |

## SHELLY'S THREE WISHES

1. To live in Colorado
2. To meet Sebastian Bach and an endless list of other incredible people
3. To marry one of the men from the endless list

## SHELLY'S FAVORITE DRIVING MUSIC

Candlebox

Pantera, COWBOYS FROM HELL

Metallica, MASTER OF PUPPETS

## SHELLY'S PET PEEVES

Whiners

Indecisive people

Hypocritical people

I lived in Tulsa when I was really little, but I grew up in Oklahoma City. I went to high school at a place called Putnam City North. Ugh! I hated high school. I had a few friends, and a lot of enemies. I don't know why, but a lot of people were intimidated by me. The big social scene was the grunge/alternative/punk scene. The "act" was to have no act, which is bull. I guess the only real thing I got out of high school is an appreciation for music, art, acting, and literature. I enjoy all the "artsy" stuff by listening, admiring, watching, and reading. I played saxophone in the marching band for a while, until I figured out I appreciate music more than I like to play it. I was into music from a young age. I blame my uncle, who gave me a Quiet Riot album when I was five years old, for my musical tastes. I like everything about metal music.

Yeah, so high school was a drag. I believe going to school is important, but it turns out to be this big social scene, and a lot of people lose sight of the fact that you're supposed to go to college afterward and everything else.

I've been interested in criminal justice forever. I always wanted to be an FBI agent—I blame it on the true crime books! After graduation I was supposed to go to college at a school down here with the best criminal justice and law enforcement program. I was actually enrolled, but then my financial aid didn't go through, so two weeks before school started I had to find something else to do.

Mom actually heard about THE REAL WORLD, LONDON on the radio. I guess they were looking for somebody from Oklahoma. Mom's always been really cool, and she thought I'd be OK, I'd be safe because there would be other people with me, looking out for me. So I sent them a videotape of me hanging out in my room, showing them my posters.

I have a cool room. I don't care what anybody else says, I just love my room. I used to have so many posters up that you couldn't even tell I had a wall. I had posters on the ceiling. It was crazy. I've got every poster of Sebastian Bach, and lots of movie posters—SINGLES, HELLRAISER....It's my little sanctuary; I feel that it represents me well.

I didn't get on THE REAL WORLD, but then they called me back and asked me to be on this new show called ROAD RULES. They probably liked me because I hadn't ever been far from Oklahoma. I'd gone to Colorado, New Mexico, Dallas, and San Antonio for some band trips. That's it.

I'm lucky enough to be a full-blooded Native American—that might have had a lot to do with why they cast me. I'm three-quarters Kiowa and one-quarter Creek.

**Native Americans haven't been on something like MTV before, and I think it's really good for people to see both sides of us.**

There's a side to me that's absolutely normal, but my culture is something completely different; even my roommates don't know much about that side. I think everybody has a culture, and it's up to each person to decide how much it influences his or her life. I am who I am because of things I was taught—things that my grandmother's told me, things that my mother's told me—morals, values. Yeah, you could probably get that in any family life, but do you?

Shelly

Oklahoma City

OK

Carlos

Stone Mountain

GA

| | |
|---|---|
| **DOB** | 3/7/74 |
| **HEIGHT** | 5'11" |
| **EYES** | brown |
| **HAIR** | black |
| **HOMETOWN** | Stone Mountain, GA |
| **CAR** | 18-speed hybrid wheeler (bike) |

I'm Los. I don't go by my full name, Carlos, because people pronounce it wrong, without the Spanish accent. The "a" is supposed to be a lot lighter and there's supposed to be a trill on the r, so it's Carrrlos. My parents were trying to be different; they wanted to give me an ethnic name, something other than Christopher or John. I was born in the '70s, what can I say? If I'd been born in the '80s or '90s when African names were "it," I would have had something from Malawi or the Ivory Coast.

I'm originally from Stone Mountain, near Atlanta, Georgia. Now I live in Washington, D.C. My dad is an ambitious fellow, I think his official title is deputy chief of police. My mom works in human resources. She's really, really light-skinned; **when I was a kid, people would always make jokes like, "When**

the revolution comes, you're going to have to straddle the fence."

Always, always. That's kinda been the greater theme in my life.

I was a swimmer in high school. When I first started, black people gave me a hard time about being on the swim team. They were like, "You need to run track or play basketball." I stuck with the swim team because I just happened to be good at it and liked it. But it didn't change who I was, or the household I was in.

What I'd like to be doing is making motion pictures. My ultimate wish is to be a D.P.—that's a director of photography—or a cinematographer

on some features. Maybe I'll direct one or two of my own.

I saw a flier for ROAD RULES at Howard University, where I go to school. I was curious right away because I've always wanted to see typical America with my camera. A lot of people are into a lot of different things, but pretty much there's that common bond that makes them all Americans. They all value the same essential things, and they all take interest in making themselves happy and being individuals. My goal is to capture that on film.

**I'm especially passionate about images of black people and the politics around those images.**

I should hope that people see my images and meet them with some apprehension and some skepticism. I don't want to be taken for granted. I don't want them to sleep and take me lightly.

**LOS'S FAVORITE THINGS**

Shooting film
Hanging with girls
Watching movies
(without sound)
Getting lost
Listening to loud music

**LOS'S FAVORITE DRIVING MUSIC**

Brand New Heavies
Jamiroquai
Incognito
A Tribe Called Quest
Pearl Jam
Outkast

**LOS'S THREE WISHES**

1. World peace
2. To have ten million dollars
3. For Howard University to be 45% white in enrollment

**LOS'S PET PEEVES**

Smoking
Stupid people

## STATS

| | |
|---|---|
| DOB | 7/7/73 |
| HEIGHT | 5'5" |
| EYES | blue |
| HAIR | blond |
| HOMETOWN | Huntington, NY |

My name is Allison. I grew up moving back and forth between my mother and my father. Moving schools a lot pushed me to mature at a young age. I always felt bad for kids who thought high school was the whole world; the most important thing was being cool, and if they weren't cool, they were nothing. When you move around a lot, you realize that there's a real world out there, full of things more important than what a select group of people think of you. I learned at an early age to make my own decisions and not worry too much about what everyone else thinks is right.

I tried out for ROAD RULES because I was finishing school at Columbia University in New York and I didn't know what I was going to do. I was looking for a job, but I wasn't really into anything. I wanted to do something different. One day I was late for my philosophy class, and I was waiting outside the door to see when the teacher would turn around so I could sneak into a seat. He wouldn't turn around, so I started reading all the fliers tacked up next to the door. One of them was a casting call for THE REAL WORLD, LONDON. It said, "Do you want to live in London, rent-free, for six months?" I was like, "Yeah, sure."

So, I sent in a video of myself and I made it to the finals. At that point, they told me, "Allison, we really like you, but you just don't do anything; you're not a race-car driver, you're not a dancer....If you want to work in a lab over in London, that's not too visual." But they called me up a couple of weeks later and asked me to try out for ROAD RULES.

### I think I'm a good role model because I want to go to medical school, yet I'm not all work and no play, I balance it out.

I will probably go into emergency medicine because it's fulfilling, but its also very challenging. Each day will be completely different from the day before. As a doctor, you're constantly on your feet, having to think, having to figure out problems. I like that. I like that challenge.

I'm very opinionated, I don't back down from an argument; if I think something is right, I want to discuss it and come to some kind of conclusion. I care about things, a lot of things, very deeply.

Sometimes I'm not good at expressing them to others, but I've got my convictions. Also, I try to judge people by who they are inside. So much of this world is based on image, but I like to look at what people base their lives

on—their morality, their strength of character.

I had a blast going to college in New York. There's so much to do and see. In the summer, it's really nice to go into Central Park and watch everyone Rollerblading and doing tricks. There's always somebody playing music or putting on some kind of show, something to see. I started running races in Central Park my sophomore year. It helped me to focus, it made me feel good, and with all the people around, there was a feeling of camaraderie. Pretty soon I decided I was going to run marathons, so I really set my mind to it and trained every day. By the time I graduated, I'd run in four. I had never really considered myself athletic before, and all of a sudden, I realized that I could do something I never thought myself capable of. Best of all was when people would say, "What did you do yesterday?" And I could answer, "Oh, I ran a marathon."

Allison

NY

Huntington

Mark

Satellite Beach

| | |
|---|---|
| DOB | 6/2/71 |
| HEIGHT | 6'2" |
| EYES | blue |
| HAIR | blond |
| HOMETOWN | Satellite Beach, FL |
| CAR | Nissan pickup |

I was an Air Force brat—born in Philadelphia, lived in California and San Antonio before I was eight. That's when my dad got transferred to Patrick Air Force Base in Satellite Beach, Florida, and we stayed put. Growing up, I always tried to emulate my brother. Whatever he did, I tried to do. Now I'm kind of the black sheep, trying to do all these crazy things, and he's the one who my parents can turn to for normalcy.

I've always got a kick out of dancing and keeping in shape. I would like to try my hand at male dancing or erotic dancing. I love the feeling of performing in front of hundreds of girls—especially with no clothes on. I also would like to try being a talk show host or something like that. I'm a real big fan of a lot of the lighter actors.

## You'll hear people go, "Oh, I want to be like De Niro, I want to be like Pacino," but I'm more of a sitcom kind of kid.

The FRIENDS show cracks me up. I would love to do something like that.

A while back, I tried out to be a roommate on THE REAL WORLD. I was a production major at University of Florida in Gainesville, so I did a real elaborate audition tape. I taped a role-reversal spoof on THE REAL WORLD, LA episode when David yanked the covers off Tami. We filmed it exactly like THE REAL WORLD was filmed, with music and the whole nine yards. I had a friend who's a black girl rip my towel off when I came out of the shower. I was halfway bawling, "I just don't feel safe in this house." I don't know if they thought that was in bad taste or not, but they must have liked it, 'cause they asked me to try out to replace Puck when he left the San Francisco cast.

Not to badmouth THE REAL WORLD cast at all, but I just didn't click with anyone, except Mohammed, who was way into athletics. If I had been chosen, I think I would have done my own thing anyway. Judd was just not me. Pam was really sweet, and

Pedro was really nice, but the other girl, Cory, I don't know what her story was. So that didn't work out, but the producers called me a few months later and said they were going to do a pilot for this new type of show, like THE REAL WORLD but on the road with a bunch of crazy adventures, and they wanted me to be in it. So I did the pilot on Catalina Island with four other awesome people. It was fun, I even got a little lovin', had a little thing with one of the female cast members. Nothing serious, but they made it look like this huge drama.

I didn't hear from MTV for a while, so I figured either the show didn't get picked up or they were going to cast all new people. Then I got the ultimate phone call. It was the producers again. They were calling to tell me, "We talked it over with the people in New York and they allowed us to keep one person from the pilot: that's you. If you want it, you can have it." I was like, "S**t, yeah!"

## MARK'S FAVORITE DRIVING MUSIC

"This Is How We Do It,"
by Montell Jordan
Any hip-hop
Dave Matthews Band
Oasis
Snoop Doggy Dog
Pearl Jam

## MARK'S SATELLITE BEACH DIGS

POPULATION: 9,900

FAVORITE PIZZA JOINT:
Pappagallo's, "They serve the coldest beer."

FAVORITE HANGOUT:
Conchy Joe's

Now starts a new beginning. Nervous I'm not. Questioning and curious I am. -SHELLY

On the night before it all started, we five still hadn't met. They put us in different hotels. I wrote in my journal and went to bed with no idea what to expect. I didn't know I would be blindfolded until the crew picked me up the next morning. They said they wanted to capture the moment when we realized where we were. When they whipped out that blindfold I was like, "No, you're kidding." They were like, "Nope, sorry." After that, I shut up. You can't see, you've gotta shut up. Then the sound lady put on the mike. She said the best place to put it inconspicuously was on the bra, so she lifted up my shirt, and I felt like I was flashing the entire world. I remember thinking, "What's going on? What are they going to do? How is this gonna look?"

# That's when it really hit, "Oh my God, I'm going on a road trip with four complete strangers." -SHELLY

We took our blindfolds off and I looked around and thought, "OK, these people are just as lost as I am." Nobody seemed to have any inside information or have a clue as to what we were supposed to do next.

I saw Allison first, and she looked very nervous. Immediately, I could relate to that. I was trying, myself, not to appear as nervous as I felt, but I could see it on her. I never would have guessed she was from New York—almost wanted to call her a hippie, but that was before we spoke.

I could see right away that Mark was the type who wanted to make money with his looks and his charm. In our first couple of conversations, there was nothing I could gather about him that was unique.

Kit reminds me of Delta Burke, from DESIGNING WOMEN. Her face anyway. And that southern attitude. I thought Kit was going to be this real bitch, I thought she was going to want to run everything and run everybody, but I soon found out she's the total opposite.

I didn't know what to make of Shelly. She was so quiet, I was like, "What's wrong with this kid?"

It was wild up there, it was just beautiful. I snapped one or two pictures, but I'm used to buildings and dirty pavement; the pictures I took were bum because this was my first time seeing this stuff and it's gorgeous and you get excited and you want to put it on film, but the beauty doesn't come out. I think I'm going to have to slow down, calm down a little bit and just get a little bit more intimate with my surroundings before I try and photograph them. -LOS

**KEY TO SYMBOLS**

⬤ ......days since last shower
♥ ..................romance
💵 ..............money trail
💻 ..............welcome to
M ..................mission
🌀 ....empty Winnie septic tank
2 ......................lost

## CLUE

555TH

KIT, CARLOS, SHELLY, MARK, AND ALLISON, YOU MUST PLACE ALL OF YOUR CASH AND CREDIT CARDS IN THE BAGS. YOU'LL GET THEM ALL BACK AT THE END OF THE TRIP. THIS SUITCASE CONTAINS YOUR KEYS AND A COMPASS. BRING THE KEYS AND FOLLOW THE DIRT ROAD DOWN TO YOUR VEHICLE; FURTHER INSTRUCTIONS AWAIT YOU INSIDE.

The first person I saw was Mark, definitely. I was like, "This guy is probably so full of himself." He literally looked like he'd walked off the pages of one of those teen magazines. Shelly was very standoffish, she just did not seem like she wanted to be there at all. I didn't think that we'd get along, she seemed too unemotional. With Kit, I said right off the bat, "Oh, this girl's going to be fun." And Carlos, I don't know what I thought of Carlos, I just saw him taking pictures, so I guessed he was artistic. -ALLISON

I had no idea where we were. As far as you could see it was just hills, grass, bushes, and paths leading all over the place. Everyone looked completely different, but in a way the same—we were all sporting jeans, a couple of us had on leather jackets. Mark looked really put together, like he'd planned out his outfit, and Shelly looked like one of those people you'd see in school, smoking by their locker. Allison looked kind of like a sorority girl, like she should've had a bow in her hair, and Los just looked kind of chill with his goatee action going on. My hope was that we were all different, but were all going to get along great.

We were all standing on top of the mountain, and this huge helicopter flew up and dropped a suitcase. Inside that suitcase was a tape and keys. We had our first clue, so as a group, we decided to split up and try to find our car. I was a little worried about us when it took an hour to find something as large as a Winnebago. First Los and I went in one direction, Shelly went off by herself, and Mark and Allison went another direction. After about 20 minutes, we ended up back where we started because none of us found anything. Then Los spotted the thing through his camera lens and we were home free. **-KIT**

**MALIBU**
POPULATION:
11,700

TRIVIA:
M*A*S*H and
PLANET OF THE APES
were both filmed at
Malibu Creek State Park

BEST BEACHES:
Malibu Surrider State Beach,
Zuma Beach, County Park,
Point Dume State Beach

# FIRST IMPRESSIONS
## are never what they seem...

When I dropped the blindfold, I said to myself, "My girlfriend has nothing to worry about. I know I'm not going to be attracted to any of these girls." It was weird because I still had in my mind the four other people who I did the ROAD RULES pilot with. This was going to be totally different. We all tried to dress up a little when we met for the first time. I thought we were going to meet in a nice room, maybe an executive suite, throw our bags in a truck, and go. When I saw where we were at—mud everywhere—I was like, "Oh God, this is my worst nightmare."

**CLUE**

NOW, DOWN TO BUSINESS. GO TO YEATS WELL'S GATES AT IVANPAH LAKE, NEVADA. GET THERE BY EARLY AFTERNOON BECAUSE I WANT YOU TO GET IN AT LEAST ONE SAIL BEFORE YOUR BIG RACE TOMORROW.

Finally, after about an hour of dredging around in knee-high mud and water, we found the Winnebago, with all our gear lying out in front of it, marked for each of us by name. I ran over, delved into my stuff; I probably lost half of it throwing things all over the place. There were jackets, boots, sunglasses, pants, slickers, bikes, a tent—anything you could think of, we had. Kit found an envelope with $1,000 in it. It looked like a lot of money, but we found a tape that said it had to last us for about three weeks, so in my estimation, that's about $10 a day per person, and we're going to run out before that time's up. The tape also gave us the clue to our next destination, so we got in the Winnebago and cruised.

I wanted to be the first to drive, since I'd been living in Hollywood for a couple months and I sort of knew the roads. Not to sound chauvinistic or anything, but I don't trust women behind the wheel. That's just me—unless I'm sitting holding on to the steering wheel, I don't feel safe. **-MARK**

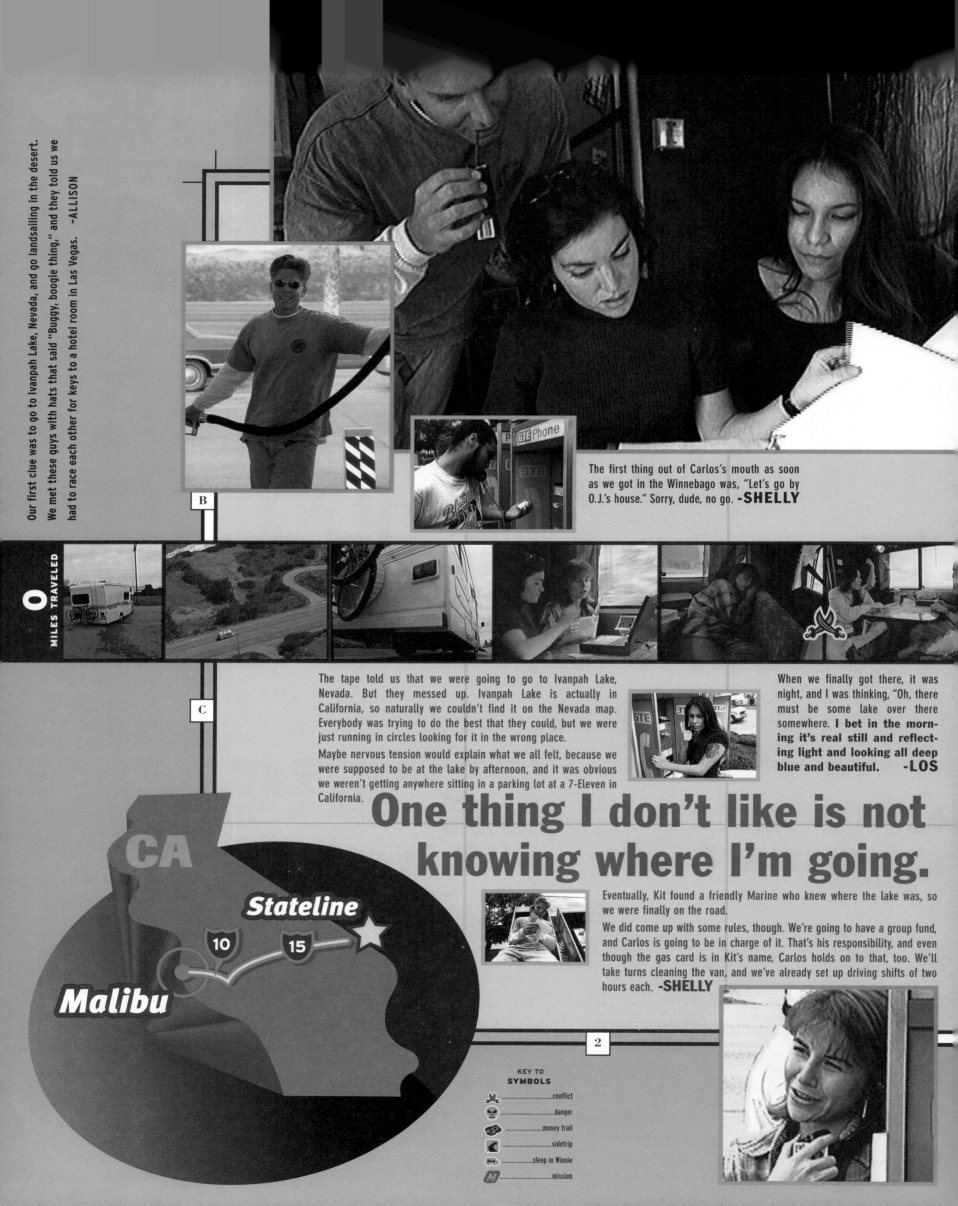

Our first clue was to go to Ivanpah Lake, Nevada, and go landsailing in the desert. We met these guys with hats that said "Buggy, boogie thing," and they told us we had to race each other for keys to a hotel room in Las Vegas.   —ALLISON

B

The first thing out of Carlos's mouth as soon as we got in the Winnebago was, "Let's go by O.J.'s house." Sorry, dude, no go. -SHELLY

**MILES TRAVELED**

**0**

C

The tape told us that we were going to go to Ivanpah Lake, Nevada. But they messed up. Ivanpah Lake is actually in California, so naturally we couldn't find it on the Nevada map. Everybody was trying to do the best that they could, but we were just running in circles looking for it in the wrong place.

Maybe nervous tension would explain what we all felt, because we were supposed to be at the lake by afternoon, and it was obvious we weren't getting anywhere sitting in a parking lot at a 7-Eleven in California.

When we finally got there, it was night, and I was thinking, "Oh, there must be some lake over there somewhere. **I bet in the morning it's real still and reflecting light and looking all deep blue and beautiful.**   —LOS

# One thing I don't like is not knowing where I'm going.

Eventually, Kit found a friendly Marine who knew where the lake was, so we were finally on the road.

We did come up with some rules, though. We're going to have a group fund, and Carlos is going to be in charge of it. That's his responsibility, and even though the gas card is in Kit's name, Carlos holds on to that, too. We'll take turns cleaning the van, and we've already set up driving shifts of two hours each. -SHELLY

## CA

### Stateline

10   15

### Malibu

2

**KEY TO SYMBOLS**

- ................conflict
- ................danger
- ................money trail
- ................sidetrip
- ................sleep in Winnie
- ................mission

3/5 1995

The conflict between the guys and the girls is definitely going to be a problem. The guys took control of the wheel, then they said that because they drove that day they should be able to sleep in the top bunk. I didn't want it to be one of those trips where the guys call all the shots, but I wasn't going to cause any trouble right off the bat. I figured there was already enough arguing going on. **-ALLISON**

Whenever we have to camp out in the RV, Mark and I are always going to get the top bunk. The girls like to complain and mope, "Oh, you guys slept up there last night." But we're always going to sleep up there, and they can get by however best they can. **-LOS**

When I woke up the next morning and peeked outside, I realized there was no lake anywhere. I was asking everyone, "Where's the water?" Then one of the landsailer dudes whipped up in this little buggy with a giant sail, and I said, "What the heck is this?" I jumped out of bed, all excited. He said, "You want to go for a ride?" So I put on my jacket and went right out there and he gave me a ride on the buggy. I was screaming, "Go faster, go faster." We went up to about 65 miles per hour. It was just amazing. Like nothing I've ever done before.

I went for the longest run of my life in that desert—almost killed myself looking for a bush to go to the bathroom behind. **-KIT**

## MISSION 1
### LANDSAILING

**OBJECTIVE:** Race across a dry lake at the fastest speed possible

**CHALLENGE:** Whatever you do, don't flip

**TOOLS:** Landsailers

**REWARD:** The winners sleep at the Excalibur Hotel in Las Vegas

B

# I love the speed. Faster, yes.

265 MILES TRAVELED

When I got out on my own, the instructor kept saying, "Just spin into it, turn into it. Put the sail into the wind." But all I knew was when I pulled the string, I went faster. When I first flipped, I was going really fast and, honestly, I didn't know what to do. I started to stick my foot out and put my arm out, but I could have broken my legs. I thought it was so funny. It was only afterward that I realized I could have hurt myself. **-ALLISON**

In landsailing, the biggest thing is you have to play the wind. You have your foot pedals to guide the Landsailer, but you never really know what's going to happen because no one knows if the wind's going to pick up or not.

At first, I was moving like a snail across the lake, so when the winds suddenly picked up, I got a little too loose trying to do different things, and my wheels went up in the air. There was a limbo period when I didn't know if I was going to land or flip over and I actually took a pretty bad spill and broke one of the Landsailers. Apparently, that has never happened before— the metal breaking in two pieces—but I seemed to do a pretty good job at it. They gave me a different Landsailer, which I managed to keep in one piece and win the race with. It was exciting as hell. **-MARK**

C

**RED HOT CHILI PEPPERS'**
TOP TEN ROAD TRIPPIN' CDs

1.................................................P.J. Harvey, DRY
2.................................................Lou Reed, BERLIN
3..David Bowie, THE RISE & FALL OF ZIGGY STARDUST
4.................................................Joni Mitchell, BLUE
5.................................N.W.A., STRAIGHT OUTTA COMPTON
6.................................................Miles Davis, KIND OF BLUE
7.................................Led Zeppelin, PHYSICAL GRAFFITI
8.................................Tower of Power, BACK TO OAKLAND
9.................................Fela Kuti, SUFFERING AND SMILING
10.................................Spain, THE BLUE MOODS OF SPAIN

**NAME:** Scott Dyer
**TITLE:** Landsailing instructor
**MOTTO:** "My job is to take your worst weather and turn it into our best sailing day."

Landsailing has been around for a long time as an alternative to sailing for people who are not near the water. The current landsailing speed record was set in Europe. It's 94.6 miles an hour. We're trying to set a new record, here on Ivanpah dry lake.

Landsailing is relatively safe. The Landsailer's masts are very strong, they're made of aircraft-quality tubing, so they take tremendous wind pressure. The only one I've ever seen collapse totally was Mark's. He just had all the combinations in the wrong spot and flipped over with enough force that it bent the mast over and he got a little closer to the ground than we would have liked.

After we finished landsailing, we headed toward Las Vegas to stay at the Excalibur Hotel and Casino, did some gambling, lost some money, and got our next clue. -MARK

**265** MILES TRAVELED

A

B

# Bright Lights,
## Small City

Kit seemed to blow her money away. She and I hung the whole night. We got our picture taken as two wild angels. **The two of us were starting to notice how easy it was to be around each other.** -MARK

A whole city consisting of only casinos and hotels is just overly decadent. That's like one person having a house with 17 bedrooms. **-LOS**

C

▼2 I never knew how nice a hot, clean shower was. I took a long shave, relaxed, took my time getting ready, clicked the AC on. It was the best feeling I've had since the trip started. **-MARK**

**KEY TO SYMBOLS**
...days since last shower
...scamming/cheating
...sleep in motel
...welcome to
...sidetrip
...missing

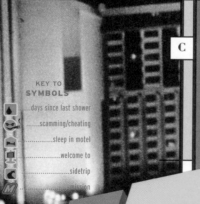

**NV**

**Las Vegas**
15

**Stateline**

**CA**

The Excalibur looks like this huge castle, and as soon as you walk in you can hear the casinos, which I couldn't go to because I wasn't 21. **-SHELLY**

2

**WHERE TO HAVE FUN WHEN YOU'RE UNDER 21**

MERLIN'S MAGIC MOTION MACHINE, AT THE EXCALIBUR:
Strap yourself into the bleacher-style seats and get ready to twist and bob in sync with an onscreen bobsled or roller coaster ride.

THE LIBERACE MUSEUM:
One word: kitsch-o-rama.

MGM GRAND ADVENTURES THEME PARK:
Get your kicks on rides like Lightning Bolt, Deep Earth Exploration, Parisian Taxis, Haunted Mine, and others.

GRAND SLAM CANYON:

**HOW TO SURVIVE BLACKJACK FEVER**

• Stay away from the free drinks while you're gambling. It doesn't take an Einstein to figure out why they want to get you trashed.

• Talk to your dealer. She knows what's going on, and will more than likely help you.

• You can tip your dealer, either by giving money directly to her, or putting it directly above your bet, so that she will have some incentive to give you good advice.

• Keep low average bets. If you go in with $50, a good idea would be to keep every bet at $5 or under. The wins won't be as big, but you won't run the risk of losing all of your money in 10 minutes.

• Once you get ahead, put away the money you came with and just play on the winnings.

• Set a time limit. About an hour or so is realistic for each gambling session.

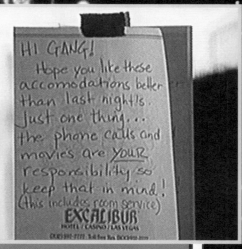

I thought I was going to win big in Vegas. I love gambling, I love betting on football games and stuff. In the past year, I've toned it down, though. I don't use a bookie anymore. Not because I don't love it, but for two reasons: because I absolutely suck, and because I'm a little low on the cash flow at this point in my life.

The group decided to take 50 bones out of the fund for each of us to spend, and I spent every bit of mine, plus most of Mark's. I had this theory that I was just going to take a little bit of everybody's money and win it back for them. But the drinks sort of kicked in, it didn't go as planned, and I lost big.

Meanwhile, Shelly, Allison, and Los decided to go shopping. Who shops in Vegas? They came back with money, and I came back empty-handed. I swear if they'd just given me a little bit more I could have won. I told them I could get on my rolling streak. My problem was that Mark would only let me gamble at the $2 table, and it just went too fast, you can't win your money back. But me and Bonehead had so much fun chilling out at the blackjack table that it didn't matter. The cocktail waitress even brought us our next clue there, on the tray with our cocktails. Everyone dragged me away from the table and to our room to listen to it. **-KIT**

## CLUE

I WANT YOU TO VISIT THE YOUNGEST MAYOR IN AMERICA AND DO WHAT IT TAKES TO WIN THE KEY TO HIS CITY. YOU HAVE TWO DAYS TO GET THERE. THE HONORABLE MAYOR EXPECTS YOU IN HIS OFFICE THE MORNING AFTER YOU ARRIVE.

30 miles south of Vegas off HWY 15 lies Good Springs, the kind of ghost town you thought only existed in John Wayne's eeriest westerns.

    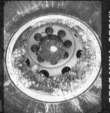

**311** MILES TRAVELED

## Unwanted Guests

I couldn't sleep, I kept thinking about the clue and who was the youngest mayor, and it was really bothering me so I woke up early and decided to go for a run in Vegas. As I was jogging I would say to every person I met, "Hey, do you know who the youngest mayor is?" All of a sudden this guy started jogging alongside of me and I started talking to him and the next thing I knew, his friends were all jogging along with me. They were from Australia and they seemed fun. Three of them jumped on the back of a car because they didn't want to run all the way to the Excalibur. They wanted to have breakfast with us, so I brought them up to the room and I told them to stand outside, but the next thing I knew they were on the bed, drinking beer, and it wasn't even 9:00 in the morning. Shelly got all pissed off, so I asked them to leave. **-ALLISON**

## An Honest Day's Work

We decided to split up and get things done faster. So the three girls went together to do the laundry and the two guys went to go clean the Winnebago. They absolutely hated us at the laundromat. Apparently our stuff was just too dirty—we had to clean the rain slickers, we had to clean the shoes from hiking and landsailing the day before, and basically they kicked us out. So we washed our shoes outside with the help of a crazy wandering guy named Rosco. At least the guys did the really gross work—the Winnie was a disaster. **-SHELLY**

We had it all mapped out that we'd do the carpet and spray off the Winnie ourselves, but we actually found a nice little place where we could do it cheap, only $40. So we paid to have it cleaned and played it off to the girls that we'd worked really hard. **-LOS**

C

LAS VEGAS
POPULATION:
329,800
TRIVIA:
Home to nine of the ten largest hotels in the world;
Elvis's favorite was the Las Vegas Hilton, where he frequently shot out the TV sets in his suite

NOTORIETY:
From the '30s through the late '60s, Vegas was primarily owned and operated by the Mafia. Las Vegas Boulevard, or "The Strip," was developed by Mafia kingpin Benjamin "Bugsy" Siegel in 1946. The city was legitimized in the late '60s by billionaire Howard Hughes, who invested $300 million in its hotels and casinos.

4

### MOVIES SHOT IN VEGAS

LEAVING LAS VEGAS
SISTER ACT 2: BACK IN THE HABIT
INDECENT PROPOSAL
HONEYMOON IN VEGAS
HONEY, I BLEW UP THE KIDS
COOL WORLD
RAIN MAN
HEAT
ROCKY IV
LOST IN AMERICA

Our clue said that we were to find the youngest mayor. So we skipped down to Nogales where we met Louie, the 23-year-old mayor. To win the key to his city, we had to compete in a pentathlon. -KIT

**A**

No one knew off the top of their head who the youngest mayor in America was; in fact, we were having a hell of a time finding out. Finally, we got a page from the crew saying, "Call the public library reference desk, dummies." Oh my God. Never in my life have I had such a problem trying to get through to anybody. Finally, I got the lady on the phone and I said, "How busy is the reference desk? It's really an emergency, I need to know the youngest mayor."

**B**

"Why?" she asked. "Well, we're on a scavenger hunt."

That got her all excited, and she found me the answer. **-ALLISON**

♥ I don't think there's any serious romantic interests among anybody in the Winnie. There's a lotta flirting going on 'cause we have a lotta beautiful people. People who are like-minded are gonna start hanging out more and more. But that physical stuff, man, I don't see it. **-LOS**

I was driving on the way to Phoenix, and Carlos stayed up with me. He was getting into his deep, philosophical, "Let's talk about your culture and my culture" thing. He thinks we should stick together because we're "oppressed peoples." Well, I believe that somebody like Los should not be concentrating on ignorance and racism, but focusing on what he can do for his culture, for his people— we just don't see eye to eye on racism.

That night we drove all over Phoenix looking for a motel until everybody got so tired and cranky we wound up sleeping on some corner in the middle of nowhere. **I was sleeping in between Mark and Carlos, and Carlos suddenly kissed me. I pushed him away and turned around and just tried to stay away.** After that he wouldn't talk to me, so I figured it was more of a big deal on his end. I figured it would blow over. But we still haven't talked, and nothing is the same. **-SHELLY**

**311** MILES TRAVELED

**C**

💰 It took us about three days to spend half of our $1,000. I guess Vegas really did it to us. **-MARK**

# House Rules

♨ As far as the bathroom's concerned, Mark is the only one to admit that he's used the crapper, so it was his job to empty it before we left Vegas. Yet, I do know that Allison ran into a little trouble in Vegas, she took some Ex-Lax, but instead of taking one Ex-Lax, she took six. So maybe she should have been the one out there helping instead of me. But we'll let her slide this time. **-KIT**

As soon as we got to Nogales we went to the city hall and met the mayor's receptionist, Christina, who also let us stay at her house. So she was very cool. We didn't meet Louie until the next day. I remember thinking he carried himself very well.

**It was completely amazing to think that this guy was 23 years old, and he was telling us what we needed to do to win the key to his city.** **-ALLISON**

**NV**

**Las Vegas**

93 40

**Flagstaff**

17

**Phoenix**

10

**AZ**

**Tucson**

19

**Nogales**

KEY TO SYMBOLS

🛏 ............sleep in motel

❤ ...................romance

💰 ............money trail

🎫 ............welcome to

Ⓜ .................mission

♨ ...empty Winnie septic tank

🐋 ..........scamming/cheating

🛏 ...........sleep in Winnie

**DUMP STATION** Registered RV Resort Guests

**How to Lighten Your Load**

1. Remove drain hose from rear bumper or exterior storage compartment.
2. Attach hose to Winnebago.
3. Place the other end of hose in disposal opening.
4. Open the (large) sewage valve with a quick pull. Open one valve at a time! Move hose gently about to dislodge any waste.
5. Close sewage valve and open (small) waste water valve with a quick pull. Close valve handle as soon as tank is empty.
6. After both tanks have been drained, run several gallons of water into the sewage tank through the toilet. Close valve.
7. Rinse sewer hose thoroughly with water and stow.

# CLUE

**THE KEY TO THE CITY IS NOT GIVEN TO JUST ANYBODY, BUT IT CAN BE YOURS IF YOU WIN OUR ANNUAL PENTATHLON. YOUR COMPETITION IS THE POLICE DEPARTMENT, THE SHERIFF'S OFFICE, THE FIRE DEPARTMENT, AND THE FOURTH TEAM, WHICH WILL BE ALL HIGH SCHOOL SENIORS.**
**-LOUIE**

## MISSION NUMBER 2

### WIN KEY TO THE CITY IN A PENTATHLON

**OBJECTIVE:** Complete a rowing event, a biking event, horseback riding, a jog, and a jog with a steep climb

**TOOLS:** A horse, a rowboat, a bike, running shoes, and a pickup truck???

**REWARD:** The key to the city

**NOGALES**
POPULATION:
19,500
NICKNAME:
Ambos Nogales (Both Nogales)
TRIVIA:
Port of entry for 75% of the US and Canada's winter fruits and veggies
CLAIM TO FAME:
Has the youngest mayor in the US
MOST NOTORIOUS RESIDENT:
On the Mexican side, bandito Pancho Villa
HOMETOWN OF:
Jazz great Charles Mingus

On the day of the race everybody's nerves kind of went out—we just wanted to finish, forget the key to the city. Los Man took the bike, Mark was on a semi-run, and I was going to pull the anchor leg. In the rowing event, Shelly beat the fire department, who kept rowing in circles. Los ran a strong leg on the bike. Allison had never been on a horse before, and I heard she rode great.

Bonehead didn't actually run in the race, he jumped in a truck; I knew something was up when he came juking across the lawn singing a song with his Walkman, because I had gone running with him earlier and he was completely out of breath.

For my part, I had to run maybe three-fourths of a mile and then shimmy up this mountain. It just about killed me. My legs got all cut up and I was exhausted at the top of the hill, so I asked for some water and this chick gave me this glass of old ice. I took about three gulps before I realized it was vodka and water, so I went and threw up and that was about it for me and the race. We finished third, but Louie ended up giving everybody a key to the city.     **-KIT**

I got stuck with half of the run. It was hot out, I was tired, what can I say? I stretched the rules a little (wink, wink). Hey, the others can be mad at me, but I did what it took to finish the race, and thanks to me, we didn't come in last.     **-MARK**

**792 MILES TRAVELED**

After the pentathlon, we went to a celebration dinner and had margaritas, beer, great food. Louie even serenaded Kit; she brings out the playfulness in people.

Then we went to a nightclub called Señor Amigos where we all went a little bit nuts. I didn't dance with Louie at all that night. He was sitting in the corner for most of the time, so I figured I'd go over and chat with him. We hung out until Louie brought us outside the restaurant and we got in a big huddle and he told us exactly where we had to go next. Then we dropped everyone off at Christina's, and he and I stayed up. I wasn't that attracted to him. Everybody makes mistakes. I'll make sure I don't drink as much next time, but it wasn't what everyone blew it up to be.

You know the game "Telephone," when one person tells someone something and they exaggerate it a little bit? That's what happened in Nogales. It's a small town and all of a sudden Louie and I were this hot item, big couple. Louie came by the Winnie and gave me a red carnation and he gave Kit and Shelly white ones. I threw them in the garbage pail in the gas station. I guess I just wanted to forget that anything happened and get the hell out of Nogales right away.

The one thing I definitely regret is putting it point-blank to Louie: "I never would've kissed you, but I was drunk." That only did more damage.     **-ALLISON**

# CLUE

**WHEN YOU LEAVE NOGALES, YOU'LL NEED TO HEAD NORTH ON I-19. YOU'LL BE STAYING IN FLAGSTAFF. ON THE WAY, LOOK FOR YOUR NEXT CLUE.**
**-LOUIE**

**THE OTHER NOGALES**

Across the Mexican border from Nogales you'll find the other Nogales, a less-sedate version of the orderly streets on the US side. It's basically a giant street fair, and a fun place to buy a hammock or sandals.

## What's wrong with a little BOOTIE-WOP,

especially if it's with a political figure? **-KIT**

# The Louie Incident

We went from desert to winter wonderland. It must of been through divine influence that we got the idea to take a picture outside of our hostel in Flagstaff, and there was the clue, hanging behind us on a big old banner. -LOS

## The Ring ♥

At Four Corners you could buy Indian jewelry, and Carlos tried to cut a deal so both of us could get rings. I think in his own way he was trying to push us one step up, even though we still hadn't talked about what happened in Phoenix. Considering that our money flow wasn't too good, I decided not to spend $12 on a ring, but I thought Los should get one, 'cause he really wanted it.

Later on, we had a talk about finances. We were tired of asking Los for money. I told him it wasn't fair that he could go out and spend $20 on jeans, spend money on music, film, and a ring, and then give me a hard time when I ask for $3 to buy a pack of cigarettes.

## I understand he doesn't agree with smoking but, hey, it's my life.

Kit made a comment, "Well, I think there's something a little bit more personal going on between you," which was completely true. But at least the money problem we could fix. We decided that each of us would get $20 to spend, no questions asked, and I would get my mom to send cigarettes. It wasn't going to be as easy to make the friendship work, I knew that.
**-SHELLY**

**KEY TO SYMBOLS**

......................danger
......................sidetrip
......................sleep in Winnie
......................romance
......................conflict
......................sleep in hostel
......................welcome to

At first, we thought Carlos was in love with Shelly because he was so sweet to her, always stroking her hair and going, "Honey, come sit next to me, honey." Then, just recently, he started pushing her the wrong way.

## I think that because Shelly has this tough-girl attitude he's trying to push her as far as he can to see when she's going to break, and she's going to break soon.

She said to me, "I'm trying my hardest to be nice, but this is not going to last very long. He's just driving me crazy." **-ALLISON**

**CO**

**Gunnison** ☆

**Montrose**  550  50

**Durango**

160

**Flagstaff**

**AZ**  89

**Phoenix**  17

**Tucson**

19  10

**Nogales**

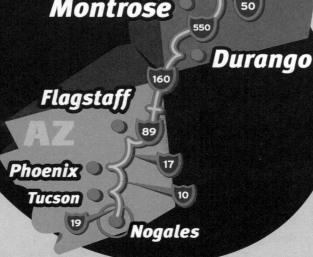

CLUE

**SILVERTON**
POPULATION:
700
POPULAR HANGOUTS:
Farquhart's, Carver's Bakery and Brewery
HISTORICAL TRIVIA:
Named when a miner shouted: "We ain't got much gold, but we sure got a ton of silver."
MUST SEE:
Re-creation of wild west shoot-out every day on Main Street at 5:30 P.M.

A

We tried to make it all the way from Flagstaff to Gunnison, but the driving conditions were as bad as you can ever imagine. The roads were slick, there was ice, it was dumping snow, it was late at night, and we were going at a straight decline.

I took my glasses off and didn't look out the window at all because everybody else was looking out and they were scared to death. **-ALLISON**

## I thought for sure we were going to take the Winnie over a cliff and tumble down to our deaths.

Finally, one of the cameramen took over and drove us to Silverton. That was one of the only times that the crew stepped in, but it was a matter of life and death, for real.    **-KIT**

B

**1278** MILES TRAVELED

All five of us were sitting by the fireplace in the restaurant looking for Gunnison on the atlas, and everybody started going off to do their own thing until there was just me and Carlos, sitting in the room and not speaking to each other. I tried to get him to talk to me about some things that were going on, like his attitude toward me, but he just sat there and said, "Shelly, you can't get everything you want." I know I can't get everything I want. All I wanted was for him to talk to me so we could lay it out and say, "OK, it's over."

I ended up walking off. When Allison came out to the Winnebago, I just lost it. When somebody won't talk to you, it makes you feel like it's your fault, though you know full well it's not.    **-SHELLY**

C

Remember elementary school, when you used to go up and kick the girl you deep down really liked? That's Los.    **-MARK**

Shelly has a very selfish, very strong-willed personality, and when she says she's ready to talk, that means she's ready for her to talk and for you to listen, and that's not how I operate. When I'm ready to share some ideas with her and when she's ready to listen, then I'll talk to her.    **-LOS**

**SEDONA**
From Flagstaff, US-89A rolls 28 miles south to Sedona, the New Age town that is said to be a locus of psychic vortices.

PORTRAIT OF
**THE LUCKY CAT
DOG CREW**
BREED:
Alaskan Husky
TEAM:
10 to 14 dogs per sled
QUALITIES:
Strength, toughness,
a good, calm brain,
ability to learn, and patience
WORKING LIFE:
Eight to 12 years

We weren't really sure what we were in for, but we finally made it to Gunnison and found Becky at the dog farm and did some snow camping and mushed the dogs back to the trading post. **-SHELLY**

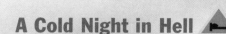

## To set the record straight, this is where the actual "first kiss" took place.

Kit and I were flirting in the laundromat, and I said, "I could swing one on you." She said, "Bull! You're too much of a wimp." I was sitting on top of a washer, and I wrapped my legs around her and yanked and it felt like breaking ice. Then we went back to the hotel and went into the hot tub. We knew we had to play it down because we had other people at home. **-MARK**

## A Cold Night in Hell

I thought maybe Becky would let us sleep in her house, but she gave us a little Honda and told us to drive to the nearest camping area. I don't think any of the five of us knew what we were in for. The sun was going down, and by the time we got up there it was pitch black and we were all fumbling around with our flashlights, trying to find a flat spot to put the tent. You would take one step in the snow and sink 4 feet down. Finally, Allison, Mark, and I pitched ours on the side of the mountain. Shelly and Los had had enough, so the two of them together decided they'd put up their own tent and cook their own dinner.

It was interesting that Shelly and Los went off together, since they'd been butting heads earlier, but they actually worked well as a team.

**When it's two in the morning and you want a warm place to sleep, it's amazing how well you can work together.**

Allison lasted half the night, and then snuck off to the car. Mark and I woke up to find that our tent had collapsed in the back and our sleeping bags were soaked in dew. **-KIT**

## MISSION NUMBER 3

### DOG SLED BACK TO CIVILIZATION

**OBJECTIVE:** Get the dogs (and yourselves) back safely

**TOOLS:** Dogs, a sled, warm clothes

**RULES:** Never let go of the sled, never let go of the sled, never let go of the sled

**REWARD:** Canine amore

**GUNNISON**
POPULATION:
4,600
TRIVIA:
1.7-million-acre Gunnison
National Forest has 27 peaks
that are 12,000 feet or higher

POPULAR HANGOUTS:
The Trough, Kochevar's Bar,
Idle Spur

FANFARE:
Fat Tire Bike Week, a huge
mountain bike celebration
that takes place in June

Definitely the worst experience of the whole trip was snow camping. I never have been so miserable in my life—couldn't sleep, felt claustrophobic, freezing, absolutely miserable. Thank God I had the good sense to go into the car and put the heater on, because I didn't think I would have lasted throughout the night. **-ALLISON**

Crested Butte is this cool little western ski town, probably about 40 minutes from Gunnison. A lot of college people take a semester off and live there and ski. It's nothing like Aspen, just really quaint, really real. We went there and had a few beers 'cause Gunnison was just so small.
**-KIT**

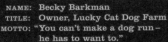

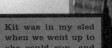

NAME: Becky Barkman
TITLE: Owner, Lucky Cat Dog Farm
MOTTO: "You can't make a dog run— he has to want to."

Kit was in my sled when we went up to Mirror Lake and she's a great athlete, she could run, and run, and run at 10,000 feet. That's definitely impressive.

However, the group as a whole didn't have any ability to solve problems. Quite frankly, I was amused by them. When they found out they were going to snow camp, I said, "Why don't you take the time to go through your equipment? It's probably going to be 10 degrees below zero. If you don't have the right equipment, you're going to die." I was exaggerating, trying to get their attention. I suggested they practice putting up their tents, because it was going to be a pain in the butt to figure it out in the dark. When I came back to check on them, they had set up the fly, the rain cover that goes over the tent and has no floor to it. They were very pleased with themselves, saying, "See, look what we did." I said, "That's nice, but where's your tent?"

So, I finally convinced them to find the real tent, then I said, "OK, now take off all your cotton and when you get there, use your stove, make warm food, and you're going to need to hydrate." Well, two of them figured it out and three of them didn't.

FARM
# 2WOOF
COLORADO

We had a really clear blue sky, and Mirror Lake was pure white. The sunlight made it look so beautiful. But the highlight for me was meeting the dogs. It put some wind back into my sails just to play with them and be out with them. They were real well-mannered and organized, just like little people—when it was time to get down to business they were right there.

I was worried about Kit and Shelly on the sled because they didn't seem to have much control. All of a sudden, their dogs started to run off the road, and the sled tilted over on its side. Neither one of the girls would let the sled go, so they got dragged behind. They were in a serious predicament, so I ran over and steered the dogs straight. It was nothing, really.

When we made it back to the trading post, a dog named Clue came running over, and in the back of his collar he had a message: Our next mission was to go to Shelly's house. Shelly's reaction was, "Damn!" She didn't mean it in a negative sense, she was just surprised and unprepared. **-LOS**

The night that we left Gunnison, Los and I got into a big fight. While the others were taking a hot tub at the hotel where we parked the Winnie, he decided to take the Winnebago and drive to get Chinese food. I was reading a book in the back, so I had to go along. I said to him, "Los, how much are you planning on spending on this?" He said, "Oh, probably about $10." Meanwhile we were all scrounging every penny we had just to get Ramen noodles or jelly sandwiches for dinner. I wouldn't even get a cup of coffee in the morning because I didn't want to spend the group's money on things like that. So when Los was inside eating his meal, I flipped out, I was so angry. I left him a note and started to walk back to the hotel. When I was halfway there, he passed me right by in the Winnie. **-ALLISON**

When we left Gunnison, I gave the money to Ally because I was just tired of the responsibility of it. It's a thankless job. Everybody wanted someone to handle the money, but they would always give me lip when I offered my advice about how they should spend it. I mean, it was a group fund and we needed it to do group things. **-LOS**

### THE LAST GREAT RACE

Known as The Last Great Race on Earth, the Iditarod commemorates the 1925 journey in which mushers transported medicine from Anchorage, AK, to stop a diptheria epidemic in Nome. The Iditarod has been run every March since its inception in 1967, and in 1976, Congress designated its course a National Historic Trail. The longest dog-sled race in the world covers two mountain ranges—the frozen Yukon River and the iced-in Norton Sound—on its 1,049-mile course. Most recently, the top finishers have completed the race in 10 days and 15 hours.

CLUE

Visit Oklahoma City.
Let Shelly show you
around her home town

### COLD AS ICE

Human beings are "homeotherms," meaning they must maintain body temperatures within a range of 96 - 101 degrees to properly function.

Chronic hypothermia is the lowering of the core temperature below 95 degrees for over a period of six hours.

Frostbite is the freezing of tissue. To avoid it, you must first avoid:

- Constricting garments
- Dehydration
- Inadequate nutrition
- Fatigue
- Smoking during exposure to cold

So we left Gunnison and headed for Oklahoma City to finally meet Shelly's mom and check out her famous room. -MARK

SHELLY'S
ROAD STAPLES
Comfortable shoes
blue jeans
leather jacket
music
photo album

It was my duty to try and schmooze the women at the front desk into another free breakfast. They looked like easy prey, so I went for it. Gave them the song and dance that we'd been traveling across the country, staying at all the Best Westerns. "Best Western's the best." They gave us five tickets for break-fast. -MARK

B

By the time we got to Oklahoma we had about $20 for the five of us. -ALLISON

**1278** MILES TRAVELED

VISITOR INFORMATION

SHELLY'S FAVORITE
ROAD FOOD
Ramen noodle soup,
peanut butter and jelly, 7-Up,
Hawaiian Punch, brown sugar
and oatmeal, microwave pizzas

C

# Shelly

WELCOME TO
OKLAHOMA

My Oklahoma City might not be your Oklahoma City. As a Native American, I go to a lot of powwows. Powwows are just the same as going to a con-cert, they're pretty big here. In general, life is pretty hum-drum in Oklahoma City. Family is very important, but it's harder than it used to be to get us all together. When my great-grandmother passed away it was one of the first times in a long time that I'd seen us all together. People were getting into limos and going to the church just like at any funeral, and we saw two hawks fly above us. Something like that, we as Native Americans would see dif-ferently, as a sign. Everybody point-ed it out, and people started crying because it just touched us. It's this kind of experience that has a lot to do with who I am as a person.

Because of my heritage I definitely feel added responsibility sometimes. I know I'm not quite the way that my grandmother wants me to be. There's a lot of pressure to do traditional dancing, to run for Princess or other titles, but it's something that I would much rather do for fun.

I think there's a false relevance placed on being Native American in the United States today. It's very commercialized, and everywhere you go people ask the dumbest questions like, "Oh, wow, you're full-blooded, how did you get full-blooded?" and, "Do you still live in tepees?" Give me a break. -SHELLY

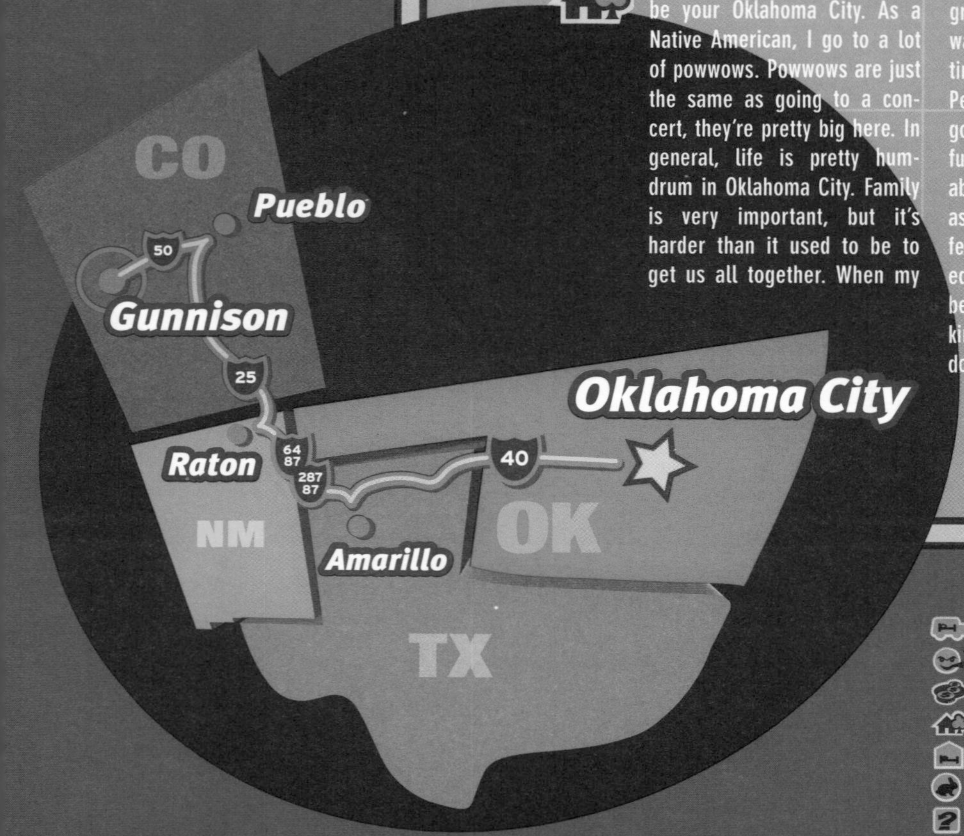

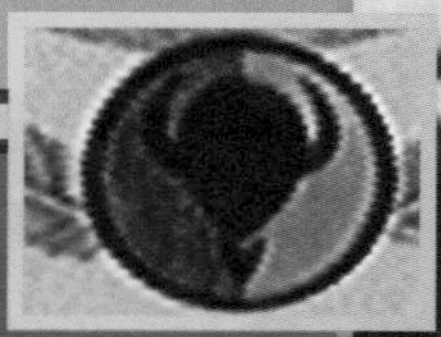

CO

Pueblo

50

Gunnison

25

Raton

64
87
287
87

40

Oklahoma City

NM

Amarillo

OK

TX

KEY TO
SYMBOLS

................sleep in Winnie
..........scamming/cheating
................money trail
...............hometown stop
................sleep in motel
................roadkill
................lost

## Shelly told me that she thinks I'm a total bitch and that's why she feels close to me.

I thought that was pretty nice. She is such an incredible person. She is very caring, she's very sensitive, and very insightful—but since she's often unhappy on this trip, people tend to judge her as being a bitch or a big baby. I've heard many things said about Shelly in the heat of the moment, but she's really the only person that I'll talk to about anything deeper or more meaningful than, "What are we doing today?" and, "How are we going to afford this?"   **-ALLISON**

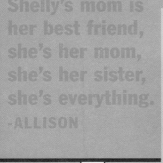

I don't know if it's her being an only child, but Shelly's not a morning person. She needs her space, she needs her music and to go off by herself with her Walkman and have a cigarette. I think that she takes things a little more seriously sometimes than she should and maybe that's because she's younger or maybe it's 'cause she's not used to dealing with so many different types of people.

I'm really envious that Shelly's got a culture to identify with. I think it's neat that she's given an Indian name and she dances with other members of her family. I think it definitely brings them closer together.   **-KIT**

**6**

When I first saw Shelly, I thought, "Hardcore, psycho rocker, maniac." Then I got to talk to her and see photos of her family and I realized that I'd been wrong. She's really a deep person. She appreciates and loves her heritage, and I've never had a friend like her before.   **-MARK**

The reason I call Shelly "Pocahontas" is number one: she lets me, and number two: she is the emergence of two different cultures. Pocahontas was from this Indian tribe and she fell in love with a conquistador, a Spanish soldier. And that's just Shelly in a nutshell, man. She's from an ancient tribe and she's into heavy metal. I think she's dating this guy in a rock band. Yo, if she ain't Pocahontas, who is? She says I'm the only person she lets call her Pocahontas, and I believe that. I guess it's just my way of connecting with her on an ethnic basis.   **-LOS**

### OKLAHOMA CITY
**POPULATION:**
444,700
**HISTORICAL TRIVIA:**
Oklahoma City was created in one day when white settlers claimed the land and drove the Native Americans out
**FANFARE:**
National Finals Rodeo is nine days of hard riding by the best cowgirls and boys in the country
**MUST SEE:**
National Cowboy Hall of Fame

**B**

2002 MILES TRAVELED

## Mom

My mom and I are very close, and when something's wrong or something's bothering me, she'll lay it out for me. I get teased a lot about calling my mom all the time, but at least I know she's going to tell me the truth, either way. She is the only person who can say, "You're being too bitchy," or "Why don't you loosen up?"   **-SHELLY**

## Shelly's mom is her best friend, she's her mom, she's her sister, she's everything.
**-ALLISON**

It's good that Shelly can talk to her mom on the phone as much as she does because she can take different problems or gripes to her mom instead of bringing 'em to the group.

Shelly's mom was a little overwhelmed and maybe a little worried about Shelly after meeting us all. She was definitely interested in seeing what Los was all about.

When we showed her the inside of the Winnie, I think right then and there she wanted Shelly to stay where she was and let the four of us go on our merry way.

**D**

I think the home stop was harder than Shelly had expected because it was kind of a tease. We pulled in there and she got to see her mom for a whole day and got used to seeing her again, and then we shoved off to our next destination.   **-KIT**

**4**

### SHELLY'S OKLAHOMA CITY DIGS
**FAVORITE HANGOUTS:**
Bricktown (like New York's East Village, but smaller); powwows

**FAVORITE LOCAL BAND:**
Aranda: "The rave scene is strong, but I prefer live music."

## CLUE

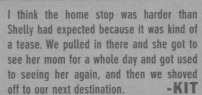

I KNOW YOU'RE RUNNING LOW ON MONEY, SO I'VE ARRANGED A JOB FOR YOU. GET TO THE KLIEBERT FARM IN HAMMOND, LOUISIANA BY TOMORROW NIGHT SO YOU CAN START EARLY THE NEXT DAY.

The 10-hour drive to Hammond took 14 hours, thanks to Los's directions. When we finally got there, we did some work and got paid in cash and Taco Bell coupons. Mark and Kit got our next clue off a drugstore jukebox. -ALLISON

**A**

I think Los was the only one that fit in in Shreveport. We were definitely the only white people running around there. Los actually stayed in the car just 'cause he didn't feel like dealing with all of us in the grocery store. **-KIT**

One thing about being brought up black is that you learn how to be respectful of other people's cultures. Just because you're black doesn't mean that you fit in with every black culture. Black people down there were BLACK. The culture was pure Southern, and people were 50 years behind everyone else. Folks was still wearing Jheri curls, and McDonald's was the only thing new on the block. **-LOS**

**2002**
**MILES TRAVELED**

NOT GUILTY!!

**C**

**KEY TO SYMBOLS**
- ........scamming/cheating
- ........sleep in motel
- JOB........job
- ?........lost
- ........welcome to
- ........conflict
- ........money trail
- ........sleep in Winnie

Went to Bennigan's for a brownie and ice cream. The waitress took too long bringing my brownie, so I didn't tip her. Then the girls started in on me about that and whatever else they could come up with. "Los, every time we go somewhere you never want to do anything with the group."

**Well, no matter where we are, Kit's looking for a place to have a drink and some laughs, Shelly wants a smoke and a shower, and Mark will go whichever way the wind blows.** For a while I wanted to be a team player, but it's just not happening anymore. **So what am I going to do? Shake things up a little.** I may pretend to be a racist for a little while, something like that. I'll most definitely hurt people's feelings. If they try hard enough, they might even be able to hurt mine. **-LOS**

**MS**

Oklahoma City

**OK**

**Jackson**

35

20

55

**Dallas**

**TX** **LA**

**Hammond**

3

HAMMOND
POPULATION:
20,000
TRIVIA:
Named for Peter Hammond,
a Swedish settler and
barrel-maker
FANFARE:
Each October, Southeastern
Louisiana University sponsors a
monthlong salute to the arts

NAME: Harvey Kliebert
TITLE: Owner, Kliebert's Turtle and Alligator Farm
MOTTO: "If they wanted to eat me, they would've already."

At Kliebert's Turtle and Alligator Farm, we raise turtles and alligators for a living. We started the farm I guess back in the early '50s. We produce 3,000 to 4,000 baby turtles and 1,000 to 1,500 alligators every year.

We sell most of our alligator skins to tanneries. We ship the baby turtles overseas, mostly to China, Taiwan, and Japan, because we don't have the rights to ship them in the United States. I don't know what they do with them; to tell you the truth, they might be eating them.

Alligators are tremendous in smarts. They like to eat nutria. If you feed them good, they don't bother you, but if you stop feeding them, they start getting hungry, they start getting closer and closer.

When we pulled up to Hammond, our grand total was $1.10.
**-MARK**

**The alligator meat tasted kind of like chicken.** It was cooked in a spicy batter. I couldn't help thinking while I ate it that I'd never even seen alligators before, except in the zoo. **-SHELLY**

## JOB Packin' Gators

OBJECTIVE: Los and Shelly, roll up your sleeves and pack some meat; Allison, give a good tour and don't get bitten

HAZARDS: The live ones bite, the dead ones stink

REWARD: $280 each

2373 MILES TRAVELED

When we were serving ice cream we met this one cat who was the Oyster King and he insisted that the Oyster Festival was about the biggest thing since Mardi Gras. He kept sayin', "The Oyster Queen's just as purty as she can be," and going on and on about this oyster thing that no one has ever heard of. I think maybe he'd been sippin' on a little bit o' nectar. **-KIT**

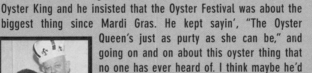

## JOB Scoopin' Ice Cream

OBJECTIVE: Kit and Mark, put on your aprons, you'll work at a soda fountain

PERKS: All the ice cream you can eat, plus an air-conditioned workplace

REWARD: $280 each

NAME: Judy Williams
TITLE: Co-owner of People's Rexall with husband Jimmy
MOTTO: "I like a place where you can drive across town in five minutes and you never have to wait in line."

Many of the little towns here in Louisiana are known for their festivals. We happen to have the Oyster Festival. It was founded by the Italians, who started the oyster industry here. Our latest Oyster Queen is Nancy Thomas. She's a senior at Amite High School. The King is Bill Owen, who's now retired. His wife, Marie, is the Oyster Pearl.

People's Rexall has been here more than 50 years. Our best-selling flavors are plain old vanilla and chocolate, and walnut is a close runner-up. Kit didn't like walnut, though.

The honest truth, I wouldn't hire Kit and Mark again. I'm glad the show didn't air until several months after they worked here because they were sticking spoons in everything, which isn't exactly sanitary. You could see the romance, they were pretty charming, he was popping her with the towel, picking on her, they picked on each other.

## CLUE

AMITE
[pronounced A-MEET]
POPULATION
5,000
POPULAR HANGOUTS:
The Amite High
School bleachers
at the Amite Warrior's
home games;
Popeye's and McDonald's
FANFARE:
The Oyster Festival

START DRIVING TO NEW ORLEANS TONIGHT SO THAT YOU CAN START LEARNING ABOUT THE FIRST MAN OF JAZZ TOMORROW. A GOOD PLACE TO START WOULD BE THE CABBIES ON THE CORNER OF BOURBON AND CONTI. FIND OUT EVERYTHING YOU CAN, BECAUSE YOU HAVE TO SPEND THE NIGHT WITH HIM.

New Orleans had a pulse, that city just thumped. Everyone was ready to ride it and relieve all the tension that had built up. –MARK

**1** **2** **3**

**A**

Kit and Mark kissed on our first night in New Orleans, and it was pretty funny because Kit came right up to me and said, "Don't tell anybody, but Mark, out of the blue, just planted a kiss on me."

And then Mark came up to me about five minutes later and said, "Don't tell anybody, but Kit told me that she wanted to tell me a secret, and the next thing I knew she started kissing me." So, they had a little conflict of stories there.

**B**

I honestly know nothing's going to develop out of it, because Kit has her man at home who she's in love with, and Mark is constantly talking about his girlfriend, too. I think they were just feeling affectionate and drank too much and by mistake things went too far. That's about it.
**-ALLISON**

Kit and Mark are just inseparable anyway. I swear those two are like Beavis and Butt-Head, Wayne and Garth, something or other. If you try and squeeze in there, you feel like an oddball.     **-SHELLY**

Don't know about any kissing, but it doesn't surprise me. I've never seen Kit so out of control. She just had too much to drink. She wanted me to keep an eye out for her and make sure she didn't do anything too stupid. Hell, there's a little daiquiri place every two damn doors. You know what I'm saying? It's like a drunkard's paradise.     **-LOS**

# The Kiss

## Aaagh, we got caught!
OK, it wasn't our first kiss, but the first was in New Orleans, just earlier that night.

**C**

Knowing that it wasn't our little secret was very upsetting because I am like really, really serious with Andy—so in love with Andy. If it was just me, I would not care about how I came out looking, but I never wanted to hurt anybody else.

Still, I don't regret having these unbelievable experiences with an awesome guy who is definitely my friend. More than anything physical, it's just a friendship thing on my end. Mark'll make up all kinds of stories. He'll probably say something like I told him a secret or something stupid like that, but all I can say is, how can someone 5 feet tall plant a kiss on someone who's 6 feet tall? He's pullin' all kindsa tricks. Basically, the guy can't keep his hands off me, and we're gonna have a little talk because you know, we can never smooch again.

The only thing I can compare it to is camp. Like you might have a boyfriend at home and you go away to camp and you're in this weird environment with all new people and you're doing cool activities and you get a crush on a boy and you might kiss him, but when camp's over, you go back to your boyfriend and your normal life. The difference for Mark and me was they caught it on TV and exposed us. We just got busted. **-KIT**

Hammond
LA
55
10
New Orleans

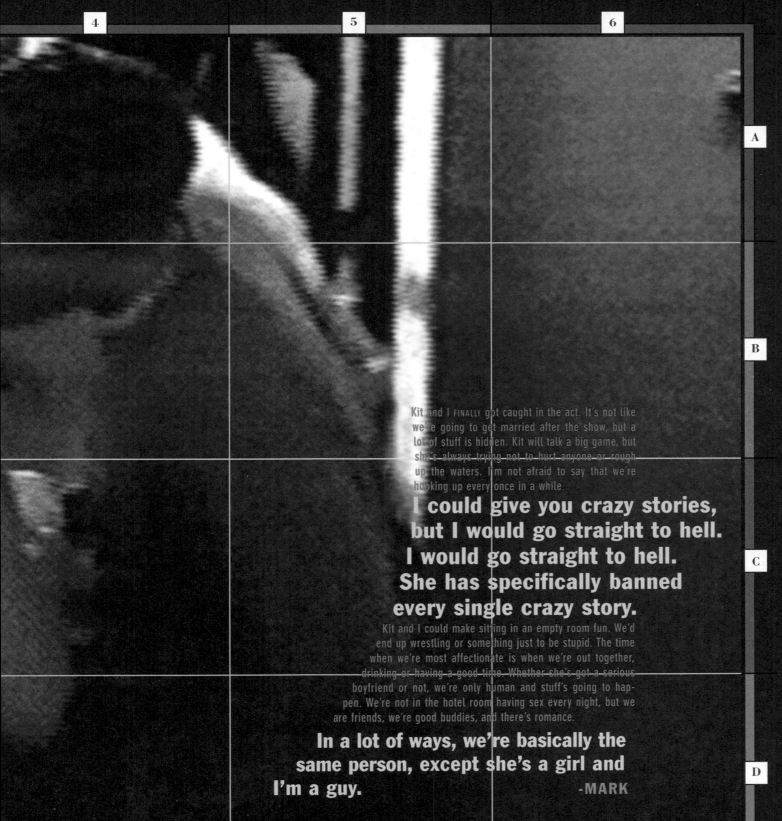

4 5 6

A B C D

Kit and I FINALLY got caught in the act. It's not like we're going to get married after the show, but a lot of stuff is hidden. Kit will talk a big game, but she's always trying not to hurt anyone or rough up the waters. I'm not afraid to say that we're hooking up every once in a while.

**I could give you crazy stories, but I would go straight to hell. I would go straight to hell. She has specifically banned every single crazy story.**

Kit and I could make sitting in an empty room fun. We'd end up wrestling or something just to be stupid. The time when we're most affectionate is when we're out together, drinking or having a good time. Whether she's got a serious boyfriend or not, we're only human and stuff's going to happen. We're not in the hotel room having sex every night, but we are friends, we're good buddies, and there's romance.

**In a lot of ways, we're basically the same person, except she's a girl and I'm a guy.**
                                    **-MARK**

**NOMS DE PLUME IN NEW ORLEANS**

Samuel Clemens came up with the moniker Mark Twain while working in New Orleans as a journalist; novelist William S. Porter was inspired to become O. Henry one afternoon in 1896 as he sipped a beer and heard someone call to the bartender, "Oh, Henry!" But New Orleans does more than inspire pseudonyms: Anne Rice lives and works in a spooky mansion in the Garden District, and the cult classic A CONFEDERACY OF DUNCES, by John Kennedy Toole was based here.

**NEW ORLEANS**
POPULATION:
496,900
POPULAR HANGOUTS:
Tipitina's, Café du Monde, and Café Brasil
TALK OF THE TOWN:
Legalized gambling
FANFARE:
Mardi Gras, Jazz and Heritage Festival
HOMETOWN OF:
Anne Rice, Harry Connick Jr., Ellen Degeneres, and John Goodman

Money is a really strange thing. It stresses people out amazingly, very easily. I hope we can handle it better the second time around. **-KIT**

We decided as a whole to split up all of our money. I personally didn't feel like it was a good idea, but Carlos, he fought for this. **-SHELLY**

we were supposed to find the first man of jazz. Ron the cool ass cabbie drove us around and showed us all the places our man, Buddy, used to hang out. After we found out Buddy was dead, a voodoo priestess told us the only way we could find him was to go visit his gravesite, which was unmarked in a decrepit little cemetery. —LOS

## MISSION

### NUMBER 4

# FIND BUDDY BOLDEN

**OBJECTIVE:** Sleep with him
**TOOLS:** Taxicab, voodoo séance
**REWARD:** Spiritual enlightenment?

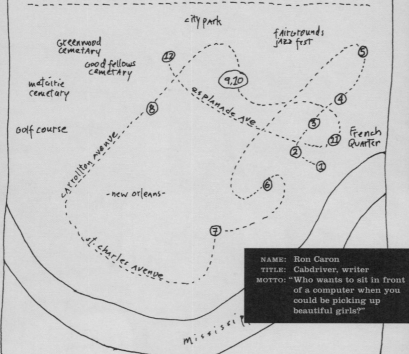

The Search for Buddy Bolden: The cab ride with Ron

1. kit, mark, allison, shelly, los meet ron at the corner of bourbon and conti next to Lucky Dog vendor. 11 A.M.
2. basin street at bienville. location of 'storyville', the old red-light district circa 1900. now a housing project. adjacent to saint louis #1 cemetery, the oldest city of the living dead's including marie laveau, voodoo priestess.
3. congo square/ Armstrong park, old perseverance hall. rampart @ st. ann st.
4. ron's house, built 1890. we didn't actually stop here.
5. jelly roll morton's home 1895. 1443 Frenchmen street.
6. The 'birthplace of JAZZ.' corner of s. rampart and perdido, once the location of union hall and 'Funky butt hall, now city hall. Louis Armstrong arrested here and taken to waif's home. New Year's eve, 1910.
7. buddy bolden lived here. 2309 1st street near simon bolivar. close to the chicken mart.
8. site of old Lincoln+ Johnson Parks, carrollton avenue @ Oleander st. where bolden performed. Gert town area.
9. bayou st. john. we stopped for strategy discussion?
10. parkway bakery on hagan street. poboys' for lunch.
11. voodoo museum. 724 dumaine. séance. the meter ticks, ron waits.
12. Holt cemetery on city park avenue. pauper's graveyard and location of bolden's unmarked grave. 9 p.m. ...fare: $228.10.

**city park**
**fairgrounds jazz fest**
**Greenwood cemetery**
**Good fellows cemetery**
**metairie cemetery**
**esplanade ave**
**golf course**
**French Quarter**
**carrollton avenue**
**—new orleans—**
**st. charles avenue**
**mississippi**

illustration: ron caron 4·1·96

**NAME:** Ron Caron
**TITLE:** Cabdriver, writer
**MOTTO:** "Who wants to sit in front of a computer when you could be picking up beautiful girls?"

We went to the corner of Bourbon and Conti and we met a taxi driver there—very chill, very cool—and we asked him if he knew who the Father of Jazz was, and he said,

# "Yeah, I think I can help you, come on."

Buddy was your typical unsung hero. His music was well known all across the region, yet he never recorded a song. It's a shame. The man's the Father of Jazz, and there's only one photograph of him left, and nobody knows anything about him. I mean, really knows anything. -LOS

I think it was by accident that Ron let the cat out of the bag... **Buddy was dead,** finito, finished, sent up the river. -MARK

I'd consider the birthplace of jazz to be New Orleans, specifically the corner of South Rampart and Perdido, where Buddy Bolden played his cornet along with some of the other best musicians—mostly black—at the turn of the century. **The Funky Butt Hall was here, named after Buddy Bolden because that was his big song, "The Funky Butt."** Louis Armstrong was arrested on the same corner as a six-year-old for firing a gun. He was put in a home for waifs, and that's where he eventually learned to play trumpet. -RON CARON

## The Séance

Walking into that room reminded me of Christmas Mass, with incense burning and a lot of candles.

## The priestess seemed to be the really deep, deep, deep spiritual one, sayin' stuff under her breath, doin' the old Charlie Manson jive.

### VOODOO WHO-DO?

Originating in Haiti, voodoo is a religious system brought to America by African slaves in the 17th, 18th, and 19th centuries. 20,000 people in New Orleans alone believe in voodoo, which is a combination of African religion and Roman Catholicism. Though movies like the cult classic ANGEL HEART sensationalize certain voodoo practices, only occasional animal sacrifices are made. More often, gris-gris, or potions and powders, are used in worship.

She had her tarot cards laid out and she was doin' her karate motions, trying to grab Buddy's spirit.

I chose my spiritual guide to be a guy by the name of Josh. Josh is an old friend of mine who I've known since the third grade. He passed away a couple of years ago. He was one of my best friends in the world, so he came to mind first.

When I asked the priestess what was in the bowl of water she said, "Holy water, flower petals, and blue balls." Kit kicked me under the table and I almost busted out laughing, 'cause that's the last thing I need right now. My sexual tank's on full; I think it's fillin' in the reserve tank right now. **-MARK**

My grandfather passed on a few years ago, and I picked him for my spiritual guide because he was the only dead person I knew. But he wasn't exactly a protective, insightful, knowledgeable kind of grandfather. And that's the reason I was a believer, because they had pointed at everyone else and said something about their saints, the people watching over them, and then they looked at me and said, "We just don't sense a lot of people watching over you." **-ALLISON**

### SPIRITUAL GUIDES TO THE FIVE

SHELLY:
Ancestors; Michael

LOS:
None

ALLISON:
Grandfather

KIT:
Best friend, Cameron; both grandfathers

MARK:
Josh

NEW ORLEANS HISTORIC VOODOO MUSEUM
Brandi Kelley
Public Relations Representative / Ritual Performance
724 Dumaine, New Orleans, LA 70116 (504) 522-5223

## Graveyard Shift

I thought we were going to come and visit Buddy, give him the nine pennies from the priestess for luck, drop a couple flowers on his grave, and be out. But that's not what we did. We ended up grabbing the sleeping bags and spending the night out there. It was so hellish, it could only be superseded by the night we spent in Colorado sleeping under 6 feet of snow. **-LOS**

**CLUE** IF YOU THOUGHT SLEEPING IN THE CEMETERY WAS SCARY, WAIT 'TIL YOU GO TO ETHOS TRACE IN PACE, FLORIDA, WHERE YOUR NEXT CLUE WILL BE REVEALED.

The paupers' graveyard where Buddy Bolden lies borders the old Storyville, which is now a ghetto and not especially safe. We've had a couple of problems with tourists getting their purses snatched. Nothing too serious—except there was one person murdered in daylight. **-RON**

To sleep in a cemetery where I didn't know anyone seemed pointless. I wasn't comforting anyone's soul. The cemetery looked so lonely and depressing, I didn't feel comfortable. I feel that cemeteries are meant for paying respects, to ease the soul.

I have had to deal with a lot of things in the past year and a half. I had a friend who died, Michael, and it was very untimely and very tragic. In a lot of ways I haven't healed myself. But I feel like I'm a better person than I was when he was alive. His death brought out something in me that wasn't there before. That's the only thing that I can thank him for—making me see a few things in a different light. And right now I see I have to take care of myself.

Out of respect to Michael, and to his family and the other people who have lost loved ones, I could not stay there for recreational fun. **-SHELLY**

### OTHER CITIES OF THE DEAD

You can pay your respects to the legendary voodoo queen Marie Laveau at St. Louis Cemetery No. 1.

Much of INTERVIEW WITH THE VAMPIRE was shot at Lafayette Cemetery.

Lakelawn Metairie used to be a racetrack; now it's a drive-through cemetery.

We went to a nudist trailer park and partied with the old naked man, George, and his horseshoe-throwing buddies. From there we turned it up to a different level and went to work in Americus, Georgia, for Habitat for Humanity. We built a house with some college kids, ate some Pixie Sticks, and headed to Hotlanta, my hometown. –KIT

ΣΤΗΟΣ ΤΡΑΣΣ

**B**

## "Ooh, oh my God! Look at his thing!" –ALLISON

I was crossing Pensacola Bay for the second time. The first time, I was little and my family was moving again. We were driving through the same swamps in the pouring rain, and the bridge seemed huge. When we crossed it in the Winnie, it was really sunny, but I could still see the rain coming down on the windshield, me and my dad in the moving truck, and my mom in front of us in her car.

I was kind of lost in that world when we pulled up to Ethos Trace and met George, who was Florida's version of Big Foot. When I first saw him I instantly thought to call HARD COPY and report seeing Sasquatch roaming the flatlands of Florida. –MARK

### 2442 MILES TRAVELED

**C**

**KEY TO SYMBOLS**

🐰 ............................roadkill
🚐 ............................sleep in Winnie
❓ ............................lost
⚔ ............................conflict
Ⓜ ............................mission
♨ ......empty Winnie septic tank
🛏 ............................sleep in motel

Kit and Mark were expecting beaches, sand, and young, naked bodies. That is not what we got, I'm telling you.
The game was:

## George had our clue in a plastic bag, nestled against his privates underwater,

so the only way to get to it was to get butterball, go into the pool, and grab it.
I was the only brother, and I was not getting naked for them old folks. George was a nice guy, and as long as he's a happy man, more power to him, but I was out, I was definitely out.
Of course Kit was up for it.
"Kit, are you going to go nude?"
"Like, it's my job."
That's her line.

With Shelly, everything's cut and dry. If she's not already thinking about it, you're not going to persuade her to do anything. Then there's Mark with the usual, "I'll go, but I'm not going by myself." Mark is the "I'm not going by myself" dude. Finally, Kit, Mark, and Allison stripped and got the clue, and I think I've pretty much summed up everybody's feelings about the nudist trip. –LOS

## CLUE

GO TO AMERICUS, GEORGIA, TODAY SO THAT YOU CAN LEND A HAND TOMORROW AT HABITAT FOR HUMANITY. THIS TIME YOU'RE REALLY GOING TO HAVE TO HIT THE NAIL ON THE HEAD.

**NAME:** George Eckenroth
**TITLE:** Manager, Riviera Naturist Resort
**MOTTO:** "Everybody's got the same thing, so why hide it?"

My name's George, and I became a nudist in 1980. I met my wife right here six years ago in a hot tub, and we've been together ever since.

People think that more goes on at a nudist resort than what really does. They think there's orgies under all the trees, and it just don't happen that way. When you have a man and a woman together with no clothes on they get less excited than if they're wearing a little bikini or a tight T-shirt.

Nudism isn't for everyone, but some people who don't think they can do it come here and say, "Wow, I didn't know it was going to be like this, I should have started out 30 years ago."

The ROAD RULES kids were real fine people. They bought us out of shirts. I bet if they had stayed a couple more days, they all would have had their clothes off—except Shelly. After their visit, we had inquiries clear from France, Scotland, and Switzerland.

### BEING BARE
Nudism began in the United States in 1929 when Kurt Barthel and his wife formed the American League for Physical Culture. Unfortunately, their outings were always subject to raids by local officers. It wasn't until the late '50s that it became safe to enjoy nudism in private parks. Today, the American Association for Nude Recreation has 46,000 members who belong to more than 200 nudist clubs in North America.

**MS** **AL** **GA**

Opelika 280
Montgomery 27 **Americus**
29 85
LA 65 **Richland**
New Orleans 10
65
**Pensacola**
FL

No Clothes
NO Food-Drink
NO ANIMALS

# MISSION 5

## BUILD A HOUSE WITH HABITAT FOR HUMANITY

**OBJECTIVE:** Use your muscle for a good cause

**HAZARDS:** Bonding games

**REWARD:** Plaque of achievement from Habitat for Humanity

We were driving along, trying to find Americus, Georgia. **All of a sudden, splat! A bat commits suicide on my windshield wipers.** Of course, we pulled over and gave it a proper burial. **-ALLISON**

Funny thing about these road trips is we're in the car all day and can't wait to get to our destination, and when we finally pull up we have to stay in the Winnie, 'cause that's our lodging. At this point in our journey, the word "house" brings back good memories, but this place makes Gunnison, Colorado, look like party capital of the world. Amigo House had separate rooms for the guys and the girls. Of course, Mark kept trying to coerce me to sleep up in his bunk, but I couldn't break the rules. **-KIT**

Habitat for Humanity is a non-profit organization; I guess I would say it's based on Christian principles. They provide housing for people who otherwise couldn't afford it, using volunteer builders and suppliers. **-LOS**

B

**2764 MILES TRAVELED**

I really liked building the house, but the group that we were with was really into sharing their spiritual feelings and it kind of turned me off.

I think my main problem was that I felt like I was being preached to. I said one thing about getting a drink and this girl turned to me and said, "Drinking is against the rules here. Why would you want to do that, anyway? Do you want to escape reality? Do you have a problem?"

So I said, "Listen, I was just making a comment, I thought I'd go out for a drink." I didn't really want to be counseled and I wasn't asking for her advice.

Later, they had a group discussion in a circle, and they said I didn't have to participate, but I could watch. I said, "OK, I'll watch." So I sat there and the leader wanted everyone to go out and get a rock. I didn't want to get a rock because I just wanted to watch. And every single person in the group turned and said, "Come on, get a rock, get a rock."

I'm just different from them. I don't really believe in organized religion. A lot of my ideals are Christian ideals, but I want to be a doctor and I'm very scientific and the things that I have learned through science almost point away from religion. **-ALLISON**

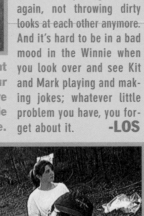

We were embarrassed that they rewarded us for our work when we spent more time sleeping in the Winnie than building a house. **-MARK**

I think we're family right now. We've had our fist-fights and temper tantrums, and every now and then Allison and I may get pretty heated, but after we're finished we can kick back and laugh about it. Pocahontas and I are palling around again, not throwing dirty looks at each other anymore. And it's hard to be in a bad mood in the Winnie when you look over and see Kit and Mark playing and making jokes; whatever little problem you have, you forget about it. **-LOS**

C

D

## CLUE

CONGRATULATIONS ON A JOB WELL DONE. YOU'VE EARNED YOURSELVES A BREAK. TAKE A COUPLE DAYS TO FIGURE OUT WHY THEY CALL IT "HOTLANTA," AND MAYBE SEE SOME RELATIVES.

**AMERICUS**
POPULATION: 17,278

POPULAR HANGOUTS:
Forsyth Bar and Grill, Pat's Place

TRIVIA:
Nine miles from Jimmy Carter's house

FANFARE:
The Sumpter Swine Fest in late April is two smoky days of barbecue

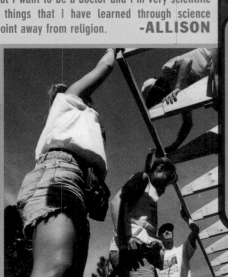

Kit and Los were really excited to see their parents. We had a good time in Atlanta, went out a couple nights, filled up our tanks. Oh, me and Kit told our respective others about the smooch. Let's just say they each handled it in their own way. -MARK

## ♥ What Hotlanta Means

One of my biggest problems is that when something bothers me, instead of confronting it, I just make a joke about it and go on my way. I'm not really good at expressing my feelings, especially if the feelings are sad or bitter. The whole Andy situation was something that I knew I had to confront. Andy was leaving to go out of town, so I was only going to see him for a couple of hours. I decided to tell him about Mark planting one on me in New Orleans. We went on a walk down the street and I just blurted it out. I thought he'd be a little upset, but not as mad as he was. He jumped in his car, and I jumped in after him and tried to explain some more, but he just drove me to my house and asked me to get out of the car. After he left, I decided I could sit and sulk or I could make a stiff drink and take everybody into town. We went to Clarence Foster's. I didn't dance all night, but on the very last song Mark pulled me onto the dance floor and we were dirty dancing, being funny. I should have known better.

If the tables were turned, if I was Andy, I would hate my guts. **I suck at relationships.** I should never get involved. Hurting Andy is my biggest regret ever. I think I got my walking papers. -KIT

I thought Randy, I mean Andy, would be bigger. I think he was maybe buck-40 or buck-50 tops. Kit could kick his ass, that's why she has him in the palm of her hand.

Kit told me he didn't take it that well that we kissed. She told me he yelled, then took off down the street.

**Geez, imagine if he would have found out all the other stuff that's been going on off-camera.**

Tracy took it a little better. She and a couple of my buddies came to Atlanta and we all went to Fellini's for pizza and beers. I thought it was going to be kind of weird, having Kit and Tracy there at the same time, but Tracy basically laughed it off. We're not that serious as it is. She lives 3,000 miles away from me, so when we're together, we're together, but when we're apart she can do what she wants and I can do basically what I want.

## 2764 MILES TRAVELED

The group wanted to stay at Kit's house, which suited me fine, I wanted to stay alone with my family. I've never been into having a whole bunch of people in my house, but everyone was big on meeting my folks, so I let them come over, shake hands, and be on their way.

I think the gang was sort of surprised at how nice my mom was and how friendly my dad was. They were like, "Oh, Carlos is so mean, he's got to come from this hellhole of a home where everybody grunts at each other, throwing dirty looks." It's not like that at all. Most of my "attitude," I guess you call it, comes from experiences that I've had dealing with people in D.C. and other places. It just works for me. -LOS

Los's dad was the Denzel Washington type, real smooth, laid-back, didn't lower or raise his voice at all the whole time, just kept that cool feel about him. -MARK

After we left Fellini's, Tracy was driving and a car pulled out and smashed up her jeep. So by the time we patched things up with the cops and got home it was 4:45. Tracy was all upset, she was just bawling, so it kind of broke the mood. But when we finally got back to the hotel, I connived my friend Pat into giving us his room and **I finally got some loving after about six weeks on the road, so I was very, very happy.** -MARK

At Fellini's I kissed Mark's friend because I'd decided that I would do a little survey on the Top Ten Best Kisses in the United States for U.S. NEWS & WORLD REPORT. I think he was better than Louie. I have to say that Kit was ahead of me in the kissing game that night: she kissed four guys. -ALLISON

### KEY TO SYMBOLS

🏠 ........................hometown stop
♥ ...............................romance
🎨 .........................money trail
📋 ...........................welcome to
Ⓜ ................................mission
〰️ ......empty Winnie septic tank
❓ .....................................lost

## Atlanta
★
75
27
## GA
## Americus

3

Kit is very fun, but at the same time a little bit self-absorbed. She's just so enthusiastic about things, she gets so caught up that she doesn't even get a chance to consider the consequences of her actions.

But when it comes down to it, Kit really cares about other people, and every now and then I can get her on a serious level.

She doesn't really like to argue much because it's just not that important to her. She's got a great outlook on life. Everything's fine, everything's happy.    **-ALLISON**

# Kit

ATLANTA
POPULATION:
394,000
TALK OF THE TOWN:
The "Olympic Ring,"
built specifically for
the 1996 Olympic games,
is 3 miles wide and
seats 85,000 people
HISTORICAL TRIVIA:
Margaret Mitchell
was a journalist in
the city until she
sprained her ankle
and freed up plenty
of time to write
GONE WITH THE WIND

B

2926 MILES TRAVELED

Kit keeps the energy high, and I like that, I like her. She's really sweet, sexy, cool, all three.    **-MARK**

Kit Kat is the leader of the group. She has no limitations. She's not the loudest, she's not the most demanding, but she seems to have the ideas that work. Not to mention that she's the oldest in the group and we respect that. So when she says something it carries a little bit more weight.  **-LOS**

Whether we admit it or not, when someone's missing from the group the aura is just off. It was good to pick up Los from his folks' and be a group again. It's weird, because when we're all together, everyone's like, "God, I just want to be alone." But then when we do end up being apart, everyone's like, "Geez, I wish Los was here, I wish Allison was with us."**-MARK**

Kit's humorous and fun to be around, but I can't tell her my problems and I can't share certain things with her. Sometimes she doesn't listen, and conversations usually end up revolving around her. To be honest, I let her talk and put half my heart into conversations.    **-SHELLY**

C

KIT'S ATLANTA DIGS
FAVORITE AREA:
Virginia Highlands
FAVORITE BAR:
Mosen Joe's,
"They only serve
Pabst Blue Ribbon."
FAVORITE SUNDAY-
AFTERNOON SPOT:
Fulton County Stadium,
to watch the Braves
(but get there soon,
before it's torn down)
BEST HOT DOGS AND BURGERS:
The Varsity

# CLUE

AHOY YE LANDLUBBERS, SCRUB THE BARNACLES OFF YOUR HULL AND SET SAIL FOR OLD BALDY ON BALD HEAD ISLAND.

**1 / A**

I was really anxious because we were so close to Florida and I thought maybe the next stop would be to my parents' house or to my college to see all my friends. Satellite Beach is a cute town, a lot of little stores, little restaurants, little yogurt shops. It's an awesome place to raise your family. We used to live on a canal, and we had a pool, so we had three different water choices in the summer. Should I take my little boat out and ride around in the canal? Should I invite friends over and swim in the pool all day? Or should we lug our surfboards on our bikes up to the beach and go surfing?

So like I said, I was disappointed to find out there wouldn't be a hometown stop for me. We could have gone skiing, wave running, active stuff that would have pulled us together as a group. **The gang would have loved my mom.** She is the sweetest mom in the world, very hospitable. Whenever I call her, she says, **"I don't want you kissing girls on TV."** Oh well. **-MARK**

**B**

So I bid farewell to my mom and brother and dad and we got a clue at Los's house saying we had to go to Bald Head Island to find some bald-headed dude (Old Baldy), who turned out to be a lighthouse. Mark was a little bitter because we didn't get to go to his hometown in Florida, but he pulled through. **-KIT**

**2764 MILES TRAVELED**

**C**

When I first met Mark, all I remember is that he had so much hair spray in his hair. I was thinking, "Oh my God, who is this guy? What's going on?"

**There's no way Mark can get that 'do to stand up without using an entire can of hair spray.**

But he turned out to be the funniest guy. From the second or third day on we hit it off completely. We have the exact same sense of humor. I mean, he can get funny quotes out of THE SILENCE OF THE LAMBS.

Both of us seem to know you've got to laugh at yourself, you can't take yourself too seriously, and I think that's a good quality. **Thank God he's on this trip with me, my partner in crime.** I think we have the best time out of the five of us. If I could start the whole trip over, I wouldn't change our friendship, but as far as romantic involvement, I definitely would change that because I just feel like it's hurt too many people. **-KIT**

Washington, D.C.
Richmond 95
VA 64
17
Norfolk
NC 158
Elizabeth City
Washington
Wanchese
17 264
Florence
211
Atlanta SC
20 501 Bald Head Island
GA Myrtle Beach

---

I could see the disappointment and the hurt in Mark's eyes when we found out we were going to Atlanta and not his hometown.

I think I can read Mark pretty well simply because we're both

# Mark

guys. That's the biggest thing we share, but we get along chill. He's not the person he looks like, obviously. He looks like your average golden boy who wants to profit from his image. But I don't think that's what he's about, I think he's just a big kid at heart, kind of like myself in a way. **-LOS**

Mark has a problem when it comes to voicing opinions. If something is causing a dilemma, he would rather someone else say it than himself.

I don't know how to explain how I feel about him. He's the surface type of guy. **Looking at him is like looking at an illusion. I'm not sure if anyone knows him.** He's got a great sense of humor, but that's all that's there. He doesn't have a serious side—I don't talk to him very much, and I'm glad he's not connected to my side like he is to Kit's. We have nothing in common, no similar interests, nada. **-SHELLY**

Mark is just, "Hey!" Mark is just Mark.

The only thing that bothers him is Shelly. Within the group I think Mark and Shelly talk the least out of everybody. I'm just waiting for Mark to blow up and go off on Shelly. I don't think it's anything particular, it's just that Shelly is very serious and doesn't get visibly excited about anything. Mark is the total opposite extreme. He's always got a smile on his face, he just wants to have a good time. **-ALLISON**

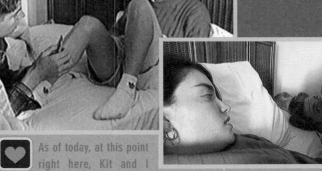

❤ As of today, at this point right here, Kit and I haven't slept together. I don't know whether it's in the future or not. There's a chance of it. There's a lot of times when there's a heavy chance of it. **-MARK**

I don't know what those two are up to, but I do know that yesterday afternoon, there was a missing Kit, a missing Mark, and a missing Winnebago that ended up in a church parking lot. They said they were going to the gym, but they never went to the gym. They did, however, get their exercise. **-ALLISON**

There was a big stink because Kit and I shared a room at the Ramada and only used one bed (go figure). **-MARK**

Kit talked the captain into letting her drive the ferry out to Bald Head Island. She did an OK job, considering she had to sit on a couple phone books to see over the steering wheel. **-MARK**

🖥 **WANCHESE**
[pronounced: *WAN-CHEESE*]
POPULATION:
1,400

ONLY RESTAURANTS:
Queen Anne's Revenge,
Fisherman's Wharf

MUST DO:
Go to nearby Outer Banks for 130 miles of beaches, hang-gliding, fishing, surfing, windsurfing, and offshore fishing

FAME:
Orville and Wilbur Wright took their first flight nearby in Kitty Hawk

## CLUE

BE IN WANCHESE, NORTH CAROLINA, BY TOMORROW NIGHT. I'VE GOT YOU A JOB TEMPING AT THE MOON TILLETT FISH COMPANY. GET A GOOD NIGHT'S SLEEP AND BE READY FOR YOUR WAKE-UP CALL.

**4061** MILES TRAVELED

We hit the channel, and they began pulling in the nets. That's where Los turned into a chameleon, changing colors all over the place. He finally lost it over the edge of the boat. At about 9:00 A.M. they took pity on the poor man and we headed back. It was just gorgeous out and we were sunnin' and chillin'. The rest of the gang had to package fish all day, so we didn't feel so bad about our morning outing. **-KIT**

We all wanted to fish, but there was one stipulation: the boat left at 4:00 A.M. We drew straws, and Kit and I won, so we got to go out on a boat called HANDFUL. A handful of what? We didn't catch jack all day. **-LOS**

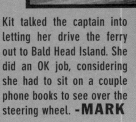

C

◀ **CAPE FEAR**
The movie was filmed in Wilmington, NC, where there is an actual Cape Fear. This town is also home to the Laney Eimsley High School basketball team, where Michael Jordan did not make varsity.

## CLUE

HEAD TOWARDS OUR NATION'S CAPITAL TO SEE THE MONUMENTS. THEN YOU MUST GO TO THE CITY THAT NEVER SLEEPS, WHERE YOU WILL FIND THE GARDEN THAT HAS NO FLOWERS, AND TALK TO THE CLOWN WITH THE POWER.

## JOB
**Go Fishing; Gut, Clean, and Fillet Fish for Moon Tillett**

**OBJECTIVE:** Don't lose your cookies
**HAZARDS:** Rough seas, fish slime
**REWARD:** $200 cash each

I didn't mind cutting up the fish, getting all slimy, but I think Kit minded 'cause I was wearing her shirt. **-ALLISON**

NAME: Ryan Tillett
TITLE: Owner, Moon Tillett Fishing Company

Wanchese is a very small town. We're just 9 or 10 miles from the Nags Head and Kill Devil Hills beaches. They pack in somewhere around 350,000 people a week during the summer. It gets hectic sometimes. It's kind of amazing to see someplace this small be so busy.

The fishermen, they go out in the mornings and come back late at night; some boats, like the trawl boats, stay out two to five days. Then there's the people who pack fish—they come in around 8:00 in the morning and pack until they're done, no matter how much there is to do. We clean the fish, we box 'em, we also do a lot of freezing. We sell fish fresh to the markets in New York, Philadelphia, and Baltimore. You can earn an average of about $7 an hour cleaning fish. I'd hire those ROAD RULES kids to do it again. Heck, I'd hire you off the street if I needed the help.

4

KEY TO
SYMBOLS

❤ ..........................romance
🖥 ....................welcome to
◀ ...............................sidetrip
🛏 ..................sleep in motel
🏠 ................hometown stop
JOB ...................................job

Kit thinks I'm gonna have a field day in D.C. 'cause of all the politicians. **-ALLISON**

On the way to New York we made a stop in D.C. and I got to see a couple of my friends. We got pulled over by the police trying to see the great national monument, great phallic symbol in the middle of the nation's capital, painted white, go figure. Then we got back in our ride and headed to New York. -LOS

Los was driving around without his lights on, so he got a ticket. What did he expect? There was nothing racial about it; **we got pulled over because his lights were off. We didn't get pulled over because he was black. -SHELLY**

I wouldn't necessarily call it an agenda, but I did have one or two friends that I wanted to visit while we were staying the night in D.C. I called up a sister named Michelle and asked her if she could come by and pick me and Shelly up to see the town.

## Pulled Over

I really wanted to take Shelly out 'cause she'd never seen the monuments before and Kit and Mark were planning to go to Georgetown and have a few beers. I wanted to take the opportunity to show Shelly how the other half lives.

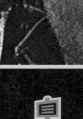

We were having a great time, cruising the monuments, when this cop came up to the car, "Can I see some ID?" Just totally rude, disrespectful. "You're driving around with no headlights on. Do I smell marijuana in the car?" Those girls were smoking cheap cigarettes, but there was no bud in that car. Now, let me tell you something.

## If I'd had on my little Georgetown cap and had a couple white faces in the backseat, that cop wouldn't have had a problem. -LOS

Los has often said to me, "Look around, Mark. Look where we're at. I don't belong here." I try to understand, but being a blond-haired, blue-eyed white boy, I don't usually experience people looking at me like, "Who the hell is this guy in my city?"

The tables turned in Washington, D.C. It was our only night there, and Los went off with Shelly and his ex-girlfriend Michelle. I was sitting on the subway with Kit, and I had this snow hat on and little dreadlocks coming out the top, which might have looked like I was trying to be someone that I'm not. There was a black guy sitting across from me,

### WASHINGTON, D.C.
**POPULATION:**
606,900

**HISTORICAL TRIVIA:**
Martin Luther King, Jr. gave his "I Have a Dream" speech on the Mall in 1963; In 1968, riots touched off by his assassination torched areas of the city, some of which still lie unrepaired

**TALK OF THE TOWN:**
In 1985, Tipper Gore fought alongside George Packwood at the US Capitol to censor violent and sexually explicit rock 'n' roll lyrics; on the defense were Frank Zappa, John Denver, and Dee Snider; the meeting resulted in the "parental advisory" stickers you see on many CD covers

**NOTORIETY:**
John Hinckley, the guy who shot Reagan at the Washington Hilton, is currently serving his insanity stint at St. Elizabeth Hospital in D.C.; his work release was denied when Secret Service agents found a letter requesting nude drawings of Jodie Foster

**MUST SEE:**
The city's famous cherry trees, a gift from the Japanese after World War II, bloom triumphantly in springtime; the National Air and Space Museum is the most popular branch of the Smithsonian

I don't know why he hates me, exactly. In the beginning, it seemed we had so much in common. He was philosophical, I liked him, and I think he liked me. But then I stood up to him about the money issue. He refuses to pay for the hotels because, "It's a waste of money," and then he winds up in my bed in the middle of the night. We're all eating jelly sandwiches, and he takes himself out to dinner....He was getting away with it because no one wanted to start a fight. When he realized that I was the only one who was going to put up a fight with him, he vowed to make my life miserable, and it's working.

But I also think that he is miserable on this trip—it's not his style. And he has all of these aggressions, so he takes them out on me. **-ALLISON**

## Carrrlos

Why he acts the way he does toward Allison, I will never know. It just blows me away. I get along with him well, and

looking at me the whole time, and he looked mean. I was thinking, "This guy is going to say something because he doesn't approve of me wearing this stuff or being on his turf." But somehow, I sparked up a conversation, and he was about the nicest guy ever. We did the handshake when we got off. The stories you hear about crazy things on the subway, they might sometimes be true, but I think if you can just be down to earth, if you don't have many walls up, you can get along with everyone.

(By the way, Los rolled in about 6:30 the next morning, so I think he got some loving that night, finally.) **-MARK**

**LOS'S D.C. DIGS**
FAVORITE BARS:
In the Closet,
State of the Union
FAVORITE PLACES TO CHILL:
The Mall
(Washington's
longest lawn)
in springtime,
the Quad at
Howard University

He thinks of me as a minority, so I'm supposed to understand him. He knows nothing about how I grew up, but he presumes to tell me what I am like, or supposed to be like. I can only shake my head and say, "Carlos, you don't know my life."**-SHELLY**

I've tried and tried to talk to Shelly about her heritage, but she wants to keep it private. Why would you want to do that? You leave room for people to be even more ignorant when you don't explain things to them or at least point the issues out. **-LOS**

I have my little mood swings. I think it's a chemical imbalance in my body, where one day I'm real hyper and crazy and ready to go and then other days I just wanna sit down and lounge and listen to some real music. I think if everybody else would be more themselves, then I probably wouldn't have these mood swings. **-LOS**

Los isn't funny-cocky...Los is just cocky in general. I thought he was going to be the laid-back one, the floater in the group, and he was actually the one that stirred things up. I really thought we'd end up being better friends. **-KIT**

Even when Los is moody, he is never moody to me. I think he just gets a kick out of getting those two girls riled up. I think music brings out like a lot of positive energy in Los. Every time he dances to "This Is How We Do It," I almost pee my pants! **-MARK**

Fairness is an imaginary word. Anything that I want done or anything that I need accomplished, I have to do it myself, and a lot of times I have to go to extremes, I have to upset people.

I started believing in this idea—that you can really cuss somebody to their face and not care about it—when I entered college. I didn't realize how bad it had gotten until I came on this trip. You have to really be self-centered, a pretty cool individual, to think only of yourself when you're around people who may be pretty nice. In a way it's bad, but for me it's like a survival mechanism and it's worked pretty well. **-LOS**

I don't believe in destiny or the guiding hand of fate.

I don't believe in forever or love as a mystical state.

I don't believe in the stars or the planets or angels watching from above.

But I believe there's a ghost of a chance we can find someone to love—and make it last. -LOS

# Through the Los Lens

Whenever you see images of America, you're not seeing Gunnison, Colorado, or Nogales, Arizona. You're basically seeing LA, New York, Washington, D.C., maybe Atlanta because of the Olympics. That's something that I need to be cognizant of from now on when I'm creating images. What image am I showing people? Am I showing people what really exists, or am I showing them something that I've been sold, something someone fed me?

My photography is very important to me, and at times it gets neglected. I haven't made any images that I think are worth printing in a while, and that hurts. It's like being a boxer and not going to a match in six months, or like Michael Jordan not playing basketball. He's back now, because that's what he was meant to do. So that's what I have to do. I have to get back in there and start shooting more.

Traveling across the country is definitely doing my eye for photography a world of good, but the disadvantage is that you're only seeing it for a second, and it's hard to get to know something in a second. **-LOS**

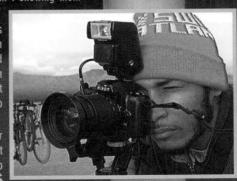

**LOS'S FAVORITE PHOTOGRAPHERS**

Roy DeCarava
Michael Kenna

**LOS'S FAVORITE BOOKS**

THE MIDDLE PASSAGE, by Tom Feelings
TIME OF THE DRAGONS, by Robert Shea

NAME: Chris Allison
TITLE: Clown, Ringling Bros. and Barnum & Bailey Circus
MOTTO: "Being a clown is about passing through that curtain and leaving your worries on the other side; people don't come to the circus to see a clown with problems, they want to be taken away from theirs."

Ringling Bros. and Barnum & Bailey travels the country by rail; we actually have two shows of the same size traveling crisscross across the United States. We have about 300 employees in our traveling city. It's an unbelievable lifestyle. We do up to 13 costume changes a show. When the ROAD RULES kids came to town, it was my job to dress them up and make them into clowns. I checked out their attitudes, tried to evaluate what kind of people they were, and gave them each the equivalent of an agent suit, which is the suit that a clown chooses to wear in public—the one costume that represents who he is the best. Los, for example, seemed like a cool cat, so I incorporated his sunglasses into his chef costume and highlighted his light moustache; Shelly had a serious side, so her clown character was older than the others'.

**1**

Driving in New York was insane, I about killed us a million times. -KIT

## MISSION NUMBER 6

### BE A CLOWN AND GET ON TELEVISION

CHALLENGE: Smile through your hangovers and don't make any babies cry

TOOLS: Makeup, wigs, rubber noses, clown shoes, and fake butts

REWARD: A good meal and showers at Allison's house

**3**

## CLUE

YOU'RE TO GO TO QUANTICO, VIRGINIA, WHERE YOU'RE GOING TO HAVE TO JUMP THROUGH HOOPS IF YOU WANT TO ACCOMPLISH THIS MISSION. LACE UP YOUR BOOTS, YOU'RE GOING TO CAMP.

In New York City, you have to be a taxicab driver to get any respect. -SHELLY

**4061 MILES TRAVELED**

RINGLING BROS AND BARNUM & BAILEY

KRYOLA CLOWN

**C**

## A Brand-New Face

I guess when we are little, everyone wants to be a clown, wants to goof off behind the face paint. At clown college we learned it takes a certain type of person to be a clown—basically you've got to be a total kook.

The first time we dressed up, we actually got to perform—we were the warm-up act. It's a lot of work making little kids laugh. That night we went to a bar called Bourbon Street, and Allison of course ran around all crazy with her friends. The owner had some balloons up and a little sign in the front saying "Welcome Back Allison." He gave us free drinks, and I'd have to say we got pretty trashed. Too trashed.

We went to Ally's old dorm at Columbia to spend the night. The girls' room was clean, cozy, and very nice. The guys' room was, well, to put it nicely, nasty! The bed was damp, the sink was disgusting, and the blanket we had to use was a 50/50 cotton/cigarette ash blend.

**The dude had so many cigarette butts around, Shelly would have been jealous.**

We went to sleep at 4:30 A.M., which was awful because we had to be at Madison Square Garden at 6:30 A.M. to clown up and get on TV. -MARK

There were about 15 minutes left of THE TODAY SHOW, and the security guard said that we couldn't get in because we were in costume. Now being the Columbia liberal that I am,

**I said that was discrimination against people with red noses and yellow hair.**

Finally, at the last minute, the cameras came outside and filmed us and we got on the closing credits.

-ALLISON

**NY**

*New York City*

NJ

95

MD

DE

VA  *Washington, D.C.*

**2**

KEY TO SYMBOLS

........sleep in motel

........romance

........hometown stop

........welcome to

M ........mission

........conflict

2 ........lost

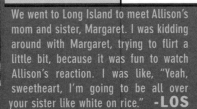

🏠
**4/9 1995**

**ALLISON'S NEW YORK DIGS**
FAVORITE RESTAURANT:
Mo's Caribbean Bar and Grill for margaritas
FAVORITE BARS:
Bear Bar, West End Bar
FAVORITE HANGOUT:
Central Park
FAVORITE PLACE TO GO ON A DATE:
The Empire State Building

Becoming clowns was part of our mission, but the second part was to get on two national TV shows. At the last minute, we got on THE TODAY SHOW. Then we ran around like crazy trying to get tickets to ROLONDA or RICKI LAKE. Finally we got aged by the crew. They said, "Guys, ROAD RULES is a TV show! You've got the second show covered." So then we got to relax and meet Allison's family. -SHELLY

I was nervous, but I wasn't nervous about being a clown, I was nervous that everyone wasn't going to have a good time or have a good place to sleep at my house, and to me that was the toughest part. But it was really good to be home. Being put into a new environment, you kind of lose sight of yourself because you're trying so hard to compromise, and you can't always have your way.

We went to Long Island to meet Allison's mom and sister, Margaret. I was kidding around with Margaret, trying to flirt a little bit, because it was fun to watch Allison's reaction. I was like, "Yeah, sweetheart, I'm going to be all over your sister like white on rice." -LOS

# Allison

## Being home helped me remember who I am, and to feel like I belonged again.

Allison's a funny one. When I first heard that voice, it absolutely killed me. In the beginning she was probably my least favorite. I remember we got in the Winnie, and she broke out her photo album and then said, "Let's play Twister." I was thinking, "You got to be kidding me. This girl is going to drive me absolutely batty."

But we really get along great now, and I admire her drive for medical school. So it's funny that in the beginning she was probably my least favorite, and now she's probably my favorite. **-KIT**

I wanted to stay at my house as long as possible, but the others wanted to go back to Manhattan, so I dropped them at the train station, and I remember sitting there thinking, "This is the first time I've had to myself since I can remember, and I'm going to miss them." The next morning I woke up and I was by myself and it was quiet and I didn't have to fight over the remote control with anyone and it was the weirdest feeling, it was just so strange. **-ALLISON**

Allison is very analytical; sometimes she tries to look at things from too many angles. She's the smarty pants in the group. Maybe not so much street smart, but book smart. She's definitely the best at Trivial Pursuit. I get along with her fine, I just wish she'd learn to let things roll off her back more, and not take certain people and certain situations so seriously. **-MARK**

Ally was so happy to be home she was like, "Oh yeah, I forgot to introduce you guys." **-KIT**

**B**

**4310 MILES TRAVELED**

Allison is a hiker, climber, just an athletic woman. Allison can do anything and everything that she puts her mind to.

## She should be on AMERICAN GLADIATORS.

We talk a lot. We are going through almost the same dilemmas with our love lives at home—just at different levels. Through our long conversations, I feel I've connected with her in a way that I haven't with anyone else. I think of her kind of like a sister. We even fight like sisters; she annoys me.... I'm sure I annoy her, but she is honest with me, and that's all I can ask for. **-SHELLY**

## Passenger Six

I think Kermit felt things for her, I'm not sure. He was always with us. We'd hang him on the rearview mirror and he'd ride along with us. Mark was really good about making him look like he was throwing up. Kermit did everything that we did. **-SHELLY**

**C**

📋

**NEW YORK CITY**
POPULATION:
8,000,000
POPULAR HANGOUTS:
Here, Twilo, Giant Step, The Cooler, Nuyorican Poets Café
HISTORICAL TRIVIA:
Bought from Native Americans in 1624 for under $24
FANFARE:
Wigstock, a September drag queen parade; a thriving theater arts scene off-Broadway and off-off-Broadway, where Shakespeare meets BLADERUNNER on basement stages

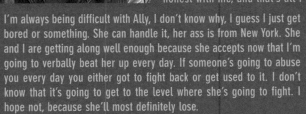

I'm always being difficult with Ally, I don't know why, I guess I just get bored or something. She can handle it, her ass is from New York. She and I are getting along well enough because she accepts now that I'm going to verbally beat her up every day. If someone's going to abuse you every day you either got to fight back or get used to it. I don't know that it's going to get to the level where she's going to fight. I hope not, because she'll most definitely lose.

On the rare occasions when I clean the Winnie, I always stick Kermie's ass in a closet somewhere. Allison starts to miss him, so now she takes him on a lot of the adventures that we go on. Kermit's been holding up pretty well. **-LOS**

**D**

## I don't mean her harm.

Hopefully she'll get into med school. If not, I'm sure she's going to be OK. She's very independent and fairly headstrong. I think she's got a lot of pride in herself that she's not going to let herself fail. **-LOS**

**4**

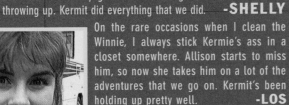
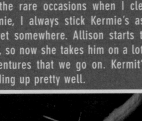

**THE CHELSEA HOTEL**
A stomping ground for the likes of Mark Twain, Tennessee Williams, and Dylan Thomas, the Chelsea also put up Jack Kerouac while he banged out the first draft of ON THE ROAD on a customized typewriter. Other colorful boarders were Edie Sedgewick, Andy Warhol, and Sid Vicious, who killed his girlfriend Nancy Spungen there. Still a haven for both wayward and upwardly mobile bohemians, the Chelsea Hotel stands as a landmark to New York's rich literary and artistic culture.

**ALLISON'S FAVORITE ROAD FOOD**

McDonald's salads, McDonald's frozen yogurt, the "Lite" menu at Taco Bell, fruit, turkey sandwiches, jelly sandwiches, Cup-a-Soup, Power Bars

NUMBER 7

# MISSION

## GO THROUGH QUANTICO MARINE TRAINING CAMP

**OBJECTIVE:** Complete each course without losing any teammates

**TOOLS:** Communication, teamwork

**REWARDS:** MREs (meals ready to eat), sore muscles

We found out from the ringleader at the circus that we were to go to Quantico, Virginia, and run through some hoops. We knew there was a marine base there, so we figured we were in for some heavy physical stuff. -SHELLY

A

B

Watch the demonstration! Marine Corps! Flying Angels! Go combat! Marine Corps is cool. Marine Corps Base Quantico, Virginia, is where they train the officers for the Marine Corps. It's called OCS, Officer Candidates School. The marines there were real nice people, strictly military, but real friendly—not at all what you'd expect.

I have family ties to the Marine Corps. My dad and my grandfather were in the military, and my attitude is, you got two of us, that's all you're getting. My dad went in because he was from the rural South, and at the time there wasn't much else a black man could do where he could have some self-respect. The armed services were something positive because your color didn't matter.

I respect them for what they're trained to do. I respect them for their skills, but I'm just a different kind of person. The odd thing about my generation is that we've grown up in the relative comfort of the baby boomers and there's nothing for us to really struggle for, nothing worth dying for. I think that what unites all of the Generation Xers is our lack of allegiance to anything, even to this country. **When you don't feel that strongly about anything, then anything can go, anything can fly, you do not bat an eye.** -LOS

## 4310 MILES TRAVELED

I was excited about going to Quantico because that's where the FBI Academy is. I did everything I could to get in there. Carlos even made a few phone calls for me because his dad's a police officer. When that didn't work, I was almost ready to sneak in and risk getting my head blown off or something crazy. They've got it all sealed up.

Getting a tour of the academy was so important to me because in high school I was planning on going into the FBI. It was the first major decision I had made in my life about what I wanted to study in college and pursue careerwise.

**Unfortunately, I found out I wasn't going to qualify for the FBI because of my tattoos and my eyesight and all these other things.**

I felt like I deserved to go by the academy and look inside and see what I was missing, but it didn't happen.

The marine base...that I was scared of. I knew that whatever they were going to put us through, it was going to be hell. And sure enough it was. But I knew that I had to endure it, that it was going to be a good experience for me. Although I knew I wasn't physically strong enough to do the obstacle course without help, mentally I was willing to go ahead and go through the pain, the suffering, the humiliation, and I did. -SHELLY

**KEY TO SYMBOLS**

🛏 ...............sleep in Winnie
💬 ...............romance
💰 ...............money trail
💻 ...............welcome to
Ⓜ ...............mission
💨 .......empty Winnie septic tank
❓ ...............lost

New York City

NY

MD 95

NJ

DE

Quantico

VA

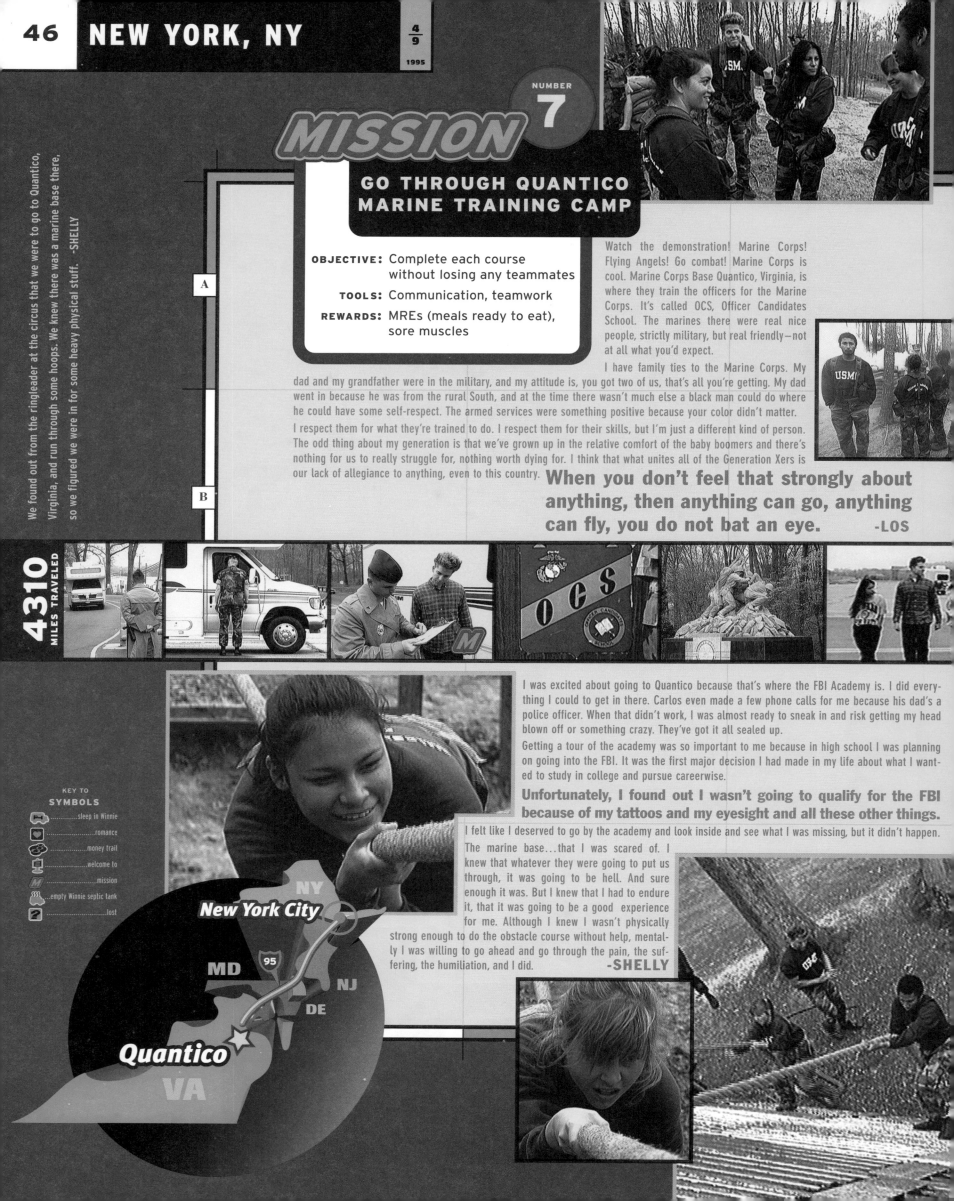

4

Captain Sweitzer met us at the gates of Quantico. He looked pretty stern, had the marine cut, the shaved head, fatigues on. But he didn't stay at attention—all squared-up and stiff—the whole time. He chitchatted, told us a couple of jokes, and set us at ease. Then he brought us into a little room and gave us a briefing on what the candidate school was about. I had flashbacks to Tom Cruise in TOP GUN.

We loaded up on fatigues and went out to the leadership course, which is basically a process to find out who is the leader of the group and who are the followers. No one in particular emerged as a leader. I think we all put in our two cents, and we all failed pretty harshly. **-MARK**

6

The marines were cool and definitely had some rock-hard bodies.

**If I had been in the market for a few good men I would have been in heaven, but my looking days are over for a while.** I'm still trying to smooth things over with cute little Andy. **-KIT**

## USMC
### OFFICER CANDIDATES SCHOOL

The OCS trains, evaluates, and screens about 2,100 officer candidates a year. About 80% successfully complete their training at OCS.

Training days start at 5:00 A.M. and end at 10:00 P.M.

The most difficult of the obstacle courses is the endurance course, which is a little over 4 miles long and contains 21 obstacles, including the infamous "Quigley."

Candidates must pass the program with at least an 80% grade in three categories: physical fitness (25% of the grade), academics (25% of the grade), leadership (50% of the grade).

A

B

**4588** MILES TRAVELED

C

Marine training was a good opportunity for me because I was thinking of applying for a naval scholarship for medical school, and I may have to go into the navy a few years down the road. They were definitely soft on us, but the obstacle course was really tough. I thought I was in better shape, that I would be able to do it to complete it, but the marines had to help me over some of the obstacles. I was really surprised at how well Shelly did. She didn't complain at all, and usually Shelly complains about crossing the street.

When we got to the final course, the combat course, the soldiers went through and demonstrated it for us. I honestly thought it was a joke. It was freezing cold out, and they were going under barbed wire, through mud, into a moat, and through another lake bed. It was funny, because for once, Los and I agreed on something: Neither of us were going to do it! Then I started thinking about the fact that I'd probably never get the chance to do this again in my life, and I have to try everything once, so I just did it.

Oh God, at the end of the day, I was so sore. I had no idea I would be that sore. That night at the hotel, I just lay in bed and didn't move at all. I didn't even want to get up to get something to eat. The next day, I slept in the Winnie all day. **-ALLISON**

**MREs are meals ready to eat. They're one fry short of a Happy Meal, definitely.** -KIT

### ALL THAT YOU CAN BE

The Marine Corps were formed on November 10, 1775, when the second Continental Congress drew up plans for a navy.

The marines' longstanding nickname, "leatherneck," goes back to the leather collar, or neckpiece, which was worn from 1775 to 1875. The band was intended to ensure that the Marines kept their heads erect. It is symbolized today by the high collar on the dress blue uniform.

In 1833, the Marine Corps motto, "Semper Fidelis," was officially adopted. This is a Latin term meaning "always faithful."

42.1% of Marine's are 21 & under

95.3% are male

4.7% are female

## CLUE

TALK TO A PERSON NAMED MICHAEL FROM THE MOUNTAIN RIVER TOURS UP IN HICO, WEST VIRGINIA, SO THAT HE CAN TEST YOUR SKILLS IN THE WATER.

Vertical text (left margin): We pressed on to Hico, West Virginia, for some white-water rafting. At the end of the run, one of the crewmates yelled, "Hey, you guys, pick up that litter over there!" So one of us swam out and picked up a floating bottle. Inside was our next clue. -MARK

**1**

**A**

When we pulled up to Hico, my first reaction was, "This town's too small, I want to go home." -SHELLY

We put the boat in the water, and I jumped into the front. I was proud of myself for doing that because usually if somebody else wants the front seat I'll just let them have it. As soon as we started paddling, Los started complaining: my strokes were too short, Shelly wasn't in sync.... Meanwhile, I turn around, and he's not even paddling, he's taking pictures!

Our instructor, Mary, pulled us aside and gave us this little talk. She said we all had to buckle down and paddle, and we all turned on Los, the obvious culprit.

**B**

## Los wanted to get into the front, so we made a deal: I'd give him the front and he'd be nice to me for a few days.

Little did he know that really, by this time, I was dying to get into the back because it was so cold and wet in the front. But, as soon as he got in the front, he transformed and he was a champ, he was going nuts with those white-water rapids. -ALLISON

## 4588
**MILES TRAVELED**

Welcome to Mountain River Tours Hico, W.Va.

RAPID FUN

**C**

Halfway through the trip, I decided that I'd had enough of being in the back and I didn't want to follow Shelly anymore. So Allison finally broke down and let me get up front. I was paddling like a madman! I was handling things, it was a rush. The best thing about leading is that you can set the pace.

We stopped a ways down the river for a break. I guess everybody thought I was being a jerk, so they circled me with their oars and were going to push me off the front of the boat. They failed, but I was not going to let that go unnoticed. I wanted to get Shelly real bad, but I knew she'd be mad for the next two weeks and just be a pain to live with. So I kind of jabbed Kit Kat with the oar and she started rolling. I didn't think she was going to fall in because Mark was right there, he'd catch her. He didn't catch her. She went in. She didn't like that and she tried to push me back in, but she just wasn't strong enough, she just wasn't pushing the Los monster in.

After Los pushed me in, I was freezing for the rest of the ride. I learned pretty quick that the harder I paddled, the warmer I got. -KIT

The past couple of days at the Marine Corps and at Mountain River Tours has been a lot like what I thought the entire trip would be like. We're out in the weather more, out in the sunshine, roughing it a bit. I felt at times on the trip we were actually being coddled a little too much. I hope we get to do more stuff like this. Up until now, I rated landsailing as our most enjoyable experience, but white-water rafting is neck and neck for the best mission ever. -LOS

**KEY TO SYMBOLS**

⚠ .............sleep in campsite
☠ ...............................danger
🏠 ...............hometown stop
▣ ..........................welcome to
Ⓜ .................................mission
Ⓔ ..........scamming/cheating

WV

Quantico

Hico  64  95

Richmond

VA

**DANIEL JOHNS OF SILVERCHAIR'S**
TOP TEN ROAD TRIPPIN' CDs

1.................................Shellac, LIVE AT ACTION PARK
2.................Deep Purple, DEEP PURPLE IN ROCK
3...................................................Helmet, BETTY
4.......................................You Am I, HI-FI WAY
5...................................................Tool, UNDERTOW
6.........Magic Dirt, SIGNS OF SATANIC YOUTH
7.............................................Velvet Underground,
BEST OF THE VELVET UNDERGROUND
8..........................Jimi Hendrix, SMASH HITS
9...............Big Black, SONGS ABOUT F**KING
10.......................Midget, THE TOGGLE SWITCH

# MISSION 8

## WHITE-WATER RAFTING

**OBJECTIVE:** Work together to get down the river in one piece

**CHALLENGE:** Persuading Los to paddle

**TOOLS:** Wetsuits, oars, white-water rafts, the rapids

Each city that we go to, everybody has their preconception of what it's gonna be, but the only way to really feel a place is to get off your bystander kick and get as excited as the locals do about the local stuff.

In any situation you find yourself in you've got to adapt and try to make yourself happy with what you got. **-LOS**

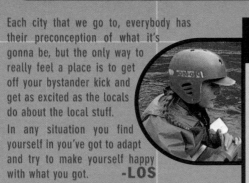

NAME: Mary Bethune
TITLE: River tour leader, Mountain River Tours

The history of white-water rafting in West Virginia started 23 years ago. Today, Mountain River Tours takes over 21,000 people a year down these rivers. You can't paddle to your own rhythm in this sport. Some groups pick up on that and others fight each other the whole way down. In the ROAD RULES case, it was Los who didn't want to paddle, he was really lazy, and that threw everyone off. I think they were in the middle of their trip at the time, and they were having problems getting along.

Remember when Mark put on that pink jacket, and he was acting all weird, like he didn't want a pink jacket? He asked for that jacket. I told him that he could have a different color, but he insisted on the pink one. I thought that was pretty funny.

If we hadn't been so concerned about looking out for ourselves, I think we could have pulled together more as a group; it would have been easier and there wouldn't have been so many words said and so much attitude given. **-SHELLY**

B

### RAPID FACTS

Each year, 250,000 people raft down West Virginia's rivers.

The Grand Canyon portion of the Colorado River is rated the #1 rafting river in the world.

The #1 injury in white-water rafting is sunburn.

White-water rafting has 1/10 the number of injuries as downhill skiing.

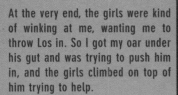

M

### 4926 MILES TRAVELED

At the very end, the girls were kind of winking at me, wanting me to throw Los in. So I got my oar under his gut and was trying to push him in, and the girls climbed on top of him trying to help.

**Suddenly, I saw a perfect opportunity to push them all in with one big bulldog charge.**

In a matter of seconds, all four of them were in the water and I was paddling to shore, trying to run away and get in the bus so they couldn't push me in. **-MARK**

### GREAT RIVER RIDES IN THE US

New River, Cheat River, and Gauley River, all located in WV

Colorado River in AZ

Arkansas River in CO

Snake River in ID

Rogue River in OR

Rio Grande in TX

### HICO
POPULATION: 2,500

POPULAR HANGOUT: Rose's Hideaway

TRIVIA: Named after popular brand of tobacco

MUST DO: Mountain biking, hiking, white-water rafting

## CLUE

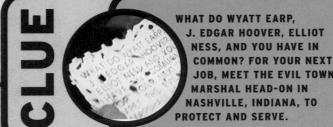

WHAT DO WYATT EARP, J. EDGAR HOOVER, ELLIOT NESS, AND YOU HAVE IN COMMON? FOR YOUR NEXT JOB, MEET THE EVIL TOWN MARSHAL HEAD-ON IN NASHVILLE, INDIANA, TO PROTECT AND SERVE.

**4/13 1995**

## JOB: Town Marshals for a Day

**OBJECTIVE:** Enforce the laws of Brown County and keep yourselves out of jail

**PERKS:** Badges, cool uniforms, and the power to write tickets

**REWARD:** $180 each

So we go to Nashville, Indiana, and we're cops for the day. We direct a little traffic, give out a few tickets, and even manage to get into a little mock trouble with the boys upstairs. —ALLISON

**A**

Nashville is about four blocks by three blocks small. There's four policemen on duty, one at a time, so if you've got a big crime going on, you probably have to call and wake up your backup. We met Officer Sanders, "the Evil Marshal." He was a good guy, in spite of his title. He gave us all duties. Los, Allison, and I did traffic detail and monitored an Easter egg hunt, because you never know when big things are going to happen at an egg hunt. **—MARK**

**B**

It was fun driving the cop car and being on the other side of the law. It was Easter, so I couldn't give a ticket, but I did try to shake folks up a little bit. I, myself, seem to have a heavy foot. In the past I've had a couple of little speeding tickets. And a couple of fender benders. When I was 15, I wrecked my best friend Cameron's car. She was 16 and she took the blame. I always seem to be in hurry for no reason. I'm just thankful those Nashville cops never checked my record.

I'm sort of quick with the tongue, but I have never been able to talk my way out of a ticket. I've tried everything from the tear shed to the "I'm late for the doctor," and never succeeded. Once I got caught for going over 100 in South Dakota. I said, "Oh well, it's just South Dakota," and I didn't pay the ticket. Well, six months later I got a call from my dad; my license had been revoked, my insurance company dropped me, and Dad was livid. I ended up paying, like, $300. It was a nightmare. So a word of warning: No matter what state you get a ticket in, just pay it immediately and you're good to go. **—KIT**

**4926 MILES TRAVELED**

**JOB**

**KEY TO SYMBOLS**

- JOB ............................job
- 🏠 ..............sleep in motel
- 👁️‍🗨️ .................money trail
- 🖥️ .................welcome to
- M .........................mission
- 👁️ ..........scamming/cheating
- 🦀 .........................sidetrip

**C**

Mark and Los, the biggest meal-scamming, fast-talking hypocrites of all time, pulled over a 16-year-old driver for going 41 in a 40 zone that had just switched to 30. It seemed ridiculous for those guys to be out there giving tickets when they're regularly breaking the law in every other way.

When they were done terrorizing, we checked out the Dillinger Museum. Dillinger is kind of a local legend. He was a gangster from the 1920s who was shot, and they really milk his story for all it's worth. I mean, the guy was shot, OK? They had diagrams and pictures of him, and a big model of him to show where he got shot. Then, in the back they had a picture of how the bullet went through his skull. It was pretty funny. **—ALLISON**

**IN**

*Nashville*
**46**
**65**
**64**
*Louisville*
*Hico*
**WV**
**KY**

**NOTORIOUS IN NASHVILLE**

Nashville's most notorious historical figure was John Dillinger, the US gangster who terrorized the Midwest in 1933 after escaping from jail. He is remembered as the criminal at large who robbed 13 banks and killed 16 people, including several police officers, before he was shot in Chicago in 1934. Dillinger's legacy of terror is well documented at Nashville's Dillinger Museum. He is buried at Crown Hill cemetery.

The morning I went in to work in Nashville I had 30¢ left. **-MARK**

I didn't know where Nashville was at, much less where Indiana was at. **-SHELLY**

I bet you thought Nashville was in Tennessee, but it's not, it's in Indiana. Just kidding, there's two Nashvilles. **-LOS**

## Dine 'n' Dash

We went out to dinner in Bloomington and had yards of beer and lots of food. I was hanging out in the corner, a little bit tired and just minding my own business, and next thing I knew, everyone was getting up and walking out the door without paying. It wasn't anything we really discussed. I think that if I'd had a little bit more time to think about it and realized that I was stiffing this poor waitress with a $100 check, I probably wouldn't have walked out. But at the time it was the funniest thing, because the last thing Kit said before splitting was, "Just act natural," then she bolted down the street in her big, noisy, high-heeled clogs. **-ALLISON**

**BLOOMINGTON**
POPULATION: 60,000
HOMETOWN OF: The Indiana University Hoosiers, five-time national college basketball champions
POPULAR HANGOUTS: The Crazy Horse, Mars, Rhino's
FANFARE: A Taste of Bloomington brings together local bands and local foods for a Bacchanalian summer blast

A

B

**5290** MILES TRAVELED

C

# Book Her

The officer took Kit and me into the mug shot room and said, "OK, so who wants to get thrown in jail?" I immediately said, "I'll do it." Why not? Never happened to me before. Then he said, "OK, put all your belongings out." I was like, "All of them?"

There would be no dodging, I was going to go through the whole process. So I emptied my pockets and he started fingerprinting me. Then he took my picture and told me to wash the ink off my hands. I followed him upstairs and saw the chapel room they have for Sunday services with people who are in for a little bit longer than me.

I talked with some of the inmates. There wasn't a whole lot to say. "What are you in for?" and "Have a nice Easter" sounded a little callous, but that was all I could think of.

I got a cell all by myself in the women's section. It was cramped—like the Winnebago, but much worse. I wanted to call my mom from jail just to say, "Hey mom, I'm in jail." She would have freaked out. It would have been great. But I don't see myself in a jail, and I really hope I don't end up back in one.

When I went to pick up my belongings I found a tape in my stuff. The officer put it in his tape deck, and we heard some Van Halen tunes and then our next clue. I started screaming, I couldn't believe it. I was going to a concert. **-SHELLY**

**Carlos had been talking about shaving his head, but we didn't think he was going to do it.**

When we went out to the Winnebago and saw him it was a big change. I thought he looked like an Easter egg, I thought it was very festive. Everybody rubbed his head, and of course when I went to rub his head he told me to get off him. **-ALLISON**

**NASHVILLE**
POPULATION: 873
POPULAR HANGOUT: Brown County Inn
NICKNAME: "Log Cabin Country"
LOCAL ROCKER: John Mellencamp
MUST SEE: Dillinger Museum, Country Star Walk of Fame, Bill Monroe Bluegrass Hall of Fame

D

**INDY 500 OR BUST**

If you're in Indiana on Memorial Day weekend, travel to Indianapolis and take a vicarious joyride at the Indy 500, where speed racers careen at a deafening 225 mph around the Indianapolis Motor Speedway. The rest of the year, you can ride a tour bus around the 2.5-mile track—not exactly as thrilling, but of interest if you've seen the race on TV.

4

## CLUE

**GO TO FORT WAYNE, INDIANA TOMORROW NIGHT. YOU'RE OPENING UP FOR VAN HALEN.**

6

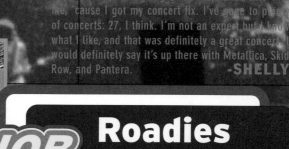

back in Nashville when we heard that we were going to be opening for Van Halen, we all figured we'd get there, meet the band, maybe have dinner with them, then introduce them at the show. We had no idea we were actually going to be roadies for the day. -KIT

It's past the halfway point, we've reached our pinnacle and now we're kind of going downhill. We're realizing that the end is coming and we have to make the best of it and keep our spirits up. **-MARK**

**3**

The Van Halen gig came along at the perfect time— I really needed it. I was so tired of all the music I brought on the trip. I'd been listening to the same stuff forever and was getting really, really sick of Tears for Fears, the SINGLES sound track, and Candlebox, believe it or not. I was just dying to go to a concert. I still bought my METAL EDGE, but I couldn't ask to buy music or tickets to a show out of our group fund; that would be a little too selfish.

The best part of the experience was I had great conversations with the roadies—talked about music and tattoos and their jobs: how much money they make, how much time it takes, the usual schedule, who to work with, not to work with.

I didn't mind meeting the band, but I was a little bit selfish. I wanted to go out to the concert, I wanted to see the opening band. Sammy was hyperactive, just bouncing off walls, absolutely crazy. Him and Kit got along—I could definitely see that one coming.

**B**

## Patrick, the head roadie, gave me some advice

**5290** **MILES TRAVELED**

**C**

**KEY TO SYMBOLS**

⚠️ .............sleep in campsite

🚐 .............sleep in Winnie

🏠 .............hometown stop

📱 .............welcome to

💰 .............money trail

**JOB** .............job

The stadium was nuts, people were running around every which direction. As soon as we got there, they immediately assigned us jobs. Mark worked the floor, Los was in the office, and Allison and Shelly got the stage ready. It turned out I wouldn't be performing that night, so I called off the search for my dressing room. I was in the rigging department. We did everything from building the stage to hoisting the lights and speakers in the air and running the stage underneath. We worked our tails off. It was the hardest work I did on the entire trip. And we didn't even get paid for it. There was no green stuff flying on that one.

The head rigger, Kevin, was a cool dude; he let me go up on the catwalk, which is about 90 feet above the stadium. I knew something was fishy, though, when he tried to get me to flash the people down below. I think he wanted to see my WonderBra. That's when I called ball game and went back down to work. **-KIT**

Sammy gave me his Van Halen album on cassette, and we got so psyched we put it on stereo and popped in the tape and found out we were going to smash some stuff up.

Wherever we were going would have been fine with me, 'cause I got my concert fix. I've gone to plenty of concerts: 27, I think. I'm not an expert but I know what I like, and that was definitely a great concert. I would definitely say it's up there with Metallica, Skid Row, and Pantera. **-SHELLY**

**Fort Wayne** ⭐

69

65

46

**Indianapolis**

**2**

**JOB** # Roadies for a Day

**OBJECTIVE:** Set up the stage today so that you can see the show tonight

**PERKS:** T-shirts, picture with the band

**REWARD:** Killer seats for the show

4

NAME: Patrick Ledwick
TITLE: Stage manager for rock 'n' roll bands
MOTTO: "Why would anyone want to do this job?"

We worked those kids hard and they did very good. No-holds-barred, there was no favoritism or nothing, we just put them to work. I noticed, come the afternoon, that some of them were passing out, but they all stuck in. We were quite impressed, actually, because it's a high-pressure environment and they didn't crack.

If you want to get involved in this business, and don't ask me why you'd bother, you pretty much have to start at the bottom and work your way up. The bottom is basically loading and unloading 18-wheeler trucks, until you can specialize in a certain department. (On average there are four to 10 trucks per show, but the Stones had 80 on their Steel Wheels tour.) If you're serious about it as a kid, you need to get involved in your local town, find out who the local stagehands are. Once you learn the ropes, then it's a question of finding a production manager who's willing to take you out on the road.

Our main guy was Patrick, he was a pretty cool dude. He told us some stories about the groupie girls that follow Van Halen around. The roadies keep a bunch of photos of these girls underneath one of the equipment trunks. I was hoping he could hook me up with one of them later in the evening. But my pickings weren't to my liking, so I changed my mind. When we met the band, they were just as anxious as us. They were all in really good moods, they were very talkative. Michael Anthony was a trip, he was way cool. I didn't think they'd be up for us little people, but they were really open, they even let us look around their tour bus.

Going from our Winnebago to that baby was like night and day. The interior was plush leather, they had their own little private sleeping compartments on either side of the bus, a big area with an open bar, a TV, a VCR, and a bathroom with actual tile instead of plastic. So we all sat there for a while and got a little jealous, but that's why they make the big bucks.

When showtime came, I kept thinking that all the ticket holders had no idea how much work it takes to get a concert going. The lights were going everywhere, the sound was perfect, and they had no problems with anything. We accomplished a lot.                    **-MARK**

## He said, "Don't be a roadie."

B

**5475 MILES TRAVELED**

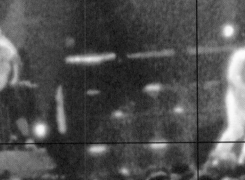

As we're heading to Rockford, the money situation is going downhill and downhill quick. We have enough to enjoy ourselves a little bit in the city, but we can't go wild.   **-KIT**

4

# CLUE

YOU HAVE TWO DAYS TO GET TO THE SPEEDWAY AT ROCKFORD, ILLINOIS, AND HAVE A SMASH-UP TIME.

**4/18 1995**

**CHICAGO**
POPULATION:
2,783,700
POPULAR HANGOUTS:
Hamilton's, The Metro, Billy Goat Tavern, Mad Bar
FANFARE:
Chicago Gospel Festival, two mid-June days
of gospel music in Grant Park
HOMETOWN OF:
Chicago Bulls, Bill Murray, Gilda Radner,
John Belushi, Oprah Winfrey

We found out on the way to Rockford that we were going to have a day or two to kill, so we stopped in Chicago and had a wild time. We actually got a hotel room, and shockaroo, Los chipped in to pay for it. From there, we went out to the Rockford Speedway and worked out some aggressions by smashing up some cars. —KIT

**A**

Naturally, Kit had friends in Chicago, just like everywhere else. I met up with her and some of her "guy friends" at a bar. Kit was being a puss. I think she worries too much about what people in Atlanta are going to think. A friend from home told her that everyone was bad-mouthing her because of the thing with me and her, so I basically hung back that night.
**-MARK**

The only real fight Mark and I had was in Chicago. I was dancing on top of the bar with these guy friends of mine, and Mark was just getting way too possessive. He was being a big baby. I tried to tell him, "We're not boyfriend/girlfriend, let's just have fun." I even tried to set him up with my hotty friend, Jules. I'm not a jealous person, that's just not in my nature.

After we finally left the bar, I told the gang, "I'm going to spend the night with Jules, and I'll be home in the morning." So Jules gave me this little T-shirt to wear to bed, I crashed out, and the next thing I knew, I found myself outside in this teeny T-shirt and my panties shoving THE WALL STREET JOURNAL under someone's door.

That's when the blood went to my head and I came to. I remember thinking, "Oh my God, I'm freezing!" Then, "What am I doing with this paper?" Then, "Son of a bitch, what am I doing outside?" It was pitch-dark, and I didn't know which building I came out of.

I started knocking on doors with Easter decorations, because I figured those would be the nice people. Finally, the Nicest Girl in America opened her door. She let me use her phone, but I didn't even have Jules's number, and no one answered in our room at the hotel. So the Nicest Girl gave me a pair of shorts and sent me back outside to look for Jules. At 4:30 A.M., not too many people would open their doors to help me find her, so I went back to Nicest Girl's house and got some shut-eye on her couch.

Finally, old Jules woke up and came to rescue me. So I don't know what kind of stuff they slipped in my drink in Chicago, but I think everybody got their paper that morning. **-KIT**

♥ I thought guys understood that if a girl isn't looking in your eyes, she doesn't want to kiss you. I was dancing with some guy, and out of nowhere, these lips started coming at me… I had to duck out of the way! That guy got a zero for approach on my Top Ten Kisses list. The guy I met at Mad Bar did better. He was a romantic, took me for a ride around the city and showed me Lake Michigan. **-ALLISON**

**5475 MILES TRAVELED**

The People of **Illinois** welcome you

**C**

## CHICAGO BLUES

Chicago wasn't very much fun. I had such a hard time there. Allison and I went to the Hard Rock Cafe for dinner, and the conversation centered on Carlos the entire time because she needed to get a lot of things off her chest. It made me sad that things had gone so far wrong between them. Later, I couldn't get into the bar everyone was at, because they were checking ID, so Allison got me a cab and the driver ripped me off; by accident I gave him a $20 bill instead of a $1 for a tip, and he wouldn't give it back.
**-SHELLY**

**KEY TO SYMBOLS**
........sleep in motel
........sleep in Winnie
........hometown stop
........welcome to
........mission
........scamming/cheating

## MISSION NUMBER 9

### DEMOLITION DERBY

As we rolled into Rockford, the weather definitely matched our mood. It was rainy and cold and dark out, and the five of us were beat from turning it up a little too high in Chicago. **-KIT**

**OBJECTIVE:** Be the last car running

**CHALLENGE:** Drive with your head in a brown bag, and let your partner be your eyes

**TOOLS:** A hearse, a Chevy, and the Rebel

**REWARD:** $200 each

**Rockford** ★ 90

Gary

**Chicago** 65

30

**Fort Wayne**

IL

IN

NAME: David Deery
TITLE: Owner, Rockford Speedway
MOTTO: "It's a business."

Those ROAD RULES kids must have had a hell of a party the night before, 'cause they were pretty much on their way out by the time they got to Rockford. Their attitudes changed big-time after experiencing the derby, though. One of the first things I heard Los say was, "These people are a bunch of rednecks." After the derby, he was more pumped than anybody.

Mark drove a converted Chevy Monte Carlo in the Road Runner race. Mark's driving was very good. I've been here 49 years, and I've seen butch guys that would never race as hard as he did their first night. **He was a hard charger, he was that kind of kid, he'd try anything.**

**THREE GREAT CHICAGO MOVIES**
FERRIS BUELLER'S DAY OFF
THE UNTOUCHABLES
THE BLUES BROTHERS

**DEMOLITION FEVER**

County fairs nationwide host traditional derbies, in which the winner is often the sole car to survive the final demolition.

USA Demolition Derby, based in Michigan, is one of the largest regional groups in the country.

Most demo cars come from junkyards and the participants' grandparents.

Minimum age for participation is 16.

5

**ROCKFORD**

POPULATION:
139,426

POPULAR HANGOUTS:
LT's, Stash O'Neil's

TRIVIA:
Nicknamed "Forest City" because each block averages more than 100 trees

MUST SEE:
Magic Waters Water Park, the go-cart track

After getting some sleep, we were psyched for the derby—all of us except Los, who didn't want to take part. David let us pick out our cars and paint them all crazy.

## Kit and I gave our car the number 69, don't ask me why.

Shelly and Allison chose a hearse and numbered it 666, I thought that fit perfectly with Shelly's whole shtick. The derby was one of our happiest times, we were all hyped up.

That afternoon, I took a test drive and they approved me to drive in the Road Runner race. I was kinda nervous and edgy about going out on the track with ten other drivers. I hoped I wasn't going to cause them to wreck. When I got in my car, my knees were shaking. Kit got to be the announcer for my race, but I didn't hear her. It was loud as hell, one touch to the accelerator rocked the whole car. So I was tensed up, all pumped up, it was a constant rush. In fact, I did an extra lap because I didn't know we were done, it went by so quick. When I got out of the car, my legs were still shaking. **-MARK**

**5721 MILES TRAVELED**

## Bagging It

In the Bag Derby they put a bag over the driver's head, and then the passenger has to direct the driver as you get all smashed up. We were really jumpy about the competition because the winner got $200.

### I decided I was not going to stop for anything and I was just going to go kamikaze, balls to the walls, going to win the 200 bones.

Then we fired up the Rebel to go into the race, and my girl conked off. The Rebel literally coasted down into the speedway. All the other engines were roaring, and the announcer was counting down while I was frantically trying to start the Rebel back up. I finally said, "The hell with it," and ripped off my bag. Mark and I were target practice, we were sitting ducks.

Then we saw the hearse flying into people, back and forth. There was little Shell Belle's bag-head over the wheel, and Allison screaming out directions. And they just kept slamming into people, it looked hysterical. They bumped into one car so hard they knocked it over part of the wall.

Then there were three cars left, the hearse being one of them. Mark and I of course hadn't left our position from the get-go. We were cheering on the hearse, thinking about those 200 bones, when all of a sudden, out of the blue, she smacked full dab into us, and she died right there. **Then came Shelly, slithering out the window onto the hood of the hearse with her long black hair and smoke everywhere.** She had a huge case of the bitteries because apparently Allison wasn't giving her good directions. **-KIT**

After we crashed into the Rebel, I slammed on the brakes and shouted at Allison, "What the hell? Where am I?" She took over the wheel and steered us totally out of the race. Whenever I'm not in control of a situation I get much bitchier. **-SHELLY**

# CLUE

YOU'RE GAINING MOMENTUM AS YOU MOVE WEST. VISIT THE PALACE MADE OF CORN IN MITCHELL, SOUTH DAKOTA.

D

4

**NASCAR**

The National Association for Stock Car Auto Racing boasts 50,000 members.

The largest NASCAR tracks are in Talladega, AL—they are 2.66 miles long.

The Daytona 500 is the Superbowl of NASCAR.

A Premier Series Winston Cup Stock car costs approximately $100,000.

In Mitchell, South Dakota, we did a tour of the Corn Palace. That's where we found our next clue, on the top of a little statue of Mount Rushmore. Guess where we went next? You guessed it. After that, we went skydiving in Gillette, Wyoming, and gave a face-lift to a big pink dinosaur at the Dine-A-Ville Motel in Vernal, Utah. –SHELLY

I don't think anybody can imagine unless they've done it what it's like to be over 12,000 feet up when they open up the back of the plane and tell you to jump.

When I opened my eyes I saw land, sky, land, sky.... Me and my tandem guy brought a beer up with us and we were about to crack it when Mark went flying by me. My guy said, "That's your buddy, they're having a malfunction." **-KIT**

Before we went up, the instructor read through a bunch of safety precautions and gave us this long, drawn-out waiver to sign.

### Sky diving's not safe; if you ever thought it was safe, you're wrong.

But then again, there's no 100 percent guarantee in anything.

I saw Kit go before me, and she just went tumbling out. It was the weirdest thing I've ever seen. When they open the back door you hear this big rush of wind that goes through the whole plane. It pumps you up and gets you ready to go. My tandem instructor triple-checked the gear, and we prepared for the jump. We did two backflips and then opened up into a freefall, kind of like a bird.

**It was like going down a roller coaster, turned up 12 notches.** I looked at my altimeter at around 5,000 feet and felt my instructor jerking around in back of me, so I figured the chute would open soon. Then I felt him reach over the top of me and start pulling on mine. Something was very wrong. At 3,500 or 4,000 feet he started grunting and shifting me all around. That's when I became a little bit more frightened. He reached down for the reserve chute, which was by my hip, and he was struggling with that when I looked down and saw we were almost at 2,000 feet. I could pick out people on the ground and their cars real precisely. We were almost in the red, which means that even if your chute does open, you're going to splatter, just not as fast. Suddenly, I felt the chute jerk up, and Bob gave me the thumbs up.

My first thought when my chute opened was, "Where's Kit?" She'd jumped before me, and when I looked up, she was still falling; I could barely see her up in her parachute. That's when it finally hit that we'd had the biggest malfunction ever. As I found out later, a $CO_2$ cartridge goes off automatically when you hit a certain height in the sky. That's what saved my ass from dying. **-MARK**

**5721** MILES TRAVELED

Mount Rushmore was originally conceived as a memorial for local heroes like Lewis and Clark, Buffalo Bill, and Kit Carson, but the sculptor finally settled on the four presidents Washington, Jefferson, Roosevelt, and Lincoln. 90% of the carving was done with dynamite, and in 1941 the nearly completed head of Thomas Jefferson had to be blasted off and moved to the right of Washington's due to insufficient granite.

The Corn Palace in one word: conceptual. -LOS

The Corn Palace in two words: good God! -MARK

### CRAZY HORSE

To let "the white man know the red man has heroes, too," Sioux Chief Henry Standing Bear initiated a project to memorialize the great Sioux war-leader, Crazy Horse. The sculpture, measuring 563 feet high, 641 feet long, with an outstretched arm long enough to support 4,000 people, was started in 1947 by sculptor Korczak Ziolowski. Visitors are welcome to view this wonder under construction or they can wait until its projected finish by the century's end, (though some insider's are skeptical about this date).

**CLUE** **REACH NEW HEIGHTS ON TOP OF THE MOUNTAIN OF PRESIDENTS. SEE THE RANGER.**

## Dead Presidents

After some twisty driving, we made it to Big Daddy Mountain. We met Ranger Mark, who took us up a trail usually reserved for VIPs, presidents and stuff. We got to go straight up to the top of George's head. -MARK

MITCHELL CORN PALACE

I bought some moccasins at Wall Drug. They had some cheaper ones made by US companies, but I wanted the ones made by a Native American, like the ones I got. It kills me that the whole time that we've been traveling out West, I've seen all this artistry and images of native people, but I haven't seen any Indians anywhere. -LOS

**CLUE** You Reached Noble HEIGHTS TODAY, But the Next Stop MAY SCARE the DEVIL Out of You Visit BOB at Black Hills SKYDIVERS in Gillette, WYOMING & FIND Out WHY

WY
**SD**
Devil's Tower — Rapid City — Sioux Falls
Buffalo
**IA**
Rockford
Mitchell
Casper
Rock Springs
Rawlins
Missouri Valley
Davenport
**IL**
Vernal
**UT**

On the way to Mount Rushmore we stopped at a motel and asked if we could see one of the rooms. We got the key and from there it was a no-brainer. Kit, the littlest one, stayed in the room and let us back in. We got a shower and a free bed, watched LETTERMAN, and spent the night for free.

Oh yeah, we got busted the next day by a maid. The crew had to pay for the room, 'cause we were out of money, but they kept promising we'll pay for this later. -MARK

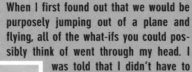

# MISSION NUMBER 10
## SKYDIVING

**OBJECTIVE:** Fly, then come back to earth gently

**HAZARDS:** There's always a chance the chute won't open

**TOOLS:** Plane, tandem instructors, parachutes

**REWARD:** Adrenaline rush

I've never done drugs or anything like that, so I couldn't tell you about feeling high that way. But I suppose if I had done drugs, then I might have felt a little something like skydiving, but not as good. **-LOS**

When I first found out that we would be purposely jumping out of a plane and flying, all of the what-ifs you could possibly think of went through my head. I was told that I didn't have to do this...I needed to.

Since my friend, Michael, fell off a building and died, there's been something within me that keeps me away from any type of danger. **Skydiving, free-falling, was something that I needed to do for myself. It was definitely a form of therapy.** A lot of it has to do with thinking about Michael and relating to him. So it was much more than an adventure for me. I feel very much at peace. **-SHELLY**

## CLUE

**I'VE ARRANGED ANOTHER JOB FOR YOU. YOU HAVE TWO DAYS TO GET TO THE DINE-A-VILLE IN VERNAL, UTAH. TRY THE PINK BRONTOSAURUS.**

Native Americans believe that Devil's Tower, featured as the landing strip in CLOSE ENCOUNTERS OF THE THIRD KIND, was created when a little boy turned into a bear and scared his seven sisters, who scurried up a tree stump, which then grew up into the sky. The park asks that hikers allow the area's Native Americans to peacefully hold religious ceremonies at the site in the month of June.

**7624 MILES TRAVELED**

## JOB — Painting Dinosaurs

Skydiving must have been the medicine that Los needed to brighten up and be more sociable with everyone. You could see it as we were painting the dinosaur; the sun was out, he was laughing, goofing off, being himself. That's the part of Los that I like to see. **-MARK**

**OBJECTIVE:** Paint the Dine-A-Ville brontosaurus Pepto pink

**HAZARDS:** Prehistoric carnivores nearby

**TOOLS:** Rollers, brushes, crane

**REWARD:** $240 each

We got paid $240 a person for painting Dine-A-Ville. We also got this nice little note from the people up above saying that they'd subtracted the money we owed them for dining and dashing and for scabbing a hotel room at that lovely little establishment in Indiana. So we're paying the fiddler, but you see, when you get low on your cash, it's amazing the things that you have to do. You're pushed to a certain limit and reduced to a life of crime. **-KIT**

## CLUE

YOU'RE ALMOST THROUGH, BUT THIS NEXT ONE'S REALLY TOUGH. ONLY THE STRONG WILL SURVIVE. GO TO BOULDER, UTAH TOMORROW, AND FIND THE B.O.S.S.

**VERNAL**
POPULATION: 6,700

NICKNAME: "Dinosaur Capital of the World"

MUST SEE: The Dinosaur Gardens at The Dinosaur Museum of Natural History feature a bevy of sorta-realistic model dinosaurs; the Dinosaur National Monument is just outside of town

TALK OF THE TOWN: Dinosaur fossils

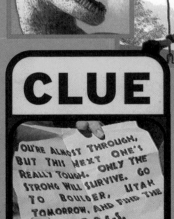

Mark shaved his hair. He decided to go for the semi-bald look. It looks better than the big hair. I just hope he's going to cut back on the hair spray now. But yeah, it looks half decent—with a hat on. **-KIT**

# MISSION 11

# B.O.S.S.

**OBJECTIVE:** Stick together to find your way back to the Winnie

**CHALLENGE:** Use your wits, not technology, to stay alive

**TOOLS:** Ponchos, rice, oats, lentils, compass

A

B

We started off to Boulder in a cold rain. After we'd been driving awhile, the sky cleared and we stopped to take photos on the side of the road. We went on and climbed into some blinding snow, but as we crossed the peak and came into Boulder the weather changed again to sun. Seeing the country has really helped me to see that not only are things rough all over, but there's beauty all over also. It kind of helps you appreciate where you're from when you're able to go out and see other places and see what they have to offer as well as what they're missing. **-LOS**

We left Vernal and spent the night in Richfield, where Los found a local outdoor store and asked them what B.O.S.S. stood for. It looked like we were in for some serious communing with Mother Nature. -MARK

## 7624 MILES TRAVELED

## On the Trail

C

When I found out that the initials B.O.S.S. stood for Boulder Outdoor Survival School, I thought, "You've got to be kidding me." I'd heard about these things where they drop you off in the wilderness and you have to survive as a team, and I knew the four that I'd been traveling with—there was no way we were going to be able to survive out there, we couldn't even find the Winnie the first day of the trip. I was definitely a little concerned.

We did two days of training, and the day before we were going to leave, they took us out to a stretch of land that would be similar to where we would be camping out, to give us a crash course. We learned the tricks of the trade: map reading, building a fire, and all those good things. I got more than a little concerned when they said we couldn't bring any of our camping gear, except sleeping bags. They gave us a little bit of food and these sorry little ponchos and that was about it. No cute little stoves to fire up or any of that.

**So I was definitely worried that**
**a) I would freeze and**
**b) I would starve.**

The logistics of this particular mission were that we would be dropped off in a remote area and have one day to reach our first checkpoint, which was about 5 miles as the crow flies. We were supposed to camp at the checkpoint that night, refill our water tanks, eat, and take care of our mess so that we didn't leave any scars on the terrain, and then start off the next day to make it to our final checkpoint. **-LOS**

Mark and I decided to buddy up; my thinking was, "Of course I'll buddy with him, he'll do all the work and I can just chill by the fire." His thinking might have been completely different. He wanted me to get in the poncho tent to do the funky gnarly, which I was having no part of.

The next day we were flown into the valley by helicopter and dumped off in the middle of nowhere and we were off on a trek. **-KIT**

### KEY TO SYMBOLS

- .............sleep in Winnie
- .............danger
- .............hometown stop
- .............welcome to
- M.............mission
- .............scamming/cheating

Vernal

Helper 191

72 12 6 10

Boulder ★ UT

2

3

### TO BUILD A FIRE

To build a bow-drill fire, take two nonresinous softwoods and create friction between the two surfaces; that friction will create an ash, and as that ash gets hotter, it finally ignites, which creates a coal. Then you take that coal and transfer it to a fibrous bundle that will allow the heat to transfer from the coal to a flame. Then you blow it up into a fire.

-DAVID, B.O.S.S. INSTRUCTOR

Canyon

**5/4 1995**

NAME: David Wescot
TITLE: B.O.S.S.
MOTTO: "We teach people how to use their natural ability to solve problems as opposed to depending on technology."

In our culture, we go with the idea that problems are instantaneous and solutions to those problems can be instantaneous as well. That's a real scary proposition.

The ROAD RULES group learned the basic skills they would need to be comfortable: how to set up a pontoon shelter so they would have protection from rain; how to build fires so they could cook their food; how to pack their gear so they could travel comfortably; how to navigate cross-country. They learned this all in the two days we spent together before hitting the trail.

I think one of the lessons they picked up a little bit, but never addressed directly, was how much they needed each other. They were used to ignoring each other and getting in tiffs and not ever dealing with it. A survival experience gave them an opportunity to address the idea that it takes a lot of teamwork and facing hard times and working together and using the strength of everybody to get the problem solved.

**BOULDER**
POPULATION:
100 in winter, 130-140 in summer
HISTORICAL TRIVIA:
The Anasazi people, descendants of the Hopi and Zuni tribes, lived in this area from 1050 to 1200 A.D.
MUST SEE:
A prehistoric Anasazi village remains intact at the Anasazi State Park, a 6-acre nature center
MUST DO:
There is no downhill skiing in this area due to its remote location, but some of the locals do enjoy cross-country skiing, fishing, and hunting elk; Boulder hosts a Bluegrass festival in July

I was kind of worried, because there's five of us, and we only had enough food to feed Mark. Allison was worried too, obviously. Somehow she smuggled in a loaf of bread, plastic utensils, matches, who knows what else. We started off hiking along a creek that took us to a huge wall. We were actually supposed to, like, climb up this wall. I didn't think I could do it, I was terrified. I was completely, completely, utterly scared, but Carlos and Allison talked me up it, told me when to step up, when to step sideways, and I made it. **That night we had a lovely little cuisine going. We had rice and beans with sand.** And for dessert, we had our breakfast. I don't know. All I wanted was a peanut butter and jelly sandwich. Everybody else wanted Power Bars, bananas, something healthy. I wanted a peanut butter and jelly sandwich with no sand. B.O.S.S. cleared some things up for me, though. I used to think I was this "city girl." There were a lot of things I hadn't allowed myself to do. Sitting by the campfire, I realized how easy life could be. I think I make things hard for myself sometimes. **-SHELLY**

There's definitely something admirable in being able to survive out in the wilderness with the bare essentials. But I think it's almost a bit hypocritical. We've developed all these things to make life easier and yet we're trying to deny ourselves all these things and put ourselves out in the woods with nothing. If an animal learns a new survival technique, it's not going to forget about it, it's going to use it. We did use bug spray and these little drops to put in the water to clarify it, so it seemed that we were trying to forget about all this technology, yet there were some pieces of technology that were necessary.

**7930 MILES TRAVELED**

At one point we were climbing straight up the side of a mountain, and I reached up and there was Los grabbing my hand. We had been fighting the whole week before, and I looked at him and said, "Los, you're not going to let me go, are you? You know we've been through a lot together, don't let me down." I was really scared, 'cause here I had to trust him with my life, and the week before he'd threatened to kick my ass when the trip was all over. But Los, he came through that time, he did the right thing. **-ALLISON**

**CLUE**

When we finally reached the end of the mission and saw the highway, I threw my trusty walking stick away. It had served its purpose, like many things have along the way.

On the front of the Winnie was a bottle of champagne and a trophy with our next mission engraved on the side. Everybody was too tired to celebrate. I would probably rate this as the second hardest physical workout on the trip, after Marine Corps training. **-LOS**

**D**

**THE END MAY BE NEAR, BUT FIRST YOU'VE GOT TO GO TO CALISTOGA VILLAGE INN AND SPA IN CALISTOGA, CALIFORNIA**

**6**

**KEEP YOUR HEAT**
To conserve heat when you're camping out, wear anything other than cotton, because cotton is breathable and allows heat to escape your body. Heat loss can also be decreased by huddling together with the other members of your group.

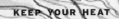

5
4
1995

While the drinking age (21) is average, Utah's other drinking laws are unusual. Alcohol cannot be brought into Utah from another state. Most restaurants and all bars serve only beer. Some establishments are licensed to sell mini bottles and splits of wine, but the customers must make drinks themselves. Only private clubs requiring membership fees are allowed to serve mixed drinks. Sometimes, licenses and zoning laws can split a room, forcing drinkers to move a few feet down the bar from non drinkers in order to get a mixed drink.

After completing B.O.S.S., we were hoping for a little pampering, and they must have read our minds because we got a clue to go to a spa in Calistoga, California. On the way, we stopped in Salt Lake City and celebrated Cinco de Mayo. We were getting closer to the Handsome Reward. -ALLISON

We were staying in the old section in a place that was just cluttered with really cool little bars and cool bands. It was Cinco de Mayo, and they were going nuts. I remember the next day I went running 5 or 6 miles out of town. I loved it there. It was really clean and I saw the Mormon Tabernacle. I went inside, and there was a wedding going on that was really gorgeous. That reminds me, I also bought my second WonderBra in Salt Lake, an orange one in honor of Cinco de Mayo. When you live this close to people, they know everything about you. I'm one of those people who goes, "Hey guys, check out the WonderBra." I was so excited about having a little bit of cleavage. **-KIT**

Our night in Salt Lake was...memorable. Kit and I kept going farther and farther away from our hotel, hitting bars. And at one point, we were upstairs at a bar, and we sneaked out the exit door up top and totally lost everyone. We were so far away from our hotel, I said, "Screw it, let's get our own room. Of course the frantic calls all over town followed: "Where's Kit? Where's Mark?" **-MARK**

# The Great Salt Lake Escape

**7930** MILES TRAVELED

The Mormon Tabernacle, built in 1867, is the home of Salt Lake City's famed choir and a 11,623-pipe organ. The structure is located in the symbolic center of the Mormon religion, Temple Square. The acoustics are among the best in the world.

**SALT LAKE CITY**
POPULATION:
159,900
POPULAR HANGOUTS:
Bar X, The Bay, Java Jive, and Squatters Pub
TRIVIA:
The Great Salt Lake is the only remaining remnant of a massive, 20,000-square-mile inland sea
TALK OF THE TOWN:
Strict drinking laws
FANFARE:
9:30 P.M. Sunday performances by the world-renowned Mormon Tabernacle Choir
HOMETOWN OF:
Roseanne

I'm still having nightmares about the Marine Corps. **-SHELLY**

The night that Kit and Mark got lost, I had a conversation with Los that explained a lot about what had happened on this trip. I think Allison was sleeping, and Carlos and I were up talking in the hotel room. I said, "You know, I understand why you don't hate Mark and Kit—they let you get away with everything, and they don't really care what you do 'cause they're off in their own little world—but Allison and I don't put up with you when you're not nice. So why do you hate Allison, and not me?"

**He said, "Why do you think?"**
**I said, "Well, I think it's the color of my skin."**
**And he said, "You're right."** Los favored me because I wasn't white. He and Allison would never be friends because he would always be black and she would always be white. **-SHELLY**

Calistoga

NV UT

Tahoe

80

89

Provo
Helper

Boulder

15

6

6 10

72 12

15

CA

**KEY TO SYMBOLS**

............sidetrip
............romance
............conflict
............welcome to
............mission
............empty Winnie septic tank
............sleep in motel

# MISSION NUMBER 12

## KICKING AT THE SPA

**OBJECTIVE:** Achieve total relaxation

**TOOLS:** Mud baths, herbal wraps, steamrooms, masseuses, masseurs

**REWARD:** The Handsome Reward in sight

Los and Shelly are so naive. That they didn't know about Kit and Mark before this just amazes me. It all came out at the dinner table one night in California. Kit and I were having this ridiculous conversation that started when Kit said something to me like, "Oh, well, you kissed the mayor."

I couldn't believe she was bringing up the mayor, which was months ago. Once again, she was trying to draw attention away from her thing with Mark by making up stories about me getting it on with guys. So I was trying to laugh it off, but it got to a point where I thought, "OK, enough is enough. I'm not covering up anything anymore." So I said, "Yeah, well, you kissed Mark."

## "Well, you saw Mark's peter."
## "You did more than see his peter."

**8926 MILES TRAVELED**

Los was in total shock. He was like, "What are you talking about?" And Shelly was like, "Wait, what's going on here?" It was the last week of the trip! I couldn't believe that they did not know. True, Kit and Mark had confided in me, and not in Los and Shelly, but I thought it was obvious.

Mark confided in me the most. He would tell me his real feelings. Kit didn't share her feelings, she just told me things that I wasn't supposed to tell anyone else. I don't think either of them was in deeper than the other, it just appeared that way, because what Kit told Mark and what Kit told the rest of the world are two completely different stories. You'd have to be inside Kit's head to know what's really true. **—ALLISON**

At the spa, Mark and I totally beefed it up for the camera—just to be jackasses. By that point, we'd been hounded for so long, we decided to give some great footage and shut everybody up. When we both ripped off our towels, it was meant to be funny, like ha ha. And we staged our final kiss, you could see us looking into the camera, it wasn't like they caught us in a room! We were doing it for the camera. That was not my best move. It didn't come off quite like I wanted it to. We were just in such a giddy mood that we forgot that the world would be watching—and judging. **—KIT**

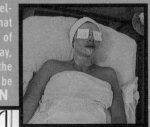

# CLUE

**YOU'RE NEARING THE END OF YOUR JOURNEY. STOP IN SANTA BARBARA FOR YOUR NEXT CLUE. YOUR ADVENTURE IS OVER, BUT ANOTHER ONE AWAITS YOU.**

**CALISTOGA**
POPULATION:
4,500

TRIVIA:
Name is a combo of Saratoga and California

SPECIAL SPAS:
Indian Springs, Calistoga Spa and Inn, International Spa, Nance's Hot Springs

MUST SEE:
Old Faithful Geyser, Clos Pegase Winery

MUST DO
Canoeing, white-water rafting, and inner tubing on the Russian River; bi plane and glider rides; hot-air balloon rides over the area's many wineries

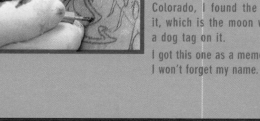

**8926** MILES TRAVELED

From Calistoga we drove to San Francisco, where Allison and I each got a tattoo, then we drove through Santa Barbara, where we got our next clue. We were to go to our Final Destination to receive our Handsome Rewards. The best surprise was seeing our parents on top of the mountain in Malibu. It was more than a full circle—it was a full circle with icing on top. –SHELLY

1    2

A

We didn't spend much time in San Francisco. I guess they thought there was enough of that on THE REAL WORLD. I think what everyone remembers most about that leg of the trip was feeling quiet, and kind of sad that it was almost over. For me, San Francisco was and always will be the place where I got my "Shelly" tattoo. For Allison, it was where she finally broke down and got the tattoo she'd been talking about the whole trip. I knew before Allison that we were going to stop at the tattoo parlor; they told me not to say anything to her. I finally told her when we were coming into San Francisco, and she was kind of stunned. Her response was, "Well, it's one thing to tell someone you're going to get a tattoo, but another to tell them, you're gonna get it today." She was right, but she did it. Me and Kit and Mark were all there for her, I don't know where Carlos was. Her tattoo looked like one of those little paste-ons, like you get through the 25¢ machines. The guy did a wonderful job. His name was Nalla. I'm going to name my kitten after him.

-SHELLY

# New Tattoo

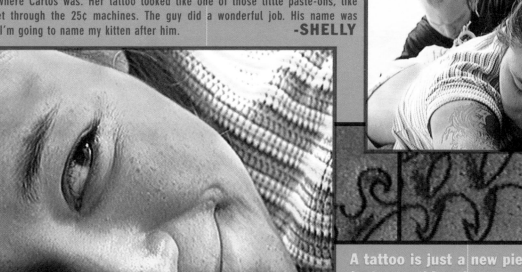

**KEY TO SYMBOLS**

△ ............sleep in campsite

☻ ..................danger

🏠 ............hometown stop

Ⓜ ............welcome to

Ⓜ ..................mission

☻ ............scamming/cheating

A tattoo is just a new piece to show off. Just something that says, "Look, look, look."

I'm a Sagittarius, so that's on my navel.

On my arm is the two faces of theater, because there's two sides to every story, and then right in the middle you have the eye, which means Truth.

The one on the back of my neck represents wholeness, it's the sun and the moon.

Then there's the sun on my stomach, which was a picture my boyfriend drew. When I went to Colorado, I found the perfect moon to put with it, which is the moon with the wizard, and it has a dog tag on it.

I got this one as a memory of the road trip. At least I won't forget my name.

*Calistoga*

101

*San Francisco*

CA

**MUIR WOODS NATIONAL MONUMENT**

560 acres of ancient redwoods are accessible from Route 1, just north of San Francisco. Secluded hiking paths lead out of the woods to Stinson Beach and Mt. Tamalpias.

2

# New You

Shelly thought I was a wimp because I wanted to get a small tattoo where people wouldn't see it. She kept insisting, "Nah, you got to get a big one across your arm or the back of your neck." I got a little Kermit with a stethoscope; I think both are important to me for obvious reasons.–**ALLISON**

**A**

**B**

**8996** MILES TRAVELED

**6**

TATTOO CITY
FRISCO

NAME: Nalla
TITLE: Tattoo artist, Ed Hardy's Tattoo City
MOTTO: "You're an anarchist today, but tomorrow you might be a Republican. You got to ask yourself: 'Do I want to wear this symbol forever?'"

Every tattoo artist excels in certain things, but some artists are more well rounded than others. No matter what, they usually apply a certain aesthetic to the design of the tattoo. If you're looking for a good tattoo artist, you're going to look for stylistic and personal compatibility. Do you get along with the person? Do they give a s**t about your tattoo? Do they care if it's going to look good? Do you get a sense they're into the project? If someone is just going to slap it on, then the price of admission is all they're looking at, not the art. If you've covered the bases of having a good artist and a good tattooer, the rest usually follows suit, but no matter what, make sure they are licensed by the health board, and that they have an autoclave sterilization process, which uses both pressure and steam. Disposable needles are always a plus.

Sometimes getting a tattoo hurts, sometimes it doesn't. It depends on the individual–on how well you slept the day before, how well you've been eating, or how stressed you are. It can be a breeze, but then again the littlest tattoo can be a living hell. If you're getting your first tattoo, it's really important to make sure your head space is clear, and you have set aside a good amount of time for it. If you've already had the experience of being tattooed, then most likely you've already dispelled all the ghosts and demons that go along with it.

**4**

**6**

SAN FRANCISCO
POPULATION:
724,000
POPULAR HANGOUTS:
Café du Nord,
Muddy Waters, Noc Noc
TRIVIA:
Named after Saint
Francis of Assisi
FANFARE:
The International Lesbian
& Gay Film Festival is the
world's largest, and it takes
place in mid-to late June;
The Chinese New Year
celebration takes place in
Chinatown in late February
HOMETOWN OF:
Lisa Bonet, Jerry Garcia,
and Clint Eastwood

## CLUE

CONGRATULATIONS, YOU HAVE SUCCESSFULLY COMPLETED YOUR JOURNEY. RETURN TO WHERE YOUR ADVENTURE STARTED IN PUERTO CANYON ROAD IN MALIBU, WHERE YOUR REWARD AWAITS YOU. THIS TAPE WILL SELF-DESTRUCT IN 30 SECONDS.

# Completing the Circle

All of our parents were at the top of the hill, waiting for us. Shelly was just hugging her mom for dear life, and I think we were all happy for ourselves—but extra proud of little Shell Belle, our youngest. Shelly by far learned the most from this trip because it was all new for her, she hasn't been to college yet. Just think how much you learn in college—that's your growing time.

Our Handsome Reward was two round-trip, first-class tickets to either Paris or Amsterdam. And they gave us a three-month Eurobus pass for two, and three nights in a five-star hotel. I already couldn't wait to cash in that pretty prize.

The feeling at the end was just overwhelming. I guess the trip can be compared to climbing a mountain; we'd climb a little bit and then get knocked down a little bit, and then climb a little more.

## Through it all we had our ups and downs, and I feel like finally now we're at the top, we've reached the peak.

I want the Winnie for my handsome reward. Hook it up, put a kit on it, put some mags on it, get the windows tinted darker, paint it red, put me in some carpet, throw me in a CD player, some 12-inch woofers, all that jazz. Turn this baby into the Los Mobile, scoot around campus, pick up brothers, might even go back across the country again, acting stupid. -LOS

## 8996 MILES TRAVELED

### KEY TO SYMBOLS

......days since last shower

......romance

......money trail

......welcome to

M ......mission

$$$ ......empty Winnie septic tank

2 ......lost

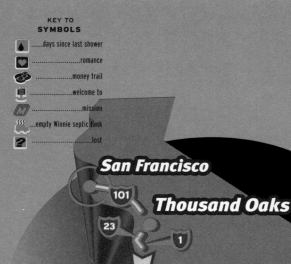

San Francisco

101

Thousand Oaks

23

1

Malibu

CA

I'm sad that it's finally wrapping up. This has been my family for ten weeks, and we've been through so much, it's going to be bizarre not having the four of them to share everything with. I'll miss the crew as well. I loved being in front of the camera.

I think Mark and I both realize that it was just one of those things, and we will probably go our separate ways now that it's over. But we will always remain friends and always look back on this as an unbelievable experience. I've been cross-country many times, but speaking from experience,

## it was a

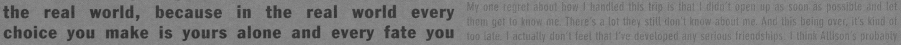

There's no comparing our microcosm in the Winnie to the real world, because in the real world every choice you make is yours alone and every fate you suffer is yours alone. There were times when I wanted to take the Winnie and drive somewhere by myself and never come back. In the real world I could have done that. And whatever happened would have been totally on me and it would have been my responsibility and my fate. I would have survived or died by my own wit and cunning. But on this trip, certain elements didn't allow you to leave. You were never totally alone, you always had other people to your right and to your left.

More than conquering or climbing a mountain, this show felt like descending one. Everything we did was so swift, like get here, do this, get here, do that. It's been a nice little departure from the everyday life of a Howard University student. It was great, and now it's time to move on. **-LOS**

My one regret about how I handled this trip is that I didn't open up as soon as possible and let them get to know me. There's a lot they still don't know about me. And this being over, it's kind of too late. I actually don't feel that I've developed any serious friendships. I think Allison's probably the only one I may keep in touch with. But, honestly, I expect I'll lose touch with all of them. Kit and Mark are obviously going to keep in touch, and Kit's going to keep at arm's distance from everyone else. We know the

least about Carlos, and I probably know more than anyone else, so I doubt if anybody's going to keep in touch with him.

I'm looking forward to going on with my life. I haven't found any of the answers I wanted. I've seen another side of myself and my reactions to situations. I've tried to develop relationships with my travel mates, but in reality, the most that has developed is just enough for us to survive. **-SHELLY**

Our generation, Generation X as they call it, has been stereotyped as kind of lazy, unmotivated, lost. And just by meeting different kinds of people in our age group I realize it's really not about that at all. I think that we're just motivated by something different than previous generations. Previously, people have been motivated by things more like money and success and a good career, but we're motivated by happiness. We want to find out what we're really meant to do, what's going to make us feel complete. And once we find that we can move on, and we can do more with our lives. But right now, it's not that we're lost, it's just that we're kind of searching...searching for what we're really all about and what life's really all about. **-ALLISON**

**9432 MILES TRAVELED**

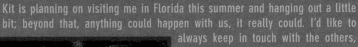

Kit is planning on visiting me in Florida this summer and hanging out a little bit; beyond that, anything could happen with us, it really could. I'd like to always keep in touch with the others, see what crazy things they're doing.

I don't actually have one word to describe ROAD RULES. I have a phrase. And the phrase would be "Once in a lifetime," because it just blows me away how many chances we had to do new things. People work for years and years for a chance to drive in a race, mush a dog, jump out of a plane, climb the VIP trail to the top of Mount Rushmore...the list goes on and on. We got to see so many areas, meet so many people, and do so many different things that no one gets to do. And that's why the people who bitched and moaned at things are going to look back on this and kick themselves in the foot for not appreciating every moment.

# It's been a blast. Thanks for the ride. -MARK

# kick-ass road trip. -KIT

## The Debut of Road Rules

MTV came to us and asked for a spin-off of THE REAL WORLD. After discussing a number of ideas, we decided to try and create some kind of a road show. We had some experience doing a show on the road during THE REAL WORLD, LA, when we followed Tami, Dominic, and Jon across the country in a Winnebago. It was sort of like turning THE REAL WORLD inside out. This time, instead of moving a group of kids into a city, we would send them out into America. To create a spine for the show, we decided to have the cast tackle a series of missions—some adrenaline-producing, others humorous. These missions would assure us a beginning, middle, and end to each episode as well as give us something on which to hang the inevitable personal drama. **-JONATHAN**

The main thing that we learned from shooting the pilot of ROAD RULES was that when the camera is around, everybody tends to overthink things. The cast had trouble figuring out some of the riddles that were meant to help them along their way, so we made the clues a little easier for the first season. But we were still learning; we learned from shooting the first season that our schedule was much too ambitious. Not only was the crew wiped out but the cast was always tired. Literally for ten weeks, we were on the go. We never had a breath. It wasn't anything like THE REAL WORLD as far as what was required of the crew. THE REAL WORLD has a control room in the house where the director can observe the cast, so it's more like a normal job than shooting ROAD RULES.

I think that their confusion during the first few weeks of shooting hindered the first group's development as a team, but Kit, Mark, Los, Allison, and Shelly finally hit their groove four weeks into the show at the alligator farm. Before that, I was pulling them off camera to remind them, "If you spend all your money, we're not to give you any more. This isn't a joke. This is real."

And sometimes they would get totally lost because none of them took charge of the computerized mapping system, so I'd page them from the crew Winnebago and say, "Guys, you're two hours in the wrong direction, double-check the map. But that was as much help as they got. If someone had a problem completing a mission, that was their problem. We didn't interfere at that point. They were told at the start that if they felt they couldn't handle something physically or emotionally, they didn't have to do it, they just had to explain why to their travel mates. **-CLAY**

**Clay Newbill**
Producer and Director, ROAD RULES, and former Coordinating Producer, THE REAL WORLD

## Casting the Net

It took four or five months to find the right people for ROAD RULES, and we cast our nets pretty wide. We found this group among people who had applied to THE REAL WORLD and, for whatever reason, were not right for that setting. We went back to revisit people who had seemed interesting on their own, and explored whether they had an adventurous spirit and a sense of humor, and were expressive. We looked for people who were inventive and curious about each other and about the world—no shrinking violets. Not that they had to promise to go through with every mission—each cast member's process of overcoming fears and phobias would be an important part of the show—but there had to be that sense of adventure, that love of the unknown. Finally, the cast members had to be telegenic, but we didn't require that they be classically beautiful.

The casting directors could tell pretty quickly who was even possible. If applicants were self-conscious in the casting process, they generally didn't go on. People who took a little time to warm up were better served by sending in their own video than by coming to an open call, because they could introduce themselves as they wanted. The 30 finalists were flown into LA or New York for further interviews. By the time we got to the final five, we knew them really well. **-MARY-ELLIS**

**Mary-Ellis Bunim and Jonathan Murray**
Creative and Executive Producers,
ROAD RULES and THE REAL WORLD

**Biff Bracht**
Director of Photography

**Andrew Perry**
Researcher and
Associate Producer

**Adam Cohen**
Director

## Crossing the Line

We have a term, "crossing the line," which was what the crew members were NOT supposed to do. They were told in no uncertain terms not to let their lives intersect with the cast members'. Clay and I were the only crew members who talked to the cast on a regular basis, because it was our job to know what was going on in their personal lives. But it was a hard rule to enforce because we were going through the same experiences together, sometimes living in a one-restaurant town for a week at a time. I carried a torch for not "crossing the line," because I really believed there should be separation—kind of like the separation between church and state. There were a couple of times when a crew member, after a 17-hour day, when there was only one bar in the town, would socialize with one of the cast members. I would come over and act as a crowbar and wedge them apart. It was inevitable that the line would blur over time, because the cast became the crew's children. Maybe that's how we came to call them "the kids." Every time we watched them run across the street we wanted to yell, "Watch out for the traffic!" But we couldn't. So it was really difficult. **-ADAM**

**Crew Winnie**

# The Cast

**During the casting process, I loved interviewing every member of this cast. I didn't want our talks to end; I wanted to go out and spend the entire evening learning more about each one of them, and I think that says something very positive about who these people are. -JONATHAN**

It was very obvious to me that Kit and Mark were falling for each other, be it love or lust, but they both had serious relationships at home. They are so alike, it was inevitable that they would become involved. And when they did, they set a precedent. Now people aren't afraid to get into a relationship with someone on the road while the cameras are documenting it. That has never happened between cast members in THE REAL WORLD.    **-CLAY**

I pretty much fell, so to speak, in love with Kit's personality. She's extremely articulate, and she had a way of tying up any controversy, any excitement, any interaction, with one of her southern belle metaphors. For instance, if she had to go to the bathroom, it was, "I have to shake the dew off the lily." And we loved that. That's what people want. They want a strong personality to come across. **-ADAM**

The first thing that really grabs you about Mark is his body. He is a well-built guy and he has the sweetest smile to boot. He reminds me a lot of Eric Nies from the first REAL WORLD: they both are young, and they plunge into things instead of worrying about the consequences or second-guessing themselves.    **-JONATHAN**

Wow, Shelly is a very special person. What attracted us to her first was how she breaks so many stereotypes. She really holds her Indian heritage close to herself, yet, at the same time, she embraces the Rock 'n' Roll lifestyle. After watching her, it's difficult for Caucasians to maintain any stereotypes about what a Native American should or should not be.    **-JONATHAN**

It was great to see Shelly come out of her shell on the road. You could see her crossing a threshold from childhood into adulthood, and it was interesting to observe her emotional growing pains in the process.    **-ADAM**

In every scientific experiment, there is something they call the control subject. For every three mice they operate on, they simply cut open one mouse and don't do the surgery. They just close it up again. That, to me, was kind of what Allison was. She played the straight man. But she showed you that you can never judge a book by its cover, because in some ways she was the wildest one. In Nogales, there were a lot of rumors as to what happened between her and the mayor, and I think that kept everyone guessing at every turn, "What is Allison going to do in this situation?" I don't think Allison would deal with a guy like Carlos in her normal life. It was great to see them forced together in this situation and to see her confronting him.    **-ADAM**

Carlos is the son of a deputy police chief from a fairly affluent community. He is also a student at Howard University, where he sees a very different black world—very northern, very urban. He is dealing with a lot of questions about who he is in Atlanta, versus who he is in Washington, D.C., and he definitely thinks a lot about how white people react to him.    **-JONATHAN**

Los always wore T-shirts with messages. He was using the show as a platform for his point of view. I don't know that there's anything wrong with that, but it proves that the kids are aware of the power they have on the air.    **-ANDREW**

# Mark

I just finished filming ROAD RULES TRIPPIN' THE AMERICAS with Kit and MTV. I also got a part in a Saturday morning TV show called SWEET VALLEY HIGH. I play a drummer in a band. I currently-ly have a manager and agent and have started acting school. I'm living in LA and I'll be here for a while, anxiously awaiting my next project.

# Shelly

I have a job at Edmund Motor Freight as a clerk. It's OK. I'm saving up extra money for my ROAD RULES prize, the trip to Europe. My mom's going to come with me, and we're going to spend a lot of time in Italy, just looking. I've been listening to the new Metallica and the new Rage Against the Machine, nonstop since it came out in June. I can finally go to concerts without people crowding around me and asking about ROAD RULES, so that's nice—I'd rather hear the music. The guy from Skid Row was watching the show and he saw the band's poster on my bedroom wall, so he gave me a call to say, "Hey." That was cool.

I put college off again until the spring, but I'm still interested in studying criminal jus-

# Los

I'm going into my last year at Howard University, and thinking some about what to do after that. Mostly, I'm studying set lighting for motion pictures. At school I have access to lights and camera equipment, but I won't have that outside, so I'm trying to get as much experience as I can now. I spend a lot of time watching movies without sound—it's the best way to study light.

# Allison

I got into Columbia Med School! I've got a boyfriend who I'm really happy with, and I'm sick of being asked about Louie. I want to go on with my life.

# Kit

I'm living in Chicago with my boyfriend, Crowley. He's a trader at the mercantile exchange, but he's just as crazy as me—he likes to wear a red sequined jacket that he got from a Neil Diamond impersonator. I just finished filming the ROAD RULES TRIPPIN' THE AMERICAS home video with Mark, and I've been commuting back and forth to LA for auditions. Right now, I'm in negotiations to be a host on a Generation X morning show, and Mark and I are getting ready to do ROAD RULES TRIPPIN' EUROPE. I don't want to be an actress, I'm just milking ROAD RULES for all it's worth. Considering my track record with long-distance relationships, I'll be staying in the Windy City with Crowley until LA really needs me.

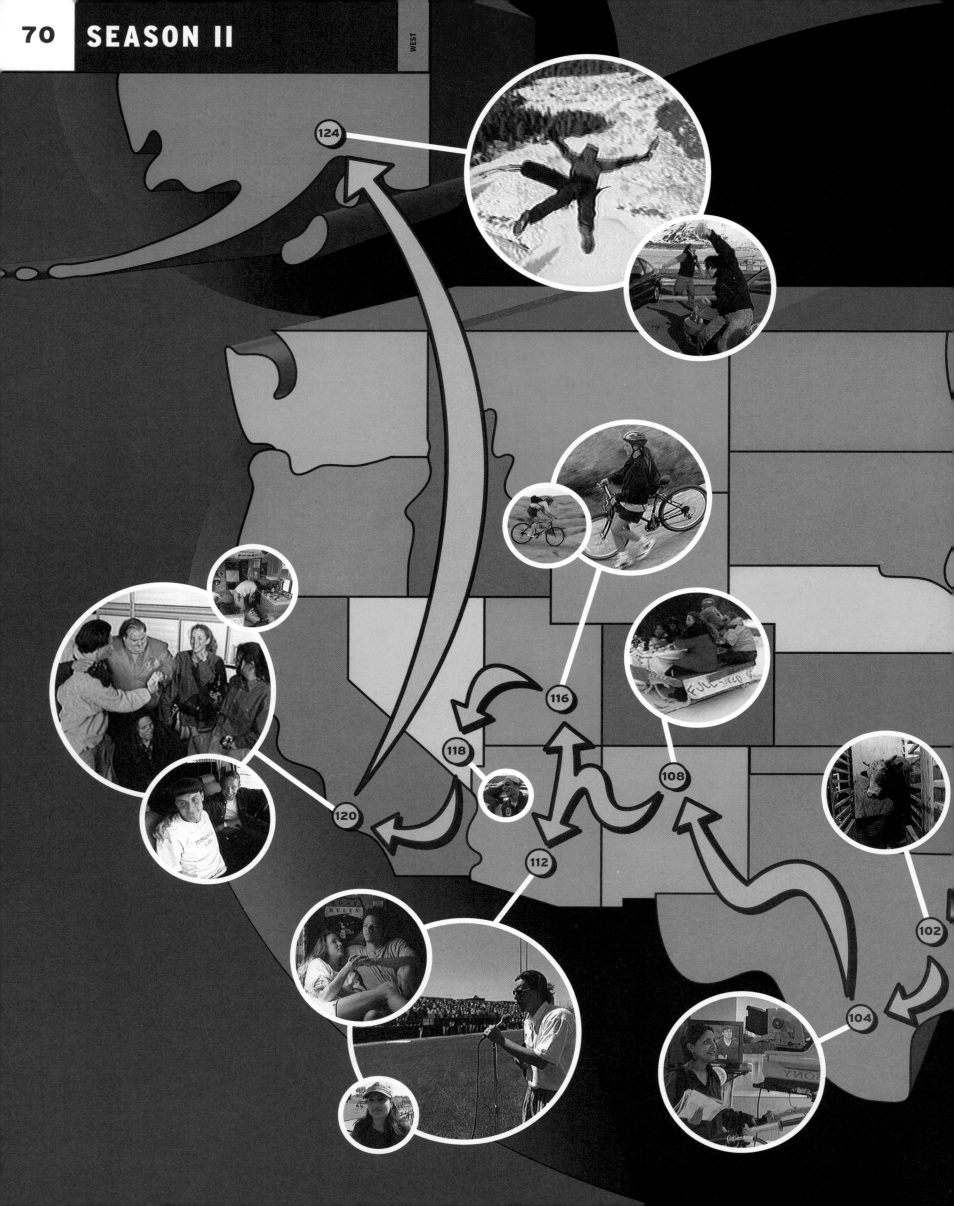

94

96
CHOOSE

90

86

84

82

80

8

78

The Winnie's trusty navigator, on the rearview mirror

NORGE

Christian

Nesøeya

## STATS

| | |
|---|---|
| DOB | 12/2/74 |
| HEIGHT | 5'6" |
| EYES | blue |
| HAIR | blond |
| HOMETOWN | Nesøeya, Norway |
| CAR | 1995 Fiat Uno |

My name is Christian, and I like to have it 100 percent. I'm very positive. I see no reason for being negative. I like socializing, and I can't stand being alone. I am often very direct—maybe too direct for some people. If people think that I'm like the average Norwegian, they are not right. If they really think that they would meet four million Christians when they come to Norway, they're wrong.

I grew up in Nesøeya, which is a little island just outside Oslo, the capital of Norway. I learned English at school and from television and radio. I feel comfortable most of the time speaking English, but sometimes I want to be a perfectionist and I get frustrated because I can't find the right words.

I go to the Norwegian School of Management, and there I study business; in two years my title will be master of business and economics. I work for two firms also. One is a communications firm. I also work as an assistant for a real estate broker firm. As for my future, I've not figured out one way to go. I've always wanted to act for a living. I've done a lot of acting previously—theater, commercials, and a Viking movie that was big in Norway called "Sigurd the Dragon Killer." I have thought about going to the state theater school in Oslo. But then again, there are a lot of actors in Norway, and it's a very small country, so there is a lot of competition and not a lot of money. You have to be permanently hired at one of the state theaters to make money. But that means doing too

much HAMLET and all that. I want to do crazy stuff. I can't help it—I like the idea of making money. I've felt that business is also a lot about acting all the time, in negotiations, in dealing with people. I know I can use my skills there, and have fun too.

My father is very much like me. He wanted to become an actor, but became a businessman. My father got his MBA and master of science in the United States, so I'm not the first one in my family to be drawn to America. My father and mother divorced when I was seven. He's with another woman now and they have a son, one-year-old, called Jan Fredrik. My mom is a secretary at a real estate office. I've lived with her until now. I have a brother, who is 25. I've traveled a lot with my family, and I've been to very many places with both my mom and my dad, but not both of them together.

I have been in love two times in my life. I have problems settling with girls. I've never had a girlfriend for a long time. I'm way too picky, or too demanding. I'm never satisfied, and that's stupid, because I'm not perfect myself, and I'm trying to look for the perfect girl.

## What I look for in a girl is somebody that shares my interest in doing weird things, like waterskiing in the middle of the night or swimming naked in a lake.

She has to be a little bit crazy, but, at the same time, really reflective. There are some things you just can't share with friends, and I really feel I need a girl to share these with. I hope when I return from ROAD RULES I can start looking, if not for Mrs. Right, then for Mrs. Right Now.

### CHRISTIAN'S ROAD STAPLES

Good-to-wear underwear
English dictionary
Goat cheese
Vitamins
Sports coat and tie
Lederhosen
Music
Camera

### CHRISTIAN'S FAVORITE DRIVING MUSIC

The Waterboys
Jamiroquai
Stereo MCs
Keziah Jones
Lillbyørn Nilsen

## STATS

| | |
|---|---|
| DOB | 5/10/77 |
| HEIGHT | 5'7" |
| EYES | green |
| HAIR | brown |
| HOMETOWN | Flora, IL |
| CAR | Chevy Beretta |

My name is Emily, I'm 18, and I'm a farmer's daughter from Flora, Illinois. Flora is basically a farm community. I've lived there my entire life—I was born there, my parents were born there.

When you hit 13 in Flora, you start counting ways to get out. Everyone feels like that. Ever since I was old enough to have my own mind and think about my future, I've felt like that. There is so much out there—so many places I want to see.

### There are so many things I want to experience that you just can't get living in a small town in the middle of southern Illinois.

It's a great place to raise a family, not a great place to be a teen-ager, though.

I come from a high school of like 400 people. I think a lot of kids in my school ended up losing their virginity a little bit too soon or turned to alcohol for a source of entertainment. I was really restless, always wanting to go, go, go, always on edge. Being on the pom pon squad helped, because I just loved to dance, it took me away. My best high school memory ever was when we went to St. Louis at the Kiel Center; 10,000 people were in the audience, and there we were, dancing in front of all of them. It was the best, best rush. I also tried to involve myself in sports—basketball, softball, volleyball—just to be able to travel a couple hours away from Flora maybe a couple nights a week.

Right after high school, I was taking classes at the community college, and I saw this ad for ROAD RULES on MTV. I was like, "That should be me." A couple weeks later I was watching some kind of race on TV—it was the pentathlon on ROAD RULES. And I just fell in love. I was so jealous of those people. I thought that would be so freaking great. At the very end of it, one of the VJs came on and said they were looking for new contestants, so I shouted to my roommate, "Get a piece of paper." That's so unlike me—I don't enter contests and stuff like that. I felt so silly. But I have a friend

who makes videos so I just asked her, "Why don't you help me make a video?" We went out and filmed me around the farm one afternoon. I knew there would be thousands of tapes and I wanted them to notice me, notice mine, so I told them I might do something crazy if they didn't pick me. When the casting directors called me, I was like, "This isn't ROAD RULES. This is some kind of cruel joke." They were like, "No, this is real." I kept going, "Get out of town, get out of here." Finally they convinced me it was real, and the neighbors below must have thought I was getting kidnapped or something, because I was screaming and jumping up and down. I just knew that this was going to be bigger than anything I used to consider big—even bigger than being elected Homecoming Queen in high school, which I considered a great honor. I don't mean to say I'm superambitious, I just always knew I would find a way out of Flora.

### EMILY'S PET PEEVES

- People who pick their nose in front of people
- People who sing louder than the radio
- Negative people

### EMILY'S ROAD STAPLES

- Favorite pair of Lucky jeans
- White T-shirt
- Leather cut-off boots
- Certs
- Goo Goo clusters

### HOW EMILY DESCRIBES EMILY

- Honest
- Down-to-earth
- Opinionated
- Spontaneous
- Conceited (at times)

Emily

IL

Flora

Devin

Cleveland Heights

OH

STATS

| | |
|---|---|
| DOB | 11/2/77 |
| HEIGHT | 5'7" |
| EYES | brown |
| HAIR | brown |
| HOMETOWN | Cleveland Heights, OH |
| CAR | 1984 Volksagon Jetta |

I grew up in Cleveland Heights, Ohio. It's a suburb. It's not small, but it's not huge. Most of the Cleveland Heights-University Heights area is Orthodox-Jewish, but over the years more people have moved into the neighborhood. I went to school with all kinds of people, from elementary school up. In my childhood, I faced a little tension because I'm such a light-skinned black guy. I didn't look like all of my black friends, and I didn't look like any of my white friends, either. I used to get into a lot of fights and stuff when people called me "white boy"; I used to have a temper on me.

I think it helped a lot that I grew up doing tae kwon do, a style of karate. My father started teaching me when I was four years old, and then I went on to teach. Martial arts was a really sound structure that kept me away from a lot of the experimenting that other kids did. I had a lot of discipline. You learn to respect your opponent, and to respect your teacher; at the same time, that teacher was my father. When I was 17, I was getting ready for my black belt and doing a lot of sparring. Then I got led away from it with senior-year stuff. I'm sure I'll pick it up again sometime. I just don't know when.

I'm not a big party-guy. I can party and will party if given the chance to, but I was in a relationship consistently for my whole high school experience and it was my choice to get to know somebody inside and out rather than be out partying.

## You can't take parties with you through the rest of your life, but you can take people.

I think that going to a movie or sitting at home playing cards or just hanging around and talking is a lot more fun, and it means a whole hell of a lot more than going out dancing or drinking.

I used to watch ROAD RULES and say, "Wow, I wish I could do that." It attracted me because I needed to meet some new people; I needed to see this country; I needed to know if Cleveland was for me for the rest of my immediate life. Mostly I just needed to get away. When I told my friends I got picked for ROAD RULES, they were like, "Yeah. You look like somebody who'd be in that. You have tattoos and you're crazy and you've got all of that hair. Yeah, that's why they picked you." But I like to think it was more than that. I think they picked me because my mom raised me to be who I am. I really wasn't influenced that much by my friends. I think I'm well spoken, I think I'm intelligent, and at the same time, I look like a freak. So, I've got balance.

I knew that leaving home was going to be easy and hard at the same time. There was a girl-friend in the picture. I told her if I came back to Cleveland after ROAD RULES, she would be the only reason. There was also my mom and little sister, then my father and his wife, who all hold very different roles in my life. My little sister's name is Dinah. She's four years younger. We had to take care of each other during our parents' really long and drawn-out divorce. I was there for her, and she was there for me. We've been through a lot of stuff, and I know she needs me. And I'd love to be there for her. I mean, whether it's a ride, or just to talk or whatever. It's my job.

### DEVIN'S CLEVELAND DIGS

FAVORITE HANGOUT: The Flats

FAVORITE LANDMARKS: Rock and Roll Hall of Fame, Jacobs Stadium (where the Indians play)

FAVORITE BAR: "None, 'cause I'm only 18."

FAVORITE PLACES TO WORK OUT: "Wherever I can skate or Rollerblade."

### DEVIN'S PET PEEVES

Loud breathers

Hysterical laughter

### DEVIN'S FAVORITE DRIVING MUSIC

Lenny Kravitz

Bob Marley

Jimi Hendrix

Nirvana

The GREASE soundtrack

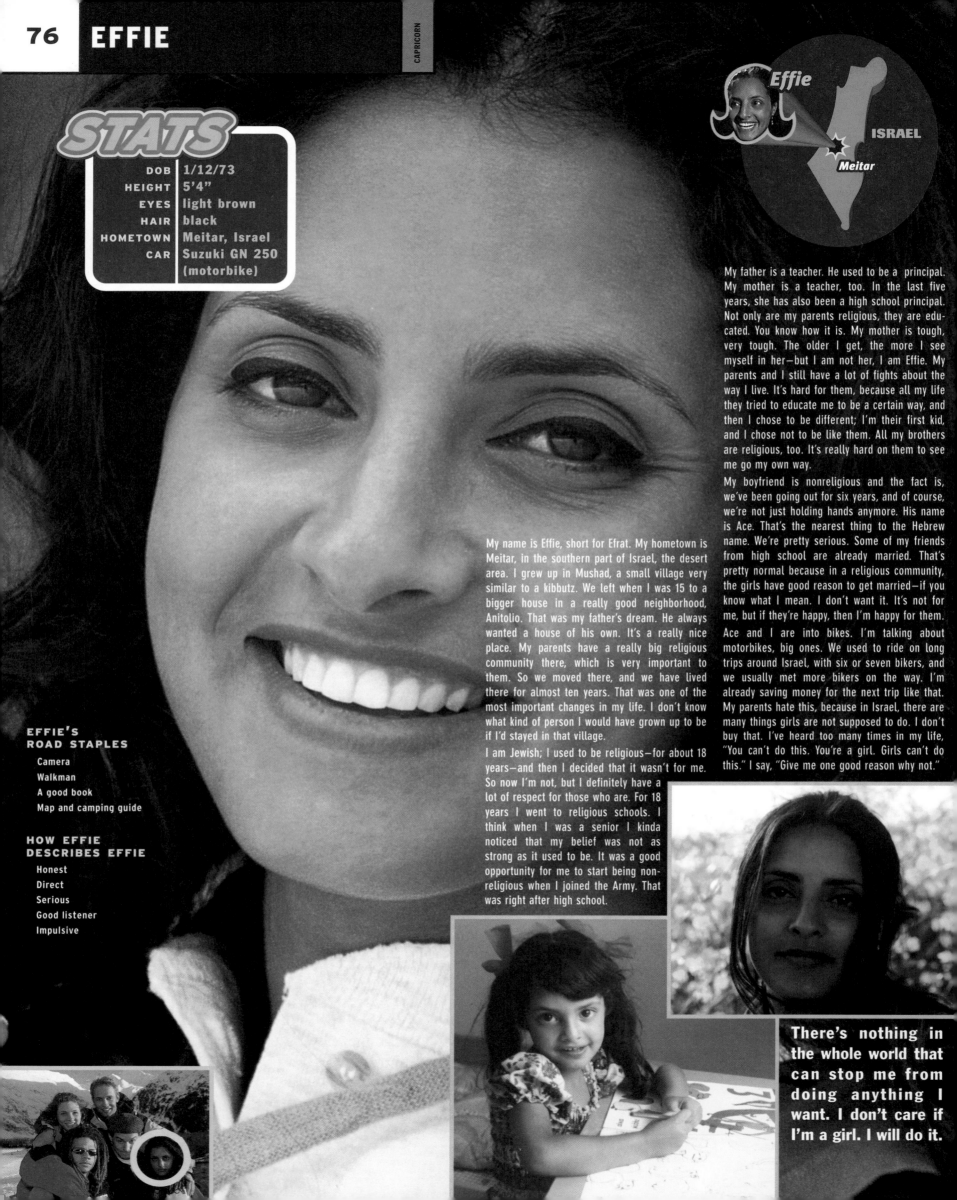

Effie
ISRAEL
Meitar

## STATS

| | |
|---|---|
| DOB | 1/12/73 |
| HEIGHT | 5'4" |
| EYES | light brown |
| HAIR | black |
| HOMETOWN | Meitar, Israel |
| CAR | Suzuki GN 250 (motorbike) |

**EFFIE'S ROAD STAPLES**

- Camera
- Walkman
- A good book
- Map and camping guide

**HOW EFFIE DESCRIBES EFFIE**

- Honest
- Direct
- Serious
- Good listener
- Impulsive

My father is a teacher. He used to be a principal. My mother is a teacher, too. In the last five years, she has also been a high school principal. Not only are my parents religious, they are educated. You know how it is. My mother is tough, very tough. The older I get, the more I see myself in her—but I am not her, I am Effie. My parents and I still have a lot of fights about the way I live. It's hard for them, because all my life they tried to educate me to be a certain way, and then I chose to be different; I'm their first kid, and I chose not to be like them. All my brothers are religious, too. It's really hard on them to see me go my own way.

My boyfriend is nonreligious and the fact is, we've been going out for six years, and of course, we're not just holding hands anymore. His name is Ace. That's the nearest thing to the Hebrew name. We're pretty serious. Some of my friends from high school are already married. That's pretty normal because in a religious community, the girls have good reason to get married—if you know what I mean. I don't want it. It's not for me, but if they're happy, then I'm happy for them.

Ace and I are into bikes. I'm talking about motorbikes, big ones. We used to ride on long trips around Israel, with six or seven bikers, and we usually met more bikers on the way. I'm already saving money for the next trip like that. My parents hate this, because in Israel, there are many things girls are not supposed to do. I don't buy that. I've heard too many times in my life, "You can't do this. You're a girl. Girls can't do this." I say, "Give me one good reason why not."

My name is Effie, short for Efrat. My hometown is Meitar, in the southern part of Israel, the desert area. I grew up in Mushad, a small village very similar to a kibbutz. We left when I was 15 to a bigger house in a really good neighborhood, Anitolio. That was my father's dream. He always wanted a house of his own. It's a really nice place. My parents have a really big religious community there, which is very important to them. So we moved there, and we have lived there for almost ten years. That was one of the most important changes in my life. I don't know what kind of person I would have grown up to be if I'd stayed in that village.

I am Jewish; I used to be religious—for about 18 years—and then I decided that it wasn't for me. So now I'm not, but I definitely have a lot of respect for those who are. For 18 years I went to religious schools. I think when I was a senior I kinda noticed that my belief was not as strong as it used to be. It was a good opportunity for me to start being nonreligious when I joined the Army. That was right after high school.

**There's nothing in the whole world that can stop me from doing anything I want. I don't care if I'm a girl. I will do it.**

GEMINI

## STATS

| | |
|---|---|
| DOB | 6/9/72 |
| HEIGHT | 5'11" |
| EYES | two |
| HAIR | brown |
| HOMETOWN | Pittsburgh, PA |
| CAR | 1977 Hornet and 1973 Hornet |

Timmy is my name. I'm 100 percent Irish and I grew up in Pittsburgh, Pennsylvania. I have one sister and too many brothers—two. I was the youngest, so I got picked on a lot. My defense was always humor. No matter how they picked on me or how bad a mood they were in, I could always turn it around with humor. I've always wanted to write a sitcom called TABLE MANNERS about my family meals. It's hard to get all six of us together at the dinner table, but when you do, it's just magic.

We had a pretty pampered life, a suburban dream. I was never really like that, though. Everyone played golf, but I'd go to the basketball court for eight hours. I was in my own little world, and pretty independent. When I left home

for college, I said to myself, "I can do it on my own, so I should." My family put me through how many years? And I'd given them hell, so I felt I should put myself through college.

I've had so many jobs in my lifetime, just all over the spectrum. I played college football at Dusquesne University, so every fall, I had to quit my job.

## I don't think there's a person in Pittsburgh I haven't served a drink to.

There's a strip of 20 blocks and every block has like three, four longshipper bars. I've worked in most of them—Rodeo, Clark Bar, Next Fat City, Lone Star, Dingbat's, Mario's, Boolou's, Jack's and Bar 11.

Pittsburgh is a unique town in itself. It's just really cool people. It was an old Polish steelworking town, and now these artistic people are coming in—many musical people, many artists, painters, people from all walks of life—just a young crowd about my age, with many of them now pretty much taking over. There are alternative stores coming in left and right. It's great. I've never lost my sense for it, or for the people. I get very attached to people. I've had tons of roommates. I get very attached to all of them. I'm just a little sappy, a little sentimental.

I don't know how many times in the last five years I almost got out of Pittsburgh, almost packed my bags and headed to New York or Hollywood to follow my dreams. But something always held me back. Then one day I was sitting at a friend's house and I just looked at the screen and saw ROAD RULES was having a call for auditions. I had to do it. The deadline was one week away. It took me forever to get a camera, 'cause no one really took me seriously. I told my friends, "Look, you get me a video camera, I'm getting this job." I was that confident. I finally got the camera on a Saturday, and the video had to be there on Monday. I taped me, walking around my dump of an apartment in Pittsburgh

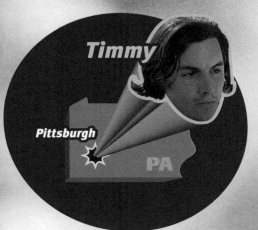

talking about what a mess my life was.

I FedExed it in and they mailed a questionnaire right back. As soon as it came in the mail, I started crying. I said, "Mom, I'm elated, they got in contact with me, I'm out of here." She really didn't believe me. I called all my friends, employers, family, and told them I was going to be on this show. I wasn't even picked yet, but I knew if they'd watched my tape, I would get it. I knew. It sounds horrible to say. I don't know what would have happened if I was wrong. It would have been interesting to see what would've happened to me.

### TIMMY'S ROAD STAPLES

- Wool cap
- Long johns
- Two pairs wool/cotton undies
- Gold Bond foot powder

### TIMMY'S PITTSBURGH DIGS

FAVORITE HANGOUTS: Any of the longshipper bars on the South Side

FAVORITE PLACE TO WORK OUT: Sam Shannon's Hall of Muscles

FAVORITE PLACE TO MEET GIRLS: Church, aisle three

FAVORITE PLACES TO GO ON A DATE: Fort Pitt Bridge, Hank's Dog House

### TIMMY'S PET PEEVES

- Know-it-alls
- Whiners
- Prejudiced people

## The Meeting

The five of us came to Key West having no idea what we would find there. First, we each found a postcard telling us to travel to the southernmost tip of the US. Then we found each other. Kit and Mark from last year's show gave us our first clue to help us find the Winnebago, and then I found a tape, which said we had to go find a doctor in the Bahamas. **-EMILY**

The night before I was supposed to meet the other guys, I slept kinda good. I just woke up one time, at 2:30, and then I slept until 6:00, when I had to stand up and be ready. Then I was very tired. I'm not a person who likes to stand up early in the morning. I like to sleep in. When I checked out, the man at the front desk gave me a postcard. I said, "Thanks!" I thought that was a nice American custom. Then I saw the note on the back: "Christian, go find your friends at the southernmost point."

The first of the other people I met was Tim, and I couldn't help it, I thought, "I don't know if I'm going to get along with this guy—he's tall, dark, he's not like me." Devin had very large reggae hair, twisted and so. He was not very tall, he looked fit, that's about it. Emily had long hair and she was good-looking and also pretty. Effie was brown and her hair was very dark, almost black. I thought she was kind of mysterious. When I discovered she was from Israel, I thought that was cool, but I would have thought it was just as cool if I was the only one not from the United States.**-CHRISTIAN**

## I saw Devin first, standing across the street from me. I couldn't figure out if he was one of us or if he was just hanging out.

Then I saw his backpack, and that's how I knew—he's with me. Then I met the rest of the group, and they all seemed very open, which is important for something like this.

All of a sudden Kit and Mark pulled up in a little sports car. I was stunned, because I really admire both of them a lot. Kit told us that we had to hurry, 'cause we had a flight to catch. When we found out we were going to capture the most feared creatures of the deep, there was some argument about what those creatures would be. Someone said sharks, and Tim brought up the idea of crabs being the most feared creatures; he said he learned that from a friend on spring break. **-EMILY**

I clicked with Christian right from the start. We looked at each other and laughed—that's usually what I do, and that's what he does, too.

Then he gave me some orange juice, and there was no question we'd be friends. As I looked at the group as a whole, I could see why everyone was chosen for the show. Being a guy, I of course noticed that both Effie and Emily were beautiful creatures, and charming, delightful, as well.

When we came upon the Winnebago, I couldn't believe some of the gifts we got. The trunk was full of all the goodies and hoards of great apparel that would help us out along the way.

We found an envelope with $1,750 that was supposed to last about four weeks, but we'll have to do a lot of budgeting. The group elected me to be the responsible one and hold the money and the keys. We even found beepers, and there was even a bottle of champagne. We had a big discussion on whether or not to christen the Winnebago; we didn't know if we should smash and litter or save it for a special moment, so we decided to save it. I hope we do save the bottle of champagne for a special moment. That would mean a lot to me. **-TIMMY**

I had a 41-kilo backpack, so I packed 41 kilos exactly. I nearly fell backward, but I got used to it. The first person I saw was Christian, and the minute I looked at him, I knew that he was a European. You could tell by his shirt, by his pants. He was cute. He gave me his orange juice, and I just said, "Oh, a happy person. Wow." I felt like we came from the same place, because I consider Israel part of Europe. I met everyone else all at once. I liked the way Devin looked, but it was not an attraction, I knew that right away.

Me and Tim were clearly the oldest ones, but I didn't know that Devin and Emily were only 18. When I found out how young they were, I hoped I wouldn't start mothering them, because I'm five years older and I have a natural instinct to do that.

**-EFFIE**

**KEY WEST**
POPULATION
**24,800**
POPULAR HANGOUTS:
**Mango's, Margaritaville**
FAMOUS RESIDENTS:
**Ernest Hemingway, Jimmy Buffet**
TRIVIA:
Only 90 miles from Cuba, Key West is the southernmost community within the continental US. The actual point, located at the intersection of Whitehead and South streets, is marked by a buoy. Hemingway's estate is home to six-toed cats—direct descendants of the writer's own pets

Devin wasn't really interested if Effie or I had boyfriends. He was more concerned with if we had girlfriends, or if the other guys had boyfriends. He said he had left his girlfriend at home, and that he was the type of person that needed somebody there with him. He said it was hard to leave her.
**-EMILY**

I left Cleveland in the middle of a big snowstorm, and the temperature was below zero. I just couldn't wait to get to someplace warm. I'm a warm-weather guy.

The first thing I noticed about Emily was her over stuffed bag and all of her hair. She looked high-maintenance. Christian bounded right up in my face—a surprisingly friendly person. He said hello in Norwegian; I thought he was saying his name. And then Effie, she was looking really nice. She had on these little bitty shorts and she got in the Winnie before me and I just saw her ass looking at me in the face. For some reason some lady asked us if the horns on the front of the Winnie were real, and Timmy started getting in this conversation with her like, "Oh, yeah, we hit that back in Mexico. Can you still see the blood?" I was thinking, "This guy's gonna be full of it the whole trip. There's never gonna be a serious moment with this guy." These are things that pretty much set the tone for the trip.

I was the first one to drive, and I started asking them questions. I wanted to know, in particular, if anybody had left a significant other at home. I guess I asked that question for two reasons: **I wanted to know if anybody was available, and I particularly wanted to know if any males were gonna say, "Yeah, I left my boyfriend at home."** I've never lived with a person who was gay before, and I just wanted to be prepared. Nobody answered me except Emily, who I immediately liked for her openness. I knew right away we were going to get along really well. I don't have a lot of close, tight guy friends. All of my life I've been good friends with girls, so I think Emily and I might have a couple of heavy discussions. That would be cool.

**-DEVIN**

## CLUE

**WELCOME TO ROAD RULES, THE SECOND ADVENTURE! ALL RIGHT, ROOKIES, HERE'S THE DRILL: JUST FOLLOW THE CLUES I GIVE YOU, AND WHEN YOU COMPLETE THE MISSIONS, YOU CAN EXPECT THAT HANDSOME REWARD. YOU'VE GOT FOUR HOURS TO REACH THE EXECUTIVE AIRPORT IN FORT LAUDERDALE. YOU'RE FLYING TO BIMINI TODAY TO MEET THE INFAMOUS DOC GRUBER. YOUR MISSION IS TO ASSIST HIM IN CAPTURING THE MOST FEARED CREATURES OF THE DEEP.**

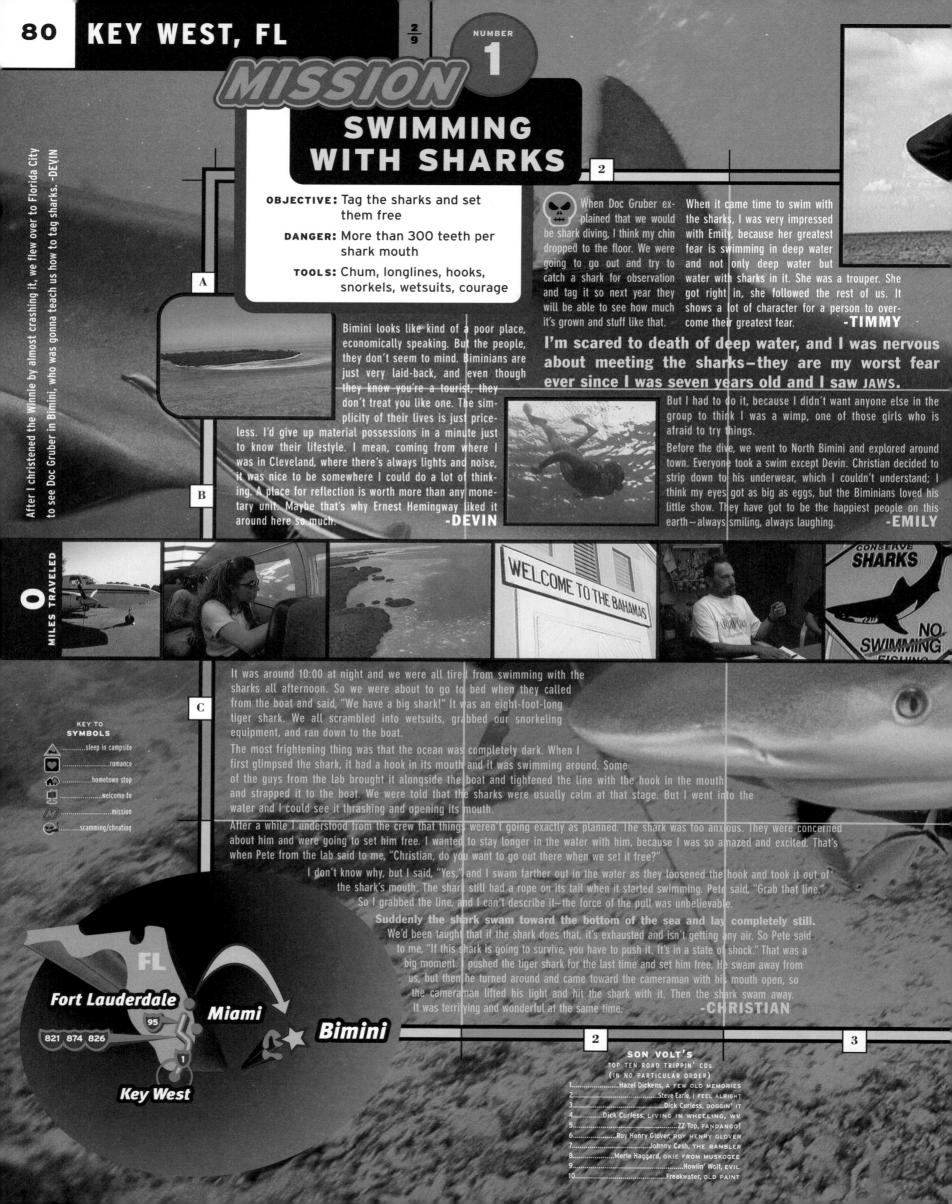

# MISSION

## SWIMMING WITH SHARKS

**OBJECTIVE:** Tag the sharks and set them free

**DANGER:** More than 300 teeth per shark mouth

**TOOLS:** Chum, longlines, hooks, snorkels, wetsuits, courage

**A**

**B**

After I christened the Winnie by almost crashing it, we flew over to Florida City to see Doc Gruber in Bimini, who was gonna teach us how to tag sharks. -DEVIN

Bimini looks like kind of a poor place, economically speaking. But the people, they don't seem to mind. Biminians are just very laid-back, and even though they know you're a tourist, they don't treat you like one. The simplicity of their lives is just priceless. I'd give up material possessions in a minute just to know their lifestyle. I mean, coming from where I was in Cleveland, where there's always lights and noise, it was nice to be somewhere I could do a lot of thinking. A place for reflection is worth more than any monetary unit. Maybe that's why Ernest Hemingway liked it around here so much.
**-DEVIN**

**2**

When Doc Gruber explained that we would be shark diving, I think my chin dropped to the floor. We were going to go out and try to catch a shark for observation and tag it so next year they will be able to see how much it's grown and stuff like that.

When it came time to swim with the sharks, I was very impressed with Emily, because her greatest fear is swimming in deep water and not only deep water but water with sharks in it. She was a trouper. She got right in, she followed the rest of us. It shows a lot of character for a person to overcome their greatest fear.
**-TIMMY**

**I'm scared to death of deep water, and I was nervous about meeting the sharks—they are my worst fear ever since I was seven years old and I saw JAWS.**

But I had to do it, because I didn't want anyone else in the group to think I was a wimp, one of those girls who is afraid to try things.

Before the dive, we went to North Bimini and explored around town. Everyone took a swim except Devin. Christian decided to strip down to his underwear, which I couldn't understand; I think my eyes got as big as eggs, but the Biminians loved his little show. They have got to be the happiest people on this earth—always smiling, always laughing.
**-EMILY**

**O MILES TRAVELED**

WELCOME TO THE BAHAMAS

CONSERVE SHARKS

NO SWIMMING

**C**

**KEY TO SYMBOLS**

△ ............ sleep in campsite
♡ ............ romance
⌂ ............ hometown stop
▭ ............ welcome to
M ............ mission
☺ ............ scamming/cheating

It was around 10:00 at night and we were all tired from swimming with the sharks all afternoon. So we were about to go to bed when they called from the boat and said, "We have a big shark!" It was an eight-foot-long tiger shark. We all scrambled into wetsuits, grabbed our snorkeling equipment, and ran down to the boat.

The most frightening thing was that the ocean was completely dark. When I first glimpsed the shark, it had a hook in its mouth and it was swimming around. Some of the guys from the lab brought it alongside the boat and tightened the line with the hook in the mouth and strapped it to the boat. We were told that the sharks were usually calm at that stage. But I went into the water and I could see it thrashing and opening its mouth.

After a while I understood from the crew that things weren't going exactly as planned. The shark was too anxious. They were concerned about him and were going to set him free. I wanted to stay longer in the water with him, because I was so amazed and excited. That's when Pete from the lab said to me, "Christian, do you want to go out there when we set it free?"

I don't know why, but I said, "Yes," and I swam farther out in the water as they loosened the hook and took it out of the shark's mouth. The shark still had a rope on its tail when it started swimming. Pete said, "Grab that line." So I grabbed the line, and I can't describe it—the force of the pull was unbelievable.

**Suddenly the shark swam toward the bottom of the sea and lay completely still.**
We'd been taught that if the shark does that, it's exhausted and isn't getting any air. So Pete said to me, "If this shark is going to survive, you have to push it. It's in a state of shock." That was a big moment. I pushed the tiger shark for the last time and set him free. He swam away from us, but then he turned around and came toward the cameraman with his mouth open, so the cameraman lifted his light and hit the shark with it. Then the shark swam away. It was terrifying and wonderful at the same time.
**-CHRISTIAN**

**FL**

**Fort Lauderdale**
95
821 874 826
**Miami**
1
**Bimini**
**Key West**

**2**

**3**

**BIMINI**
POPULATION
1,639
TRIVIA:
One of the smallest islands in the Bahamas, it lies 50 miles off Miami
CLAIM TO FAME:
The big-game fishing capital of the world
HISTORY:
Island was a liquor haven for people fleeing prohibition laws in the 1930s
FANFARE:
Hemingway Billfish Tournament and Bacardi Billfish Tournament

NAME: Doc Gruber
TITLE: Shark expert, researcher, Bimini Biological Field Station
MOTTO: "An ocean without sharks is a sick ocean."

Primarily, we work with lemon sharks in our tagging program. The young sharks are dying at a rate of 60 percent, and we want to know why so we can explain to fisheries exactly what they can do if they really want to manage the shark stocks that have been so heavily impacted by commercial fishing.

We introduced the ROAD RULES kids to the sharks by letting them observe while we hand-fed them. That helped get the group over some of the fear and see how beautiful the sharks are. Even though the kids were frightened, they very quickly realized they were not going to get killed or eaten or anything like that. They were a receptive group. One of them got a little crush on my daughter, and she has been communicating with him quite a bit.

The next thing we did was set longlines, which are half a mile long, with 15 hooks, and we caught a big tiger for them to swim with. Even though tigers are dangerous sharks, once you catch them they become demoralized. They don't realize that they can easily kill you.

Everyone was nervous. Some showed it, like Emily, but I kept it to myself. There's a difference between being nervous and being scared, and I wasn't scared—sharks are just big beasts, after all.

We had to throw pieces of fish in the water to bait them, and we relieved a little tension by having a fish fight. It was disgustingly fun. The funny part was that my mother is always trying to get me inside a kitchen so I can see how to cook things, and I say every time, "No way, I hate the kitchen." She tried to show me how to cook fish, but I told her, "Mom, I'm not putting my hands inside of that." I didn't mind chopping up the chum in Bimini, though. It's not that disgusting—I'm just spoiled at home—and it was fun getting all messed up, all bloody. -EFFIE

A

**ROAD KEY**

This shark is a little memento of your first mission. It's called a Road Key. It's the first of five you'll get on your journey, so be on the lookout. And don't lose them, 'cause they're the keys to your reward. They fit the puzzle in the Winnebago. Look for your next clue on the mainland. Have a nice flight.

**240 MILES TRAVELED**

We celebrated our successful mission at the Sand Bar. I'm not a drinker, in fact I'd never had a drink before, but I had a Bahama Mama, followed by a piña colada with a rum float, followed by a rum and coke, and my first shot of tequila. Then I did a shot of Southern Comfort followed by some Sprite, and I was right back on with another Bahama Mama to finish the night off. I was flying high, man. We listened to some nice island music and did a lot of dancing. Then Ayla and I went back to the shark lab and fell asleep waiting for Emily to come back from her walk with Kelly, 'cause I was worried about her. Ayla was cool, she was a little woman with a big voice. She sounded like she meant business, and I liked that, but nothing happened between us. -DEVIN

Kelly worked at the shark lab for Doc Gruber. He took me down by the ocean where the waves were crashing against the rocks and he kissed me—it sounds so corny, it sounds like I'm 12, but it was really romantic. -EMILY

**CLUE**

D

NOW FOR SOME REAL FUN. THIS TIME YOU'RE THE PREDATOR, AND YOUR PREY IS THE CAST OF THE REAL WORLD. YOUR MISSION IS TO STEAL THE EIGHT BALL FROM THE POOL TABLE OF THE REAL WORLD HOUSE IN MIAMI BEACH WITHOUT GETTING CAUGHT. NEVER LET THEM KNOW YOU'RE WITH ROAD RULES. EVERYTHING YOU NEED IS IN THE DOSSIER. YOU HAVE TWO DAYS. GOOD LUCK.

**LEMON SHARKS**
There have been less than ten documented unprovoked lemon shark attacks on the open sea.
The lemon must consume 20,600 calories daily in order to maintain body weight.
In captivity, the lemon can grow at ten times its natural growth rate.
The lemon has a litter of 4-17 sharks.

**TIGER SHARKS**
The tiger shark is second only to the great white shark in the number of known attacks on people and boats.
The jagged teeth enable the tiger to tear flesh easily, leaving a unique curved wound on its victim.
The tiger has a litter of 10-82 sharks.
One tiger shark weighed in at more than three tons.

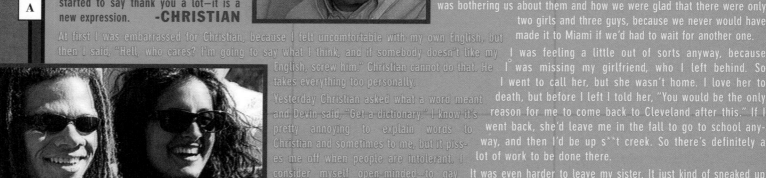

Our mission was to infiltrate the REAL WORLD house in Miami and take the eight ball from the pool table without them knowing we were from ROAD RULES.

So we dressed up like maintenance people and pulled a good one over on them. —CHRISTIAN

**1**

**A**

🗡️ I think I may have a different view of what is to be polite than the others. They tease me because I say thank you a lot, but now they have started to say thank you a lot—it is a new expression. **-CHRISTIAN**

At first I was embarrassed for Christian, because I felt uncomfortable with my own English, but then I said, "Hell, who cares? I'm going to say what I think, and if somebody doesn't like my English, screw him." Christian cannot do that. He takes everything too personally.

Yesterday Christian asked what a word meant and Devin said, "Get a dictionary." I know it's pretty annoying to explain words to Christian and sometimes to me, but it pisses me off when people are intolerant. I consider myself open-minded—to gay people, to black people, to mixed couples, to anything that is different from me—and I wish everyone in the group would show the same tolerance to the foreigners. **-EFFIE**

When we got to the hostel in South Miami, we split up into guys' rooms and girls' rooms. The guys had just about had it with the other two. We vented for about half an hour straight. We just totally went off on what was bothering us about them and how we were glad that there were only two girls and three guys, because we never would have made it to Miami if we'd had to wait for another one.

I was feeling a little out of sorts anyway, because I was missing my girlfriend, who I left behind. So I went to call her, but she wasn't home. I love her to death, but before I left I told her, "You would be the only reason for me to come back to Cleveland after this." If I went back, she'd leave me in the fall to go to school anyway, and then I'd be up s**t creek. So there's definitely a lot of work to be done there.

It was even harder to leave my sister. It just kind of sneaked up on me. I live with my father, so the night I left I went over to Mom's house to say goodbye, and as soon as I hugged my little sister, we both broke down. I miss her to death, I worry about her lot. And every time I think about it, I get all, like, teary and stuff, because she means the world to me. **-DEVIN**

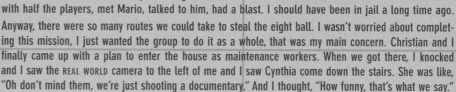

**240** MILES TRAVELED

**MISSION 2**

### PRANK THE REAL WORLD

**CHALLENGE:** Talk your way into the REAL WORLD house, and make off with the eight ball

**TOOLS:** Blue coveralls, photos and descriptions of the REAL WORLD cast, blueprint of the house, getaway car

**REWARD:** The satisfaction that you've pulled a fast one on MTV's other heroes

When we got the clue to steal the eight ball from THE REAL WORLD, everyone was flipping out, because what could be more fun? Personally, I live for practical jokes. I've done this kind of stuff my whole life. One of the best pranks I've ever pulled was when the Pittsburgh Penguins won their first Stanley Cup and I wanted to go to the celebration party at Mario Lemieux's house. At the time, I was working security at Three Rivers Stadium, so I put on my rent-a-cop uniform and knocked on Mario's door, pretending to work for him. I bulls**tted with half the players, met Mario, talked to him, had a blast. I should have been in jail a long time ago.

CONFIDENTIAL

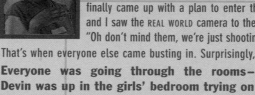

Anyway, there were so many routes we could take to steal the eight ball. I wasn't worried about completing this mission, I just wanted the group to do it as a whole, that was my main concern. Christian and I finally came up with a plan to enter the house as maintenance workers. When we got there, I knocked and I saw the REAL WORLD camera to the left of me and I saw Cynthia come down the stairs. She was like, "Oh don't mind them, we're just shooting a documentary." And I thought, "How funny, that's what we say." That's when everyone else came busting in. Surprisingly, Cynthia really didn't react too much.

**Everyone was going through the rooms— Devin was up in the girls' bedroom trying on their underwear, Emily was putting tape on outlets, Effie was lost, and Christian was doing circles around a ladder.**

Then I came around a corner, and there was dapper Dan at the door with this giant grin, and he knew something was going on. The game was almost up, and I didn't know whether the eight ball was picked up. **-TIMMY**

**FL**

**Miami** 🎱 **Bimini**

**2**

KEY TO SYMBOLS

🗡️ ............scamming/cheating

🔥 ...............conflict

💰 ...........money trail

📖 .............welcome to

Ⓜ ...............mission

🛏️ .........sleep in motel

**?** ...............lost

2/14 1996

**4**

We all decided to go to dinner, and we were, you know, waiting. Waiting for everybody to get ready is always a big challenge, because we all take different amounts of time to get ready. All I have to do is…I don't have to do anything. I'm comfortable lookin' like whatever, but the girls take a while, and Christian has a weird habit of shaving with an electric shaver and then shaving with a razor. He showers and deodorizes and puts on the after-sun lotion and contacts and all of that good stuff. I think he might take as long as the girls sometimes. Effie had met up with some freako suave character from Israel that she was chatting with, so she just said screw us, basically, and blew off the dinner with us, which was kind of a big deal, because it was the first dinner we had as a group. **-DEVIN**

**5**

After dinner, the subject of money came up. We decided to take a good portion of our money and put it into a group fund for necessary things like food and lodging, and the rest we would divide among us to do as we pleased. Tim and Christian are the drinkers of the group, so we didn't want to pay for their alcohol. I think that everyone was happy with the agreement we made—$600 in the group fund and then $120 for each person until our next allotment. **-EMILY**

We didn't have a lot of money—we never do—so we agreed on borrowing some hangers from the hotel. I feel kind of sorry we did that. If we had asked, we probably could have got some for free. But I'm gonna return the hangers after we have used them for a while. **-CHRISTIAN**

I didn't feel too good about stealing hangers and an ashtray, but Christian talked me into it. I'm going to have to put all the blame on him. He can be a bad kid sometimes. **-TIMMY**

**B**

**290** MILES TRAVELED

My only job was to walk around. Don't talk to anybody. Just look for the pool table. I saw the swimming pool. I saw everything but the pool table. It was there, but it was so huge I didn't recognize it. Finally I saw it, and I picked up Devin, and he grabbed the eight ball. After we got out of the house, everybody touched it. We were so proud of ourselves, and we knew our film crew was very proud of us, too.

## The five of us were ecstatic; we felt really, really good about ourselves.

**CLUE**

TO COMPLETE THE NEXT MISSION, HEAD NORTH TO OKAHUMPKA. EACH OF YOU MUST FINISH A COURSE AT INTERNATIONAL TOURNAMENT SKIING.

It was time to return our uniforms to the prop shop, but Devin kind of liked his, so he bought it. When we got the receipt, our next clue was written on the back. We didn't know where the hell Okahumpka was, but we were happy to know our next step. **-EFFIE**

**MIAMI**
POPULATION: 358,500
BEST BEACH: South Beach
FAMOUS RESIDENTS: Madonna, Gianni Versace
POPULAR HANGOUTS: Clevelander, Bash
MUST SEE: Parrot Jungle, which holds daily parrot talent shows in its Parrot Bowl Amphitheater; Miami Beach Police and Fire Station, where early MIAMI VICE episodes were shot

**5**

### STORY OF THE EIGHT BALL

The balls used in pool weigh 5.5-6 ounces and measure 2.25 inches in diameter. At one time the pool billiards were made of ivory. These days most are made of a plastic material.

### BRANDY'S
TOP TEN ROAD TRIPPIN' CDs

1. ...................Boyz II Men, II
2. ...................Jodeci, THE SHOW, THE AFTER-PARTY, THE HOTEL
3. ..Alanis Morissette, JAGGED LITTLE PILL
4. ...The Cranberries, NO NEED TO ARGUE
5. ...................Mariah Carey, DAY DREAM
6. ...................SWV, NEW BEGINNING
7. ...................Faith Evans, FAITH EVANS
8. ...................Hootie and the Blowfish, CRACKED REAR VIEW
9. ...................Total, TOTAL
10. ............soundtrack, THE BODYGUARD

2 / 14
1996

1

Driving down the highway, we kept spotting all these really beautiful orchards dripping with tons and tons of oranges, so we hopped out with a couple of bags and got us some vitamin C.

When we borrowed the oranges I had the same feeling as when we borrowed the hangers. It's this Robin Hood feeling that: "You have so many oranges and we have none." But I think this is not a good justification. -CHRISTIAN

When we got to Okahumpka, we stopped at Dave's Chevron and got directions. They showed us where we could find some groceries, 'cause the last dinner we had in Miami Beach cost us $85, and it was time to start eating in the Winnie. Christian bought some goat cheese and made us try it. I'm sorry, but goat cheese tastes like Play-Doh—funky, salty, nasty. He took it personally that I didn't like it. You'd have thought he milked the damn goat himself. I have to watch hurting that guy's feelings. I don't know what his deal is; he's always in overdrive. I mean, I'm just not like that.

Later, we were all kicking back in the Winnie, resting and drinking juice from our Florida oranges, and Christian decided to bring these two kids and their mom inside. He played music for them and they climbed around with their shoes on until I told them to leave. I was tired, and we had to get up early the next morning to ski. I just couldn't see how all that was necessary. -DEVIN

A

B

In Okahumpka we had to complete a course at the International Tournament Skiing camp, meaning we all had to get in freezing-cold water and be dragged around by a boat until we turned blue. -DEVIN

290 MILES TRAVELED

At Aunt Bea's Trailer Park, me and Devin hopped up on top of the Winnie and had a big, long talk. I think he was trying to plant a little seed in my head.

He said, "I figure two people were picked to hook up with each other on this trip, and I think it was me and you." We realized we really had a lot of things in common. A lot, a lot, a lot. This was the first time we were openly attracted to each other, but he has a girlfriend, first of all, and I don't really want to start anything with anybody, second of all. It would just be too awkward to start anything. It would complicate everything and it might dampen our fun a little bit, so I think we'll just remain friends.

We sat up there until the others hollered that dinner was served. This was the second group meal that Effie skipped out on. She was upset and took off to have some time away from everybody. Effie feels like she is a lot farther away from home than most of us, and she misses her boyfriend of six years. It really hit her hard that night, because it was the first time we had time to settle down and let our minds think about home. Tim went to find her and the rest of us decided to go ahead and eat. When Effie and Tim came back she seemed to be feeling better, and we all stayed up late. The management yelled at us two or three times before we finally turned in. I don't think anyone in the RV resort was under the age of 85. They didn't appreciate a bunch of teenagers running around on their bicycles hooting and hollering all night. The next day Aunt Bea told us that our slot had been taken. -EMILY

Okahumpka

29

FLORIDA'S TURNPIKE

FL

27

Miami

KEY TO SYMBOLS

........sleep in Winnie

........romance

........money trail

........scamming/cheating

M........mission

$$$........empty Winnie septic tank

........danger

2

FORT LAUDERDALE
Only 27 miles from Miami, Fort Lauderdale's lagoons, waterways, and beaches make it one of the most popular destinations on the Gold Coast. Once the original college spring break hot spot, Fort Lauderdale has been eclipsed by Daytona Beach and Panama City.

## SKI THIS

National waterskiing tournament events include jumping, slalom, barefooting, knee-boarding, tricks, and wake-boarding.

The jumping event involves going over a ramp. The distance measured is how far you fly after jumping. Jumps range from 60 to 150 feet.

The slalom course involves skiing through six buoys at different speeds. The women ski from 26-34 mph and the men ski from 28-36 mph.

Wake-boarding, similar to surfing, involves skiing on one board into the waves of the boat.

4

## MISSION 3 NUMBER

## WALK ON WATER

**OBJECTIVE:** Choose between master jumping, slalom, barefooting, knee-boarding, and wake-boarding to complete the course that suits you best

**CHALLENGES:** Whitecaps, wind, freezing temperatures

**REWARDS:** Hypothermia, sore muscles

# Waterskiing: Take One

**I don't like water, OK? I'm a mammal, I want to be outside water.**

But I volunteered to waterski first because I didn't want to spend all day watching the others do it and lose my courage. I had never done anything like this before. I put my gear on and Jack gave me some instructions. Then he put me in the water. But the board kept sinking, and once the front of the board is in the water, you sink no matter what. **I tried twice, and on the third time the damn board hit me in the face.** I was so pissed, I didn't want to try again. I just got out of the water and went back to the Winnebago. Half my face was numb and I was afraid I broke my nose. I did that once. I don't want to do it again. I didn't want to see anyone. I wanted a few seconds with myself.

It was a bad day to ski in the first place. It was extremely windy. Everyone was dressed up in two jackets and it was really cold, so Jack finally decided it wasn't fair for us to try skiing for the first time in such weather. We had to wait for the next day.

**-EFFIE**

# Take Two

**Christian is the best skier in all of Norway, so he completed his mission with flying colors, of course.**

Effie and Devin and Tim convinced Jack to let them try and try and try until they got up on their skis, and it paid off—they completed their missions the second time around.

Considering that Timmy had never waterskied before, I thought that he made a great accomplishment by jumping part of the ramp. It seemed to me that everyone should be satisfied with themselves, but back at the Winnie, Timmy kept saying, "I really wanted to go all the way." I can understand that. I would have wanted that, too. **-CHRISTIAN**

Jack instructed me that I should go over the side of the jump first because I'm a beginner and it's very tough— it's a six-foot jump or something. We kept circling around and hitting the jump and WHA-POW, I'd do the same nice little facial in the water again and again. Eventually I managed to land on my butt instead, so I gained a little bit of confidence. I just kept repeating what my mother told me when I called her the night before: "Let the boat pull you, let the boat pull you."

At that point Jack wanted to get me out of the water for fear of frostbite, but I was kinda on a roll and I was very determined and mad because I hate failure and I knew I could do this. I told Jack to speed up when I was going off the jump so that when I landed it would kind of jerk me upright. This seemed to work, and I thought, "I'm accomplishing something. I'm getting somewhere." But Jack pulled in, let me off, and told me to go inside and get a really hot shower, stay in there for a while and warm up. **-TIMMY**

**NAME:** Jack Travers
**TITLE:** Owner and waterski teacher, International Tournament Skiing camp
**MOTTO:** "The biggest challenge is breaking from routine."

The ROAD RULES kids had a pretty unique challenge in the respect that only one or two of them had any waterskiing experience whatsoever. To make that challenge even greater, a cold front came through, and our first afternoon was a blowout. We ended up finishing the next morning, when it was about 38 degrees without the windchill factor. The kids actually got out in the water and skied when it was bone chilling. They were determined, and they did an excellent job.

There was a time when the world's top waterskiers were all about the age of the ROAD RULES group, about 18 years old. Now our current world-record holders are in their 30s. That's due to the fact that today you can make a living out of this sport. 25 years ago, once you achieved your title at 17, 18, 19, years old, it was time to go out and get a real job and make some money.

C

## OKAHUMPKA

**POPULATION:** 400

**NICKNAME:** Okahumpka means "Deep water"

**POPULAR HANGOUTS:** Sally's Place: The Recovery Room; Ramshackle Cafe, down the road in Leesburg

**TRIVIA:** Home to Bug Springs, a natural spring more than 300 feet deep

# CLUE

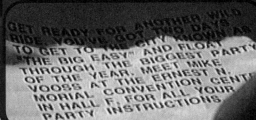

GET READY FOR ANOTHER WILD RIDE. YOU'VE GOT TWO DAYS TO GET TO THE CITY KNOWN AS "THE BIG EASY", AND FLOAT THROUGH THE BIGGEST PARTY OF THE YEAR. MEET MIKE VOOSS AT THE ERNEST N. MORIAL CONVENTION CENT... IN HALL F. FOR ALL YOUR PARTY INSTRUCTIONS

We packed up and headed to New Orleans. It was everybody's first Mardi Gras, so we had no idea what we were coming into. But as soon as we got into the city, we hit a parade, and that set the pace for a wild time. —TIMMY

**A**

**B**

In Mobile we slept in the Winnie in a hotel parking lot, because we didn't have much money. That's where Timmy did his naked midnight dash. I don't know why he did that, but I had a great laugh. Timmy has a strange background. He has done a lot of things in his life that he regrets. I think we both share an interest in doing weird things for the fun of it, and sometimes it gets us into some trouble; sometimes it doesn't. **-CHRISTIAN**

When we woke up in Mobile, we needed some form of shower before we started our day off, so we all jumped the fence and went in the hotel hot tub. Devin, Effie, and me still had a bad case of chiggers from Bimini. Chiggers are these little-bitty bugs that get underneath your skin and itch like crazy. They didn't show up until a week after we left the Bahamas, then they hit hard. We were all itching, scratching, and just trying to get rid of them. I called my parents and they said to get in a hot tub and the chlorine would kill them off.**-EMILY**

**556** MILES TRAVELED

LOUISIANA WELCOMES YOU

**MOBILE**
POPULATION:
96,300
TRIVIA:
Site of the first Mardi Gras
POPULAR HANGOUTS:
Hayley's, Judge Roy Bean's
FANFARE:
Azalea Trail Festival,
February and March
tour of a blooming,
27-mile trail

**C**

NAME: Mike Voos
TITLE: Public relations director,
Orpheus Krewe
MOTTO: "If you can't have fun at
Mardi Gras, you can't
have fun."

Mardi Gras is the monthlong celebration before the dawn of Lent, a Catholic holiday. In 1857 the Anglo-Americans introduced the krewe system, in which secret carnival clubs would parade wildly exotic floats throughout the city. The krewe system was once a function of people with lots of money, mostly men, called maskers, who would ride through the streets of New Orleans, throwing trinkets and doubloons (coins) to the crowd. A few years back, there began to be talk in New Orleans about what seemed to be discriminatory practices within some of the old krewes—if you weren't a white male, you weren't in any of these organizations. Eventually the old-time krewes were told to open up their membership, but many pulled out of the regular parade schedule rather than do so. And that created the opportunity for some new blood, so Harry Connick, Jr. decided to start his own krewe, which was open to all, no matter what race, religion, or gender. The name of the parade was chosen as Orpheus, because it was musically attached, and music is the one element that brings everyone together.

**MISSION** NUMBER **4**

**COMMAND A FLOAT
AT MARDI GRAS**

**OBJECTIVE:** Have a ball, throw some beads, and wave to a crowd of 750,000

**HAZARDS:** Drunk people with roaming hands, flying beads

**PERKS:** Hobnob with Harry Connick, Jr., and other famous faces, get a killer view of the Orpheus Krewe parade

LA
MS
AL
FL

New Orleans
Mobile
10
10
75
Leesburg
Okahumpka
27

2

KEY TO
SYMBOLS
M..............mission
♥..............romance
..............sleep in hotel
..............welcome to
..............sleep in Winnie
..............days since last shower
..............sidetrip

**HIALEAH PARK
RACETRACK**
See the incredible spectacle of flamingo racing in Hialeah, FL, off I-95

There is a Jewish prayer that we say whenever we go to a faraway place. It asks God to save us from things that might happen along the way. My mother gave it to me and she said, "Just keep it with you." So I took it and I glued it to the dashboard of the Winnie. I figure if it doesn't help, it won't hurt, either. Hopefully it will keep us from getting into really big trouble.

It was good to have this prayer in New Orleans. I didn't like the city so much. We had a great time, but I have the impression that people are not so tolerant there. You don't see any mixed-race couples, everyone stays in his corner. One more thing—it's much better to be the one that throws the beads than the one who tries to catch them.

This country has strange traditions. In order to get beads at Mardi Gras, girls must expose their breasts. I wanted to see someone do that, because I didn't believe it.

## I actually said to one of the girls, "You want my beads, show me your breast."

And she was like, "You want me to show you my breast?" And I was like, "Yeah, show me." So she did, and I gave her the cheap beads, and she was like, "You bitch!" The whole idea of girls showing their breasts—of course it's degrading, but it's fun. If she wants to flash, who am I to stop her? **-EFFIE**

### CLUE

A HOUSE DIVIDED AGAINST ITSELF CANNOT STAND... IT'S BROTHER AGAINST BROTHER IN THIS NEXT MISSION...ARRIVE IN COLUMBUS, MISSISSIPPI IN TWO DAYS...SEE COLONEL DOBBS FOR YOUR ASSIGNMENTS... AND UNIFORMS.

B

**1160 MILES TRAVELED**

Devin was definitely having a great time throwing beads off the float at all the topless girls. I think he was finding it hilarious. I hated it. I get so fed up with girls degrading themselves. I didn't see many men doing that.

Mardi Gras is not anything like I thought it was going to be. Overall it wasn't a good experience for me. If I'd never gone down to the French Quarter, it would have been OK. The parade was great, and the banquet was unbelievable, but downtown on Bourbon Street was just disgusting. Unless you're the type of girl that likes to be grabbed and hit on, it's not the place to be. Overall, I really couldn't wait to get out of New Orleans. I was scared the entire time. **-EMILY**

Emily had never been exposed to a lot of the things that were going on down in New Orleans. Not that any of us had, but she is from a really small town, and Timmy and I, being from Pittsburgh and Cleveland, have a better hold on what to expect in cities. When guys approached her, she didn't bite her tongue at all. I had to explain to her that if she didn't back down a little bit, I was gonna be the one to get in a fight. Later on we were in a bar and some guy touched her butt, and she turned around and said, "If you touch my butt again, I'm gonna knee you in the balls." Then the guy elbowed her in the eye. That was the end of her night. She was just done. I think she could have avoided it by handling the situation a little bit better. But now she knows. **-DEVIN**

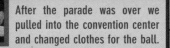

After the parade was over we pulled into the convention center and changed clothes for the ball. Mike gave us each a mask, and told us that we wouldn't have to look far for our next clue. It took a while for us to notice there was a message broken apart among the masks, so we put them all together, and that's when we found our next clue. **-TIMMY**

D

**HISTORICAL TRIVIA**
New Orleans was originally settled by the French, but it was secretly taken over by the Spanish in 1762. Eventually, the city was returned to France and finally purchased by the US government in 1803.

4    5

### BILLIE JOE OF GREEN DAY'S
#### TOP TWELVE ROAD TRIPPIN' TAPES
##### (IN NO PARTICULAR ORDER)

1. Neurosis, THE WORD AS LAW
2. Screeching Weasel, MY BRAIN HURTS
3. The Muffs, THE MUFFS
4. Crimpshrine, DUCKTAPE SOUP
5. The Replacements, anything by
6. The Beatles, WITH THE BEATLES
7. Phantom Surfers, WITH DICK DALE
8. Nirvana, NEVERMIND
9. The Ramones, ROAD TO RUIN
10. Hüsker Dü, WAREHOUSE...SONGS AND STORIES
11. Fifteen, SWAIN'S FIRST BIKERIDE
12. The Hi-Fives, WELCOME TO MY MIND

**2/23 1996**

When we finally got to Columbus, it was past dark. I don't even know how long we were on the road, but there were several fights along the way, and lots of debate about who Colonel Dobbs was.  -Devin

**1**

**A**

**B**

## Effie's Army

In Israel it is the law that all girls and guys have to join the Army when they turn 18. Some girls just make coffee, some do promotional work, but all girls join the Army. The only exception is for very religious people.

I started as a medic. Then I posted at a base near Gaza Strip, and they asked me if I wanted to try to be an officer. I tried, and I am now a lieutenant. I never took part in a battle in the Israeli Army, but I know that armies are not different from each other. Even though the Civil

Before we left New Orleans, I borrowed a squeegee from a gas station and washed some shop windows for some extra cash. Christian went to the gas station and washed car windows. We each earned about $20. When we checked out of the hotel, the bill came to $200, plus a couple of phone calls, and it really put a dent in the old group fund. I think we had $100 to get us through about eight more days. We vowed not to buy groceries until we'd eaten everything in the Winnie—that came to a jar of peanut butter, a box of Total, and some spaghetti sauce.  **-TIMMY**

I've got about $100 in my pocket. I think I'm the one with the most money right now, partly because I don't spend it on alcohol, and partly because I'm used to living off nothing, just fending for myself, and living off what I make. I'm a penny-pincher. What can I say?  **-DEVIN**

## 1160 MILES TRAVELED

### ISRAEL'S ARMY

Israel founded its own army when it gained independence as a state, in 1948. The rules established at that time are still enforced today. Men and women must join at the age of 18, men for three years and women for two. While mandatory service is an accepted part of Israeli life, religious women, married women, and male members of some very religious groups are exempt. The Army provides its people with food, housing, and 300 shekels (approximately $100) a month, which often goes toward cigarettes and social activities.

Both men and women must serve in the reserves. Men must serve 30 days a year until the age of 51, and single women must serve in the reserves until they turn 24.

Women do not engage in combat. The female military role generally includes work in the fields of medicine, intelligence, computers, communications, and technology.

**C**

War was a hundred years ago, the drills and the tactics and the strategies were just the same as today. The only things different are the weapons and the uniforms—the rest is the same all over the world, in every army.

When we met Colonel Dobbs in Columbus, he told us that the Civil War was not about slavery—it was about money, and a thousand different things, but not slavery. He said that only 5 percent of the population in the southern states

owned slaves. But I think it was about slavery. I didn't see one black person besides Devin at Waverly Waters. Everyone was white and southern and had long blond hair. I love blond hair, but not when it is the only thing I see. Even me, I felt like a stranger. I felt they were trying to make a big happy picture of an unhappy time.

### I never thought about this black-white issue in Israel, but in America, it's a big deal.

In the Civil War, the Americans were fighting for the economy, which was driven by slavery in the South. Some people try to compare that war to the ongoing conflict in Israel between the Jews and the Arabs. But Israel is fighting for a

country, not for money, OK? Right now, two peoples claim Israel, the Jews and the Arabs. If the Arabs leave Israel, they have five or six different Arab countries they can live in. If the Jews don't live in Israel, we don't have another place to go. We can't live in the States. We can't live in France. We don't have the options they do. That's how I feel.

I miss home more than I expected, because when I was in the Army I didn't miss home. I was never really attached to my parents, but I guess it's a big difference when you are out of the country. I really miss my parents now, I miss my friends, I miss my boyfriend a lot. It's pretty new to me because I'm used to being very independent. I'm really proud of me for doing things on my own. I don't like to miss people. It's new to me. I'm learning how to deal with it right now.  **-EFFIE**

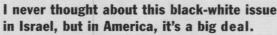

**2**

MS

**Columbus**

45

82

**Meridian**

20

59

10

**New Orleans**

LA

### KEY TO SYMBOLS

🌢 ......days since last shower

♡ ..................................romance

🖐 ...................money trail

🖥 ....................welcome to

Ⓜ .........................mission

🐾 ...empty Winnie septic tank

**2** ...................................lost

**EFFIE'S THREE WISHES**

A house of my own
Peace and quiet in my life
To travel around the world
whenever I want to

**5**

**Sometimes Effie can seem hard-edged and untouchable, but she also has a really nice, giggly, happy side. The group is pretty convinced that she's got two separate personalities. We've even given the bitchy Effie a name, we call her Daphne, after that character on** SCOOBY-DOO.

Lately, Effie's been saying, "I think I feel Daphne coming on" or "Here comes Daphne" whenever she feels her other self coming on. On the one hand, it's funny, but on the other, it's kind of scary. I've never asked Effie why she seems so guarded or why she isn't as open as some of us. I don't feel like I have the right to ask her a question like that any more than she has the right to question why I'm so open about what I'm going through or what's happening in my life.

The beautiful thing about Effie and me is that we butt heads a lot but we can hang out together. We love dancing together. If there's music around, and there's Effie and there's Devin, we just dance. It's nice to just let loose with somebody who's a friend. **-DEVIN**

**Efrat**

**A**

When I'm together with other people, I'm very, very influenced by their moods. Of course, when Effie is in a bad mood or is bored, it creates bad feelings within the group. **I must admit that we tend to make fun of Effie and talk a little bit behind her back, which obviously is not good at all, but hard to help.** I've told her that she should consider the fact that she's with four other people and try to work with us and not against us. Effie only sees us as five individuals, but we're also a group of five people. **-CHRISTIAN**

**B**

**EFFIE'S NICKNAMES**

F-Rat
Effie
Daphne
Coffee Queen
F-Troop
Kosher

**1447 MILES TRAVELED**

Effie's got a lot of big words for a foreigner. She uses bigger words than I do, and that kind of scares me. She is very intelligent, and she knows exactly how to get under my skin. Sometimes she treats me like a little girl, and sometimes I let that get to me, especially since she told me from the beginning that age didn't matter to her.

Effie's very opinionated, but my impression is that, where she comes from, women aren't given the chance to stick up for themselves and have minds of their own. So I admire Effie for having her own thoughts and her own philosophies. She knows what she wants and she goes after it. I never have to wonder if something I'm doing is pissing her off, because she'll come right out and tell me. I can't be sure, but I think we're gonna be great friends by the time this is over with. **-EMILY**

I think by far I'm the closest person to Effie. Now and then the group treats her rough, and she needs someone to be close to, so I'm there for her. We have a game where we make faces back and forth at each other, trying to make each other laugh. Making her smile once in a while is a good deed in my book.

Sometimes Effie's with the group, sometimes she's not. It's hard to tell whether she feels left out or just wants to be alone. I think it's 50/50. Sometimes she wants to be there, and other times she's just like, "I've had enough of you people, stay away from me."

**People sometimes think there's an attraction between Effie and me, but it just wouldn't work–I'm Catholic, she's schizophrenic. I'm American, she's annoying.**

But I do think she's the horniest person in three nations. You can see it in the way she walks down the street. She's hinted to the group a couple of times that she's a bit lonely and she can't wait to get back to her certain partner friend. She's missing a certain spice of life that we all enjoy. **-TIMMY**

**D**

**COLUMBUS**

POPULATION:
23,800

NICKNAME:
Originally called "Possum Town," because local Indians thought the town founder was extremely ugly

POPULAR HANGOUTS:
Thunderbird, Portabella's, Browne's Downtown

TRIVIA:
In 1866, women began decorating graves of both Confederate and Union soldiers, a tradition that evolved into Memorial Day; Columbus is home to the first state-supported women's college, the Mississippi University for Women

Colonel Dobbs was a scary character. He was almost like plastic, and he didn't look like he had any feelings. He just spat out some directions and we followed suit. We were actually going to get dressed up in uniform and fight in a Civil War reenactment. The camp was set up like a real Civil War–period camp. **There were cloth tents and campfires and tin cups, and people everywhere screaming and whooping and hollering and shooting guns—it was just really wild, like walking into the twilight zone.**

In Columbus we went to a place called Waverly Waters, an authentic imitation of a town from 1860. We were told we had to fight in a reenactment of the Civil War, but Devin felt uncomfortable doing that, so we said, "If you want to stay out, we're out with you." In the end we completed the mission and got our next clue, at the Confederate Ball.  —CHRISTIAN

# Devin's Dilemma

While everybody was running around excited about putting their costumes on, I took some time to think about the whole situation and feel out how comfortable I was, because I was the only person of color there.

One of the Civil War reenactors was talking to Christian and Timmy, and the part that really bothered me was that this guy kind of sounded like he wanted the Confederacy to win. He started talking about states' rights and said that if one state wanted to charge a tariff on another state for importing or exporting stuff, then that would be that state's right. He said that the Confederates believed if you didn't like the laws in your state, then you should just move to one where they had stuff that you liked. I immediately drew the parallel that what if those states had continued to want slavery?

I had a frog in my throat, and I was really wound up, and that's when I realized that I needed to just get away. I took a little walk and weighed everything out. Finally I decided it was an opportunity to learn something that you can't get out of a textbook and I could take whatever I learned and share it with others.  —DEVIN

I didn't realize that Devin was bothered by what was going on at the Civil War camp. It was just a big game to me; I didn't even think about the possibility of it upsetting him. I thought he just didn't like the uniforms—they weren't the most attractive things you've ever seen, and Devin hates dressing up. Basically I blew him off until Tim came up to me and explained what was going on.  —EMILY

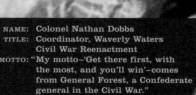

**NAME:** Colonel Nathan Dobbs
**TITLE:** Coordinator, Waverly Waters Civil War Reenactment
**MOTTO:** "My motto–'Get there first, with the most, and you'll win'–comes from General Forest, a Confederate general in the Civil War."

To set up a good battle scene, I study the battles that happened a hundred or so odd years ago and then I write something like a screenplay that blocks out each step of the action for my troops. I do this because I think the ultimate way to teach about war is to set up an authentic imitation of one, where everybody is friends and no one has to die. I try to stress to the younger people who come and attend how terrible war is. This is one of the main reasons why I do what I do–to educate the public. If you don't know your history, it could happen again, and we don't ever want a war like that to happen again.

**ROAD RULES UNION**
Timmy
Effie
Devin

**ROAD RULES CONFEDERACY**
Christian
Emily

## MISSION NUMBER 5

# FIGHT IN THE CIVIL WAR

**OBJECTIVE:** Conquer and capture the opposing side's soldiers to win the Battle of West Point

**CHALLENGE:** Put aside ideological differences to take a living history lesson

**TOOLS:** Military uniform, .58 caliber rifle muskets, blank charges of gunpowder

Devin immediately felt uncomfortable there. I think he had no reasons for that. Nobody there was like, "Look, a black guy." But he had a pretty hard time when he was supposed to put on his uniform, so he went for a little walk and called his mom. While he was gone, Timmy said that if Devin didn't do it, we wouldn't do it either. I was a little annoyed, because it was only a reenactment—we weren't really fighting for or against slavery. But on the other hand, I understood that Devin's feelings were certainly real, and I agreed with Timmy that either we do this as a group or nobody does it.  —CHRISTIAN

At breakfast Devin pulled me aside and told me he really was having a good time and he was very glad he went through with it. I think the night before, he became more and more comfortable, and then after he saw how much fun it was going to be, he was pretty happy.

I didn't know what was going on from the start. I didn't know we were going to be attacked from all angles, and I didn't even know we were going to shoot guns. But we kind of got the hang of it—ripping the gunpowder and putting the caps on and smack, **smack, smack!**

I was running and shooting at the same time, screaming, "Your mother eats goat cheese!" And then I stepped in a giant pile of horse honkey and went down on my arse. Overall our company lost 73 men, but we hung on to Effie. That was our biggest victory.

Later on, two horsemen delivered us an invitation to the Confederate Ball. We got to the party late, 'cause that's how we arrive everywhere we go—late. There was dancing, singing, a band playing, and everyone wanted us to drink their own type of moonshine. I had about six different types of liquor in my system in about six minutes. Devin got drunk on moonshine that night. I think this was the second time in his life being drunk. Of course, we've had the honor of witnessing both occasions on this trip. He didn't hold it very well this time; it kind of gave him the shivers. But he didn't throw up. I was proud of him.

From what I understood, we had to dance with the person at the party who had our next clue, but it was our job to discover who that person was. With a little help from Christian, Emily finally danced with the right partner, and she got the clue, which was embroidered on the gentleman's handkerchief. It told us that we were going to Emily's home, the House of Corn, and she couldn't be happier. It was just the little punch in the arm she needed to keep her going, 'cause she's been a little homesick lately. **-TIMMY**

## CLUE

**YOU ARE CORDIALLY INVITED TO ATTEND THE CONFEDERATE BALL TONIGHT AT EIGHT.**

## CLUE

**YOUR NEXT MISSION IS IN EMILY'S HOMETOWN. EMILY'S MOM EXPECTS YOU FOR DINNER IN TWO DAYS. AND WHILE YOU'RE THERE, GET A BIRD'S-EYE VIEW OF ILLINOIS.**

### THE CIVIL WAR

**DATES:**
1861–1865

**CAUSE:**
Differences between the North's industrial economy and the South's agrarian economy, which depended on slave labor, caused increasing antagonism. When the southern states (the Confederacy) tried to maintain their autonomy by seceding from the Union, war erupted.

**AIM:**
Restoration of the Union or independence for the South.

**OUTCOME:**
The abolition of slavery and the destruction of the South's agrarian society. Assertion of the US government's authority.

**COST:**
More than half a million lives lost in 2,400 named battles.

On our way to Flora, we stopped in Nashville for the night and went out on the town, did some partying, and visited one of my old friends, Jason. -EMILY

**1**

♥ Driving to Nashville, Emily and I were up front, and we got to talking about each other's backgrounds and the fact that I am the first black person that Emily has had any really significant contact with. It also came up that I haven't really had a serious relationship with a black girl. It's not because I don't want to or because I choose not to, it's just because that's the way the chips fell. I think you really limit yourself to people and experiences when you categorize them by color.

**I don't know if I'd call it a relationship, but me and Emily at this point are really, really, really close.**

It started out as one of those affectionate friendship things, and now it's deeper than that. I don't know what it might turn into. It might stay here or it might keep going. I'm not used to being alone, and besides, it feels good to have somebody to talk to and confide in—especially since my soon-to-be-ex-girlfriend, Amy, has basically given up on me. I've called and left messages, but she is never

home, and I just gave up. I feel like our relationship is over, and I kinda feel like there might be something worth pursuing with Emily.

I think Emily's feelings about coming home were mixed. On one side she was really homesick and really wanted to see her family—she's got three sisters, and her older sister's fiancé's name is Devin, which is weird. Then there's Erika and the little one, Liz. On the other side, Em was nervous about dealing with all of her friends and how they were gonna react to her being home for a little bit and then having to leave again. I kind of felt for her. **-DEVIN**

**1447** MILES TRAVELED

KEY TO SYMBOLS

♠ ........................romance

♣ ........................roadkill

⌂ ..................hometown stop

🖳 ........................welcome to

Ⓜ ........................mission

⛺ ..................sleep at campsite

**C**

I was really surprised when Devin told me that, out of eight of his previous girlfriends, only one of them was black. I just assumed I was the only white girl he'd had anything to do with, and it took me off-guard. But I think it's great that he has had the opportunity to have white friends and black friends and to experience both sides. I wish I had the opportunity to make more black friends like Devin.

I wanted my friend Jason from Nashville to be able to meet Devin, so I invited him to meet us at the Music Mix Factory. I wanted them to get along, but they pretty much ignored each other. Talking with Jason, I kept catching myself thinking, "I wish Devin was here."

♥ I think Devin didn't like it that Emmie talked to Jason all night at the club and basically ignored Devin. I personally feel that there's a little bit more in the air than friendship between Emmie and Devin, but we haven't reached a confession from either one of them yet. Both have announced that they will not have an affair on this trip and that we're all friends, we're all in this together. **From my point of view it looks like Devin is a bit in love with Emmie, and I think Emmie likes him very much, too, but I don't know if it's love from her side.** It's obvious that they have a lot in common—on the other hand, they have nothing in common. **-CHRISTIAN**

**So I went to look for him, and he was dancing with Effie—it looked like they were having sex out there.**

Something just went through me. I wanted to rip both their hair out. It was immature on my part. I turned around and walked back outside and told Jason, "Well, he's busy, let him have a good time." **-EMILY**

**2**

IL

**Flora** ★

64
57
45

KY

24

**Nashville**

TN

59 20
65
10

**Columbus**

MS

**Birmingham**

**Tuscaloosa**

AL

**COUNTRY MUSIC HALL OF FAME**

Elvis's "solid gold" 1960 Cadillac (equipped with a gold-plated telephone and TV, and lined on the interior with gold records), Travis Tritt's 20-foot-long Gibson guitar, original musical manuscripts, and the Pontiac Trans Am Turbo 4.9 driven by Burt Reynolds in SMOKEY AND THE BANDIT II are just a few of the items that can be found at the Country Music Hall of Fame, in Nashville, TN.

2/27 1996

Emily

4

Emily is definitely a very attractive girl. I think she looks a lot better without makeup and without a shower than she does all prettied up and stuff. But that's just the kind of guy I am. She doesn't need any makeup or any gel or none of that stuff. She's just naturally beautiful. I think one of the things I like about Emily is that she's not really prissy and she's not afraid of breaking a nail or getting a cut or a bruise. She gets real deep into everything she does. Another great thing about Emily is that she's really open-minded to any and everything.

**I honestly believe that there are few things in this world that Emily can't or won't do.** -DEVIN

Emily's most impressive quality is her bottom lip. Her worst qualities are that she swears like a sailor and she owns too many pairs of jeans. We took a look at how many jeans she packed, and it is more jeans than I have owned in a lifetime. She has a pair of jeans for every occasion, whether it be dancing, eating, filling up the gas tank, cutting the grass, combing her hair; she has a pair of jeans for everything!

She's a woman who has balls, if that's possible. She's got courage. It's funny to say, but she's the type of girl that I could see myself with—outgoing, completing every mission, just a tough girl overall. **-TIMMY**

### EMILY'S TOP THREE WAYS TO GET OUT OF A TRAFFIC TICKET

1. Say: "I'm from Flora, they only have dirt roads there."
2. Cry uncontrollably
3. Say you've had a horrible day and start crying

B

I think back to Emily on the first day: a very-good-looking girl with a huge backpack and so much hair; we all thought she would spend hours in the bathroom. Well, she does, but she also has a magnificent side that is very tough and incredibly brave. In Bimini, she conquered her greatest fear to get in the water with those sharks, and I have respected her ever since then. I have maybe one or two female friends back in Norway who would do that. Emily and I don't sit down together and talk for hours, but already on this trip I am discovering things about her that I would not have guessed. **-CHRISTIAN**

The first thing I noted was that she's extremely beautiful. She was, like, white and blond, and the first thing she said to me was, "Oh, you've got great eyes." And I told her, "You've got great eyes." So I liked her. One thing I'll always remember Emily for is her big smile. I guess I'm not such a pessimist after all—I will remember her smile and forget that she called me a bitch every other day.

She's a funny girl. One day she said to me, "I will never get married, I will never fall in love, I will never have kids." I think she's saying that based on some unhappy relationships, but she's only 18! I told her that I really hope she's gonna find somebody who really cares for her and really loves her and appreciates her. If she finds this guy, it will be the best thing that can ever happen for her. I really hope she won't miss it. **-EFFIE**

4

C

It was very dark outside when we arrived in Emily's hometown. The houses were very far apart and very big. It looked kinda deserted. Emily wanted so bad to get home; she was ecstatic. She was trying to break things in the Winnebago—she actually broke the car seat. Once we got there, she jumped into the house. The meeting between Emily and her parents was too much for me, too mushy, too many tears, too private. I went away until this whole hugging-kissing thing was over, then I came back to the house.

Emily's mom cooked us a huge dinner that night, and I ate until I couldn't eat another thing. Then she brought out an apple pie, and I thought I would roll off my chair if she made me eat one more bite. But in the bottom of the pie, we found our mission. It said we were gonna do a skydive, and everybody was ecstatic. Devin had been sleeping in his chair, but once he heard this, he couldn't stop moving—he wanted this really, really bad. Me, I never wanted to do skydiving in particular, but I always say I want to try everything I haven't done before. **-EFFIE**

D

**NASHVILLE**
POPULATION:
488,374
NICKNAME:
"Tacksville," for its tackiness
MUST DO:
Visit Opryland USA for live-music spectaculars and amusement park rides; Grand Ole Opry is the place to hear country music every Friday and Saturday night
HOMETOWN OF:
Barbara Mandrell, Greg Allman, Southern Baptist National Headquarters

6

**CLUE**
TOMORROW HEAD WEST TO VANDALIA AND THE ARCHWAY SKYDIVING CENTER. IT'S TIME FOR THAT BIRD'S EYE VIEW.

I found out when I called home that my older sister, Danielle, had gotten engaged on Valentine's Day, but I had forgotten all about it until we sat down after dinner and she was like, "Oh, you want to see my ring?" I gave her a big hug, and she asked me to be her maid of honor. It was hard for me to handle, because she's my oldest sister and the first one of us to get married, and it's kind of sad, because we're growing up. I'm not too good at changes. It's also hard for my parents to deal with. My dad's not handling the whole marriage thing too well. I don't think he could be happy with any person his daughter chose to marry.

Dad really liked Devin, though, you could tell. I didn't tell him, but I think he might have had a small clue something was going on. Dads pick up on stuff like that really fast. Usually he's kind of cocky toward guys that come over to see his little girl, but he took Devin into his home and treated him really nice. Every now and then I'd catch him patting Dev on the shoulder and Devin with this scared look on his face like, "He's gonna beat the s**t out of me, he knows, he knows."

If I had told my mom and dad, I don't think they would think twice about my being in a mixed-race relationship. Some of my friends are a different story, though. My ex-boyfriend Wes called me in Flora and asked me if Devin and I were actually seeing each other. I said yes, and he was like, "Do you realize what you've done to me?" I told him, "First of all, you're taking for granted that I'm ashamed or embarrassed of anything I've done. And second of all, I feel very sorry for you, because you have the same views that I shed the moment I went on this trip and met Devin. I reckon that if you have that attitude, you're going to miss out on a lot of wonderful people like Devin." I finally just lost it and started crying. I told him I needed to go, and I made plans to see him the next day, which was a mistake, 'cause all we ended up doing was arguing.

—EMILY

## Flora sucked.

Our first attempt to go skydiving didn't work out because of the weather, but our second try was amazing. It really brought us together. There were at least 14 people I had to see in Flora, including my ex-boyfriend, so I felt pulled in every direction.

—EMILY

I mean, her place was really nice. Her family was great. We were just doing country things, jumping on a trampoline in the backyard—that was cool. But the town was dead, and I couldn't imagine growing up there—18 years in that place. —DEVIN

### MISSION NUMBER 6

## SKYDIVING

**OBJECTIVE:** Free-fall from an airplane for 50 seconds at 120 miles per hour, pull the rip cord at 4,000 feet, and parachute to safety

**CHALLENGE:** High winds may make for a false start, but don't lose heart

**REWARD:** A hero's welcome from the Flora pom pon squad

**FLORA**
POPULATION:
5,093

NICKNAME:
"Armpit of the United States"
—Emily

LOCAL HANGOUTS:
People's houses, Duke's, concerts in the park, the high school parking lot, Wolves football games

FANFARE:
Clay County Fair is the place to go if you're looking to buy a prizewinning heifer or a home-baked pie

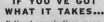

**IF YOU'VE GOT WHAT IT TAKES...**

National organizations recognize three different kinds of jumps for the first-time jumper: tandem, static line, and AFF. In a tandem jump, the student is attached to the instructor throughout. The static line is a solo jump in which the parachute opens automatically after 3,000 feet. In the AFF, or accelerated free fall, the student is attached to two instructors during a 45-second fall, after which the parachute opens and the student makes a solo descent.

**THE SKY'S THE LIMIT**

The US Parachute Association has more than 31,000 members, of which 12-15% are women.

A USPA skydiving center is referred to as a drop zone, or DZ, of which there are 330 nationwide.

Laws surrounding jumping are minimal and are generally set by each DZ.

In order to jump, you must be in good health, at least 18 years old, and under 225 pounds.

There are about 26-30 fatalities per year, or one in 100,000 jumps.

My mother said to me before I left on this trip, "Timothy, if you don't want to do any of the missions, you just tell them: 'No, I am not jumping out of an airplane.' They'll understand." Yeah, right. I couldn't wait to get up in that plane.

Well, our first attempt to throw ourselves out of airplanes was a bust. The wind was too strong, and they sent us home, visions of the Okahumpka disaster dancing in our heads. They told us to come back in the morning.

The next day, I went first, Devin was second, Emily was third, Effie was fourth, and Christian was to jump last. I had no time to think about turning back. It was like in cartoons. My ears felt like I'd swum too deep in the ocean. I felt like a newborn baby on a 747. All I could think was, "Do I still have a pulse?" It was my happy birthday, merry Christmas, happy New Year, pass-go-collect-two-hundred-dollars, bingo jackpot!

When it was time to pull my rip cord, well, I did just that—and nothing happened. My tandem guy actually had to go into the chute on his back and open it on his own. There are so many backups and reserves that it's a pretty safe sport overall: 30,000 jumps last year or something like that and, like, 17 people got hurt. I bet more people are killed by bees.
**-TIMMY**

I wanted to be the first one to jump, because I didn't want to lose my courage. But I didn't get to choose, and luckily I didn't lose my courage. I didn't have any time to hesitate or to go back. The instructor just pushed me. I didn't understand exactly that I was in the air until I felt the wind in my face so strong, and then my heart jumped out of my chest.

**I stopped breathing for a few seconds. It was double orgasm. Multiple orgasm. It kept me walking for hours, and I was refreshed and happy when we left Flora.**

I loved Emily's family, and I felt sad to say goodbye to her little sisters. Before we left, Liz gave me her favorite stuffed lion to take on the trip. I don't often see children give up their toys, especially their favorite toys, so I was flattered. I really enjoyed that week. It was boring, but it was nice. After the Civil War reenactment, we really needed somebody to take care of us, and they really took care of us.        **-EFFIE**

Flora was a very little town. Since my home is by the ocean and fjords, I feel attached to the sea. I missed the sea when I was in her country. What I liked very much about it was driving through the woods on her family's four-wheelers. That was the coolest thing I did there except for getting to know Emily's family—and of course, the skydiving.

If I had to compare the Bimini experience, when I pushed the shark on the bottom of the sea, to jumping out of that airplane, I would say that both moments were so freaking close to a ten, probably the biggest moments of my life. I felt like a bird out there, just flying.

After the dive, Emmie opened the door to the Winnie and out came 20 cheerleaders from the Flora high school, yelling our next clue and jumping up and down. I was like, "Wow." It was cold outside, and they had nothing on their legs. That's why I said wow, of course.

We couldn't take any money from Emily's parents, but right before we left Flora, they gave us almost their entire refrigerator of food—from canned salmon to steaks to tuna fish to pudding to Kool-Aid. I guess we will eat this food the next couple weeks or so, because we are really short on money right now. Emily's dad also gave us the next piece of our puzzle. I think it's a little bit too early to try to figure out what the puzzle says. The only two words we can figure out are "your" and "destination." So it can go anywhere.        **-CHRISTIAN**

## CLUE

**"THAT JUMP TOOK REAL GUTS YOU GUYS ARE TOTALLY NUTS YOU'VE EARNED YOUR SECOND ROAD KEY NEXT STOP IS TENNESSEE IT'S TIME TO CRUISE GO MAKE A DIFFERENCE IT'S CHOOSE OR LOSE LISTEN TO US BRING OUT THE VOTE GET ON THE CHOOSE OR LOSE BUS AT UNIVERSITY OF MEMPHIS"**

## ROAD KEY

# MISSION

## CHOOSE OR LOSE

**OBJECTIVE:** Register as many young people to vote as possible

**CHALLENGE:** Apathy

**REWARDS:** Political awareness, the power to rock the vote... and a free dinner for the one with the most registrations

In Memphis we had to sign up as many people as possible to vote in the country's next elections. Christian was very imaginative, and he signed up the most voters, so he won a dinner prize and took us all along, but we had to work for our supper. —EFFIE

We drove to Memphis University to meet Dave Anderson and the Choose or Lose crew. Dave told us that we had to compete against each other to get the most registrations, and the winner would have a dinner for two at the best restaurant in Memphis. I immediately thought of going into large auditoriums and making people simultaneously fill out the registration forms. So I chose some quite cute girls, and asked them if they would like to show me an auditorium which was filled up with people. **—CHRISTIAN**

## 2009 MILES TRAVELED

### IT'S YOUR VOTE

IN THE LAST PRESIDENTIAL ELECTIONS (1992):

75% of the voting-age population was registered to vote.

75% of registered voters voted.

54% of the African-American population voted.

28% of the Hispanic population voted.

63% of the white population voted.

Historically, Minnesota outvotes the other states.

Southern states, such as Texas, Alabama, and Louisiana, generally have the lowest voter turnout.

Studies indicate that voter turnout increases with age.

The morning after we arrived in Memphis, I woke up, turned on CNN, and heard about a bombing in Israel. It was the third bombing in the last nine days. It was really, really sad watching the peace process stop dead—Israel was a mess. Elections for a new prime minister were coming up in May, and it was a crucial time to keep the country at peace. I can't stand being so far away and hearing this kind of news. I couldn't help it, I started crying. Emily was trying to understand exactly what happened—it's a complicated issue, this whole Arab-Israeli thing. I was trying to make her understand that the whole fight has been going on for 1,000 years. It was kinda hard, because she's not used to this kind of history; her life is so safe compared to mine.

**Choose or Lose would never happen in Israel, because 90 percent of Israelis already vote.** Why don't people in America use their rights? The small people need to understand that they're part of a bigger thing and that they can make a difference. It's definitely an American thing, trying to convince people to know their rights and to use them. I'm glad that somebody's doing it. **—EFFIE**

We went out to a bar called Six One Six, and Christian and I became friendly with the owner. His name is Wilbur, and he took us behind the bar, showed us his pet alligator, and let me sling drinks around. I even swallowed a goldfish for $20. Being behind a bar is sort of a way of being onstage. Of course, I love to be the center of attention, making people laugh. That's the way I live my life. If you get a drink from me, you will remember my face, name, or something I did.

Christian and I ended up going out after work with Wilbur. He took us to a casino in Mississippi, and we gambled away all his money. We didn't return until the sun was up. **—TIMMY**

Tim always wants to do everything big for the camera. We're not supposed to do things for the camera. We're supposed to do what we want, but if we're thinking about the camera, then we're missing the whole point. I'm not looking to be outrageous. **—EFFIE**

### KEY TO SYMBOLS

⚠ ............sleep in campsite

♥ ............romance

🏠 ............hometown stop

📋 ............welcome to

Ⓜ ............mission

😈 ............scamming/cheating

**3**

5

Of course, I won this contest. I had already decided to share my free dinner with one of the people who helped us, as a gesture of goodwill, so I invited Missy, because she really helped out.

Part of the deal was that we got to ride to this restaurant in a limo. Well, you see all these American movies with suspicious guys in limos, turning down the windows and saying, "Give me some dough. Give me some crack. I need some—something."

**Excuse me the language, but I think limos are in some way penis extensions, somehow pornographic—but fun when you sit in one.**
**-CHRISTIAN**

Ever since we left Flora, I've been much happier. It was important for my family to know what I was going through. Now that they've had the cameras in their house, I can talk to them about it and they can relate a lot better. The first two weeks of this trip I was totally lost within myself. I met 20 new people, four of them I can never get away from, and I was going to so many new places I couldn't keep track. Going home put things in perspective, and since then my interviews have been going better, the mikes and cameras don't get on my nerves…well, every now and then they get on my nerves, but they don't upset me anymore. **-EMILY**

NAME: Dave Anderson
TITLE: Manager, Choose or Lose
MOTTO: "Choose or Lose. That's it."

The Choose or Lose crew travels the United States for about ten months of the year, registering voters and working with Rock the Vote to cover elections and candidates. There are five people on our bus and two advance people, so we definitely relate to the dramas of the ROAD RULES kids.

Our own little drama with them was that they were late, and it's very important that our volunteers be on time and start going. I know they had some stuff going on. There had been a bombing in Israel, and who knows if they got lost or whatever, but we were holding up our whole event waiting for them. Had it been anyone else, we would have started without them, but I didn't want to look like a jerk on TV, so when I walked up to the their Winnebago I just said, "Hi," when I really wanted to say, "Where the hell have you been?"

The group was happy to help if the crew was there, but when the cameras were out of sight, they were a little flaky. Also, Devin spent a lot of time chewing on Emily's hand. I was like, "Wow! People are chewing on each other's body parts." I haven't seen that on our bus before."

**2317** MILES TRAVELED

A chameleon would have exploded if it had landed on Christian in his outfit that night. He had on a striped shirt, a plaid jacket, red pants, a tie with teddy bears on it, black socks, and brown shoes. Everyone was feeling a little eccentric that night. Effie especially had been in a crazy, weird mood the last couple of days. The first time I noticed the change in Effie was the first night we got to Memphis—she was just screaming and yelling, bouncing off the walls and cursing.

**She was having crazy dreams at night, and her weirdness kept building and building and building until our dinner at Chez Philippe, when she decided to have a personal, intimate experience with a strawberry.**

Everything at the table completely stopped while we all watched her sexually assault that piece of fruit. It's been a conversation piece ever since. **-DEVIN**

During dinner, Christian asked me and Devin what was up with our relationship. I think it was kind of good to get it out in the open once and for all. Devin and I are DEFINITELY romantically involved. No more sneaking around, no more feeling awkward in front of the group. But at the same time, the restaurant wasn't the best place in the world to bring it up. I think Devin especially wishes that Christian had saved it for later, when we were all hanging out in the Winnie. But that's just Christian.

So as dessert was being served, we got a plate that was covered with some elaborate brass-covered lid, and underneath was our next clue, written in some kind of baking chocolate. It said we were supposed to go to Overton Park Theater and meet the King there. Then we got our check. It turned out to be $436, and we probably had $4.36 between us. So we all kind of just stopped and looked at Christian like, "What's up?" Apparently the hostess didn't remember their phone conversation about us paying what we could for the meal, so we ended up on kitchen duty that night. **-EMILY**

I just hope that Devin doesn't wait until we're sitting down and eating at the next nice dinner to ask Christian and me if we're dating. **-TIMMY**

CLUE

Meet The King Tomorrow At Noon At The Overton Park Theater

## MEMPHIS

POPULATION:
610,337

HOMETOWN OF:
Alex Chilton, Shannen Doherty,
Aretha Franklin, Elvis Presley

TRIVIA:
Elvis paid $100,000 for
Graceland in 1957

MUST SEE:
Sun Recording Studios, where
Elvis, Johnny Cash, and U2
have cut records; the National
Civil Rights Museum, built
around the remains of the
Lorraine Motel, where Martin
Luther King was assassinated

## BBQ

Although people have cooked
meat over open fires
throughout history, the term
"barbacoa" did not appear
until the Spanish came to
America. Caribbean natives
dried and smoked their meat
by hanging it on wooden
racks. This custom was introduced to the US when many
of these people were later
enslaved in the South. Since
that time, many different
forms of barbecuing have
emerged. The method of
rapid cooking over hot
charcoal was popularized by
Henry Ford.

## BIRTHPLACE
## OF THE KING

Peek in the window of Elvis's
birthplace, in Tupelo, MS,
then share a quiet moment
with the King at the adjacent
Elvis memorial meditation
chapel–a popular spot for

On the was to go to the overton Park theater, which is the first place Elvis ever performed live, and meet the King. The King was a fat Elvis impersonator who sang a horrible song that said we had to go to the Rendezvous Restaurant and meet a guy called Nick. -TIMMY

## JOB Rendezvous Barbecue

**OBJECTIVE:** Barbecue some ribs and
entertain the eaters at the
best rib joint in Memphis

**CHALLENGE:** Overcome your
differences to keep
the restaurant running

**TOOLS:** Elvis suits, instant camera,
aprons, ovens, secret sauce

## CLUE

CLUE
CLUE
CLUE
CLUE
CLUE

E:

I KNOW WHAT IT'S LIKE TO BE
IN A STRANGE TOWN AND NOT
HAVE ANY MONEY, SO I'VE
USED A LITTLE OF MY PULL
HERE AND I'VE GOT YOU ALL
JOBS. YOU NEED TO FIND A
GUY NAMED NICK VERGOS AT
RENDEZVOUS RESTAURANT

It was 5:00, and we had to be at Rendezvous by 6:00. Everyone was there except Effie, of course. I figured she probably just wandered off into Effie's world and forgot she was supposed to be back, so I went to look for her. I found out that Effie had not been wandering around but had talked her way into using a hotel room to shower and get ready for the night.

# I told her it wasn't very cool for her to just run off and get a shower while all of us were out there stinking.

It wasn't the first time something like this happened. I was so pissed I yelled at her, then I stormed out to the Winnie and filled the guys in on what was going on. Effie eventually came back, and all I could hear was her and Devin screaming at the top of their lungs. I hate to see us all fight, and that was the first real fight we've had. I think we were both wrong, in the end. **-EMILY**

# Memphis Meltdown

## DEVIN'S VERSION

Effie had been an island of just herself for the past couple of days. She'd been really withdrawn and wandering. She was scaring me, personally. It seemed like at any moment she might snap and release the parking brake on a hill and send us into oncoming traffic. So she was kind of in and out of our whole afternoon. While she was gone, somehow or other we got in a conversation about the change in her disposition. I had been biting my tongue with Effie up until then, but I believe it's not healthy to keep things bottled up; it was time to exhale. And when Effie came back from her shower, she got it all. We got into a screaming and cursing match, but it all died down and then we went to dinner. We had to get working. **-DEVIN**

## EFFIE'S VERSION

The whole reason I disappear like I do is to avoid shouting at the people I care about. And when people shout at me, it's like Effie with a big box on her head. I don't hear anything. I'm not listening, I'm not listening. Thank God I'm old enough not to have to answer to a couple of screaming, 18-year-old children. Emily, she's just a little girl. I could eat her for breakfast.

As for Devin, I really do like him; he's one hell of a guy. It's just that whenever we have a conversation, it goes BANG! I'm opinionated and he's very strong minded and we are OK as long as we are honest with each other. I didn't like it one bit that he screamed at me, but it's better than keeping it inside and pretending he is OK with me, I guess. **-EFFIE**

## CLUE

INGREDIENTS:
EQUINES, BOVINES,
AND THE CIVIC CENTER OF
SULPHUR SPRINGS, TX

DIRECTIONS:
TALK TO CHALK
DONALDSON OR
ROD HENDERSON.

# Before this trip, all I knew about Elvis was that he was the big idol of the '60s and some of the '70s.

He is often described as a white man singing just like a black man. Timmy was a much better Elvis than me, but I was a novelty, an Elvis from Norway. It was a living hell in the restaurant; I mean, we just screwed up things. The most funny thing was when we asked this girl if she wanted to take a picture with the two Elvises for $3 and she said yeah, and she was very, very tall. Both Tim and I just reached to her ta-ta's and Tim started singing "Can't Help Falling in Love." I can't believe she didn't get mad, but I think she didn't know what it was all about and she had fun with us, too. We sang to the ta-ta's. I wish I had better language to explain how funny it was. Dead funny. No, not dead funny. Living funny. S**t. It was funny, period.

Later, Tim and I went to a bar called Hooters, where the girls wear something like bikinis and they have to have very large—how do you say, advantages—to work there. It was a new experience. We don't have a Hooters in Norway. Then we went to Silky's and met up with a girl named Cindy and her friend. Cindy was 28 and she worked as a flight attendant. I had been on the road for three weeks, and I weighed too much in the front, what can I say? I didn't think she was very cute, but I really had to do it, because I wanted it and I needed it. She was very talkative. She said more than, "Yeah, yeah, I like that, yeah, great, yeah, let's do that."

NAME: Nick Vergos
TITLE: Owner, Rendezvous Restaurant
MOTTO: "If you like good barbecue, you need to come to Memphis."

At the end of the night, N[...] gathered us together a[...] told us we had earned our keep. [...] gave us an envelope with $1,200 [...] last us for the next three weeks. [...] was perfect timing, because we want[...] to spend a little money in Memp[...] and we were pretty much broke. N[...] also gave us a special jar of Bar[...] Clue Sauce and it told us that we h[...] to go to Texas for our next missi[...] and meet some bulls. **-TIMM**

GRACELA[...]
Elvis purchased the [...] estate at the age [...] $100,000. His platin[...] and stage costume[...] walls of the Trophy [...] dedicated fans like [...] moment of reflect[...] Elvis's grave in the [...] Gardens before mo[...] the Wall of Love, can [...] can inscribe their ow[...] message to the King [...]

I don't know about the guys from ROAD RULES, but the two girls were babes. They were cooking and they got into a little catfight in the kitchen, so I had to pull one of the Elvises back there and take one of the girls out. I didn't know what was going to happen, but I didn't want to see it get worse than it already was. There are knives and cleavers down there.

Those kids weren't the first to be filmed with my ribs. There's a barbecue contest here every year called Memphis in May. They have teams from all over the world coming here to barbecue. I was Al Gore's cook every May for about eight years before he became vice president. I've been on Air Force One to take him food. He's a good friend, and he'll walk past ten congressmen to come shake my hand.

**TATTOO CULTURE**
Modern mechanical tattooing was invented in New York City at the end of the 19th century when Samuel O'Reilly modified Thomas Edison's electric engraving pen so that it would inscribe the tattoo on the skin. Bob Wicks and Bill Jones were two of the first great NY tattoo artists.

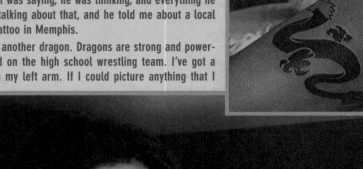

Devin got a tattoo in Memphis after meeting a guy who inspired him. It was my first time in a tattoo parlor. I thought about getting one but I chickened out. The clue we got at the Rendezvous sent us to Texas. -EMILY

**1**

# The Third Dragon

**A**

After that big blowout at the Rendezvous, Emily and I needed to get away, so we went out to get something to eat. During the course of our meal, we started talking to the waiter, Herb. One thing led to another and we ended up going back to his place and talking all night. Me and Herb vibed off one another. Everything I was saying, he was thinking, and everything he was saying, I was thinking. He was tattooed and I'm tattooed and we got talking about that, and he told me about a local artist who did a lot of his work; I made my decision then that I wanted a tattoo in Memphis.

So the next afternoon, I went to this place called Underground Art and got another dragon. Dragons are strong and powerful and beautiful at the same time. I got my first one when I was 16 and on the high school wrestling team. I've got a dragon tattoo on my back and on my right arm, and now I've got one on my left arm. If I could picture anything that I would want on my body for the rest of my life, this is it. When I called home and told my mom about this new tattoo, she said, "That's forever." I know it's forever, and that's OK. To me it's not like I got a tattoo, it's like a tattoo was missing. I'm not gonna regret anything that I do to myself or for myself.

There will always be a lot of memories attached to my Memphis dragon.

**B**

**I'm doing a lot of changing. I'm kind of finding out who I am, and I wanted something to remember this by, because nothing is ever going to be the same again.**

## 2317 MILES TRAVELED

**C**

I've learned that, after this journey, I want to travel more. I want to see more. I want to learn more. I want to meet more people. I think I'm getting a greater appreciation for different cultures. I'm becoming more well-rounded, and I'm dealing with my temper a lot better. I don't think there is anything bad coming out of this trip for me. **-DEVIN**

My first impression of Devin was so different from what he really is. I saw this guy with dreadlocks, tattoos, and a pierced bellybutton. He seemed like a hard, hard person who wouldn't open up very easily, and I thought, "Wow, I have to live with this guy?" But after I got to talking to him, he was just really intelligent, sweet, and sincere.

### KEY TO SYMBOLS
......................sidetrip
......................romance
......................danger
......................welcome to
*JOB* ......................mission
......................sleep in Winnie
**2** ......................lost

# Devin

**Devin's probably the most open-minded person I've ever met in my life.** I guess it's just because he's been in a big-city atmosphere. He's seen it all. Nothing really shocks him, and if it does, then he deals with it. When I'm talking to him, I feel like I'm talking to someone a lot older. I mean, most people my age are like three years behind me! If I had to go to someone for advice, you know, I would go to Devin.

What I like the most about Devin is that whenever I have a comment or share my views, he'll have something totally different that I've never thought of to add. **Usually, if it's coming out of Devin's mouth, it's off-the-wall.** He has a really weird way of looking at things. You can't say, "Well, Devin would like this," or "Devin would do this," or "Devin is going to be mad about this," because you never know. **-EMILY**

**2**

Little Rock    40    Memphis
AR                              TN
30
★ Sulphur Springs
TX

When I first saw Devin, I was like, "Whoa, he's cool." I mean, he dresses cool, he talks cool, and he's got a beautiful face and incredible eyes.

Later, I learned the most important thing about Devin: he's smart. I never met somebody his age so incredibly arrogant but very, very smart. I learn a lot from Devin, and he's 18 and I'm 23; it's supposed to be the other way around, but it's not. I hope he's learned from me.

**He always amazes me, all the time, over and over again.   -EFFIE**

I didn't think anything bad about him, but I didn't realize what type of person Devin was from the start. His maturity and intelligence for an 18-year-old is beyond my comprehension. He's a naturally smart person—book smart and commonsense smart. He voices his opinions very strongly, and he's extremely good at it. He knows how to argue, he knows what words are coming out of his mouth, and he knows how to use them.

He's a unique individual overall, but I think the thing that'll most stick in my mind about Devin would definitely have to be his music and the way he always sings louder than any song on the radio.   -TIMMY

Devin is very different from me, but at the same time, I honestly think that we share some of the same minds, some of the same heads. We have some way of looking at things in common. And even though I think in some way that he's younger than me, I have to add that, in many ways, in too many ways, I am younger than him.   -CHRISTIAN

**DEVIN'S ROAD STAPLES**
Hiking boots
Condoms
Lotion
Sunglasses
Sandals
Strawberry Fig Newtons

**2696 MILES TRAVELED**

**HOW DEVIN DESCRIBES DEVIN**
Sensitive
Good listener
Hardworking
Occasional crybaby

Another night in a parking lot. Living in hotel parking lots is basically just like camping out, except you have electricity. The streetlights are always shining on you. I guess it's not a lot like camping out. Sometimes it's hard watching all these people go into their nice cozy rooms and take their nice hot showers while we're stuck in this Winnie, sometimes after we've been in there hours upon hours, just ready to rip each other's heads off.   -EMILY

Driving through Texas is really weird, because it's a really big state and you kind of get in this zone where you're used to doing 70 miles an hour and just seeing nothing but farmland, but every once in a while you hit a small town, and they have stoplights and stuff. On my shift, I was in highway mode, and I didn't switch to small-town mode, and went flying through a red light and almost killed everybody. And then about 15 minutes later I almost hit a pack of dogs that was hanging out in the highway. I'm learning to pay attention.

We got into town and we picked a prime parking lot to sleep in. Living in hotel parking lots isn't that bad. You get used to living with five people. You find a place to plug in, we have a nice little heater in there, and we've got cool sleeping bags, although it does get kind of cold. It's nice to get inside every once in a while and take a shower and relax, watch a little TV.   -DEVIN

**MELISSA ETHERIDGE'S** TOP TEN ROAD TRIPPIN' CDs
1. Radiohead, THE BENDS
2. Garbage, GARBAGE
3. Heather Nova, anything by
4. Amanda Marshall, anything by
5. Janis Joplin, PEARL
6. Joan Armatrading, anything by
7. Joni Mitchell, BLUE
8. Peter Gabriel, PASSION
9. Hank Williams, GREATEST HITS
10. Glen Cambell, GREATEST HITS

I slept the entire ten hours from Memphis to Sulphur Springs. That's where we did the rodeo, and where we celebrated our one-month anniversary, kind of. We all said happy anniversary, and that was it. -EMILY

We went to the Civic Center where the rodeo takes place and met Chock, a very friendly cowboy. He told us what we were going to be doing, and gave us some cowboys to take care of us. I didn't like the idea of this whole mission, but I usually don't like things at the beginning. I never rode a horse before, and I don't like the whole idea of controlling animals. But I loved it once I understood how this whole horse-person thing worked. As I rode into the ring for the grand opening, I wasn't nervous at all—I never noticed the people, I never heard the music, I just focused on the girl on the horse in front of me and did what she did.

I wouldn't have done what Emily did, but I knew she was going to be OK. I said to the guys, "She won't bitch about getting thrown off the horse. She'll bitch about getting sand in her hair." That's Emily. **-EFFIE**

## MISSION RODEO

NUMBER 8

**OBJECTIVE:** Each Road Ruler must bravely fulfill the responsibilities of a chosen role: bareback rider, saddle bronc rider, bull rider, flag-carrier, clown

**HAZARDS:** Concussion, back and neck injury, shock, or if you're lucky, only a mouthful of dirt

**TOOLS:** Mustang, riding horse, bull, red flag

### THE RIDE OF YOUR LIFE

The saddle bronc event is responsible for 18% of rodeo injuries. Most of these are knee injuries.

Bull riding accounts for 43% of rodeo injuries. The most common bull riding injuries are groin injuries.

Bareback riding accounts for another 24% of injuries. These are usually elbow and arm injuries.

Horses buck in a straight line or circular pattern, while bulls buck in a spinning motion, throwing the rider to the side.

From 1981-1990 noncontestants such as clowns, bullfighters, and judges suffered 242 of the 2,240 injuries.

As soon as Chock explained saddle broncing, that's exactly what I wanted to do. But every time I told anybody I was going to do a saddle bronc, they would get a smirk on their face like, "Yeah, right." A lot of the cowboys had told me that I'm the first girl they've ever seen in this event and I'd be lucky if I even got out there. Then this guy came up to me and said, "We're getting ready to get your horse out here. If you're gonna back out, you better do it now." That did it—I wasn't gonna let a bunch of cowboys talk me out of riding.

When I got on my horse in the chute, they said, "If you get in trouble, use two hands." But I wanted to do it the right way. They gave me a rope, showed me how to hold it, and said to nod my head when I was ready. I tipped my hat and they opened the gate and the horse immediately started bucking. I think I felt it buck three or four times, then my knees gave out and I knew it was all over. I went flying and landed face-first in the sand. I lay there for a second, 'cause I'd forgotten where I was, and Devin came running up and dragged me over to the side.

It was tough for me to get on that horse and tackle a fear like that. The group was really concerned for me, and they helped me through a tough time that turned out to be a great time. I think these people are going to be around in my life for a very long time, hopefully for as long as I live. I found out when I went home that I might have lost some friends in Flora, but I've made four of the most wonderful friends I'll ever make during this experience, so it kind of evens things out a little bit. **-EMILY**

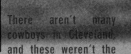

There aren't many cowboys in Cleveland, and these weren't the pretty cowboys you see on TV. These were the real deal. They get their hands dirty. After I met 50 or 60 of them, the one thing I can say about cowboys is they have really tight grips: my hand hurt after a night of shaking with them.

I was out on the floor in my ridiculous clown suit when the first bull was released. The gate opened and the bull came out, bucked the guy off, and made a beeline for me, so I hopped up on a fence, and from that point on, I knew that this wasn't a game. This wasn't about running around and tripping and falling and entertaining the crowd. It was a job: you had to keep the bull away from the rider, and there wasn't a lot of laughing involved.

I actually hate getting dressed up. That's the last silly outfit I'm putting on for the rest of the trip. I'm taking a stand. I'm putting my foot down. No more costumes for Devin.

**Another thing I want to say from this standpoint is that I stopped eating meat a couple of years ago, and it just gave me the creeps, looking that bull in the eye and thinking that I used to shovel that stuff into my mouth.**

I dealt with beef at the Rendezvous in Memphis, and I was face-to-face with it at the rodeo. If anything, these experiences have fueled my fight against eating meat. **-DEVIN**

I was able to stay on the bull for .6 seconds. I couldn't believe how powerful it was. I thought I'd be able to stay on longer. I really felt like I got ripped off. I sat on a bull for a half a second, and he threw me—end of the ride. I wish I could save that feeling in a bottle. It's like: jilted at the altar, park's closed, six out of seven numbers in the lottery, you show up to the New Year's Eve party at 12:05.

After the very last bull rides were over, Chock brought us down to the rodeo ground and we tackled a calf and ripped the clue off its neck. **-TIMMY**

## CLUE

**YOUR NEXT MISSION IS IN AUSTIN, TEXAS. CONTACT CARMEN VALERA AT KTBC-FOX 7. HURRY, YOU'RE ON DEADLINE.**

Besides falling off horses, there was not a lot to do in Sulphur Springs. It was an average town in Texas. The accent was very difficult for me to handle. I took a very long jog there. I jogged for like 15 miles, all the way to the location where Tim had an interview with the director. And on the way, I picked up a sign that said "Dawson for Judge," and I ran by Tim with it so he had to stop his interview to die from laughing. On my way back, I met two guys who said, "Hey, what are you doing with that?" Those were the guys that made the sign. So I told them a story: "I'm from Norway, and I want to do a little campaigning for this judge." I told them that I would get lots of attention, because people driving by would look twice at a jogger carrying a judge sign. The two men agreed that it was a good idea. They said, "Thank you, that's great."

Another thing we did in Sulphur Springs was dump the s**tter. We drove a couple of miles out of town and dumped it in the most deserted place we found, which was kind of not cool. As usual, Tim and I did the dumping and the others hung out of a window and looked at us. I think he and I are used to handling bulls**t, because that's the only thing that comes out of our mouth sometimes. **-CHRISTIAN**

NAME: Chock Donaldson
TITLE: Owner, 44 Bar Rodeo Company; retired rodeo rider; International Professional Rodeo Association's All-Around Rookie of the Year, 1979
MOTTO: "If you mess with the bull, you get the horn."

There have been so many misconceptions about cowboys and about rodeo livestock over the years. Some folks say that rodeo is inhumane to the livestock, but if you come to the rodeo, you'll see that the animals are treated probably better than the handlers. There's a common stereotype that cowboys are uneducated, but rodeo is now a major entertainment business, and people are starting to see that cowboys are not only athletes, but businessmen, too. We have to be, because in rodeo there are no guarantees. You don't sign a contract like a football player or a basketball player. What you are good enough to win is all you get paid.

The danger of rodeo riding varies depending on the particular sport. Bull riding is probably the most dangerous. The professional life span of a bull rider is about 12 years, but they're getting injured less today, because they wear protective vests. The least stressful ride, physically and mentally, is the team roping. Team ropers are horseback all the time, and they'll occasionally lose a finger or a thumb, dallying the rope around the saddle horn, but that's about the extent of the injuries. And I know men that have team-roped up into their 70s.

**SULPHUR SPRINGS**
POPULATION: 14,100
TRIVIA: Center of Texas's leading dairy region
FANFARE: Hopkins County Dairy Festival; CRA Finals Rodeo in mid-November
MUST SEE: The Southwest Dairy Museum, where you'll learn the real truth about how cream separates

In Austin we had a serious job to do. We were representing a news station at the South by Southwest Music and Media Festival. Between the five of us, we researched, reported, and edited a spot for the 10:00 news. —DEVIN

**1**

**A**

Christian's favorite part of the entire mission is the very beginning—finding out where we're supposed to go, who we're supposed to talk to, and getting all the details. I had never really taken control and done the detective work for a mission before, so I decided to prove to them I could do it. I called Carmen and left her a message with my pager number. When I got back to the Winnie, Christian was questioning me up and down: "Are you sure you did everything? Are you sure she knows who we are?" I thought he was insulting my intelligence, and we started getting into it. Then Effie pulled me aside and told me that I needed to be more patient with Christian, which is something I know I need to do, but it's just so hard. He's got a heart of gold, but he really gets on my nerves.

**B**

There's a lot of times when I think, "These people, they are driving me crazy." But that's normal in a situation like this. For the most part, we click, but when we're over-tired, that's when the tension starts rising. At this point, we're kind of choosing who our close friends are, and I'm closer with Tim and Devin than with Effie and Christian. That's not necessarily because they're from the States, it's just the people they are. I hope in the next five weeks I'll be able to become a little bit closer with Christian and Effie. **—EMILY**

I don't get involved in a lot of the arguments, because most of them I feel are pointless. I've hated arguing my entire life. I like being happy. I have attempted a couple of times throughout this field trip to intervene and calm things down, but I've learned through example that you really can't change things. It's best to just let them fight, let them go at it, and then let them get over it. **—TIMMY**

**2696 MILES TRAVELED**

**C**

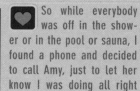

One way or another, everywhere we go, we sweet-talk, schmooze, or scam someone into letting us get a room and a shower.

Either we send one of the girls in and they flash a pretty smile, or Timmy or Christian will go in and joke around and make friends to get us into a room. There's various ways to do it. You can ask for a dirty room, and if the people behind the desk are cool with it, they'll let you go in just to shower, get warm, and get out. It really doesn't inconvenience them that much, and it's a nice favor to us.

So while everybody was off in the shower or in the pool or sauna, I found a phone and decided to call Amy, just to let her know I was doing all right and to see how she was doing. I had just found out that there was a misunderstanding during the time I was in New Orleans. I had left tons of messages, and I thought she wasn't returning my calls, but really, it was just that my pager wasn't working. I didn't find out till later that she was still really into our relationship and waiting for me. I wish I had known what I know now before I got involved with Emily—then things would've been straight from the front end. **—DEVIN**

## KEY TO SYMBOLS

⚔ ................conflict
♥ ................romance
💰 ...............money trail
🧳 ...............welcome to
M ...............mission
💩 ...............empty Winnie septic tank
❓ ...............lost

**TX**

**Dallas** — 30 — **Sulphur Springs**
35
★
**Austin**

### LONGHORN LEGACY
After defeating the University of Texas Longhorns 13-0 in a 1929 football game, the Texas A&M Aggies stole and branded the UT mascot, a steer. The Longhorns repaired the steer by turning the brand, which read "13-0" into "Bevo," thereby naming their mascot. In order to fight the power of the Aggies, the Longhorns hold a Hex Rally the night before the big UT/A&M game every season.

**3**

### GARBAGE'S
TOP THIRTEEN ROAD TRIPPIN' CDs

1 .............................Nick Cave, and the Bad Seeds, LET LOVE IN
2 ...........................................Frank Sinatra, THE CAPITOL YEARS
3 ...........Massive Attack vs. The Mad Professor, NO PROTECTION
4 .............................................The Clash, LONDON CALLING
5 ...................................................The Beatles, REVOLVER
6 .................................................Roxy Music, COUNTRY LIFE
7 .........Captain Beefheart and His Magic Band, CLEAR SPOT
8 ...................................................Patti Smith, HORSES
9 ...................................................John Cale, FEAR
10 ...................The Rolling Stones, BETWEEN THE BUTTONS
11 ...........................................Television, MARQUEE MOON
12 ..................................................Radiohead, THE BENDS
13 ..............................P.J. Harvey, TO BRING YOU MY LOVE

# MISSION 9

## DELIVER THE NEWS

**OBJECTIVE:** Cover the South by Southwest Music and Media Festival for KTBC-Fox 7

**CHALLENGE:** Find an angle on the story, then decide who gets the glory

**TOOLS:** Cameras, mikes, lights, editing room

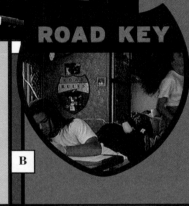

**ROAD KEY**

B

## South by Southwest

At the beginning, after they told us that South by Southwest was a big music festival where over 600 bands would be performing, everybody really wanted to be out in the field with the reporter, so we drew for it. It turned out that Devin, Emily, and I were going to be on the street, and Tim and Christian would stay in the studio and edit. But I realized that I didn't care about local bands, and I didn't much feel like going out with the two lovebirds. So I went to Timmy and told him that if he really wanted to be on the field with a reporter, then I would be more than happy to stay in the studios. So Timmy got to do it; he's so good in front of the camera; he was really the natural one to go, anyway.

My job was to choose the best video cuts from Emily and Devin's report, and match them with the audio. **It was nice to be serious for a few hours, to feel that I had a real job, that people were counting on me, like real life—but I was stressed.** How was I supposed to do it? I was dying for a cigarette. I couldn't sit, I was going up and down the stairs, in and out of the edit room, drinking tons of coffee. But I wouldn't smoke, because I had a bet with Timmy for $20 that I wouldn't smoke for a week, and I was gonna get that money—I'd already gone four days without smoking.
**-EFFIE**

Effie thought things over and decided she'd rather be back at the station, so she asked me several times to switch. Christian and I were a little bit upset that we weren't going to be able to do this part of the mission together. We thought we could really raise some heck back at the station, but I didn't want to upset Effie, because she was trying not to smoke. We'd been cracking down on her because she has trouble understanding that you can't smoke anywhere you please in America.

**Effie definitely has direction in her life, but I tried to tell her that if a person**

**2891 MILES TRAVELED**

I don't know if Emily was feeling the pressure or if she was just uncomfortable with the camera, but she choked big-time doing her stand-up story at Palmer Auditorium. She just kept putting her foot in her mouth every opportunity she got. As soon as she looked at the camera, she was a different person: she wasn't the Emily that everyone knew, she was just really laid-back and there wasn't any pep in her voice or anything.
**-DEVIN**

**wants to stop a certain habit and they can't, then they don't have very much control over their own body and mind.**

I noticed that one of the anchormen wore his nice suit with silly jogging shoes and white socks. It looked so ridiculous that I had to make a comment. He told me that he also wore jeans when he did the news. **I had to ask him, of course, if he had ever delivered the news naked.** But he never had. I asked one of the camerawomen if she had done it naked, too, but she hadn't.

**Tim was really playing the part of the reporter—he was running through the streets, yelling, "We're on deadline, get out of the way!" He was yelling at cars; he was yelling at people; he was yelling at dogs.**
**-EMILY**

When Emily was done telling about South by Southwest Music and Media Festival, she tossed the word back to the anchorwoman in the studio, who revealed the next clue. **-CHRISTIAN**

Effie tried to turn the tables and she asked me, "What kind of control do you have over your life?" She stated the fact that I really don't know what I'm going to be doing when this field trip is over. But the fact of the matter is, I'm going to do whatever I want to do. So that's about as much control as you can get. **-TIMMY**

**CLUE**

C

**FOX 7 NEWS**

**THE NEXT MISSION FOR THE ROAD RULES CREW IS TO WIN THE DERBY! THEY HAVE THREE DAYS TO GET TO RED RIVER, NEW MEXICO, AND CONTACT WALLY DOBBS. GOOD LUCK!**

**LIVE PALMER AUDITORIUM**

**NAME:** Carmen Valera
**TITLE:** Television newscaster
**MOTTO:** "Plan for everything there is, and then expect for all to go wrong."

**FOX 7 NE...**

News reporting was different than many of the other ROAD RULES missions because in order to get the job done, the group had to split up a little bit. The whole idea was to entirely produce a piece for television: write it, report it, edit it, and put the finished package on the air. It was left up to them to decide who would do each role. You could see their personalities come out as they fought for a while over who would do the stand-up; naturally, the most aggressive of the bunch won out.

It was a pretty intensive experience, because they had to learn everything in one day. They didn't realize how much work was going to be involved, and I think they expected some of the stuff to be done for them. When they figured out they were going to have to do it themselves, they became very intense and got to work. Effie, for example, had two hours to learn how to edit before Emily's report came in for editing, and she did a pretty good job. When the segment aired it was pretty clean.

Reporting is not a glamorous business at all. But if you're thinking about making a career of it, I highly recommend finding a company that you want to work for and getting an internship or an entry-level position there. I started out working as a production assistant and running camera on the floor. I proved myself that way, then I worked my way up.

Christian and I do a lot of senseless babbling together. We talk about Americana and repeat certain phrases endlessly. Earlier in the field trip, we came across some lines from the movie AIRPLANE! and it's been growing and growing ever since. We'd been on a quest for quite some time to get this movie, and in Austin, we found it. With tax, I believe it cost about $16.24. Worth every penny of Christian's money. It's a real hot item. I think there's four left in circulation in America. The others were burned. So that's half the battle. Now we have to watch it somewhere.

Right after we came from our successful shopping venture, we got a page that said, "Meet me and not 'us' at County Line Restaurant at 7:30." We all thought that it was Christian's dad, because we knew he was in the States. At the restaurant, Christian was sitting with his back to the door, and he was making me crazy turning around every five seconds, so I finally said, "Shut up, already," and traded seats with him. **-TIMMY**

# Dad

I was just sitting there watching Christian, with a big smile on his face, hugging his dad. And I could tell he was getting ready to cry, he was so happy to see him. We all just sat there and kind of smiled. We really enjoyed seeing Christian that happy. His dad was great; Christian and he are exactly the same. They talked the same, and I understand Christian a lot better after meeting his dad. **-EMILY**

When we got the page, I more or less knew it was my father. I tried not to communicate that to the others, but I knew that it was my father. I knew he was in the country. He's just as curious as me and he was curious about the other four people and how I live. I just had the feeling that it was going to be my dad; it couldn't have been anybody else.

The first thing my dad did after he hugged me was spill a glass of water all over himself, which was kind of funny, because the others have made much out of me spilling orange juice and sodas a couple of times. Tim was quiet at dinner, and I think that was kind of strange. I couldn't believe he thought he couldn't joke with my father.

Dad had presents for all of us. He brought me a pair of underwear, which everyone thought was very funny, since they like to tease me about my underwear lying around the Winnie. But I didn't care; I like that he brought me a pair of underwear, because that's what you need on a trip, a pair of clean underwear.

## Seeing Dad made me think about going home and seeing all of my friends there.

My Norwegian friends might be exceptional, because I try to choose friends that are like me—a little wacky, as you say. In the past couple years I have come to understand that I'm nothing without my friends. They mean very much to me. On this trip, I've discovered that what I miss most about Norway is being in my own safe environment. It's wonderful to travel, and it's wonderful to come back home, too. **-CHRISTIAN**

**AUSTIN**
POPULATION:
465,622
NICKNAME:
"Live Music Capital of the World"
POPULAR HANGOUTS:
Ruby's BBQ, 311 Club, Emo's
HOMETOWN OF:
Janis Joplin, Stevie Ray Vaughan, Ethan Hawke, Junior Brown
FAMOUS RESIDENTS:
Al Jourgensen, lead singer of Ministry; The Butthole Surfers
TRIVIA:
The city's laid-back college

**HOW CHRISTIAN DESCRIBES CHRISTIAN**
Curious
Creative—full of devices
Energetic
Somewhat crazy

BARTON SPRINGS

The coolest place to retreat from sticky-hot Austin afternoons is located southwest of the city center, in Zilker Park. Swim in the refreshingly cold 1,000-foot-long, 200-foot-wide spring-fed watering hole, and chill in the shade of the walnut and pecan trees.

# Christian

Christian's underwear is a regular topic of conversation with us. His underwear is always wet, and it's always lying around the Winnie. Timmy teases that he takes showers in it. I think it all started when we were in Bimini and I had a problem with him diving in the water in his underwear. Ever since then, the wet underwear jokes just seem to come naturally.

Christian's a very positive person. He's always hyper. Even right before he goes to bed, he never dies down. In the beginning I was kind of concerned about him, because he takes a lot of the things we say too personally. He doesn't know when we're joking until we say, "We're joking." His has been the personality I've had the most trouble figuring out.

**-EMILY**

## Our personalities are so similar; I believe Christian could be the Timmy of Norway.

I created a monster, he created a monster. Together, we are Frankenstein, Jekyll, and Hyde. Whatever goes on in our heads is magnified when we are in each other's presence. We both got the goofy chromosome in the gene pool. We entertain ourselves by entertaining others. He does a good job of making people smile, which is pretty much my lifelong goal. The biggest difference between us is: I'm white and he's really white. Also, I'm more laid-back than Christian. He tends to be the button-down-shirt and business-suit type. He's always wearing a very nice shirt, even when we go bike riding. I'm the sweatpants, T-shirt, big-wad-of-bubble-gum type. He has his own stuff, his own sleeping bag, his own makeup, and I'm like, "I'll sleep on that bench tonight." Ultimately, Christian is a down-to-earth person with true feelings; he cares about the people around him, and he makes sure they know that. For example, when the show started, he had T-shirts for all of us, and he gave me a tie from his business school—it's nothing, but it's everything. Christian is the epitome of thoughtfulness.

**-TIMMY**

Christian says, "It's all good," "It's all great," and "It's out of town" over and over again. He says, "I agree" four hundred million times a day. He says thank you after everything. Or "I'm sorry" or "Excuse me." He's just so damn sugar-sweet he's giving us all cavities. We have to make a real effort not to tease him too much, but he can handle it.

**-DEVIN**

Christian—he's so cute, and obviously he's very, very happy. It's a bit weird for me to be around him, but I kind of like it. He's a good influence. He is also very kind. When this trip is over and I try to imagine Christian, I'll always remember him putting his head on my shoulder as if to say, "I'm here if you want me." He's happy all the time. So we're happy and we're laughing all the time. I always thought that Norwegians were pretty stiff; you know, pretty cold and uptight. Then there's Christian saying, "Hey, dude!" Sometimes I think it's a big rig. Maybe he's the Israeli and I'm the Norwegian.

**-EFFIE**

**CHRISTIAN'S TOP THREE WAYS TO GET OUT OF A TRAFFIC TICKET**

1. Speak like a madman in Norwegian
2. Get naked and jump in the nearest river
3. Blame it on Tenje Sølsnes and Toppen Beck!

**CHRISTIAN'S FAVORITE THINGS**

Sports
Doing abnormal things
Being out with friends
Partying
"Projects"

## MISSION NUMBER 10
### SNOW-BOX DERBY

The night we came into Red River we found out that different people in the town were making snow boxes–giant, crazy sleds–out of old skis and strange materials for a snow-box derby. We built a very fine racing machine and won an award for Most Congenial Sled. –CHRISTIAN

**OBJECTIVE:** Beat a couch, a refrigerator, a reclining chair, and other household furniture in a downhill ski race

**TOOLS:** Picnic table, garbage can, food, fire extinguisher, three pairs of skis, patience, and a long stick for a brake

**HAZARDS:** 16 heavy, careening objects with no brakes or steering devices; the competition's hard-hitting snowballs

**B** Our money situation going into Red River was not too good. All of our individual funds were kind of low and our group fund was somewhere under a $100. **–EFFIE**

Red River looked like a strange combination of Norwegian mountains and the Wild West, with tiny stores and bars and so on.

We came there very late and stayed in the usual hotel parking lot. We talked with a receptionist and asked if we could see AIR-PLANE! in one of the hotel rooms. She said yes, so we brought the others and we watched the movie. Timmy and I had a blast. We thought it was very extremely funny. We were almost too excited about it.

The next morning, we met a guy named Wally, and he gave us $50 to make a snow box. My first impression of Wally was not much. I found out later that he's in many ways the same kind of guy that I'm gonna be when I'm 50 or 60—dating younger girls, like 25, and having a good time skiing a lot and enjoying life.

Back in Norway, when I was a little child, I loved to build tiny cottages and go-carts on my own. I guess that's why I took charge of building the snow box. We managed to find a total of six pairs of skis and I got the idea that if we attached those to the picnic table, it would go very fast. And it worked out. Tim thought my idea with the picnic table was a pretty good one. I think Devin liked it, too. Emily was not quite sure what she thought; she wanted us to build a shark or something. And Effie—at first she was like, "No way, uh-uh, I don't like it, I don't even want to talk about it, stay away." **–CHRISTIAN**

## 2891 MILES TRAVELED

**C** Wally sent us to find a guy named Swag in his workshop, where we were going to build the snow box. Christian and Tim found a picnic table and decided that was what we'd build upon. Effie and I thought that was just too easy. We wanted to put a lot of sweat into it. We were like, "Wow, guys, slow down, you haven't even talked to us about this idea." But after a while I warmed up to it and decided that if everyone else was gonna go with it, I would compromise. But Effie just kind of bulled up. I never heard any suggestions out of her mouth at all. She was only willing to say what she didn't like. And I think that's what really pissed us all off.

I didn't want to get into a big knock-down-drag-out fight with her so I just went to the Winnie to cool off. While I was gone, Effie and Devin and the entire group got into it, and the last thing I heard was that Effie said I was spoiled. It pissed me off that she never said anything like that to my face. **–EMILY**

**The thing is, I trust these people, I really like them, I take all my guards down, and then they hurt me.**

My conclusion from this snow box argument was that I will never again let anyone get to me the way I let Devin get to me. I thought he was my friend, but he's not my friend. Friends don't yell at friends the way he yelled at me. From now on I'm gonna be a bitch, and this way no one will get to me. I will not be vulnerable, and if somebody's gonna get hurt, it's not gonna be me. **–EFFIE**

My argument with Effie was about her negative attitude toward what we were doing. I don't know if it was that night or the night after, but she was sitting in front of the fire in the clubhouse, crying, and I was kind of shocked. I was like, "You need a hug? You want to talk? I mean, what?" And she sort of hugged me, then told me and Timmy to leave. That's OK. We don't have to be best friends, but we don't have to be enemies, either. **–DEVIN**

**KEY TO SYMBOLS**

.....sleep in Winnie
.....sleep in motel
.....money trail
.....welcome to
M .....mission
.....danger
? .....lost

Red River
64
25
84 Amarillo
Las Vegas
40 27
NM
Lubbock
84
TX
20 183
Austin

3

## A good name for our snow box might have been Andy Warhol Eats Dinner at a Bingo Parlor.

It had a bedsheet for a brake and about 12 skis to run on, plus various decorations. No one was really steering or trying to go in any direction or order. We just wanted to raise hell. As soon as Devin lightened the load by falling off, we started going haywire on the slopes. When we hit the bottom, no one even knew who had won the race, but some people were ticked off that we threw eggs and ruined their clothes. It's safe to say that an all-out snowball war broke out when we accepted our award for Most Congenial Sled. Inside our trophy there was a tape with our next clue.

Christian and Effie decided to stay with Wally the last night in Red River. Christian wasn't feeling good and wanted to stay in a warm house instead of the cold Winnie, and Effie decided she was gonna crash on the couch. They both returned the next morning with some serious goods. Effie got a really nice ski jacket from Wally, and Christian got a ski vest and a ski patrol hat. We were kind of wondering what went on at Wally's place that night that they got all of these cool gifts.

**RED RIVER**
POPULATION: 387
NICKNAME: "Dead Liver," because one out of every 40 citizens owns a liquor license
MUST DO: Ski at the Wild Rivers Recreational Area, one of the largest ski resorts in the country
POPULAR HANGOUTS: Motherlode Saloon, Texas Red's Steakhouse
TALK OF THE TOWN: Heavy tourism in the summer due to the relatively cool temperatures (about 75 degrees). "The hotter it gets in Texas or Oklahoma, the busier Red River gets in the summer."-Wally Dobbs

**3732 MILES TRAVELED**

**CLUE**
YOUR NEXT JOB'S A REAL BALL. GET TO PHOENIX MUNICIPAL STADIUM IN TWO DAYS. THAT SHOULD BE JUST ENOUGH TIME TO TEACH CHRISTIAN AND EFRAT "THE STAR SPANGLED BANNER." TEDDY SANTIAGO OF THE ATHLETICS HAS YOUR ASSIGNMENTS. BATTER UP!

After Red River, we had like $60 or $70 in the group fund, and individually I think I had $10 and Effie had $20. But Christian was doing real well after Red River, because he hopped buck-naked in this freezing-cold lake for $50, and Wally actually paid him for it.
-TIMMY

**RED RIVER FESTIVALS**
The Wheeler Pig Mountain Run is a challenging 11-mile race that takes place every June.
Mardi Gras on the Mountain takes place every February.
The Red River Memorial Day celebration draws thousands of Harley-Davidson riders every year.
Aspencade, the Red River Country Festival, attracts country folk and country vendors alike. City dwellers are welcome, too.

NAME: Wally Dobbs
TITLE: Director, Red River events
MOTTO: "If you don't have any rules, then people can't cheat."

The snow-box derby was something that we had been talking about doing in Red River to make spring break more fun. When they got into this, I think the crew from ROAD RULES thought we'd been doing it for years; they were a little concerned when I told them this was the first snow-box derby ever. The only rules were: the sled had to be on skis, it had to have some type of a body, and it had to have somebody in it or on it. I gave the ROAD RULES guys $50 to build a snow box, and they sort of cheated because they got all their materials for free and spent the money on groceries.

They decided they'd put a picnic table on skis. Christian was the engineer. Effie was the grunt, going around getting paint and looking for a candelabra to put on the table. Emily was the "I'll cook, you work" type and Tim was the money guy. It was like a five-person company where everybody had a department.

On the back of their picnic table, they built a little patio. On the patio, they had a garbage can. And in the garbage can, they had all this food they planned to throw at people. We did a Le Mans start, where the racers had to run, jump on their item, and sled down the hill. Once they were on, they started nailing the other racers with eggs and whipped cream and whatever else they had. I couldn't believe how undirected and unscripted it was. I couldn't quit laughing. I'd never seen anything come off so funny in my life.

Many National Parks in the Rocky Mountain area specifically state that sex in the outdoors is not advisable, especially in grizzly territory. Grizzly bears can detect and are drawn to sex-related smells from miles away.

Timmy has told me his story about being arrested for skinny-dipping, and I think it's a crazy thing to arrest somebody for that. It is a shame that he lost his mascot job over such a little thing, but if he hadn't, he might not be on this trip with us. —CHRISTIAN

A

B

**3732** MILES TRAVELED

# Timmy's Flashback

C

The whole way to Phoenix, I was beside myself. I couldn't believe I was going to be back on the field, involved with baseball, and in front of a crowd again. I didn't think I would get another chance to do this in my lifetime. Why? You'd better get comfortable.

My last semester in college, I got auditioned for the Pittsburgh Pirates mascot, and I got the job. I was there to provide entertainment during the peak moments of the baseball game. I went through the crowds and had a good time with them, just keeping their spirits alive. So there I was, instantly this minicelebrity in Pittsburgh. Hometown boy makes good. Have you ever made 10,000 people laugh at one time? I can't explain to you

that feeling. It was a feeling that I wanted to have for the rest of my life. It prepared me for so much. It gave me the confidence to do whatever I wanted, and that, to me, was freedom.

Well, everything changed one night when me and my friends sneaked into a public pool for a skinny-dip and the cops came. All kinds of cops. Everyone scattered, but I didn't care, I thought, "What are they gonna do? Tell me to go home? No big deal." On the other side of the building, they busted a girl, a friend of mine. She was a

little bit ornery, I guess. I don't know exactly what she said to the cops, but they're weren't pleasant. They took us downtown, me and the girl. I thought it might actually be kind of interesting, my first time being arrested.

I guess someone at the station recognized my name, and they called the Pirates. As soon as that hit the fan, they made the biggest issue of

it. Someone spread the rumor that me and the girl were having sex in the pool. I don't know how these stories get out, but the media is warped, twisted, and powerful. First of all, how could you prove something like that? You'd have to be Jacques Cousteau with an underwater camera.

So I was charged with having sex in a public pool, and I was in jail forever—almost two nights and a day. I didn't call anyone except my sister, because I was supposed to work for her the next day. I asked her not to tell anyone, because my parents would flip. I had no idea what was going on outside the jail. I thought I would get out, and no one would ever know. But it was too late. I'd already lost my job, and the press was having a field day. It was the worst experience of my life, and this trip saved me from its aftermath.  —TIMMY

**KEY TO SYMBOLS**

⚠ ...........sleep in campsite

☻ ...........danger

🏠 ...........hometown stop

💻 ...........welcome to

M ...........mission

☺ ...........scamming/cheating

Flagstaff
40
Winslow
64
Red River
17
285
84
68
40
25
Phoenix
Albuquerque
AZ
NM

2

3

Tim

**4348** MILES TRAVELED

## Timmy is a good soul.

He's trying to make everyone happy, but the thing is that when you live with five people, you're not always happy. Actually, you don't have to live with five people to know that you're not always happy. A few moments in the day you want to be serious or sad or just alone. Timmy is never serious this way. We can start a serious conversation, and somewhere along the way, he will make a joke, and that's the end of our serious conversation. I have yet to see Timmy angry about something. It's not a way to live. You have to be angry sometimes and let everything out. I don't know. Maybe he's doing it in a different way.

What the heck, Timmy makes me laugh. And I like people who make me laugh. He does it not because he's just trying to be funny, but because he really wants to put a smile on other people's faces. Especially mine. And sometimes we get along perfectly and sometimes he pisses me off, but he's the only one I consider my friend from this group.

Sometimes people mistake our friendship for a romance, but I'm just a very touchy person, and when I like people, I hug them. So if I'm hugging Timmy, it's because he's my friend. **-EFFIE**

If there's one person I want to have as my friend for the rest of my life, it's going to be Tim. From the first moment I met him, I knew he would be the most interesting person on this trip to get to know. I've had plenty of conversations with him, and we have spent many hours doing funny stuff to keep ourselves busy. I just have to say that partying with Timmy is very much fun. It's hard to keep up with that guy, because he does a lot of funny stuff. I don't want to get sentimental, but I think that the trip for me personally is so good because of Timmy. We have argued a couple of times, too, because, of course, we are not the same person. We don't think exactly alike. Maybe close, though. **-CHRISTIAN**

Timmy's just different. A little crazy. He does everything big, but it's hard to tell when Timmy's performing, because Timmy IS a performer. A perfect example of Timmy's style is his tradition of drying his wet underwear on the horns on the hood of the Winnie. A couple times we've driven with the underwear flapping in the wind ahead of us. Timmy does weird things; that's just one of them. But he can be serious if you really, really need him to be. That's why Timmy's definitely someone I can open up to.

## I think of him as my big brother, and he would never let anything happen to me. -EMILY

I think in a lot of different ways I'm gonna miss Timmy more than anyone when this trip is over. He's the big brother that I never had. He's like me in that his exterior is so different from his interior. There have been times during this trip when I've pictured myself living with Timmy when it's all over. He's so resourceful and so on top of it—he's the kind of person I want in my corner. **-DEVIN**

C

D

### HOW TIMMY DESCRIBES TIMMY
Good-humored
Giving
Unpretentious
Competitive
Stubborn
Jovial

### TIMMY'S THREE WISHES
1. To take the ultimate road trip—to the moon!
2. To be able to travel in time
3. World tolerance

## JOB Spring Training

**MISSION:** Sing the national anthem, vend peanuts, work as a bat-girl, manage the scoreboard, sling colorful commentary

**TOOLS:** A deep voice, an apron, Oakland A's uniforms, keys to the batter's box

**HAZARDS:** Practical jokes, fly balls

**REWARD:** Cash

I heard on the radio that there was going to be a really big baseball game in Phoenix. So I thought we would take part in it somehow, and I was right. We went to the stadium and met this guy named Ted who told us we were going to earn some money working for him.

As soon as I got my uniform on, one of the players, Jim, told me that in order for the game to start, I had to go to the other team and ask for the keys to the batter's box and for a box of curveballs. I didn't understand a word of what he said, but I had this feeling that somebody was making big fun of me—again. I was right. After they sent me running in circles all over the field to get these balls, Jim told me that they do this prank on every new batboy. I was pissed for a few seconds. I was like, "I'm gonna kick your ass. Just wait for me after the game." But he was so sweet. He kept saying, "Are you pissed at me? Please don't be pissed at me." So I decided to be nice. **-EFFIE**

I was pretty much by myself the whole day—I didn't get to meet any of the players, though I heard that some of them were really nice. I didn't even get to hang around with the ushers, because they were too busy getting drunk behind the advertisements at the back of the field. I wouldn't have minded getting drunk out there in the sun. Worst of all, I had to wear another stupid uniform, and I smelled like peanuts at the end of the day. Everybody else had a really good time, though. Timmy was right at home doing PR and singing the anthem. Effie was a batgirl, and Emily was working the grounds crew—it was fun to watch her raking the dirt down on the diamond. We all missed Christian. He couldn't work because he was really, really sick from jumping in that pond in Red River. We had to keep him isolated in the back of the Winnie in a plastic bubble of sorts. He wasn't to have any contact with anyone, and he was just supposed to sleep and rest all he could. So he lay there and fondled his $50 for a couple hours. **-DEVIN**

Tim got up to sing "The Star Spangled Banner," and there weren't a lot of people in the stands yet, but I think they really enjoyed his performance. Not too many of them were holding their ears. The only time I saw Tim during the rest of the day was whenever he was on top of the players' dugouts doing promotional work—he was hurling T-shirts at the crowds with a slingshot and really making the crowd laugh. I think they really enjoyed him.

Before the fifth inning, I was taking a break from raking the field, and it just so happened that I found myself standing by the doorway to the players' locker room. Naturally I was curious, so I grabbed Effie and we went in there to look for some guys in jockstraps, but we didn't have any luck. They were all dressed for the game and playing some cards. I'd pictured a locker room filled with all kinds of naked men running around in towels and jockstraps, but it was pretty boring. **-EMILY**

### BASEBALL'S TOAST TO TAFT

In 1910 President Taft stood up during the seventh inning of a baseball game. The crowd, assuming that he was leaving, stood out of respect for the president. He soon sat down, followed by the crowd, thus leading to the birth of the seventh-inning stretch.

**PHOENIX**
POPULATION:
983,400

MUST SEE:
Hall of Flame Museum of
Firefighting, the world's
largest museum of firefighting
equipment and memorabilia

NOTORIOUS RESIDENT:
Vincent Furnier, lead singer of
'60s band the Spiders, who
once played regularly at the
VIP Club; Furnier took the
advice of a Ouija board and
changed his name to Alice
Cooper, then went on to fame

TRIVIA:
During the summer, the
temperature averages 100°
and lodging prices drop 70%

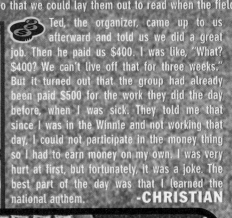

NAME: Ted Santiago
TITLE: Media relations manager,
the Oakland A's
MOTTO: "If you work hard, somebody
will notice it and good things
will happen."

My job is to handle
publicity for the A's, so
I write press releases,
set up player inter-
views, and travel with the team. There are only 28 jobs in the
country like mine, and I got where I am because I'm one of those
Never-give-up people. I pretty much started at the bottom, but I
was always on the lookout for opportunity. There's a lot of luck
involved, a lot of timing, and it's tough to launch a career in
baseball. Whether you want to play or be involved in management, you've got to be committed. There are other jobs you can
do if you like baseball but don't want to make a career of it. You
could be a ticket vendor or sell concessions, like Devin
did–although he was sort of upset, because he said he kept on
getting stuck with the s**tty jobs everywhere they went.

When the game was almost over, a guy came on the
intercom and told us to look in the stands for our next
clue. And so everyone in that section held up cards,
but all we could make out was R-O-A-D R-U-L-E-S and the rest of it was just garbled. Some people
had the cards upside down and some were shaking them a lot and it was just impossible. I think
they drank too many beers up there. Devin made a mad dash toward that section and collected
the cards from the audience so that we could lay them out to read when the field was cleared off.

Ted, the organizer, came up to us
afterward and told us we did a great
job. Then he paid us $400. I was like, "What?
$400? We can't live off that for three weeks."
But it turned out that the group had already
been paid $500 for the work they did the day
before, when I was sick. They told me that
since I was in the Winnie and not working that
day, I could not participate in the money thing
so I had to earn money on my own. I was very
hurt at first, but fortunately, it was a joke. The
best part of the day was that I learned the
national anthem.
**-CHRISTIAN**

**BELOVED
BATS**

Babe Ruth liked knots in
his bats, Joe DiMaggio
rubbed all his bats with
olive oil, and Joe Jackson
slept with his bat. In the
early days, players were
always searching for ways
to improve and lighten
their bats, such as shav-
ing wood from the barrel,
shaving the handle, and
corking (hollowing the
bat and replacing the
center with cork). The
aluminum bat, introduced
in 1970, lasts longer, hits
harder, and is lighter
than the wooden bat.

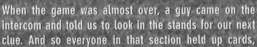

# CLUE C

ROAD RULES.
X MARKS THE
SPOT FOR YOUR
NEXT CLUE.
N. 33 DEGREES.
294 LATITUDE
BY W. 109 DEGREE
31.861 LONITUDE.
GPS WILL SHOW
THE WAY.

I rarely separated myself from the group,
but one of the best solo times I can think of
was in Phoenix, when I rode my bike I don't
know how many miles to Mount McDowell
and climbed up. I was on top of this mountain, and you could see Scottsdale, you
could see Tempe. You could see the lights. I
was so high up there. Wildlife everywhere. In a place like
that, all you do is sit and think, "This is it."
**-TIMMY**

**MONUMENT VALLEY
TRIBAL PARK**

These towering mesas and
rocks, located on the Utah-
Arizona border, are owned by
a Navajo Indian reservation.
They often serve as cinematic
backdrops for films set in the
Southwest.

Things between Devin and Emily were very very tense in Phoenix, and we were happy to move on and make a new start. We knew we were going to Moab, because we'd figured out the coordinates—north 38, west 109.  —EFFIE

**2**

I was looking forward to spending some time alone with Devin—that is, without Ms. Pac Man. He's been having an affair with Ms. Pac Man for quite a while, and I was glad she wasn't around. I thought that maybe after this campout with me, he'd like me more than her. Well, I don't get to see very many sunsets in Illinois, and the last sunset I remember seeing was in Bimini, on Shell Beach. There we were in the desert, surrounded by mountains, and I wanted to go watch a beautiful sunset with Devin. He didn't seem remotely interested. He made up all these excuses about why he couldn't go, and when he finally followed me out there, I don't think he even saw the sunset. It kind of hurt my feelings that he couldn't just sit there with me for 15 minutes and at least ACT like he was having a good time. I was beginning to sense that he was distancing himself from me.

That night, we were going to cook out; it was going to be the first time the five of us were together doing nothing in a long time. I was sitting down on the curb, trying to think things through and calm down, when Devin walked up and said, "Is there something we need to talk about?" I was searching for the right words. I was trying to think of a tactful way to come out and say that it hurt me that he was calling his ex-girlfriend Amy up all the time. I didn't want to come off as a jealous girlfriend, so I didn't say anything. Then he accused me of playing games. He said, "Fine, if you just want to play games for a while longer, we can." And that really hurt me. I really wanted to solve the problem right then and there.  —EMILY

**4348** MILES TRAVELED

## Fast Friends

KEY TO SYMBOLS

⚠ ............sleep in campsite
☠ ............danger
⌂ ............hometown stop
⎙ ............welcome to
Ⓜ ............mission
☻ ............scamming/cheating

**C**

**B**

It sucks to sleep alone. Nobody wants to sleep alone every day. So I had made it a point that we shouldn't go to bed angry. There's no point in arguing overnight and then picking up the argument in the morning. But she wanted to suck back some beers and sleep alone, so she slept in the Winnie and I slept in the tent.

Part of my personality is that I don't just drink to be drinking. There was a campfire, and everybody was having a good time. There was really no need to be drinking. Every night that we've been at that campsite, she's consistently been drinking. I don't think it's my place to pass judgment, but my opinion is that it's not cool. Especially if there's something in the air that needs to be dealt with; she can't deal with it if she's had six beers. I knew she was upset that I've been talking to Amy lately, but I couldn't talk to her about it. If we had done any talking that night, I wouldn't have been talking to Emily, I'd have been talking to some piece of her, the piece that still had her feet on the ground, not the piece that was floating high.  —DEVIN

UT

Moab ★

160  191

163

Flagstaff

89

17

Phoenix

AZ

**3**

I'm think Emily's got a problem. It seems that Devin still has a connection with his ex-girlfriend, and Emily's kind of caught in the middle. She came to me for advice, I guess because I'm older and have had a really long relationship with someone. I was surprised and happy that she wanted my advice. I told her she really had to ask Devin to give her a definition: What exactly is Emily for Devin and Devin for Emily? **-EFFIE**

Whenever one of us is really down in the dumps, we all kind of rally around the person, try and help them through their way. Emily was pretty much down in the dumps that night in Phoenix. They're kind of on the rocks, and, well, hell, we've all been there, so we all reached out to her as best as we could. But I don't know enough about their relationship to really get involved. I don't know what's going on, so I talked to both. I don't think Emily really knows where she stands in Devin's life and I think Devin is just stuck between two worlds: the one back home and the world he's living in right now. **-TIMMY**

**B**

# Fading

**4801** MILES TRAVELED

It's OK to argue and stuff. It's natural. But sometimes I think that we should all step outside the Winnie and remind ourselves what we are doing here. We're five people, strange to each other, but pretty much friends, and in a couple weeks we're not gonna see each other anymore. I was thinking this as we went through some spectacular landscapes on the drive from Arizona to Utah. There was a place called Monument Valley, where the rocks went up in the air so high it was unbelievable. We also stopped by the road where some Native Americans were selling souvenirs, and I bought a tomahawk. When I get back to Norway, I will use it in a ritual to remember all the stuff I learned in America. It was very hot, so we went dipping in a wonderful river and met this dog that had a crush on the dead horn on the front of the Winnebago.

I've traveled through Europe and many different countries, and of course I think my own country, Norway, is the best; it's very pure and untouched. But now, almost at the end of this trip, I feel that this country has so much to offer. It's more diverse in the landscapes and the people than I thought. **- CHRISTIAN**

**D**

## MOUNTAIN MAD

WOMBATS—Women's Mountain Bike and Tea Society—is a mountain-biking club that organizes rides and races exclusively for women.

The National Off Road Bicycle Association has more than 30,000 registered members, whose primary interest is racing.

Even though it was invented in the US, mountain biking is still dominated by the Europeans.

It's the law that professional mountain bike racers wear helmets.

Moab, UT, and Durango, CO, are two of the most popular mountain-biking sites in the US.

Ski resorts are following the craze by opening their lifts and trails to bikes in the summer.

**6**

### CANDLEBOX'S
TOP TEN ROAD TRIPPIN' CDs

1.................Tripl 3 Fast Action, BROADCASTER
2..........................Seaweed, SPANAWAY
3.........The Flaming Lips, CLOUDS TASTE METALLIC
4.................Truly, FAST STORIES...FROM KID COMA
5......Fig Dish, THAT'S WHAT LOVE SONGS OFTEN DO
6.................Marvin Gaye, WHAT'S GOING ON
7..........................Chavez, GONE GLIMMERING
8................Pink Floyd, DARK SIDE OF THE MOON,
                      WISH YOU WERE HERE
9...................No Doubt, TRAGIC KINGDOM
10..........................Abba, GOLD

# MISSION
## NUMBER 11
## SLICK ROCK RIDE

In Moab we spent a lot of time just admiring the nature and riding our bikes. We used our computerized map to help us find our next clue, a jack-in-the-box. —CHRISTIAN

When we arrived in Moab I slept on the roof of the Winnie—I've done that a couple of times now. Unfortunately I tend to have problems sleeping on the roof. If it's not raining, it's very windy, and that night it was very, very, very windy, and I almost fell off the roof. **-CHRISTIAN**

**OBJECTIVE:** Find your next clue on Slick Rock Trail

**TOOLS:** Handheld computerized navigator, mountain bikes, helmets, yellow kneesocks

**HAZARDS:** Treacherous trails and slippery rocks

By the time the day of the mission came around, it was pretty obvious that we were going to be mountain biking, and of course, it was going to be at Slick Rock—the best mountain biking in America. **I heard rumors about the Slick Rock trail in the town.** They said it was dangerous. The declines and inclines came at you every 5 feet. The trail was marked with white dots, which were crucial, because there were some bends that dropped off so steeply they could kill you. This was my ideal mission. It was an opportunity to act physically and mentally at once.

After riding for a while, we came up over a ridge and met an awesome sight: the walls of a giant canyon looming above us. The echo was unbelievable, and you could see a little creek down below in the trees. We hopped on our bikes and began walking toward the edge. Naturally, Christian was the first one there. We sat and looked down at the different sculptures in the rocks and the trees, and of course, when you're sitting on an edge this high, you have to spit to see how long it takes to hit the bottom. It took a while. **-TIMMY**

DANGER

**MOAB**
POPULATION:
4,000
POPULAR HANGOUTS:
Moab Diner, Eddie McStiff's Brewery
TRIVIA:
Flourished in the '50s due to uranium discoveries by prospector Charlie Sheen
MUST SEE:
Hole 'n the Rock: 5,000-square-foot, 14-room former home of Albert Christensen, who spent 20 years carving it out of solid sandstone; also, the Hollywood Stuntman's Hall of Fame
FANFARE:
The Moab Fat Tire Festival, held during the last week of October, is the best-known mountain-bike festival in the US

When we spotted the clue, everyone raced. I rode like a maniac on my bike, and I was first. Of course, I waited for the others to come so we could open it together. The box was huge, wrapped in paper, with many, many smaller boxes inside. Finally, we came to a little jack-in-the-box that popped up and gave us our next clue—to go to Las Vegas, Nevada.

At that point we were only two miles or so into the trail. The girls wanted to go back, and Devin and Tim and I wanted to go another 10 miles. So we split up and continued all the way, and that was even more fantabulous. This time, we saw an even bigger canyon, and the Colorado River floating through it. **-CHRISTIAN**

## CLUE

IF YOU THOUGHT THIS WAS HARD, YOUR NEXT MISSION IS A REAL DOGFIGHT. YOU HAVE TWO DAYS TO REACH LAS VEGAS AND LOCATE THE DESERT ACES.

In Moab, the Winnie got extra dirty, just wrecked, completely totaled. I was cleaning up, and I found a used condom of Devin's. Everybody was laughing about Devin and Emily, but we were making big fun of Devin. We kept asking him, "Why did you put it underneath the mattress? Couldn't you have thrown it in the garbage?" Emily was so embarrassed she turned around and ran out of the Winnie. **-EFFIE**

After the mission was accomplished, Emily pulled me aside to ask me a pretty big question. She wanted to know if I want to continue something with her at the end of the trip. And I can't answer that question any more than I could have answered it at the beginning of the trip. It would seem really shallow to say that what I've got with Emily is just a road relationship, but basically, this relationship isn't reality—on one hand, it's really down-to-earth, and on the other hand, it's just like make-believe. I feel like we could go one way or the other. We could realize that we don't want to get into this at the present time, and end it and remain friends. Or we could try and continue it and let it get deeper, and run the risk of ending our friendship. And I'm leaning more toward the first than the second. **-DEVIN**

## What's Important

The next day was the beginning of Passover, a Jewish holiday. You celebrate the first day of Passover with a seder, a big meal at sundown. I wanted to leave Moab really, really early that morning so I could get to Vegas in time to call the Jewish community and hopefully get invited to a seder.

I didn't expect anyone else to feel how important this was, but Timmy got it. He woke up with me, and we left on time. On our way to Vegas I called and spoke with a rabbi, and he gave me this lady's number and told me that she was having a seder. I called her and she said that she would be very happy to have me.

The main thing about Passover is that we're trying to remember the period when God took the Israeli people out of Egypt, where they were slaves, and walked them to the desert toward Israel, where He made them a nation. **-EFFIE**

**SLICK ROCK**
The Moab Slick Rock bike trail, laid out in 1969 by a group of motor-bikers, is a 10.3-mile loop that traverses an expanse of rugged, rolling sandstone. The Navaho sandstone, formed millions of years ago from the hardening of the ancient sand dunes, provides excellent traction for bikers—despite its name. The trail is known for its cliffs, which provide beautiful views of the Negro Bill Canyon and the main canyon of the Colorado River.

**SOUTHERN UTAH'S NATIONAL PARKS**
Canyonlands, Arches, Capital Reef, Bryce Canyon, and Zion are all within a two-hour drive of Moab. Each of the five is breathtaking.

We made it to Vegas in time for Effie to hit seder and for me and Christian to double the group fund at the casinos. Next we played some war games at the Desert Aces. Then we squeezed in another visit to the Vegas strip, because Effie missed it the first time. —TIMMY

When we got to Vegas, me and Christian sat in front of the computer and found the direction to the seder house. I explained the meaning of seder to Timmy and invited him to come with me, but he felt uncomfortable, because this was not the normal environment for him. It was totally his call, but as far as I'm concerned, everybody was welcome to come to seder. It was probably for the better, because I would have been insulted if he and Christian had come and not behaved themselves. I'm not a religious person, but this is my history.

Mira, who held the seder, was a really nice lady. Her family was totally different from my family—we're Orthodox, by the book, and they were not traditional at all. Still, they read all the things they were supposed to read and they ate everything they were supposed to eat and we sang songs. I can't even try to explain how important it was for me. -EFFIE

Christian and my idea of gambling was to start slow and work our way up. Our main goal was to double the group fund. Why not try and live comfortably? We started off easy, with just nickel and quarter slots and pulls, and I hit something like $20, so I thought, "Well, that's enough money to build on." From there we played the roulette wheel and broke even. Then we decided to try our hand at blackjack. That turned out to be pretty profitable. I would definitely say that we had a night of beginner's luck. We started with $10 and we made eight times that. It was a hoot to see Christian's reaction to the experience. He thought it was the best—winning money. He considered taking money from other people to be beating them at their own game.
-TIMMY

4801 MILES TRAVELED

WELCOME TO NEVADA
125 YEARS OF VISION

DESERT ACES

KEY TO SYMBOLS

🏠 ..................sleep in Winnie
❤ ...........................romance
💰 ...................money trail
🏁 .........................welcome to
M .................................mission
〰〰〰 ...empty Winnie septic tank
? .................................lost

## MISSION NUMBER 12

## FIGHTER PLANES

**OBJECTIVE:** Fly a real plane in a mock dogfight against a fellow Road Ruler

**HAZARDS:** Airsickness

**TOOLS:** Italian-built Marchetti S260 trainers, cool flight suits

**REWARD:** The winner is the Desert Ace

When we came to the Desert Aces at the airport, we met the owner, Nancy, and the two pilots, R.P. and Snake. All three had flown jet fighters in the Air Force for many years, and they knew what they were doing, fortunately. Right away it seemed to me that the language barrier between Effie and the pilots made her uncomfortable. She kept having to ask R.P. to repeat himself, because she didn't understand him, and I thought maybe she was worried that the same thing would happen up in the plane. So she got a little weird and quiet, and I knew my battle against her wasn't gonna last long.

I had the false impression that we were gonna be flying high-tech planes like the ones we saw in the briefing room. What we actually flew were propeller planes, the kind where you feel everything times ten. What had me really uncomfortable was that I couldn't hear Snake through my big hair and the helmet, which wasn't made to accommodate hair, let alone dreads. We turned the volume all the way up on my receiver and I still couldn't hear him. So by the end of the flight we had resorted to hand signals. Basically I was flying blind.

NV

UT

Fillmore
191
70
15
Moab
Las Vegas

I felt sick and nervous the minute they told me I would be flying this plane. I tried to get used to it up in the air, but I felt so bad. I lost my vision, I couldn't focus, I had a terrible headache, I was totally dizzy, and I couldn't feel my hands. -EFFIE

I was still trying to get my equilibrium when we got radioed from the other plane to turn around because Effie was done, she was out.
-DEVIN

**FIGHTER PLANES**
The US Air Force used Aermacchi Marchetti S260s as primary trainers in 1991 and 1992. The Air Force has since switched to the Swisscraft PC9 and the British Slingsby T3s, but Aermacchis are currently flown as frontline fighters in several developing countries.

I really hoped that I could dogfight Timmy—I would have spanked his butt. But Emily got to him first, so he was out of the game. Emily kicked Devin's butt next, and then it was my turn. By this time, Emily had a bunch of experience, and boy did she have self-confidence. I must admit, waiting five hours to fly was not too good for me. On the runway I already didn't feel well, and I hate that, because I wanted to experience the whole thing 100 percent.

I tried to beat her, and I won the first battle, but I was very dizzy by the second battle, and I couldn't hang with her. I guess I'm not that good of a loser after all. I was wearing the Norwegian flag on the side of my helmet, and by the time I came back to the ground, I wished it was an Israeli flag or Polish flag, so I wouldn't have to feel I'd let my country down. I'm sorry, Norway.

When the air combat was finally over, we got certificates of accomplishment, and on the back of Emily's certificate our next clue was revealed. We were going to Hollywood, California. Thank goodness, because I bet Tim that if we didn't go there, I would walk back to Norway naked.

**-CHRISTIAN**

**5258** MILES TRAVELED

Pulling G's is a great feeling—one minute it feels like you can't get out of your seat even if you try your hardest, and the next minute you just float right off it. It was a great feeling to whip Timmy, Devin, and Christian and then land the plane and rub it in their faces for a while. I was completely exhausted. I'd been in the air nine times, and my neck was killing me, but I don't think I've ever been that cocky in my life. I don't think cockiness is very attractive, but I couldn't help it.

As far as our next mission, I think it's gonna have something to do with the movies, but I don't know what. On top of the clue, we got our next puzzle piece, in the shape of an airplane. We only have one more piece left in our puzzle. It looks like an upside-down cruise ship. Hopefully the ultimate mission will be to work on a cruise ship for a while, maybe go to Hawaii. But since we started in the southernmost point, it would also be cool to finish in the northernmost point of America. It's pretty cold up there, but I've always wanted to go to Alaska.

**-EMILY**

After we were done with our mission, we figured we were so close to Las Vegas that we should let Effie give it a go with the slot machines. It will suffice to say that our beginner's luck had worn off. We ended up back where we started when we arrived in Vegas, with about $60 in the group fund.

**-TIM**

C

**NAME:** Nancy Stone
**TITLE:** Owner, Desert Aces
**MOTTO:** "I feel safer in a combat than I do in a commercial airplane."

When people come to fly at Desert Aces, the first thing we do is put them in a flight suit. Then they go into a briefing, where we give them all the information they need about air-to-air combat. In the planes, which are Marchetti S260s, they have their own controls and they actually fly the missions. The instructor sits to the right and does all the hard work—the taking off, instrument reading, and landing.

The kids were real troupers. Of course, they were surprised when they found out what they were going to be doing, but after the shock wore off, they were great. I've seen over 8,000 people do this thing, and there are certain emotional steps that you go through, from disbelief to the adrenaline excitement to a little bit of fear. And each and every one of the kids did go through that. Emily started out with the call name Desert Levi's because she had Levi's for every event, but by the end of the day they were calling her Nails. They called her that because when she first heard what she was going to do, the nails went into the mouth. But by the end of the day, she was the Desert Ace; she flew hard as nails.

**CLUE** **ROAD KEY**

HOLLYWOOD: CLOSE TO THE FINAL FRONTIER... THIS IS THE VOYAGE OF THE ROAD RULES WINNY. ITS NEXT MISSION: TO SEEK OUT NEW STARS AND NEW CLUES...TO BOLDLY GO TO THE CHINESE THEATER...TO THE FOOTPRINTS OF THE [CREW] OF THE STARSHIP [ENTER]PRISE.

In LA we spent some time with Chris Farley, helping him on the set of his new movie. I was Chris's assistant, and nobody could be happy for me because, in my opinion, they were all jealous. —EFFIE

**A**

I'd been waiting my whole life to finally make it to California. Ironically, as we were crossing the state line from Nevada, the star that Devin had taped to the antenna way back in Memphis flew right off. The wind was blowing real hard, and I was actually watching the star and wondering to myself if that star's gonna come flying off, and just then it did. I don't know if there's any meaning behind that, but I imagined it was like one star leaving and five entering.
—TIMMY

**B**

**2**

On the way to Hollywood we got stopped by something called agricultural inspection, because they have to protect all of the orange plants in California from foreign insects. Tim told them we had a coconut, but we didn't tell them we brought it from the Bahamas, because they wouldn't like that. So we told them we brought it from Florida. They checked with a knife for little creatures. It was very important to us that we passed the coconut inspection, because we were planning to crack it at our final destination.

When we came down from the hills, we saw the beautiful city and the not-so-beautiful smog. We had to go to the walk of fame at Mann's Chinese Theater and meet a stranger who would give us our next clue. When we went to park the Winnie, they wanted $5, and we were totally broke, so we had to convince the attendant to let us park for free. Then we walked all around, looking everywhere for our next clue. Someone saw the STAR TREK footprints and they were pointing in the direction of a guy selling maps, so I figured maybe he had something to do with our clue. I tried to buy a map from him, but he wanted $6 for it and once again, we didn't have the money. We tried to bargain with him, we gave him all the change we had, and we even got some change from a passerby. Emily and Effie kept saying, "Leave the poor guy alone. Forget about the map," but I just knew this guy had something to do with us. Finally, he got tired of me and said, "Take the map." Inside was our next clue.
—CHRISTIAN

### CLUE

**MEET YOUR NEW BOSS ON WEDNESDAY, APRIL 10, AT 5:30 P.M. AT NORRIS INDUSTRIES, 5214 S. BOYLE, VERNON, CALIFORNIA (GET PLENTY OF REST–YOU'LL BE WORKING ALL NIGHT).**

## 5258
### MILES TRAVELED

### KEY TO SYMBOLS

..............conflict

..............sidetrip

..............money trail

..............welcome to

..............mission

....empty Winnie septic tank

..............sleep in Winnie

**NV**

**CA**

**Las Vegas**

10   15

**Los Angeles**

**C**

## Venice Beach was all about the sun, the sand, the women, the freaks, and the skating.

When we got there, we all decided to split up. Everybody had their own thing that they wanted to do. Timmy wanted to play ball; I've seen him play a couple of times, and he's actually pretty good. Effie wanted to do some shopping. She fits in to the whole Venice thing, because she's kind of retro. Christian wanted to hop directly in the water. Emily was into walking on the beach. And I definitely wanted to do some skating.
—DEVIN

MELROSE A
720

### FAMOUS FEET

The first footprints at the original Grauman's Chinese Theater were shaped by Norma Talmadge in 1927, when, as the legend goes, she accidentally stepped in wet concrete outside the building. Since then, 180 stars have followed suit. Some of the Chinese Theater sidewalk's more novel prints include Betty Grable's legs, John Wayne's fists, Whoopi Goldberg's braids, and odd-shaped feet from the cast of STAR TREK.

# MOVIE SET

**OBJECTIVE:** Assist Chris Farley, drive a golf cart, work the refreshment table, be a grip

**HAZARDS:** Practical jokes involving Cheez Whiz, Chris Farley

**REWARDS:** All the food you can steal, cash

## 15 Minutes?

By the time we neared Norris Industries, we'd passed so many factories that we thought we were going to be working in some assembly line or something. But the lights and cameras made it clear—we knew we were gonna be working on a movie set.

We were told to sit tight in the Winnie and our boss would find us. When Chris Farley came around the corner, I almost dropped a bomb in my pants. I couldn't believe it, there was the Big Man. He's a legend. It was almost like we were watching a movie. I couldn't believe that he was actually in my presence. Everyone was going crazy except Effie, who didn't really know who he was. She just kept jumping up and down and screaming, "It's that fat funny guy, it's the fat funny guy." And then Christian said, "I don't want to work for a fat man." The fat jokes rolled and rolled.

**-TIMMY**

SMUGGLER'S COVE
Despite a reputation as a city that's open to new ideas, LA has only one nude beach. Smuggler's Cove is located near Torrance, just 30 minutes from downtown LA. Some bathers dare disrobe completely at public beaches like Venice, but they risk a fine and possible arrest.

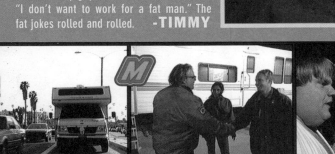

The first minute I found out I was going to work with Chris Farley, I was like, "Great, thank you very much, now I'm gonna get s**t." And I got it. Something weird was in the air. Nobody was making fun or getting excited anymore, and I got the feeling they were like, "Why did she get it?" Timmy kept saying Chris was his biggest hero and on and on. I guess Timmy expected me to give my assignment to him, but I wanted to do it. So I just left and went to meet Chris, and it was hard to understand him, because one second he's serious and the other second he's making a big joke. **Chris is a really funny guy when he's not trying to be funny.** And he's nice, he's OK.

Well, right away, Chris had to climb up a palm tree for his next scene, and there was nothing for me to do. So Dennis, the director, told me I was gonna be HIS assistant now. He let me sit next to him and shout, "Ready," "Action!" and "Cut!"

Then Dennis told me to get Emily and tell her, "The director wants some Cheez Whiz, and whatever the director wants, he gets." So I told Emily to do this, and I tried to be very serious, but it was hard, because it was so much fun to play this joke on Emily, who is used to making fun of others. She didn't believe me, so she asked Dennis and everybody she could find, "Is this a joke?" I kept thinking about me in Phoenix, looking for the keys for the batter's box. Dennis thought that we all understood it was a joke, but an hour later, Timmy came back with Cheez Whiz. Dennis was totally shocked. The only thing he could say was, "I want the nonfat Cheez Whiz, go get me the nonfat."

**-EFFIE**

To work for Chris would have meant the world to Timmy. He's been dreaming about Hollywood all his life. I was really disappointed in Effie for not giving him the opportunity to do something he's been dreaming about.

For a scene in the movie, they were trying to catapult Chris's stuntman from a fake palm tree onto a building. When it was Chris's turn to go up in the mechanical tree, it broke. So one of my jobs was to tie a rope to the tree and manually pull Chris back and forth. I felt like I was part of the crew. I figured that, being a rookie, I would have all kinds of jokes played on me, like the baseball team did to Effie, but they didn't make fun of me at all. They really seemed to like me a lot, and I really liked them, too.

Effie had on Chris Farley's jacket, and she was sitting with the director, so I was really happy for her, even though we don't get along. I was thinking, "It's about time she is having a good time. There've been umpteen missions, and she's been complaining and bitching and moaning, and now she's finally enjoying herself. Maybe running and getting coffee for directors is just her thing.

After we had supper, Chris Farley came up and said, "It's been nice working with you guys. Had a lot of fun." And he handed us a little award statue with our clue written on the plaque. It took us like probably two hours to turn the damn thing around and see our flight number and a time on the back. Chris also gave us $600 to last us until the end of the trip. We're going to Alaska, so I don't know what we'll spend it on, except maybe some crab legs, because I'm crazy about seafood.

**-EMILY**

## CLUE

**ALL RIGHT, THIS IS IT! YOUR FINAL CLUE AWAITS YOU IN ALASKA. YOU'RE BOOKED ON FLIGHT #1554, DEPARTING LAX SATURDAY MORNING, PRECISELY AT 8:00 AM. AND DON'T FORGET TO TAKE YOUR ROAD KEYS AND PUZZLE WITH YOU IF YOU WANT YOUR HANDSOME REWARD.**

50-FOOT HOLLYWOOD
In 1923, the original HOLLYWOODLAND sign was mounted atop Mount Lee as a real estate venture. The LAND portion of the sign was removed in 1949. Despite the $103 penalty for approaching the sign, the 50-foot-high letters have been both a famous suicide spot and subject to many pranks.

**5533 MILES TRAVELED**

**U2'S**
TOP TEN ROAD TRIPPIN' CDs

1. ............................................Bob Marley, EXODUS
2. ..................Underworld, SECOND TOUGHEST IN THE INFANTS
3. ...........................................Garbage, GARBAGE
4. ...Smashing Pumpkins, MELLON COLLIE AND THE INFINITE SADNESS
5. ...............Black Grape, IT'S GREAT WHEN YOU'RE STRAIGHT...YEAH
6. ......................The Beastie Boys, CHECK YOUR HEAD
7. ........Parliament, BEST OF PARLIAMENT: GIVE UP THE FUNK
8. ...............................Bob Dylan, HIGHWAY 61 REVISITED
9. ..............................................Leftfield, LEFTISM
10. ......................................Radiohead, THE BENDS

We were starting to get nostalgic already in Los Angeles—especially Timmy, whose ex-girlfriend came to visit, so she was sentimental. On our last night with the Winnie, we had a party with just the five of us and became friends all over again. Then we packed up and cleaned up and drove to the airport. –EMILY

**1**

**A**

My ex-girlfriend, Sherry, lives in San Diego. I called her before I left for ROAD RULES and said, "If I come to California, I'm looking you up." Well, guess what? I called her, and she came to see me at the RV park where we were staying. It was the weirdest experience I've ever gone through. Here's a girl I haven't seen in two years, who I still care for, and I have to tell her, "All right, before you go in the Winnebago, put this microphone on for the camera that's going to follow you." How weird is that? We went to the House of Blues, got led in through the back door, free parking, chairs brought for us. We were pampered, but it was the same old Sherry and the same old Tim.

I didn't really expect anything romantic to happen. I was hoping to stay up all night and talk with her, but you can't really talk with the camera going. At the end of the night, we go down to the beach. We're sitting there. Lovely ocean. Lovely stars. Too bad we can't see them, because there's light shining right in our faces and cameras everywhere, It's horrible. Here's a girl I haven't seen for two years, and I'm saying goodbye to her. I'm like, "OK, this is national TV. Do I kiss her?" We haven't talked about this. Of course I want to kiss her. I gave her hug and then we started kissing. Tim's first kiss on camera.  **-TIMMY**

## Leaving Winnie

Before our party in the Winnie, we wanted to find the O.J. Simpson house and just take a look at it. There were two people standing in the road, and I didn't think much about it, but when we stopped by the entrance, suddenly the two shouted at us: "Back off, pal. Get the f**k into the car and drive away right now." So of course I started walking toward the two security guards. I just wanted to ask them why we couldn't be there. But the others panicked, and starting shouting "Christian! Come back here, he's got a gun!" but the only thing he pointed at me was a flashlight.

**5533** MILES TRAVELED

**C**

### LOS ANGELES
POPULATION:
3,620,000

POPULAR HANGOUTS:
The Dresden Room, where Michelle Pfeiffer practiced her lounge act for THE FABULOUS BAKER BOYS; The Good Luck Club; Hollywood Billiards; HMS Bounty; Saturday Night Fever at the Diamond Club

MUST DO:
Bring a picnic to the Hollywood Bowl, close your eyes, and soak up the music; go for dim sum in Chinatown; hike in the San Bernadino Mountains; check out the wares on Melrose Avenue; soak with celebs in the Beverly Hot Springs

On the way back, we stopped at a roadwork site and I borrowed one of those signal lights that go, **tick, tick, tick,** to use for a disco light for our party. It was my idea to exchange gifts. I gave Timmy a present. It was the AIRPLANE! movie that I bought in Austin, Texas. I paid $15 for it out of my money, and I wanted Timmy to have that video. I must admit that I couldn't use it in Europe because of the different systems in Europe and America, but it's the thought that counts. I got a very special gift from Timmy, too. He started off by giving me a pair of socks that I found out were mine from the very beginning. Then he gave me the real present, which was one of the slippers that he had worn for a long, long time and that meant very much to him. I got only one, because he couldn't find the other. But he found it later on, and we decided to have one each and we should wear one slipper on Christmas Eve from now on.

Devin and I traded clothes, and I thought Devin looked very cool. It was funny, too, to watch Devin in my clothes, saying, "Oh, I don't feel well. The shorts is squeezing my nuts." I'm perfectly OK with people joking about my often very straight clothes, but it has a little bit deeper meaning to me, because back in Norway this is how all my friends dress, and by making fun of me, he was making fun of them, too. So that's why I suddenly got a little bit quiet and didn't enjoy the fun quite as much as usual.  **-CHRISTIAN**

I had made a big deal not to wear any more silly costumes for the rest of the trip, but that was the silliest costume that I've ever worn.  **-DEVIN**

**AK**

### Anchorage

### Los Angeles

**CA**

**2**

### MADONNA'S
TOP TEN ROAD TRIPPIN' CDs
1................Me'Shell NdegeOcello, PEACE BEYOND PASSION
2................................Soundtrack, THE MODERNS
3................Massive Attack V. the Mad Professor, PROTECTION
4................................Fugees, THE SCORE
5................................Celia Cruz, anything by
6................Cachao, MASTER SESSIONS, VOLUME II
7................Everything But the Girl, AMPLIFIED HEART
8................Joaõ Gilberto, THE LEGENDARY JOAÕ GILBERTO
9................Josephine Baker, JOSEPHINE BAKER
10................soundtrack, HENRY & JUNE

I was really disappointed at first, because I wanted to have this big dinner. We'd planned it for two days, and I thought this was no time to get lazy—it was the last night in the Winnie. But then everyone took a shower and went to the phone, and it was too late for anything but a liquid dinner, so we poured some wine and got to talking. The conversation was just wonderful. And we had a great time. It was probably the best night I've ever had in that Winnie.

Christian's idea to exchange gifts seemed corny at first, and I wasn't thrilled about giving up my stuff, but then I realized that it would mean a lot to the others, so I went with it. I gave Timmy the ankle bracelet I bought in Moab. It had little black beads on it, and when the ankle bracelet falls off, it's supposed to bring fame. I gave it to Timmy because it's his life dream to become an actor. I didn't think it would be that big of a deal to him. But it really touched him.

There's a certain pair of jean shorts of mine that Effie loves, and I broke down and gave them to her. It was kinda tough, but in return she gave me her favorite shirt, so we were even. I was trying to think of what I could possibly give Christian, and really the only thing that we've shared just between the two of us is the Norwegian phrase "freckek," which means "sweet butt," so I gave him a Polaroid that Devin snapped of my butt once. I was so embarrassed. I didn't want anybody to see it, but I knew it was probably the best present I could ever give him. It was Timmy's idea to do the final high skol, so we all got our drinks and stood up and got the high elbows going, and it was sad. **-EMILY**

**B**

Anchorage Welcomes You

**7866** MILES TRAVELED

I'm really bad with good-byes. I get really teary, so I kept asking Devin and Timmy to hug me while we were packing up the Winnie. I would dry my eyes on their shirts and then pack some more and then ask for another hug. It was like leaving your house. This was our house for the last ten weeks—a pretty crowded one, but still our home, and we were not gonna see it again. I hate packing so much. It means the end, and I don't like ends. I like things to go on. **-EFFIE**

The next morning, I woke everyone up bright and early to start cleaning. The Winnebago looked like the aftermath of a tornado / hurricane / avalanche / nuclear fallout, and we needed every second we could spare to clean the damn thing and get on our way. There were three articles that were pretty important to take along with us to Alaska, and they were of course the Road Keys, the bottle of champagne that we didn't break to christen the Winnebago back in Florida, and the coconut, which was kind of a symbol from Bimini. But the coconut was gone.

**C**

**KEY TO SYMBOLS**

..............................conflict
........................sleep in motel
...........................money trail
...........................welcome to
M .............................mission
...empty Winnie septic tank
..................................lost

Christian went and paid for the RV park for the week, and I didn't know it was going to be that expensive. We didn't really have a group fund anymore—it was all our own individual money. And of course, the ferrets were spending it like wood chips, so we had to pull the group fund back together to pay for the RV site. Most importantly, I bestowed the honor upon myself to take the last bomb in the Winnebago. I had been saving up a little special something over the day. The biggest personal touch that we added to the Winnebago was our own odor. I don't think you'll ever be able to get that smell out of the Winnebago, and I feel sorry for the sucker who buys it. **-TIMMY**

**D**

## MISSION 14 NUMBER 14

## BUNGEE JUMP

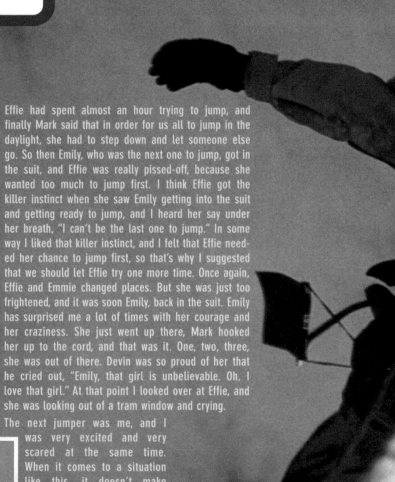

**OBJECTIVE:** Make a 220-foot bungee jump out of a tram and pick up your final clue

**TOOLS:** Tram, bungee cords, body harness

**HAZARDS:** Whiplash, rope burn

**REWARDS:** Adrenaline rush, final clue

Our plane landed in Alaska late at night, and we were taken to our most luxurious lodgings yet. The next few days we did some snowball fighting, a lot of talking, and AHHH! Bungee jumping! –CHRISTIAN

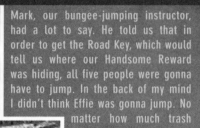

Mark, our bungee-jumping instructor, had a lot to say. He told us that in order to get the Road Key, which would tell us where our Handsome Reward was hiding, all five people were gonna have to jump. In the back of my mind I didn't think Effie was gonna jump. No matter how much trash she was talking about it being her mission and her wanting to go first, we all had in the back of our minds that if there was an ounce of doubt in Effie, she wasn't doing it. It didn't matter if we never got our Handsome Reward.

Mark told us that we were gonna be suspended 300 feet above the ground at the bottom of our jump. **I asked, "Has it ever been done before? Is this like a prototype jump?" And he said that we would be the first people to jump from the tram.** That made me a little uneasy, to be honest. But we all signed our lives away and said that our families wouldn't sue and all that good stuff. Then we boarded the tram and they locked all the doors and there was no turning back.

Effie was gonna be the first one to jump. She spent a long time, a really long time, in front of the door and at one point she broke down into tears. Mark kept saying, "You have to do this, you have to do this," and he just didn't understand that Effie doesn't have to do anything. **-DEVIN**

So here I am standing on the edge and I'm trying to gather up every bit of logic that I have. "OK," I tell myself, "Let's think it through. It's not really far, and the cord is really thick. Nothing can happen to you." That was a bad idea. The more I thought about it, the more I kept looking down, the more scared I became. **-EFFIE**

Effie had spent almost an hour trying to jump, and finally Mark said that in order for us all to jump in the daylight, she had to step down and let someone else go. So then Emily, who was the next one to jump, got in the suit, and Effie was really pissed-off, because she wanted too much to jump first. I think Effie got the killer instinct when she saw Emily getting into the suit and getting ready to jump, and I heard her say under her breath, "I can't be the last one to jump." In some way I liked that killer instinct, and I felt that Effie needed her chance to jump first, so that's why I suggested that we should let Effie try one more time. Once again, Effie and Emmie changed places. But she was just too frightened, and it was soon Emily, back in the suit. Emily has surprised me a lot of times with her courage and her craziness. She just went up there, Mark hooked her up to the cord, and that was it. One, two, three, she was out of there. Devin was so proud of her that he cried out, "Emily, that girl is unbelievable. Oh, I love that girl." At that point I looked over at Effie, and she was looking out of a tram window and crying.

The next jumper was me, and I was very excited and very scared at the same time. When it comes to a situation like this, it doesn't make sense to me to look at the ground, so I blocked that out, took a step backwards, ran out of the tram, and had the most incredible feeling that I can ever remember. **-CHRISTIAN**

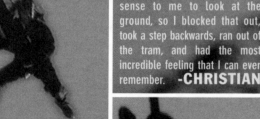

**MT. ALYESKA**
Located 35 miles south of Anchorage, Mount Alyeska is only 270 feet above sea level at its base and 3,160 feet high at its summit.

Christian had a little something planned for me that was kind of special. He had brought the eight ball for me to jump with as a memento of what we've gone through. As I was psyching myself up to jump, I thought about a friend of mine named Ty who passed away a little bit before I left for the show. And I thought about the lesson he taught me—that life is precious, and you have to be thankful and grateful for what you have. So I dedicated my jump to Ty. **-TIMMY**

I hate to say it, but I lost complete faith in Effie. I really didn't think she was going to jump. And it really, really surprised me when she did. I was so happy that she conquered her fear and didn't let herself and the group down. It was a really, really great moment for the whole group, and we were all incredibly proud of her.

The ride back down to the resort was really, really sad. I was staring out the window just thinking about everything we accomplished. But at the same time it was a good feeling, because if it wasn't at the end, I wouldn't have as much confidence and all these good memories. Even though I'd love it to go on forever, every beginning has to have an ending, and this was definitely a great ending to the trip. I've come out of the trip with four great friends and tons of great experiences, so now I can sit back and finally take it all in instead of concentrating on what's coming next. **-EMILY**

When they all finished, I knew I had to go. I had to stop thinking. I chose to do it backward, so I wouldn't have to look. Mark started to count, but I said, "No, don't count, I want to count." And I threw myself out. I think I stayed hanging out in the air for 15 minutes after the fall. He sent me the rope and I hooked it to me, but I shouted to him, "Don't bring me up, I want to enjoy this!" And I enjoyed that moment. This was definitely my mission. The best I've ever done so far.

Attached to the cord was a little bag with the clue in it. I knew that when he pulled me up everyone was gonna look for this little bag, and I didn't want them to get it. So I put the clue inside the pocket of my coat and I zipped it. I was still trying to get over the fact that I had just done a very crazy thing. It was very emotional for me, and they kept insisting, "Where's the clue, where's the clue?" So I just took it out and showed them. **-EFFIE**

**ANCHORAGE**
**POPULATION:**
226,338
**NICKNAME:**
"Crossroads of the World"
**POPULAR HANGOUTS:**
Fly by Night Club, Blondie's Cafe
**TRIVIA:**
Heaviest annual snowfall was 974.5 inches in the winter of 1951-1952
**MUST DO:**
Hike in the nation's second largest forest, the Six Million Acre Chugach National Forest

**CLUE**

**PORTAGE GLACIER IS YOUR FINAL DESTINATION.**

**NAME:** Mark Vance
**TITLE:** President, Club Way North, Alaska
**MOTTO:** "If you don't laugh, and life isn't fun, don't join Club Way North."

Club Way North caters mostly to adrenaline junkies, adventurous people, but I'd say that about five percent of those people balk when faced with bungee jumping. With Effie, it was a real balk. She wanted to go first, but that's a real tough spot, because you're jumping into the unknown. She was so intense. Once that fear factor came in, you could see it grow in her until she broke down completely. She felt a lot of pressure from the other kids and the cameras and everything. I think that's why she finally jumped at the end of the day. They were real proud of Effie. It was a big milestone for her, and they all knew it.

**BUNGEE BELIEVERS**

Bungee jumping first emerged in New Hebrides, South Pacific, where tribesmen tied vines to their ankles and jumped from high cliffs to prove their manhood. April Fool's Day in 1979 marks the beginning of modern-day bungee jumping, when the Oxford Dangerous Sports Club of Britain jumped from a bridge in Bristol, England.

There are four types of bungee-jumping platforms: bridges, hot-air balloons, cranes, and towers.

Jumping prices range from $30-$150.

There are 500 bungee-jumping sites worldwide.

The two national bungee associations, the American Bungee Association and the North American Bungee Association, are working together to formulate a bungee-jumping standard.

Bungee-jumping injuries include pinched fingers, cord burns, broken bones, internal bleeding, ruptured organs, and head injuries.

There have been five recorded deaths and four recorded critical injuries from bungee jumping.

**ROAD KEY**

**PORTAGE GLACIER**

**OLD SEWARD HIGHWAY**

The 100-mile stretch south of Anchorage is considered to be among the five most beautiful scenic highways in the world.

When we came to the glacier, we were all expecting to have to hunt around awhile for our final reward, but it was there in front of us—five shiny new cars. It was too much for us to comprehend that we were being rewarded SO handsomely for having the best time of our lives. We already miss each other. -EFFIE

I was speechless when we arrived at Portage Glacier and saw the cars. I figured we would be taking a trip or something, but this was unbelievable. Devin was probably the happiest of all of us, because he really needed a car. I decided to pick a black one, because I already have a red one at home. I don't believe we got cars as rewards. People will think we are the biggest brats in this world.

I really must thank all the Americans that I've met who have had to deal with me asking them questions about their language and about the places and all that. I must thank them for having a funny, silly Norwegian crossing their country and doing weird things. I'm very grateful for the people that I met that have taken care of me, from showing me directions to really getting to know me.

I feel it's extremely important to have some other things to look forward to, and I honestly... I'm 21, I don't want this to be the end of my life. This is not, "OK, now the funniest thing in my life has happened and now it can only go downward." I can't have that attitude. So that's why I'm really looking forward to going to Argentina in August, September. I'm confident that I will experience things later on in my life that I can compare to this, but that's a tough mission. -CHRISTIAN

I don't have to run anymore to look for something exciting. Sure, Daphne is a part of me. I'm sure she'll be around for a while. I definitely need her sometimes. She helps me avoid people that I don't want to meet. She helps me not get hurt and sometimes be really strong. But I don't want her around all the time—I like Effie, I'm not going to say, "This is a new Effie," but there are a few things I've changed for good, and it's really nice.

I've learned from everybody on this trip. Effie has taught me a good bit of patience, that's for sure. From Devin I've learned not to judge a book by its cover; there's a lot of wisdom beneath that cool exterior. From Emily I learned that you never really stop growing. She has really grown up over the past couple weeks. You can really tell from start to finish the different person she has become. She's much more worldy. Surprisingly, I think Devin and Emily's relationship together didn't take away from the group; it almost contributed. Of course, when two people become close like that, they tend to drift off and stay by themselves, but they participated and stuck with the group as much as any other person.

Christian and I have definitely developed quite a unique relationship. He's the same type of person I am. And you hate to say goodbye to people like that. I don't think the trip would have been as easy without Christian, without someone there keeping the laughs rolling and someone to joke around with the whole time. For the the rest of my life, I'll be doing the Norweigan toast, the high elbow.

The last thing I feel I must say is, "Sorry if I embarrassed you, Mom and Dad, but you're used to it by now." -TIMMY

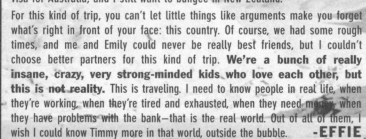

I proved over and over again that I can deal with things. It made me so strong. Nothing can stop me. I'm emotionally strong enough now to say, "I'm not going back to Israel." I used to look down on people from Israel who moved to the States. I didn't understand why they would abandon their country. Now I know that it's because it's very easy to be here, it's easier than being in Israel. I want to stay here. At least for a few years. I want to go to New York and maybe work there for a few months until I decide when to leave for Australia. I have already got a visa for Australia, and I still want to bungee in New Zealand.

For this kind of trip, you can't let little things like arguments make you forget what's right in front of your face: this country. Of course, we had some rough times, and me and Emily could never be really best friends, but I couldn't choose better partners for this kind of trip. **We're a bunch of really insane, crazy, very strong-minded kids who love each other, but this is not reality.** This is traveling. I need to know people in real life, when they're working, when they're tired and exhausted, when they need money, when they have problems with the bank—that is the real world. Out of all of them, I wish I could know Timmy more in that world, outside the bubble. -EFFIE

4/19 1996

Me and Devin are going our separate ways. He is going back to Cleveland, and I'm going back to Flora. We're both talking about moving to LA, and if it happens, I think we'll be together. But it's not really for me to decide, because if I had my way, we'd be together, plain and simple.

When ROAD RULES airs, I know that a lot of people will judge this relationship because he's black and I'm white. And they will shun it. It will be taboo to them. I feel sorry for those people because they've got a lot to learn about life. I feel nothing but pity for those people.

That's probably the biggest part of me that's changed. Before this trip, my experience with other races was limited, and I don't feel like it was really my fault. The old Emily had this wall of stereotyping and assumptions, and I've learned to be a lot more open-minded and accept that just because people are different doesn't mean that they're wrong. It's a great feeling.

If I had to sum up this whole entire trip, like, 80 years from now, sitting around my grandchildren, I would probably have to refer to it as the time in my life where everything took a turn.

**The words "I can't" or "I don't think I can" are completely demolished from my brain. I don't believe those words anymore.** —EMILY

I think that by far Emily will take more away from this trip than any of us. For 18 years, she lived in this little isolation booth. She didn't get to meet anybody. She didn't meet anybody that didn't look or sound or talk like herself. Here she met an Israeli, a Norwegian, a Clevelander, and a Pittsburgh Pirate.

If I would have thought about getting into a relationship with Emily, it never would have happened, because I would have known that this point would come, that I'd have to make the decision—or that we would have to make the decision—to let it go. But I didn't think about it when it started. I just followed what I felt, and it felt right. But right now it doesn't feel right to continue.

Now that the trip is over, I'm gonna pick my little sister up from school in my new car for a few weeks, then I'm gonna drive straight out of Cleveland. I don't know where exactly I'm headed, but I know it's gonna be west. I'm gonna go home for a month, take care of some business, and drive out to LA. And sooner or later, I gotta go to school. Pretty soon I'm gonna wake up alone. I won't have the four people I spent the last ten weeks with, and I won't have the girl that I woke up with every morning for the last eight. I'm pretty sure there's gonna be a lot of money spent in the first couple of months just keeping in touch, just needing to talk. And then we'll get to the point where it's just once every couple of weeks. And then it will be once a month. It's hard. I'm trying not to think about it, but I know it's reality. —DEVIN

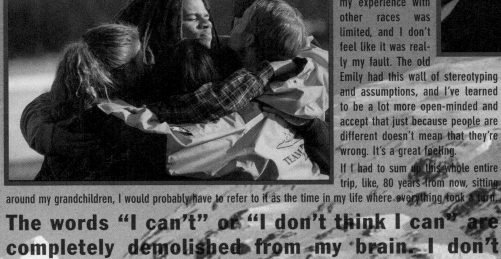

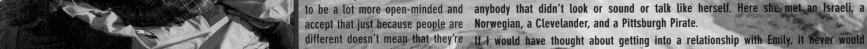

For the record, I would like to state that I am not a nudist. -CHRISTIAN

**Mary-Ellis Bunim and Jonathan Murray**
Creative and Executive Producers, ROAD RULES and THE REAL WORLD

## Learning the Ropes

The second ROAD RULES cast had an advantage over the first—they knew what to expect. They each came in knowing, "I'm going to find a Winnebago and a little bit of money, and my job is to attack my missions with enthusiasm and try to get them all done." It was a huge relief for me as the director to have a cast that showed up and wasn't confused.

Another big difference this season was that we added additional crew members to the team and we slowed the pace of the trip down—a lot. This time, they had a chance to explore their environments and get to know people along the way. In the previous season, it was like, "Hi, you are here to go white-water rafting. Boom. You're done. OK, now you are going to drive 500 miles and go jump out of an airplane. Then you are going to be dropped in the desert." **-CLAY**

**Mary-Ellis Bunim**
(pictured with cast)

**Andrew Perry**
Researcher and Associate Producer

**Anthony Dalferes**
Audio Mixer

**Mark Perez**
Director

**Clay Newbil**
Producer and Director

**Matt Sohn**
Camera Operator

**John Gumina**
Technical Supervisor

**Kathleen Kelly**
Production Assistant

**Adam Willett**
Camera Assistant

**Andy Anderson**
Camera Operator

**John Gunima**

# The Cast

I don't think any of the kids really realized it was going to be work. Every morning, we went in their rooms at 7:00 and literally shook them awake. We kept them going all the time.  **-ANDY**

This group was quite savvy as to how they would be portrayed on film, and sometimes we'd even catch them acting. There were things that they wanted us to know, and things that they didn't. At one point, a cast member said to me, "I don't want to be seen smoking on camera." And so I said, "Then don't smoke." We were with them about 17 hours a day, so we saw a lot of things that they didn't want us to see.  **-ANDREW**

Christian has the best manners of any person under 25 that I've ever met in my life. He's flawless—a genuinely good person who has very deep feelings. He tends to keep things light, but I know that the experience was hitting him very deeply.  **-MARY-ELLIS**

With Christian, what you see is what you get. He is a guy from Norway who enjoys a good time and likes to give the old high-elbow drinking salute. I would almost say he's like a Norwegian frat boy, but he's much more intelligent than that. I think he's pretty much a product of his environment in Norway, and as you can gather from his regular nakedness, he's comfortable with himself.  **-ANDREW**

The moment we saw Devin's audition tape, we knew he was very special. He had, for an 18-year-old, tremendous maturity. He also had a special relationship with women—they found him sexy because he was always comfortable around them. He's also great looking and has that unforgettable hair.  **-JONATHAN**

One of the goals of ROAD RULES is to bring a diverse group together who represent different economic, ethnic, and demographic backgrounds. That's what makes it good. That's what makes it interesting. Coming from two different worlds, Devin and Emily had a lot of curiosity about each other, and what they learned in the process of their relationship was educational for everyone watching, on the inside and on the outside.  **-JONATHAN**

Emily is used to being a big fish in a small pond. She was queen of the hill in high school; she could have her pick of anyone. This might have spoiled her a little, and I think it was a jolt for her to find herself in the outside world where she had to negotiate with people who weren't giving her as much attention as she was accustomed to. On the other hand, there were times when I expected Emily to whine, but she was up for any challenge.  **-MARY-ELLIS**

Effie reflects where she is from and how she has been brought up: She's a fighter. She's aggressive, assertive, and a very strong woman. She's not afraid to say exactly what she thinks, because she believes in herself. To me, that's the most attractive thing about her and what makes her a strong role model for women. I would say Effie's greatest quality is that she shoots from the hip. I think a lot of people in our society aren't used to that kind of straightforwardness from a woman, but more and more people are coming to respect it.  **-CLAY**

Timmy is like a class clown, but he has a much more intense side, which he seldom shows. I think he's had some hard knocks in life but doesn't really like talking about them.  **-ANDREW**

Timmy is easily the comedian of the group. He has the cast rolling constantly. You'll see that extra little jiggle in the shot sometimes when the kids are laughing, because the cameramen are laughing as well.  **-MATT**

Demily is what we called them. Devin and Emily were really tight, but too young to get serious. Toward the end of the trip, Devin was getting restless, and the inevitability of them ending the relationship was pretty obvious. Emily was crushed. She felt she had risked her reputation in the eyes of her small-town community by dating a black man, but she was smart enough to know that if you love someone, it doesn't matter—and she loved Devin.  **-ANDY**

# Emily

These days I'm trying to decide what college to go to. I want to move to a big city where there is more to do and there are more opportunities for me than in Flora. Meanwhile, I've been helping my father in the fields and trying to get my private pilot's license. I see the cast and crew from ROAD RULES whenever I can. I've already visited Timmy, Devin, and Effie, but I haven't heard from Christian. I plan to leave Flora after my sister is married. I will probably move to LA.

# Timmy

After the show ended, I wasn't ready to stop driving, so I decided to do ROAD RULES, part IIa. I went through five states in five days, and had fun fondling tollbooth operators' hands as I gave them money. Now I'm living in LA, overtipping bartenders, and hitting up comedy improv groups for a slot. I've seen everyone from the cast except Christian, but we've talked four or five times on the phone, and as soon as I save enough kroner, I'll take the trip over the ocean to see him. I really miss ROAD RULES; I wish I was still doing it.

# Christian

I plan to go to the USA as soon as I can to visit the others from ROAD RULES. I have been partying, waterskiing in the fjords of Norway, and telemark skiing; but the main thing in my life has been getting ready to participate in the Argentina Expedition '96, which is a race through the Andes. This October I plan to move to Nice, France, to live for one year. When I get back, I will take the exam to get into a law degree program in Norway.

# Effie

I'm living in the West Village in New York, trying to find a job, but it's very difficult to get work without citizenship. When ROAD RULES finished and I got some press photos taken in LA, everyone said I should look for modeling work, so I'm thinking about doing that, just to pay some bills. I'm looking forward to seeing if anything comes of my stint in ROAD RULES, but I'm not counting on it. Soon I'll go to Israel to visit my parents, and then I will travel in Australia, New Zealand, and Asia, as I've always dreamed. I'm not together with my boyfriend anymore; it wasn't fair to him to stay together when I'm living so far from home, always moving, moving.

# Devin

I live with my mom and sister in Cleveland. My little sister missed me a lot while I was on the road, and it's good to be back and hang with her for now. Since the show, I've just been sleeping. The experience spoiled me rotten and I just can't face going back to work. When they ship me the car I got for my reward, I'm going to get in it and drive until I can't drive anymore. I'll probably visit my friend Herb in Memphis, and then move to LA. So far, since the show, I've seen Emily and Timmy, but I haven't heard from Effie or Christian. Emily and I are just friends. My ex-girlfriend Amy and I are no longer on speaking terms.

READ

# We're looking for five young people, women and men, who will travel together for ten weeks and accomplish a series of adventures. We're not interested in hiring five actors-we want "real people" from varying ethnic and socioeconomic backgrounds, we want the conventional and the not-so-conventional.

We're looking for interesting people who are not afraid to express their emotions and opinions, people who want to share their lives . . . in front of cameras. You'll be living in a fishbowl, with cameras rolling almost every waking hour. You'll wear a wireless microphone and have two or three camerapeople following you around-in the vehicle, on the street, on dates, and sometimes when you are desperate to be left alone. Consider this very carefully, because we require you to sign a contract and commit to the full taping period.

While you're on the road, we will pay your expenses but you'll pay your own long-distance phone bills. We will also pay for your trip to the beginning destination and back, and you will be paid a stipend for each of the weeks that you are being taped, payable at the end of the contract.

This is a tough, emotionally exhausting experience. Please consider carefully whether you have the strength to endure it. If you are still interested, complete the application ASAP, and we will contact you further from this point. Please be patient . . . .

# ROAD RULES APPLICATION
# INSTRUCTIONS

**1.** Call the ROAD RULES hotline at (818) 754-5730. This number will tell you the latest deadline information and anything else you need to know. (You must be 18-25 years old to participate.)

**2.** Fill out the enclosed application. Answer all of the questions as honestly as you can. Please keep your answers to a paragraph in length. You can use additional sheets of paper if needed. Please be sure to type or write legibly.

**3.** Make a ten-minute videotape of yourself talking about whatever you think makes you a good candidate for ROAD RULES. Remember, we want to see if you are a person who is open and willing to express what is important to you. Sometimes the best videos are very simple. Don't overthink it, and try to be honest and sincere. (Also, make sure there's enough light on your face and that you are close enough to the mike to be heard.)

**4.** If you completed the extra credit mission described on page 5, write the first letter of each of your answers where indicated on this application. (Hint: if the letters spell a word, you're on the right track.)

**5.** **Send the application to:**
Road Rules-Casting Dept.
6007 Sepulveda Blvd.
Van Nuys, CA 91411

**6.** You should return this application as soon as possible, as we have a very limited amount of time until production begins.

# road rules
## application form

**Name:**

Address:

Phone:                    Birthdate:                    Age:

Parent's Name, Address, Phone:                    Brothers and Sisters (names and ages):

Are you or have you ever been a member of SAG/AFTRA?          Yes ◯     No ◯

Have you ever acted or performed outside of school?          Yes ◯     No ◯

Name of High School (and years completed):                    Other education:

Name of College (years completed and majors):

Are you currently in school?                    Yes ◯     No ◯

Do you work? If so, describe your job.

How would you describe your best traits?

How would you describe your worst traits?

Do you consider yourself: high maintenance? ◯     low maintenance? ◯     Why?

How long does it take you to get ready in the morning?

If you could only pack one backpack for a trip, what would be in it?

Describe your most embarrassing moment:

Do you have a:          boyfriend ◯     girlfriend? ◯          How long have you been together?

What drives you crazy about this person?                    What do you like most about this person?

How would your boyfriend/girlfriend feel about your leaving for 8 weeks?          Would you be faithful?

How important is sex to you?

Do you have it only when you are in a relationship or do you seek it out at other times?

What's the most exciting/interesting place you've ever had sex?

Is there any issue, political or social, that you are passionate about?          Have you ever done anything about it?

What is the most important issue or problem you are facing?

Are you physically fit?          Do you work out?          If so, how often and what types of activities do you like to do?

If not, how do you stay in shape?

Describe a major event that has affected your life:

What habits do other people have that you simply cannot tolerate?

Where were you born? | Where did you grow up?

Describe how conflicts were handled at home as you were growing up (Who won, who lost, was yelling and/or hitting involved?):

What are your thoughts on abortion? | Other sexual orientations?

Have you traveled outside of your state? | Describe some experiences you enjoyed and some you didn't:

If you had Aladdin's Lamp and three wishes, what would they be?

What was the last unusual, exciting, or spontaneous outing you initiated for you and your friends?

Do you smoke cigarettes? | Yes ◯ No ◯ | Do you drink alcohol?

How old were you when you had your first drink? | How much do you drink now? | How often?

Do you use recreational drugs? | What drugs have you used? | How often?

Are you on any prescription medication? | If so, for what, and for how long have you been taking it?

Have you ever been arrested? | If so, what was the charge and were you convicted?

Do you have a driver's license? | Yes ◯ No ◯

Have you had any tickets? If so, how many? | Has your license ever been suspended? | If so, why?

Do you believe in God? | Are you religious? | Do you practice religion?

Who are your heroes? | Tell us why:

What was the last silly or ridiculous thing you did?

HOW DO YOU RATE ON THE FOLLOWING? (Rate yourself on a 1-10 scale. 1 being unskilled and 10 being very skilled)

| ACTIVITY | RATING | COMMENTS | ACTIVITY | RATING | COMMENTS |
|---|---|---|---|---|---|
| Ride a bicycle | | | Ride a motorcycle | | |
| Ski | | | Run a mile | | |
| Snowboard | | | Rock climb | | |
| Surf | | | Speak a foreign language | | |
| Fix a car | | | Fix a motor | | |
| Cook | | | Sew | | |
| Tie nautical knots | | | Sail a boat | | |
| Swim | | | Fly | | |
| Skydive | | | Waterski | | |
| Scuba dive | | | Use a computer | | |
| Drive a bus | | | Rollerblade | | |
| Bungee jump | | | Set up a tent | | |
| Fix a flat tire | | | Read a map | | |

Other skills:

List 4 people who have known you for a long time and will tell us what a great person you are (excluding relatives).

| NAME | ADDRESS | PHONE | HOW DO THEY KNOW YOU? |
|---|---|---|---|
| 1. | | | |
| 2. | | | |
| 3. | | | |
| 4. | | | |

IF YOU COMPLETED THE EXTRA CREDIT MISSION, WRITE THE FIRST LETTER OF EACH OF YOUR ANSWERS HERE:
— — — — — — — —

I acknowledge that everything stated in this application is true. I understand that any falsely submitted answers can and will be grounds for removal from the application process and from the subsequent participation in the final series. I further acknowledge and accept that this application form and the videotape I previously submitted to MTV will become property of MTV and will not be returned. By signing below, I grant rights for MTVN/Bunim-Murray Productions (BMP) to use any biographical information contained in this application, my home video, or taped interview, and to record, use, and publicize my home videotape or taped interview, voice, actions, likeness, and appearance in any manner in connection with ROAD RULES.

Signature | Date

Thank you for your time and effort in completing this form. Please do not get impatient with our response time-we will get back to you as soon as possible.

Your own road trip won't be truly trippin' without tunes, especially local favorites. Check out these stations along the ROAD RULES routes, or just flip the dial—you never know what new sounds await you 'round the next bend.

## ALASKA

| | | |
|---|---|---|
| ANCHORAGE | 106.5-FM | MODERN ROCK |
| GIRDWOOD | 106.5-FM | MODERN ROCK |

## ALABAMA

| | | |
|---|---|---|
| MOBILE | 107.1-FM | ALTERNATIVE |
| TUSCALOOSA | 101.7-FM | MODERN ROCK |

## ARIZONA

| | | |
|---|---|---|
| PHOENIX | 97.9-FM | AOR |
| NOGALES | 98.3-FM | MEXICAN/ROCK |
| FLAGSTAFF | 93.9-FM | CLASSIC ROCK |

## ALIFORNIA

| | | |
|---|---|---|
| ALIBU | 106.7-FM | ALTERNATIVE |
| S ANGELES | 106.7-FM | ALTERNATIVE |
| AN FRANCISCO | 105-FM | ALTERNATIVE |
| LISTOGA | 101.7-FM | ROCK |
| KE TAHOE | 93.9-FM | ROCK-OLD & NEW |
| ANTA BARBARA | 99.9-FM | ROCK/AOR |

## COLORADO

| | | |
|---|---|---|
| SILVERTON | 94.9-FM | ROCK |
| GUNNISON | 91.1-FM | ROCK |
| CRESTED BUTTE | 98.9-FM | ADULT/ALT/AOR |

## FLORIDA

| | | |
|---|---|---|
| PENSACOLA | 107.3-FM | ALTERNATIVE |
| KEY WEST | 107.1-FM | ALTERNATIVE |
| FORT LAUDERDALE | 103.5-FM | ALT/MODERN/ADULT |
| MIAMI | 94.9-FM | ALTERNATIVE |
| OKAHUMPKA | 101.1-FM | MODERN ROCK |

## GEORGIA

| | | |
|---|---|---|
| AMERICUS | 94.7-FM | ROCK |
| ATLANTA | 97.5-FM | CHURBAN |

## ILLINOIS

| | | |
|---|---|---|
| CHICAGO | 101-FM | ALTERNATIVE |
| ROCKFORD | 104.9-FM | CLASSIC ROCK |
| FLORA | 103.9-FM | ROCK |
| VANDALIA | 107.1-FM | SOFT ROCK |
| | 1500-AM | OLDIES |

## INDIANA

| | | |
|---|---|---|
| FAYETTEVILLE | 105.5-FM | CLASSIC ROCK |
| BLOOMINGTON | 95.1-FM | ROCK/ALTERNATIVE |
| NASHVILLE | 94.7-FM | CLASSIC ROCK |
| FORT WAYNE | 103.9-FM | ROCK |

## LOUISIANA

| | | |
|---|---|---|
| NEW ORLEANS | 92.3-FM | ROCK |

## MISSISSIPPI

| | | |
|---|---|---|
| COLUMBUS | 93.3-FM | ROCK |

## NEW MEXICO

| | | |
|---|---|---|
| RED RIVER | 90.1-FM | ROCK |

## EW YORK

| | | |
|---|---|---|
| W YORK CITY | 102.7-FM | CLASSIC ROCK |
| NG ISLAND | 107.1-FM | MODERN ROCK |

## NEVADA

| | | |
|---|---|---|
| LAS VEGAS | 97.1-FM | ALTERNATIVE |
| | 96.3-FM | CLASSIC ROCK |

## NORTH CAROLINA

| | | |
|---|---|---|
| WANCHESE | 102.5-FM | ALTERNATIVE |
| WILMINGTON | 107.5-FM | MODERN ROCK |
| BALD HEAD ISLAND | 107.5-FM | MODERN ROCK |

## KLAHOMA

| | | |
|---|---|---|
| KLAHOMA CITY | 100.5-FM | AOR/ALTERNATIVE |
| | 98.9-FM | CHRISTIAN |

## SOUTH DAKOTA

| | | |
|---|---|---|
| RAPID CITY | 95.1-FM | CLASSIC ROCK/AOR |

## TENNESSEE

| | | |
|---|---|---|
| NASHVILLE | 103.3-FM | MODERN ROCK |
| MEMPHIS | 96-FM | ALTERNATIVE |

## UTAH

| | | |
|---|---|---|
| VERNAL | 98.5-FM | HITS FROM THE '60S TO THE '90S |
| SALT LAKE CITY | 1320-AM | HOT TALK |
| | 101-FM | AOR |
| BOULDER | 93.7-FM | COUNTRY |
| PROVO | 101-FM | AOR |

## EXAS

| | | |
|---|---|---|
| MARILLO | 107.9-FM | ALTERNATIVE |
| | 95.7-FM | CLASSIC ROCK |
| | 93.1-FM | TOP 40 |
| ALLAS | 94.5-FM | ALTERNATIVE |
| STIN | 107.7-FM | ALTERNATIVE |
| BBOCK | 94.5-FM | ALTERNATIVE |

## VIRGINIA

| | | |
|---|---|---|
| QUANTICO | 99.1-FM | ALTERNATIVE |

## ASHINGTON, D.C.

| | | |
|---|---|---|
| ASHINGTON, D.C. | 101.1-FM | MODERN ROCK |

## WEST VIRGINIA

| | | |
|---|---|---|
| HICO | 103.7-FM | TOP 40 |

## WYOMING

| | | |
|---|---|---|
| GILLETTE | 95.1-FM | ROCK/ALTERNATIVE |
| CASPER | 106.3-FM | ROCK/ALTERNATIVE |
| HEWLITT | 95.1-FM | ROCK/ALTERNATIVE |

# ALABAMA

Nickname: "Heart of Dixie." Capital: Montgomery. Alabama Bureau of Tourism and Travel, 401 Adams Ave., Montgomery, 36104, 334) 242-4169. Division of Parks, 64 N. Union St., Montgomery, 36130. 800) 252-7275.

MOBILE: Visitors' Center: 150 S. Royal St., 36602, 334) 434-7304.

Where to Stay: ♠ Holiday Inn, Exit 15B off of I-10, 334) 666-5600. Your basic Holiday Inn: swimming pool, restaurant, cable TV. ♠ I-10 Kampground, 6430 Theodore Dawes Rd., 334) 653-9816. Generous campground with bath facilities. Not accessible by public transportation. $12/campsite.

Where to Eat: ⚫ Dreamland, 3314 Old Shell Rd., 334) 479-9898. Ribs anyone? We hope so, 'cause that's all they serve. Delicious slabs, half or whole, are smoked right on the premises. ⚫ Lumber Yard, 2617 Dauphin St., 334) 476-4609. Hearty sandwiches, pizzas, and salads. A good place if you're looking for healthier fare.

Night Life: ☽ Hayley's, 278 Dauphin St., 334) 433-4970. Alternative bar with lively decoration. Great drink deals nightly. ☽ Judge Roy Bean's, Off Old Hwy. 98 in Daphne, 334) 626-9988. This tin-roofed bar is home to dozens of cats, goats, and barflies. Complete bar with frozen drinks, food, and frequent live music.

Attractions and Adventures: ⚫ The Exploreum, Museum of Discovery, 1906 Spring Hill Ave., 334) 476-6873. 80 interactive life science exhibits. ⚫ Azalea Trail Festival, 334) 471-0025. 3-mile-long tour of the azaleas in bloom (late March).

# ALASKA

Nickname: "North to the Future." Capital: Juneau. Tourism Council, P.O. Box 20710, Juneau, 800) 423-0568. State Division of Parks, 3601 C St., #200, Anchorage, 99510, 907) 762-2617.

ANCHORAGE: Convention and Visitors' Bureau, Corner of 4th St. & F St., 99501-2212, 907) 276-4118.

Where to Stay: ♠ Anchorage International Hostel, 700 H St., 907) 276-3635. There's a kitchen on each floor of this dorm-style hotel. ♠ Spenard Hostel, 2845 W. 42 Place, 907) 248-5036. No curfew, lots of common rooms to meet people. They ask you to perform one chore before you leave.

Where to Eat: ⚫ Blondie's Cafe, 333 W. 4th Ave., 907) 279-0698. Breakfast is served all day in this strangely decorated restaurant. ⚫ Downtown Deli, 524 W. 4th Ave., 907) 276-7116. Classic Alaskan atmosphere: woodsy and rustic. Serves up lots of local fish.

Night Life: ☽ Fly-by-Night Club, 3300 Spenard Rd., 907) 279-7726. Always features live music, usually the most popular local bands. Be aware that many of the "bars" in this area are actually strip joints.

Attractions and Adventures: ⚫ Dog Musher's Hall of Fame, along Iditarod Trail, mile 13.9 on Knik Rd., Knik, 907) 376-7755. ⚫ Alaska Experience Theater, 6th St. & G St., 907) 276-3730. Get an eyeful of Alaska's most dramatic scenery on 180-degree wraparound screen. ⚫ Old Seward Highway. A scenic 100-mile stretch of road running south of Anchorage.

GIRDWOOD: Visitors' Information: Begich Boggs Visitor Center, Portage Glacier, 99587, 907) 783-2326.

Where to Eat: ⚫ Taco's, Girdwood Station, 907) 783-2155. Mexican takeout. ⚫ Double Musky Inn, Crow Creek Road, 907) 783-2822. Cajun-style cooking and plenty of fresh Alaskan seafood.

Where to Stay: ✕♠ Alyeska Resort, 907) 754-1111. Alaska's largest winter sports complex. Includes a first-class hotel and has excellent night skiing.

Attractions and Adventures: ⚫ Crow Creek Mine, 907) 278-8060. Site of one of the earliest gold strikes in Alaska. ⚫ Tram at the Alyeska resort to the top of Mt. Alyeska (3160 ft.). ⚫ The Six Million Acre Chugach National Forest is the second largest in the country, an amazing place to hike and climb. For now, the state has banned whitewater rafting on the park's Eagle River, but call Anchorage White Water to rent a raft for use on rivers outside the area. ✕ ⚫ Club Way North, P.O. Box 1003, 907) 783-1335. Call ahead to schedule your own bungee-jumping adventure. Ask for Mark Vance. ⚫ Denali National Park and Reserve, P.O. Box 9, 907) 683-1266. Established in 1917 to protect wildlife, this park contains Mt. McKinley, the tallest mountain in North America (18,000 ft.). ✕ ⚫ Portage Glacier, 11 miles south of Girdwood, P.O. Box 129, 907) 783-2326. Not one of Alaska's most dramatic glaciers, but one of the closest to Anchorage.

# ARIZONA

Nickname: "Grand Canyon State." Capital: Phoenix. Tourist Office: 2702 N. 3rd St., Suite 4015, Phoenix, 85004, 602) 230-7733. State Parks information: 1300 W. Washington, Phoenix, 85007, 602) 542-4174.

FLAGSTAFF: Flagstaff Visitors' Center: 1 E Rt. 66, 86001, 800) 842-7293.

Where to Stay: ♠ Flagstaff KOA, 5803 N. Highway 89, 520) 526-9926. 200 campsites are available for hookup. You can do your laundry and use the on-site rec. room. ✕♠ Weatherford Motel, 23 N. Leroux St., 520) 774-2731. $12-$35/night.

Where to Eat: ⚫ Macy's, 14 Beaver St., 520) 774-2243. Right behind the Motel du Beau, Macy's serves inexpensive pasta and sandwiches in a relaxed, mostly student atmosphere. ⚫ Hassib's, San Francisco St. #211, 520) 774-1037. Serves a variety of Middle Eastern and European dishes.

Night Life: ☽ Charly's, 23 N. Leroux St., 520) 779-1919. Great live music. Tell them where you're staying and you can get special deals. ☽ The Mad Italian, San Francisco St. #101, 520) 779-1820. Great pizza and pasta.

Sidetrips: ➔Sedona, 28 miles south of Flagstaff on US-89A, 520) 282-7722. A haven for new-age practitioners of all kinds. ➔ Grand Canyon, north of Flagstaff on US-180, 520) 638-7888. You can't go to Arizona without visiting this awe-inspiring formation. Ask about access to the North and South rims. ➔ Four Corners Monument. Tell your friends you went to Arizona, New Mexico, Colorado, and Utah all in one day.

PHOENIX: Phoenix Convention and Visitors' Center: 1 Arizona Center, 400 E. Van Buren, Suite 600, 85004, 602) 254-6500.

602) 264-4553. A gay bar in a cute little house by the highway.

Attractions and Adventures: ⚫ Heard Museum, 22 E. Monte Vista Rd., 602) 252-8840. Features mostly Native American artwork. $5/person. ⚫ Hall of Flame/Museum of Fire Fighting, 6101 E. Van Buren St., 602) 275-3473. Displays of the first fire engines and some ridiculous early fire extinguishing methods. ✕ ⚫ Phoenix Municipal Stadium, 5999 E. Van Buren, 602) 495-7239. Stadium hosts a variety of events, but primarily baseball.

Sidetrips: ➔ Big Surf water park, 1500 N. Mclintock Ave., in Tempe, 602) 947-7873. Ride the 5-foot waves on those 100-degree days. ➔ Tortilla Flats, Rte. 88, 18 miles north of US-60 junct., 602) 984-1776. An old ghost town named after the Steinbeck novella. ➔ London Bridge, Lake Havasu City. From Phoenix, Take US-10E to US-95N. The bridge was shipped from Britain to the US in 1968. ✕ ➔ Nogales, Mexico, 180 miles south of Phoenix, Visitors' Center 011-52-631 2 64-46. The other Nogales. Not nearly as seedy as Tijuana, and very easy to get to: just walk through a gap in the wire fence. A great place to go if you want a quick glimpse of Mexico. ✕ ➔ Senor Amigos (Nogales, Mexico), 52) 631-22375. Mexican dive bar.

# BIMINI, BAHAMAS

Capital: Nassau. Bahamas News Bureau, 19495 Biscayne Blvd., Suite 809, Aventura, Florida, 33180, 800) 327-7678.

BIMINI: Bahamas Tourist Office, General Delivery, Alice Town, Bimini, 809) 347-3529.

Where to Stay: ♠ Bimini Compleat Angler Hotel, Kings Hwy., P.O. Box 601, Alice Town, 809) 347-3122. Hemingway visited this hotel on several occasions in the 30s.

Where to Eat: ⚫ Captain Bob's Conch Hall of Fame, 809) 347-3260. Great Bimini bread and french toast. ⚫ CJ's Deli 809) 347-3295. Great cracked conch.

Adventures and Attractions: ⚫Hemingway Championship Billfish Tournament, March, Blue Water Resort, Alice Town, 809) 347-3166. ⚫Bacardi Billfish Tournament, March, Bimini Bay Game Fishing Club, 809) 347-3391. Who can catch the largest blue marlin? ✕⚫ Bimini Biological Field Station, 9300 S.W. 99 St., 305) 274-0628. Call ahead to visit Doc Gruber, his staff, and the sharks.

# CALIFORNIA

Nickname: "The Golden State." Capital: Sacramento. California Office of Tourism, 801 K St., #1600, Sacramento, 95814, 800) 862-2543.

*road rules america*

If you thought reading ROAD RULES ROAD TRIPS was fun, why not drive it? Use this guide to follow the trails blazed by our ten fearless road trippers. If you'd like to bungee in Alaska, fly a fighter plane over the Nevada desert, or skydive from 12,000 feet, see ATTRACTIONS AND ADVENTURES for the names and numbers of the pros who ushered the casts of ROAD RULES through their daredevil missions. Every time you see an ✕, you're looking at a place where the ROAD RULES casts really ate, slept, drank, danced, or adventured. Now YOUR adventure begins.

Night Life: ☽ Fly-by-Night Club, 3300 Spenard Rd., 907) 279-7726. Always features live music, usually the most popular local bands. Be aware that many of the "bars" in this area are actually strip joints.

Attractions and Adventures: ⚫ Dog Musher's Hall of Fame, along Iditarod Trail, mile 13.9 on Knik Rd., Knik, 907) 376-7755. ⚫ Alaska Experience Theater, 6th St. & G St., 907) 276-3730. Get an eyeful of Alaska's most dramatic scenery on 180-degree wraparound screen. ⚫Old Seward Highway. A scenic 100-mile stretch of road running south of Anchorage.

GIRDWOOD: Visitors' Information: Begich Boggs Visitor Center, Portage Glacier, 99587, 907) 783-2326.

Where to Eat: ⚫ Taco's, Girdwood Station, 907) 783-2155. Mexican takeout. ⚫ Double Musky Inn, Crow Creek Road, 907) 783-2822. Cajun-style cooking and plenty of fresh Alaskan seafood.

Where to Stay: ✕♠ McDowell Mountain Regional Park, 15612 E. Palisades Dr. (in the Fountainhills area), 602) 471-0173. Park includes camping facilities, showers, picnic areas, and trails for mountain biking. ♠ KOA Phoenix West, 602)853-0537. Reliable campgrounds close to town. $14.50/site. A YMCA, 350 N. First Ave., 602) 253-6181.

Where to Eat: ⚫ Bill Johnson's Big Apple, 3757 E. Van Buren St., 602) 275-2107. 40 years in the same location. Inexpensive grub with ambiance. ⚫ Ed Debevic's, 2102 E. Highland Ave., 602) 956-2760. A '50s-style restaurant with waitresses who put you in your place. ⚫Julio's Barrio, 7243 E. Indian School, 602) 423-0058. Good, inexpensive Mexican food, in a '30s-style diner.

Night Life: ☽ Phoenix Live, at Arizona Center, 455 N. 3rd St., 602) 252-2502. This huge complex houses three bars and a restaurant. Open Tues.-Sat. ☽ Mason Jar, 2303 E. Indian School, 602) 956-6271. Head-banging metal music seven days a week. ☽ The Country Club, 4428 N. 7th Ave.

CALISTOGA: Calistoga Chamber of Commerce, 1458 Lincoln Ave., #9, 94515, 707) 942-6333.

Where to Stay: ♠ The inns and spas in the area start at about $70/night, so we recommend camping, but if you want to be spoiled, call the Chamber of Commerce for info about the ultra-comfy places to stay in the area. ♠ Bothe-Napa Valley, 3801 N. St. Helena, 707) 942-4575. Boasts 55 camping sites at around $15/night. Make reservations through Destinet, 800) 444-7275. ♠ Napa County Fairgrounds, 1435 N. Oak St., 707) 942-5111. Call ahead to reserve one of the 46 sites, which range from $10-18/night.

Where to Eat: ⚫ Big Daddy's, 1522 Lincoln Ave., 707) 942-9503. All-American fast food-hamburgers, chicken, salads. ⚫ Bosco's, 1364 Lincoln Ave., 707)942-9088. Tasty Italian food, including gourmet pizza, pastas, salads, and sandwiches.

Adventures and Attractions: 👁 Old Faithful Geyser, 1299 Tubbs Lane, 707) 942-6463. A 60-foot-high geyser that erupts at regular intervals. ✖👁 Calistoga Spa, 1006 Washington St., 707) 942-6269. 👁 Indian Hot Springs, 1712 Lincoln Ave., 707) 942-4913. Olympic-size pool with complete facilities. 👁 International Spa, 1300 Washington, 707) 942-6122. Very New Age. 👁 Nance's Hot Springs, 1614 Lincoln Ave., 707) 942-6211. Down to earth and affordable. 👁 Clos Pegase Winery, 1060 Dunaweal Lane, 707) 942-4981. A breathtaking spot for a picnic. 👁 Chateau Montelena Winery, 1429 Tubbs Lane, 707) 942-5105. A small "castle" on a beautiful lake. 👁 Calistoga Gliders of Napa Valley, 1546 Lincoln Ave., 707) 942-5000. Glider flights daily, 1 or 2 passengers.

**LOS ANGELES:** Los Angeles Convention and Visitors' Bureau, 685 S. Figueroa St., 90071, 213) 624-7300.

Where to Stay: ⌂ Banana Bungalow, W. Hollywood, 2775 Cahuenga Blvd., 213) 851-1129. Pool on premises, and a free shuttle to the beach. $15/room. ⌂ Cadillac Hotel, Venice, 8 Dudley Ave., 310) 399-8876. Dorm-style rooms available ($20), and singles ($55). Building has gym and sauna. Good location. ⌂ HI- Los Angeles/Santa Monica, 1436 Second St., Santa Monica, 310) 393-9913. Large, new hostel, in a restored building near the beach.

Where to Eat: 🐟 Toi Thai, 7505 1/2 Sunset Blvd., 213) 874-8062. A rock-and-roll Thai place in Hollywood. 🐟 El Coyote, 7312 Beverly Blvd., 213) 939-2255. Great Mexican food in West Hollywood. 🐟 Reel Inn, 1220 3rd St. Promenade, on Pacific Coast Highway, just north of Santa Monica, 310) 395-5538. A great seafood restaurant. 🐟 Rosco's 5006 W. Pico Blvd., 213) 934-4405. Chicken and waffles.

Night Life: ☽ The Dresden Room, 1760 N. Vermont, 213) 665-4294. ☽ The Good Luck Club, 1514 Hillhurst Ave., 213) 666-3524. ☽ HMS Bounty, 3357 Wilshire Blvd., 213) 385-7275. Old Hollywood bar with wood paneling and good martinis. ☽ The Diamond Club, 7070 Hollywood Blvd., 213) 467-7070. Check out Saturday Night Fever on Saturday nights. ☽ The Derby, 4500 Los Feliz Blvd., 213) 663-8979. Swing dancing lessons on Wed. and Thurs. On Fridays, the band from THE MASK plays. ✖☽ House of Blues, 8430 Sunset Blvd., 213) 650-1451.

Adventures and Attractions: ✖👁 Mann's Chinese Theater, 6925 Hollywood Blvd., 310) 208-8998. Stick around long enough and you might pick up some free movie passes. 👁 Ocean Front Walk, Venice Beach, 1800 Ocean Front Walk (18th and Pacific). You'll never get tired of looking at the bodybuilders, juggling cyclists, and Rollerbladers. 👁 The Beverly Hot Springs, 308 N. Oxford, 213) 734-7000. Soak with the celebs at this slightly pricey, but well-worth-it spot. ✖👁 Venice Beach, 18 miles southwest of downtown LA, 310) 827-2366. Packed with Rollerbladers, weightlifters, and sunbathers. 👁 Smuggler's Cove, near Torrance, just 30 minutes from downtown LA. LA's only nude beach. 👁 Redondo Sport Fishing, 233 N. Harbor Dr., 310) 372-2111. Makes whale-watching available to everyone. Take a three-hour boat ride (and a Dramamine) and watch the whales do their thing.

Sidetrips: ➜ Catalina Island, Avalon and Twin Harbors. Has a nature preserve and good camping. Wild buffalo on the island. ➜ San Bernadino Mts., one hour east of LA, 909) 889-3980. Great hiking, biking, and camping.

**MALIBU:** Chamber of Commerce: 23805 Stewart Ranch Rd., Suite 100, 90265, 310) 456-9025.

Where to Stay: ⌂ Malibu Surfer Motel, 22541 W. Pacific Coast Hwy., 310) 456-6169. Pool and sundeck, right across the street from Surfrider State Beach. ✖⌂ Malibu RV Park, 25801 Pacific Coast Hwy., 310) 456-6052. Incredible hilltop view of the ocean. ⌂ Malibu Creek State Park, 1925 Las Virgines Rd., 818) 880-0367. 60 campsites available at $14/car.

Where to Eat: 🐟 Mio, 22821 Pacific Coast Hwy., 310) 456-3132. Cheap Italian menu. Very popular with Pepperdine University students. 🐟 Van Go's Ear, 796 Main St., Venice, 310) 314-0022. Delicious omelets and sandwiches. Conveniently located down the street from Muscle Beach. 🐟 Coogie's Beach Cafe, 23755 West Malibu Rd., 310) 317-1444. Homestyle cooking.

Night Life: ☽ Harvelles 1432 4th St., Santa Monica, 310) 395-1676. Hosts excellent blues nightly. ☽ Whisky A Go-Go, 8901 Sunset Blvd. 310) 652-4202. Hopping, all-ages nightclub. Has hosted renowned performers such as The Doors, Talking Heads, and Jimi Hendrix.

Attractions and Adventures: 👁 Self Realization Fellowship Shrine, 17190 Sunset Blvd., 310) 454-4114. Come to this little Eden to get away from it all. If you feel the urge, there are meditation benches amongst the flowers. Also the home for Gandhi's ashes. 👁 Zuma Beach Country Park, 30,000 Block of Pacific Coast Highway. LA County's largest, most popular, northernmost beach. $5 for parking. 👁 Point Dume State Beach, 26,000 Block of Pacific Coast Highway. This uncrowded beach is perfect for swimming, snorkeling, and windsurfing. 👁 Malibu Surfrider State Beach, Pier 2300 Pacific Coast Highway. The surf capital of the world in the '50s and '60s. Gaze at the celebrity mansions of nearby Malibu Colony, but beware of trespassing.

**SAN FRANCISCO:** Convention and Visitors' Bureau, 415) 703-8650.

Where to Stay: ⌂ Green Tortoise Guest House, 494 Broadway, 415) 834-1000. Meet international travelers, take advantage of the complimentary breakfast. $13/single. ⌂ San Francisco International Guest House, 2976 23rd St., 415) 641-1411. Cheap, no curfew. Mission district Victorian house with four-person dorms and a few private rooms.

Where to Eat: 🐟 Kate's Kitchen, 471 Haight St., 415) 626-3984. Try the hush puppies or the peach pancakes–you won't regret it. 🐟 Amazing Grace, 216 Church St., 415) 626-6411. Great vegetarian food for about $5 a plate. 🐟 The Stinking Rose, 325 Columbus Ave., 415) 781-7673. Everything, including the ice cream, is made with garlic. 🐟 Hamburger Mary's Organic Grill, 1582 Folsom St., 415) 626-5767. Punky restaurant where the hip wait-staff serves up great burgers and sandwiches.

Night Life: ☽ Up and Down Club, 1151 Folsom, 415) 626-2388. Bi-level nightclub with a DJ upstairs and live acid jazz downstairs. ☽ Cafe du Nord, 2170 Market St., 415) 861-5016. Tragically hip, huge, happening. ☽ Noc Noc, 557 Haight St., 415) 861-5811. Features all kinds of music and crowds. ☽ Muddy Waters, 521 Valencia St., 415) 863-8006. Good coffee, drinks. ☽ The Tonga Room, 950 Mason St., 415) 772-5278, in the basement of the Fairmont. Decked out like a Polynesian village, complete with a pond and simulated rainstorms. Was a favorite of THE REAL WORLD, SAN FRANCISCO cast.

Adventures and Attractions: 👁 The International Lesbian and Gay Film Festival, the largest of its kind, held every mid-June. For info. about this, and other city festivals, call the Convention and Visitors' Bureau. 👁 Chinese New Year Celebration, late Feb./early March, Chinatown. 👁 Alcatraz Island, San Francisco Bay, 415) 563-6504. Tour the infamous island prison you saw in MURDER IN THE FIRST and THE ROCK. ✖👁 Ed Hardy's Tattoo City , 722 Columbus Ave., 415) 433-9437. Where Shelly and Allison got tattoos. Either walk in or call for an appointment.

Sidetrip: ➜ Muir Woods, Mill Valley, 20 miles north of Golden Gate, 415) 388-2596. Some of the tallest ancient redwoods in the world.

## COLORADO

Nickname: "Centennial State." Capital: Denver. Colorado Board of Tourism, CTTA, P.O. Box 3524, Englewood, 80155, 800) 265-6723. National Park Service, 12795 W. Alameda Pkwy., Lakewood, 80228, 303) 969-2000.

**GUNNISON, CRESTED BUTTE, AND NEARBY:** Gunnison National Forest, 216 N. Colorado St., 812309, 970) 641-0471. Provides valuable information about nearby campgrounds and scenic hikes. Crested Butte Chamber of Commerce, 613 Elk Ave., P.O. Box 1288, 81224, 970) 349-6438. Silverton Chamber of Commerce, P.O. Box 565, 414 4th St., 81433, 970) 387-5654.

Where to Stay: ⌂ Cement Creek Campground, Gunnison National Forest, 970) 641-0471. Has 13 campsites for $7/night. ✖⌂ Best Western, 41883 HWY 50 E., Gunnison, 970) 641-1131. Pool, spa, and complimentary breakfast.

Where to Eat: ✖🐟 The Crested Butte Brewery at the Idlespur, 226 Elk Ave., 970) 349-5026. Great selection of home-brewed beer and yummy bar food. Live music venues. 🐟 The Trough: Two miles west of Gunnison on Hwy. 50, 970) 641-3724. Excellent steak and seafood, as well as wild game and trout.

Night Life: ☽ Kochevar's, 127 Elk Ave., Durango, 970) 349-6756. An 1896 log cabin converted into a pool hall and saloon. ☽ Farquart's, 725 Main Ave., Durango, 970) 247-5440. Antique-looking bar that features local rock bands. ☽ Carver's Bakery and Brewery, 1022 Main Ave., Durango, 970) 259-2545. Serves freshly brewed beer and great food. ✖☽ Idle Spur, 226 Elk Ave., Crested Butte, 970) 349-5026. Home-brewed beer and great live music.

Adventures and Attractions: 👁 Silverton, "The mining town that never quit," 970) 387-5654. Take a tour of its ghost towns and mines. 👁 Black Canyon, Gunnison National Forest, 970) 641-0471. A 2,500-foot gash caused by erosion. 👁 Mirror Lake, Gunnison. Call the National Park Service at 970) 249-7036. ✖👁 Lucky Cat Dog Farm, 900 County Rd. 13, 970) 641-1636. Dogsled tours in winter. Mush! 👁 Fat Tire Bike Week. For info call 970) 349-6817. A great yearly event. 👁 Mountain Bike Hall of Fame and Museum, 126 Elk Ave., Crested Butte, 303) 349-7382. Opened in 1988. Features 39 inductees, hundreds of classic bikes, photos, and artifacts. Hosts several events, such as the June Bike Swap and the July Induction Ceremony.

Sidetrip: ✖➜ Boulder Outdoor Survival School (B.O.S.S.), P.O. Box 1590, Boulder, CO 80306, 800) 335-7404. Call or write for information on how you can have your own B.O.S.S. experience.

## FLORIDA

Nickname: "The Sunshine State." Capital: Tallahassee. Florida Division of Tourism, 126 W. Van Buren St., Tallahassee, 800) 628-2866.

**KEY WEST:** Key West Chamber of Commerce, 402 Wall St., 33040, 305) 294-2587.

Where to Stay: ⌂ Key West Hostel, 718 South St., 305) 296-5719. Dorm or motel rooms available, common kitchen, and A/C. Seasonal prices, never more than $18 for a dorm bed. ⌂ Boyd's Campground, 6401 Maloney Ave., 305) 294-1465. Located right on the ocean. Note: Every amenity costs extra, $31/room, $5/water, A/C is $5, you get the picture.

Where to Eat: 🐟 Gringo's Cantina, 509 1/2 Duval St., 305) 294-9215. Large platters of authentic Mexican food at reasonable prices. Try the key lime pie. ✖🐟 Mangoes, 700 Duval St., 305) 292-4606. Offers creative Caribbean fare. You'll definitely feel like you're on vacation at this place, especially if you eat outside under the huge umbrellas. 🐟 Blue Heaven Fruit Market, 729 Thomas St., 305) 296-8666. Healthy breakfasts, and good vegetarian lunches.

Night Life: ☽ Captain Tony's Saloon, 428 Greene St., 305) 294-1838. Former stomping grounds of Ernest Hemingway. This place has lots of character. Features live music every night. ✖☽ Margaritaville, 500 Duval St., 305) 292-1435. Owned by Jimmy Buffet, live music that shouldn't be missed. ☽ Rick's/Durty Harry's, 208 Duval St., 305) 296-4890. Great live rock and roll music bar.

Adventures and Attractions: 👁 Hemingway House, 907 Whitehead St., 305) 294-1575. Hemingway penned both FOR WHOM THE BELL TOLLS and A FAREWELL TO ARMS here, and if that doesn't interest you, there are 50 cats roaming the premises. 👁 Southernmost Point, where you'll find a huge concrete buoy marking the southernmost point in the United States, hence the name.

**MIAMI AND MIAMI BEACH:** Miami Beach Chamber of Commerce, 1920 Meridian Ave., 33139, 305) 672-1270. Coconut Grove Chamber of Commerce, 2820 McFarlane Rd., 33133 (downtown), 305) 444-7270.

Where to Stay: ⌂ The Tropics, 1550 Collins Ave., 305) 531-0361. A great place to meet people from all over the world. Lots of beds, and only one block from the beach. $14/person. ✖⌂ The Clay Hotel and Hostel International, 1438 Washington Ave., 305) 534-2988. ⌂ The Kenmore Hotel, 1050 Washington Ave., 305) 674-1930. A great bargain. Three blocks from the beach.

Where to Eat: 🐟 11th St. Diner, 1065 Washington Ave., 305) 534-6373. A 24-hour authentic diner serving cheap food in a silver bullet building. 🐟 Captain Dick's Tackle Shack, 3381 Pan American Dr., Coconut Grove, 305) 854-5871. Cheaply priced seafood and salads. Right across from Miami City Hall. 🐟 Lulu's, 1053 Washington Ave., 305) 532-6147. Laid-back, funky, and filled with Elvis's favorite foods and a ton of memorabilia.

Night Life: ☽ Bash, 655 Washington Ave., 305) 538-2274. Dance music on the inside, reggae on the outside. $10 cover, Sundays are free. ☽ Clevelander, 1020 Ocean Dr., 305) 531-3485. Outdoor bar with a large pool. Has great happy hour prices and covers all major sports events. ☽ The Warsaw Ballroom, 1450 Collins Ave., South Beach, 305) 531-4555. Dance club with a bar. Big nights are Friday and Saturday. Lots of drag acts, DJs, a great sound system.

Adventures and Attractions: 👁 Check out the colorful Art Deco architecture on Ocean Dr. and Washington Ave., between 5th and 16th Sts. A hot spot for fashion shoots, 305) 672-2014. Popular cafés and shops face the Atlantic Ocean. 👁 Miami Beach Police and Fire Station, 1100 Washington Ave., 305) 673-7911. A must-see. Early MIAMI VICE episodes were shot here. 👁 Parrot Jungle, 11,000

Southwest 57th Ave., 305) 666-7834. Visit the Parrot Bowl Ampitheatre and see parrots peddle tiny bicycles, pull tiny chariots, and perform other wacky stunts. 👁 South Beach, Southernmost portion of Miami Beach, call visitors' center for info. Beautiful beach with restyled 1930s Art Deco buildings. ✗👁Non Stop Prop Shop, 1800 Bay Rd., 305) 534-8771. Rent costumes and props for all your practical-joke needs.

Sidetrips: ➔ International Museum of Cartoon Art, up the coast on US-1. Minzer Park at 201 Plaza Real, Boca Raton, 561) 391-2200. Features original drawings, a simulated studio, and recreations of famous movie sets. ➔ Hialeah Park Racetrack, 2200 E. 4th Ave., Hialeah, 305) 885-8000. Take 79th. St. exit off of I-95, Features flamingo racing.

**OKAHUMPKA:** Chamber of Commerce: 3430 Hwy. 441/27, 34748, 352) 787-2131.

Where to Stay Nearby: ✗🏠 B's RV Park, 20260 US-27, Clairmont, 352) 429-9400. RV Park with plenty of hookups. ✗🏠 Southern Palms, 1 Avocado Ln., Eustis, 352) 357-8882. Huge RV Park with 1100 sites, 2 pools, a shuffleboard court, bocci space, and planned activities.

Where to Eat: 👄 Sally's Place: The Recovery Room, 607 E. Main St., 352) 728-0080. Great home cooking, Perfect for breakfast and lunch. 👄 Ramshackle Cafe, 1317 N. 14th St., 352) 365-6565. Everything: wings to skins, steaks too.

Adventures and Attractions: 👁 International Tournament Skiing, 20225 County Rd. 33, Groveland, 5 minutes south of Okahumpka, 352) 429-9027 or 800) 732-2755. Best waterskiing around. 👁 Museum of Drag Racing, exit 67 S. off I-75, 13700 S.W. 16th St., Ocala, 352) 245-8661. Racing memorabilia. Engine and car designs of the last 30 years.

**PACE:** Santa Rosa County Chamber of Commerce: 5247 Stewart St., 32570, 904) 623-2339.

Adventures and Attractions: ✗👁 Riviera Naturist Resort, 5000 Guernsey Rd., 904) 994-3665. Meet George Eckenroth at the nudist park formerly known as Ethos Trace. Make it a day trip or stay overnight.

# GEORGIA

Nickname: "The Peach State." Capital: Atlanta. Georgia Tourism, 285 Peachtree St., Atlanta, 404) 656-3590. Parks and Recreation Dept.: US Forest Service, 1720 Peachtree Rd. N.W., 30309, 404) 347-2384.

**ATLANTA:** Visitors' Center: 200 Spring St., 30303 404) 224-2000.

Where to Stay: 🏠 Atlanta Dream Hostel, 222 E. Howard Ave. or 115 Church St., 404) 370-0380 or 800) Dream-96. Has an art gallery with beer garden. $12-$30/night. 🏠 Comfort Inn Downtown, 101 International Blvd., 404) 524-5555. Inexpensive chain motel. 🏠 KOA South Atlanta, 281 Mt. Olive Rd (in McDonough), 770) 957-2610. Tent sites with water, $16/night.

Where to Eat: 👄 Crescent Moon, 254 W. Ponce de Leon, 404) 377-5623. Yummy southern breakfast, try the waffles or the Elvis potatoes, chicken, cheese, and eggs for $2.50. 👄 Mosen Joe's Bar and Grill, 1030 N. Highland Ave., 404) 873-6090. 👄 The Varsity, 61 North Ave., 404) 881-1706. Don't leave Atlanta without going here. The fast food at this huge, '50s-style drive-in will blow your mind. 👄 Fellini's, 2809 Peachtree Rd., 404) 266-0082. Great pizza!

Night Life: 🎵 Lulu's Bait Shack, 3057 Peachtree Rd., 404) 262-5220. Drink out of a fishbowl in an actual shack. 🎵 Dark Horse Tavern and Grill, 816 N. Highland Ave., 404) 873-3607. A nice place with great live music every night. 🎵 Kaya, 1068 Peachtree St., 404) 874-4460. A downtown club with a café on one side and a disco on the other. 🎵 Blind Willie's, 828 N. Highland Ave., 404) 873-2583. Best blues bar in town. Regular appearances by major artists.

Adventures and Attractions: 👁 World of Coca-Cola, 55 M.L. King, Jr. Dr., 404) 676-5151. Tours, taste-tests, and video rooms are some of the attractions at this soft drink birthplace. 👁 Martin Luther King, Jr. National Historic Site. Info Center, 522 Auburn Ave, 404) 331-5190. Visit the church where he preached, the King Center, and his birthplace. 👁 National Black Arts Festival, 236 Forsyth St., Suite 400, 404) 730-7315. Takes place in July. 👁 Fulton County Stadium, 521 Capital Ave., 404) 522-7630. Home of the Braves. Kit's favorite hangout 👁 Olympic Ring, 1.5 mile

from downtown, 404) 222-6688. This ring surrounds the center of town.

**AMERICUS:** Chamber of Commerce: 400 West Lamar, 31709, 912) 924-2646.

Where to Stay: ✗🏠 Amigo House, Habitat for Humanity, 507 W. Church, 912) 924-6935. This hostel is open free of charge to Habitat volunteer groups only. You must call in advance to make reservations. 🏠 The Windsor Hotel, 125 W. Lamar St., 912) 924-1555. $70/night.

Where to Eat: 👄 Beall's 1860, 315 College St. (in Macon), 912) 745-3663. A cute, restored Southern mansion with home cooking. 👄 Forsyth Bar and Grill, 124 W. Forsyth St., 912) 924-8193. 👄 Pat's Place, 1526 South Lee St., 912) 924-0033.

Adventures and Attractions: ✗👁 Habitat for Humanity, 121 Habitat St., 800) HABITAT. Call for information on how you can work for Habitat. 👁 Sumpter Swine Fest, late April, Sumpter County Fairgrounds, call the Chamber of Commerce for info. The largest BBQ competition and livestock show around.

Sidetrips: ➔ Duane Allman crash site. Off I-25 in Macon on the way to Atlanta from Americus. ➔ Athens, GA: The hometown and starting place for bands such as R.E.M., Pylon, and the B-52's. 👄 Check out Weaver D's Soul-Food Café, 1016 E. Broad St., 706) 353-7797. Home of the "Automatic for the People" slogan that graces R.E.M.'s 9th album.

# ILLINOIS

Nickname: "Land of Lincoln." Capital: Springfield. Bureau of Tourism, 800) 2-CONNECT.

**CHICAGO:** Chicago Office of Tourism, 78 E. Washington St., 60602, 312) 744-2400.

Where to Stay: ✗🏠 Best Western, 125 W. Ohio St., 312) 467-0800. A little pricey, but the indoor pool and a sauna are worth it. 🏠 Arlington House, 616 Arlington Pl., 800) 467-8355. Ideal location in Lincoln Park, near the center of nightlife. Open 24 hrs., $16 for nonmembers.

Where to Eat: ✗👄 Hard Rock Cafe, 63 W. Ontario, 312) 943-2252. Check out the rock 'n' roll history on the walls while you munch on fries and burgers. 👄 Giordano's, 730 N. Rush St., 312) 951-0747. Famous Chicago-style pizza, one of 35 city locations. 👄 Billy Goat Tavern, 430 North Michigan, 312) 222-1525. Diner that was the inspiration for John Belushi's Greek diner skits on SATURDAY NIGHT LIVE. 👄 John Barleycorn, 658 West Belden St., 312) 348-8899. Pub food.

Night Life: ✗🎵 Mad Bar, 1640 N. Damen Ave., 312) 227-2277. A "see and be seen" place with live music. 🎵 Hamilton's, 6341 N. Broadway, 312) 764-8133. A great Chicago bar. 🎵 Roscoe's Tavern and Café, 3356 N. Halsted, 312) 281-3355. Primarily gay, but anyone can have fun here. Pool tables, dance floor, even a clairvoyant. ✗🎵 Tequila, 2529 N. Milwaukee St., 312) 772-6266. Latin dance club.

Adventures and Attractions: 👁 Annoyance Theater, 3747 N. Clark, 312) 929-6200. Great comedy acts based on pop culture trends, often involves audience participation. 👁 Biograph Theater, North Lincoln, 312) 348-4123. See where John Dillinger got shot. 👁 Chicago Jazz Festival, late August, Grant Park, call visitors' center for info.

Sidetrips: ➔ Magic Waters Theme Park, 7820 N. Cherryvale Blvd., Cherry Valley, 815) 332-3260. An 18-acre park, open all summer. ✗➔ Rockford: ✗➔ Rockford Speedway, 9500 Forest Hills Rd., 815) 633-1500, just outside Rockford in Loves Park. Stop by and let David Deery show you the races. ➔ LT's, 1011 S. Alpine Rd., Rockford, 815) 394-1098. The ultimate dive bar. ➔ Stash O'Neil's, 4846 East 8th St., Rockford, 815) 397-4182. Great bar.

**FLORA:** Chamber of Commerce, 123 W. North Ave., 62839, 618) 662-5646.

Where to Eat: 👄 Duke's Drive-in, Jct. Routes 45 & 50, 618) 662-2002. Full line of fast food.

Adventures and Attractions: 👁 Clay County Fair, every July, Charlie Brown Park, Flora, 618) 662-FAIR or 618) 662-5646. Carnival rides and the greatest auction around. 👁 Country Music Concert in the Park, every June, Charlie Brown Park, Flora, 618) 662-5646. Live music.

Sidetrip: ➔ Archway Skydiving Center, Vandalia, 40 minutes from Flora, Exit 61 off Highway 70, Rural Route 3, 618) 283-4978. Let Kirk Verner show you how to fly.

# INDIANA

Nickname: "The Crossroads of America." Capital: Indianapolis. Indiana Division of Tourism: 1 N. Capitol #700, 800) 289-6646. State Parks and Reservoirs, 402 W. Washington #W-298, 47802, 812) 232-4125.

**BLOOMINGTON:** Convention and Visitors' Bureau, 2855 N. Walnut St., 47404, 812) 334-8900 or 317) 232-4124.

Where to Stay: 🏠 Motel 6, 1800 N. Walnut St., 812) 332-0820. Cheapest place in town. Singles for $30, doubles for $36. 🏠 Lake Monroe Village Campgrounds, 8107 S. Fairfax Rd., 812) 824-2267. $16/site, $23/hookup. Check out the log cabins for two at $42 a night.

Where to Eat: 👄 The Laughing Planet Cafe, 322 E. Kirkwood Ave., 812) 323-2233. Get burritos for $3.50. 👄 The Crazy Horse, 214 W. Kirkwood, 812) 336-8877. More than 80 beers from all over the world to taste.

Night Life: 🎵 Second Story, 201 S. College Ave., 812) 336-2582. Live alternative bands. 🎵 Rhino's, 325 1/2 S. Walnut St., 812) 333-3430. Local bands. Accepts people under 21.

Adventures and Attractions: 👁 A Taste of Bloomington. This June festival features great local bands and town delicacies. Call the visitors bureau or 812) 336-3681 for more info.

**FORT WAYNE:** Chamber of Commerce, 826 Ewing St.,46802, 219) 424-1435.

Where to Stay: ✗🏠 Holiday Inn Downtown, 300 E. Washington Blvd., 219) 422-5511. Coffee shop, indoor pool, free cable. ✗🏠 Knights Inn, 2901 Goshen Rd., 219) 484-2669. Free coffee for patrons, a pool and a restaurant next door that stays open 24 hrs. $33 and up.

Where to Eat: 👄 Don Hall's Factory, 5811 Coldwater Rd., 219) 484-8693. Delicious Greek salads. Family owned. Lunch and dinner from $4-$16. 👄 Flanagan's, 6525 Covington Rd., 219) 432-6666. Try the seafood in this Victorian-style restaurant. Beautiful grounds with a gazebo and a carousel.

Sidetrips: ➔ James Dean Memorial, Fairmount, 1 hour south of Fort Wayne. This is James Dean's hometown. ➔ Indy 500, Memorial Day Weekend, 4790 W. 16th St., Indianapolis, 317) 481-8500. Call for reservations, tickets sell out 1 year in advance.

**NASHVILLE:** Brown County Convention and Visitors' Bureau, P.O. Box 840, 47448, 812) 988-7303.

Where to Stay: 🏠 Hickory Shades Motel, 5714 W. Highway 46, 812) 988-4694. Exceptionally clean and in a green, rural area. ✗🏠 Brown County Inn, 51 E. State Road 46, 812) 988-2291.

Where to Eat: 👄 The Ordinary, S. Van Buren, 812) 988-6166. Great tavern that will satisfy any appetite.

Attractions: 👁 Brown County Art Guild, Inc., one block south of Van Buren and Main St., 812) 988-6185. 👁 Bill Monroe Bluegrass Hall of Fame, State Rd. 135 N., Morgantown, 812) 988-6422. 👁 Dillinger Museum, 90 W. Washington St., 812) 988-1933. 👁 Johnny Appleseed Festival, September, Johnny Appleseed Park, Fort Wayne, 800) 289-6646. Pioneer festival honoring the man who planted all those apple trees.

# LOUISIANA

Nickname: "Pelican State." Capital: Baton Rouge. Louisiana Office of Tourism, P.O. Box 94291, Baton Rouge 70804-9291, 504) 342-8119. Office of State Parks, P.O. Box 44426, Baton Rouge 70804, 504) 342-8111.

**NEW ORLEANS:** Welcome Center, 529 St. Ann, in the French Quarter, 70116, 504) 566-5031. Convention and Visitors' Bureau, 529 St. Ann, 504) 566-5011.

Where to Stay: ✗🏠 Avenue Plaza Hotel, 2111 St. Charles Ave., 504) 566-1212. On the edge of the historic Garden District. Has a sundeck, European spa, private courtyard with pool, and a restaurant. 🏠 Longpre House, 1726 Prytania St., 504) 581-4540. Frequented by backpackers, this relaxed inn is a great place to meet people and find out what's going on. 🏠 Lee Circle YMCA, 920 St. Charles Ave., 504) 568-9622. Easy access by public transportation, this standby is convenient and reliable. Use the gym to work off a hangover. 🏠 KOA West, 11129 Jefferson Highway, 504) 467-1792. Shuttle access to the French Quarter, clean and inexpensive.

**Where to Eat:** ◄ Cafe Atchafalaya, 901 Louisiana Ave., 504) 891-5271. This little eatery has some of the best food the city has to offer, at reasonable prices. Try the cobblers for an out-of-body experience. ◄ Mothers', 401 Poydras, 504) 523-9656. Great homestyle New Orleans food. ◄ Camelia Grill, 626 S. Carrollton, 504) 866-9573. The original 24-hour hangout. ◄ Cafe Du Monde, 800 Decatur St., 504) 525-4544, French Quarter. Have their world-famous beignets and chicory-blend coffee.

**Night Life:** ♪ Jazz and blues are what New Orleans is known for, so there's plenty to choose from. ♪ House of Blues, 225 Decatur St., 504) 529-2624. Standing room only, this place is always packed, and you won't get bored. The decor, videos, and live music should keep you occupied. Also, check out the bathrooms. ♪ Tipitina's, 501 Napoleon Ave., 504) 895-8477. Famous for its bluesy, New Orleans-style music. Frequented by John Goodman and Harry Connick, Jr. ♪ Cafe Brasil, 2100 Chartres St., 504) 947-9386. Hosts mostly Latin music, poetry readings, and film shows.

**Adventures and Attractions:** ◉ New Orleans Historic Voodoo Museum, 724 Dumaine, 504) 522-5223. Traces the history of voodoo practices back to its African roots. ◉ New Orleans Jazz and Heritage Festival, 1205 N. Rampart St., 504) 522-4786, late April. Invites more than 4,000 musicians to play on several stages. Over the years, this festival has seen the likes of Bob Dylan, Aretha Franklin, and Wynton Marsalis. ◉ Don't miss Mardi Gras, the biggest party of the year, late February or early March. ✗◉ Lakelawn Cemetery Metairie, 5100 Pontchartrain Blvd., 504) 486-6331. ◉ St. Louis Cemetery No. 1, 623 Royal St., 504) 588-9357. Beware of voodoo queen Marie Laveau. Make reservations. ✗◉ Orpheus Krewe, one of the largest parades in Mardi Gras, call the Chamber of Commerce for info.

**Sidetrips:** ✗➜ Hammond: ✗➜ Kliebert's Alligator and Turtle Farm, 41067 West Yellow Water Rd., 504) 345-3617. ➜ Fanfare, Southeastern Louisiana University, Hammond, 504) 549-2867. A monthlong salute to the arts held every October. Great music, drama, film, and dance. ➜ Amite: ✗➜ People's Rexall, 114 N.E. Central Ave., Amite, 504) 748-4591. Ask Judy Williams for a scoop of her fabulous ice cream. ➜ Oyster Festival, March, middle of downtown Amite, 504) 222-4616. Delicious oysters, chili, dance bands, and parades.

## MISSISSIPPI

Nickname: "Magnolia State." Capital: Jackson. Division of Travel and Tourism, P.O. Box 849, Jackson, 39205, 601) 359-3297. Bureau of Parks and Recreation, P.O. Box 451, Jackson 39025, 601) 364-2163.

**COLUMBUS:** Convention and Visitors' Bureau, P.O. Box 789, 321 7th St. N, 39701, 601) 329-1191.

**Where to Stay:** ✗⌂ Waverly Waters, 9 miles east and 1 mile south of West Point, on SR 50, 601) 494-1800. Interesting historic house with some antebellum furnishings.

**Where to Eat:** ◄ Harvey's, 200 Main St., 601) 327-1639. Open late. Good, cheap food. ◄ Thunderbird, 205 5th St. N., 601) 329-2882. ◄ Profabella's Diner, 309 Main St., 601) 245-1007. ◄ Browne's Downtown, 509 Main St., 601) 327-8880.

**Adventures and Attractions:** ◉ Lake Lowndes State Park, 3319 Lake Lowndes Rd., 601) 328-2110. Tons of activities like waterskiing, hiking, and fishing. Camping is also permitted. ◉ Friendship Cemetery, 1500 4th St. S., 601-328-2565. The first Memorial Day commemoration was held here.

**Sidetrip:** ➜ Elvis Presley Memorial Meditation Chapel & Birthplace. Exit US-78 at Canal St. to 306 Elvis Presley Dr., Tupelo, 601) 841-1245. This 15-acre park preserves the birthplace and meditation chapel of the King.

## NEVADA

Nickname: "Silver State." Capital: Carson City. Nevada Commission on Tourism, Capitol Complex, Carson City, 89701, 702) 687-4322. Nevada Division of State Parks, 123 W. Nye Lane, Carson City, 89701, 702) 687-4384.

**LAS VEGAS:** Las Vegas Convention and Visitors' Authority, 3150 Paradise Rd., 89109, 702) 892-7575.

**Where to Stay:** It's not hard to find cheap hotels just blocks from the main drag. Shop around. ⌂ Las Vegas International Hostel, 1208 Las Vegas Blvd., 702) 385-9955. The staff is eager to give assistance when needed. $12-$14. ⌂ KOA Las Vegas, 4315 Boulder Highway, 702) 451-5527. Free casino shuttle, slot machines on premises. $23. ✗⌂ Excalibur, 3850 Las Vegas Blvd. S., 702) 597-7777. Theme park on the premises, as well as a beauty salon, wedding chapel, 3,000 slot machines, and 4,032 rooms. ⌂ Buffalo Bill Resort, 45 miles south of Las Vegas, I-15 South at the California-Nevada border, 702) 386-7867. Pool, movie theater, and roller-coaster rides.

**Where to Eat:** ◄ Bally's Big Kitchen Buffet, Bally's Casino, 3645 S. Las Vegas Blvd., 702) 739-4930. One of the most popular buffets available; its massive selection will fill you up for the whole day. ◄ The Great Buffet, Sam's Town Hotel and Gambling Hall, 5111 Boulder Hwy., 702) 456-7777. Offers delicious buffet fare, plus live country music and dancing.

**Adventures and Attractions:** ◉ Liberace Museum features the late entertainer's rhinestone collection, wardrobe, cars etc., 1775 E. Tropicana Ave., 702) 798-5595. ◉ MGM Grand Adventures Theme Park, at the MGM Grand Hotel, 3799 Las Vegas Blvd. S., 800) 929-1111. The largest hotel in the world—5,005 rooms, nine restaurants, a food court, a roller coaster, and a riverboat. ◉ Grand Slam Canyon, at the Circus Circus Hotel, 2880 Las Vegas Blvd. S., 702) 734-0410. This amusement park has a 15-story mountain and a 90-foot waterfall. It's all about size in Las Vegas. ✗◉ BFK Sports of Las Vegas, 3111 S. Valley View, Suite A116, 702) 220-4340. Call Scott Dyer to plan your own landsailing adventure. ✗◉ Desert Aces, North Las Vegas Air Terminal, 2772 N. Rancho Drive, 702) 646-5599. Military training planes and dogfighting. Ask for Nancy Stone.

**Sidetrips:** ➜ Hoover Dam, 25 miles south of L.V. by way of US-93, Boulder City, 702) 293-8367. ➜ Good Springs, 30 miles south of Las Vegas, Highway 15. Ghost town with neat old buildings. ➜ Pueblo Grande or Lost City Museum, Overton, 63 miles north of Las Vegas, 702) 397-2193. Pueblos and recreated Indian villages.

## NEW MEXICO

Nickname: "Land of Enchantment." Capital: Santa Fe. Department of Tourism, The Lamy Building, 491 Old Santa Fe Trail, Santa Fe, 87503, 800) 545-2040. New Mexico Parks and Recreation Division, 2040 South Pacheco St., Santa Fe, 87501, 888) 667-2757.

**RED RIVER:** Chamber of Commerce, P.O. Box 870, Main Street Town Hall, Red River, 87558, 505) 754-2366

**Where to Stay:** ✗⌂ Red River Inn, 300 W. Main St., Red River, 505) 754-2930. Doubles start at $50. Hot tub available. A nonsmoking establishment. ⌂ Laguna Vista Lodge, 51 Rt. 64, Eagle Nest, 505) 377-6522. Budget-minded; suites also available.

**Where to Eat:** ◄ Angelina's, 112 West Main St., 505) 754-2211. Best to offer southwestern-style food. ◄ Texas Red's Steakhouse, 111 E. Main St., 505) 754-2964. Great steaks at affordable prices.

**Night Life:** ✗♪ The Motherlode, The Lodge at Red River, E. Main St., 505) 754-6280. Live music, cover.

**Adventures and Attractions:** ◉ Wild Rivers Natural Recreation Site, 35 miles north of Taos, 505) 758-8851. Access to rivers, hiking, mountain biking. ◉ Winnie's Museum Park, 1.5 miles east of Red River, 505) 754-6404. Tour of an old log cabin with mining tools and furniture from 1890s. ◉ Bittercreek Guest Ranch, 2.5 miles NE of Red River, 505) 754-2587. Horseback riding in an out-of-this-world setting. ✗◉ Snow box derby, Red River's newest festival. Call the Chamber of Commerce or call the Red River Ski Area at 505) 754-2223. Ask for Wally Dobbs.

**Sidetrips:** ➜ National Atomic Museum, Wyoming Blvd., Bldg. 20358, Kirkland Air Force Base, Albuquerque, 505) 284-3243. History of bombs. ➜ Tinkertown, 121 Sandia Crest Rd., Albuquerque, 505) 281-5233. Walls made of glass bottles, miniature animated Western town and circus.

## NEW YORK

Nickname: "The Empire State." Capital: Albany. Division of Tourism, 1 Commerce Plaza, Albany, 12245, 800) 225-5697. NY State Office of Parks and Recreation, Empire State Plaza, Bldg. 1, Albany, 12238-0001, 518) 474-0456. Division of Lands and Forests DEC, S. Wolfe Rd., Room 412, Albany, 12233-4255, 518) 457-7433.

**NEW YORK CITY AND LONG ISLAND:** Tourist Office, 2 Columbus Circle, 10019, 212) 397-8222.

**Where to Stay:** ⌂ New York International HI-AYH Hostel, 891 Amsterdam Ave., 201) 932-2300. The largest hostel in the US is located in a historic building that is walking distance to Central Park. ⌂ International Student Center, 38 W. 88th St., 212) 787-7706. Unlike many other hostels, this one has no curfew. $12/night. ⌂ Chelsea International Hostel, 251 W. 20th St., 212) 647-0010. This new hostel provides guests with free beer and pizza on Wed. nights. $18/night. ⌂ Wilderness camping, Fire Island, near Smith Point West, 516) 281-3010. Camping is free, just pick up a permit at the Smith Point Visitors' Center.

**Where to Eat:** ◄ Mo's Caribbean Bar and Grill, 1154 2nd Ave., 212) 650-0561. ◄ Dojo Restaurant, 24 St. Mark's Pl., 212) 674-9821. Great healthy food at affordable prices. Sit outdoors to chat with East Village hipsters. ◄ John's Pizza, 278 Bleeker St., 212) 243-1680. This coal brick oven baked pizza is known as the tastiest in NYC.

**Night Life:** ♪ Giant Step. Check the VILLAGE VOICE to locate this mobile party that plays at different clubs in the city. The live music is a mixture of funk, jazz, and hip-hop. ♪ Twilo, 530 W. 27th St., 212) 268-1600. Gay dance club where everybody struts their stuff. Friday and Saturday, dance until dawn. ♪ Beauty Bar, 231 E. 14th St., 212) 539-1389. Get "teased up" with a $5 manicure during happy hour (5-9). ♪ The Cooler, 416 W. 14th St., 212) 645-5189. Once a meat cooler, this cavernous space reverberates with the New York sound. All of the city's hottest acts pass through. ♪ Here, 145 Ave. of the Americas, 212) 647-0202. The two stages at this oh-so-hip performance space host postmodern Shakespeare and the latest plays by the city's up-and-coming playwrights. ♪ Nuyorican Poets Cafe, 236 E. 3rd St., 212) 505-8183. Sip cappuccino with the black-turtleneck crowd while you marvel at the café's fast-talking poetry slammers. $5-10 cover for readings and slams. ♪ Bourbon St. Bar, 407 Amsterdam Ave., between 79th & 80th, 212) 721-1332. Great ladies-night specials. ♪ Bear Bar, Broadway btw. 75th & 76th, 212) 362-2145. An Allison favorite. ♪ The West End Gate, 2911 Broadway, btw. 113th and 114th St., 212) 662-8830. Allison's bar of choice.

**Adventures and Attractions:** ◉ Museum of Modern Art, 11 W. 53rd St., 212) 708-9400. See original artwork by Picasso, Monet, and Jasper Johns. ◉ Museum of Television and Radio, 25 W. 52nd St., 212) 621-6800. ◉ Apollo Theater, 253 W. 125th St., 212) 749-5838. The center of black entertainment. ◉ Shakespeare in the Park, Delacorte Theater, Central Park, 212) 861-7277. Very popular summer plays that often feature celebrities. Come early, the tickets are free. ◉ Chelsea Hotel, 222 W. 23rd St., 212) 243-3700. The former home of many artists is still a hotel, but you don't have to stay there to feel the aura of the good old days, when the place was packed with famous authors and musicians. ◉ The stage at Bryant Park, 42nd St. and Sixth Ave., 212) 397-8222. The grassy field hosts free classic films, jazz concerts, and live comedy. Bring a blanket and a picnic dinner. ◉ Central Park, between 5th Ave and Central Park West from 59th St. to 110th St., 212) 794-6564. A great oasis from the city. Bring your Rollerblades, rent a bicycle, or just relax in the grass. The place to be on Sunday afternoons. ◉ Wigstock, September, Greenwich Village, call the Visitors' Center for info.

## NORTH CAROLINA

Nickname: "Tarheel State." Capital: Raleigh. Travel and Tourism, 430 N. Salisbury St., Raleigh, 27603, 919) 733-4171. US Forest Service, P.O. Box 2750, Asheville, 28802, 704) 257-4200.

**WANCHESE:** Chamber of Commerce, P.O. Box 1757, Kill Devil Hills, 27948, 919) 441-8144.

**Where to Stay:** ✗⌂ Raleigh/Durham Airport Holiday Inn, not far from Wanchese on 4810 Page Rd., 919) 941-6000. Rooms start at $89. Outdoor pool, free cable, and exercise room.

**Where to Eat:** ◄ Queen Anne's Revenge, 1064 Old Wharf Rd., 919) 473-5466. ◄ Fisherman's Wharf, Highway 345 South, 919) 473-5205. Freshest seafood around.

**Adventures and Attractions:** ◉ Moon Tillett Fish Company, 4703 Mill Landing Road, 919) 473-2323. Ryan Tillett might be able to help you if you're looking for work and you don't mind smelling fishy.

◉ World's Largest Ten Commandments, Fields of the Wood Bible Theme Park, outside Murphy, 714) 494-7855. ◉ Outer Banks, 122 miles of North Carolina coastline, 919) 441-8144. Beautiful beaches with great surfing, windsurfing, and fishing opportunities.

**WILMINGTON:** Cape Fear Coast Convention and Visitors' Bureau, 24 N. 3rd St., 28401, 910) 341-4030.

**Where to Stay:** ♠ Camelot Campground, 8 miles north on US-17, 910) 686-7705, $15/tent. ♠ Comfort Inn Executive Center, 151 College Rd., 910) 791-4841. Free continental breakfast, pool, and Nautilus on premises.

**Where to Eat:** ◑ Riverboat Landing, 2 Market St., 910) 763-7227. Good seafood and pasta on the menu. Nightly jazz and a great view. ◑ Pilot House, Chandler's Wharf, 2 Ann St., 910) 343-0200. Awesome Sunday brunch on the outdoor patio should not be passed up.

**Night Life:** ♪ Thalian Hall Center for the Performance Arts, 310 Chestnut St., 910) 343-3664. This amazing building opened in 1799, and has been hosting all kinds of performances ever since.

**Adventures and Attractions:** ◉ Wilmington Jazz Festival. The turnout is huge. 910) 343-4030. ◉ Cape Fear Blues Festival in the summer should not be missed. 910) 343-4030.

## OKLAHOMA

**Nickname:** "The Sooner State." **Capital:** Oklahoma City. Tourism and Recreation Dept.: 500 Will Rogers Blvd., Oklahoma City, 73146, 800) 652-6552.

**OKLAHOMA CITY:** Chamber of Commerce: 123 Park Avenue, 73102, 405) 297-8900.

**Where to Stay:** ♠ Little River State Park, 405) 360-3572. Sites $6. Swim or fish in the lake. ♠ Motel 6, 4200 W. I-40, 405) 947-6550. $32/single. Huge rooms with access to spa and pool.

**Where to Eat:** ◑ Sweeny's Deli, 900 N. Broadway Ave., 405) 232-2510. Pool tables, food available until late, friendly atmosphere. ◑ Cattleman's Steak House, 1309 S. Agnew, 405) 236-0416. Steaks from the largest cattle market in the US.

**Night Life:** ♪ Bricktown Brewery, at Sheridan Ave. and Oklahoma St., 405) 232-BREW. Full menu, fresh beer, live music upstairs, and bar games.

**Adventures and Attractions:** ◉ National Cowboy Hall of Fame and Western Heritage, 1700 N.E. 63rd, 405) 478-2250. John Wayne display, history-based exhibits. ◉ Red Earth Festival, 405) 427-5228. Country's largest Native American celebration, held in early June. ◉ Oklahoma City Stockyards, 2500 Exchange Ave., 405) 235-8675. The busiest cattle auctions in the world are held here on Monday and Tuesday mornings. ◉ International Rodeo Finals, every January, Fairgrounds, Oklahoma City, 405) 235-6540. Watch the greatest cowboys on earth compete in this world renown festival. ◉ Bricktown, 315 East Sheridan St., 405) 236-8666. Revitalized warehouse district with charming restaurants and shops.

**Sidetrips:** ➜ National Wrestling Hall of Fame and Museum, 405 W. Hall of Fame Ave., Stillwater, 405) 377-5243. ➜ Big Peanut Statue, 3rd & Evergreen, Durant. The world's largest peanut.

## SOUTH DAKOTA

**Nickname:** "The Mount Rushmore State." **Capital:** Pierre. Division of Tourism, 711 E. Wells Ave., Pierre, 57501, 800) 952-3625.

**RAPID CITY:** Chamber of Commerce: 444 Mt. Rushmore Rd., 57701, 800) 487-3223.

**Where to Stay:** ♠ Rapid City YMCA, 815 Kansas City St., 605) 342-8538. Separate rooms for guys and girls. A great deal at $10/night. ♠ Ranch House Motel, 202 E. North St., 605) 341-0785. Fridges and micros, downtown locale. $32 and up.

**Where to eat:** ◑ Sixth St. Bakery and Deli, 516 6th St., 605) 342-6660. Yummy sandwiches, good coffee. Next to cheap movie theater.

**Night Life:** ♪ Firehouse Brewing Co., 610 Main St., 605) 348-1915. Beers, full menu, most popular bar.

**Adventures and Attractions:** ✕◉ Mount Rushmore National Monument, 24 miles south of Rapid City, 605) 574-4104. Dubbed "The Shrine of Democracy." Total cost to build: $989,000, 1/2 million tons of rock.

**Sidetrips:** ✕◉ The Corn Palace, 604 W. Main St., 605) 996-7311. Huge domed arena that seats 3,500, surrounded by scenic murals. ◉ Crazy Horse Monument, 17 miles southwest of Mount Rushmore on US-16/385, 605) 673-4681. Enormous memorial sculpture to Crazy Horse carved out of a mountain. ◉ Explore the nearby wonders of South Dakota, such as the Badlands, the Black Hills, Mount Rushmore, and the Crazy Horse Monument. Call the Visitors' Center for info.

## TENNESSEE

**Nickname:** "Volunteer State." **Capital:** Nashville. Tennessee Dept. of Tourist Development: P.O. Box 23170., 615) 741-2158. Tennessee State Parks Information: 401 Church St., L&N Tower, 7th Floor, Nashville, 37243, 800) 421-6683.

**NASHVILLE:** Nashville Area Visitors' Bureau, 161 4th Ave., North, 37119, 615) 259-4700.

**Where to Stay:** ♠ Hallmark Inn, 309 W. Trinity Lane, 800) 251-3294. Free continental breakfast, pool, and cable, $29.88/single. ♠ Opryland KOA, 2626 Music Valley Dr., 615) 889-0282. 460 sites, but gets crowded. Pool and live summer music, $19.95 and up.

**Where to Eat:** ◑ The Iguana, 1910 Belcourt Ave., 615) 383-8920. You have no choice but to order the amazing chicken fajitas. ◑ Slice of Life, 1811 Division St., 615) 329-2525. Healthy fare, yuppie hangout. ◑ The Loveless Cafe, Rte. 5 off Hwy. 100, 615) 646-9700. Don't miss their breakfast biscuits and homemade jams. ◑ Rotier's, 2413 Alliston Place, near Vanderbilt, 615) 327-9892. Southern style.

**Night Life:** ♪ Blue Bird Cafe, 4104 Hillsboro Rd., 615) 383-1461. Country, blues, and folk. Garth Brooks started here. ♪ The Connection, 901 Cowan St., 615) 742-1166. High energy dancing at Nashville's foremost gay club. ♪ Grand Ole Opry, Opryland, 2808 Opryland Dr., 615) 889-3060. The birthplace of the nation's Country Music show.

**Adventures and Attractions:** ◉ Country Music Hall of Fame, 4 Music Sq. East, 615) 256-1639. Artifacts from the early days of country, such as Elvis's solid-gold Cadillac. ◉ Opryland, 2808 Opryland Dr., Rm. 4787, 615) 889-3060. Theater, theme park. Minnie Pearl, and Reba McEntire perform here. Home of the Grand Ole Opry. ◉ The Museum of Tobacco Art and History, 800 Harrison St., 615) 271-2349. Check out some cool Indian pipes and the surprisingly interesting history of cigars, pipes, and tobacco.

**Sidetrips:** ➜ National Knife Museum, 7201 Shallowford Rd., Chattanooga. 423) 892-5007. ➜ Dollywood, 1020 Dollywood Lane, Pigeon Forge, foothills of Smokey Mtns., 423) 428-9488. Dolly Parton's theme park is a must-see.

**MEMPHIS:** Visitors' Information Center: 340 Beale Street, 38103, 901) 543-5333.

**Where to Stay:** ✕♠ French Quarter Suites, 2144 Madison Ave., 901) 728-4000. Single and double suites starting at $110. Outdoor pool and continental breakfast included. ♠ Motel 6, 1117 E. Brooks Rd., 901) 346-0992. The basics for $33.99/night. ♠ Memphis/Graceland KOA, 3691 Elvis Presley Blvd., 901) 396-7125. Right next door to Graceland, $19 and up.

**Where to Eat:** ◑ Front Street Delicatessen, 77 S. Front St., 901) 522-8943. Right downtown, outdoor patio, very cheap. ◑ The North End, 346 N. Main St., 901) 526-0319. Delicious tamales and creole dishes, $3-$10. ✕◑ Chez Phillipe, 149 Union St., 901) 529-4188. ✕◑ Rendezvous Restaurant, 52 S. 2nd St., 901) 523-2746. The biggest ribs around must not be missed.

**Night Life:** ♪ Kudzu's, 603 Monroe Ave., 901) 525-4924. Downtown, live music, packed on weekends. ♪ Oasis, 567 S. Highland., 901) 320-7020. Alternative music, open till 3:00 AM ✕♪ Hooters, 2653 Mt. Moriah, 901) 795-7123. Has a great selection of import beers. ✕♪ Six-One-Six, 901) 526-6552. Come on by and meet Wilbur's pet alligator. ✕♪ Silky O'Sullivan's, 183 Beale St., 901) 522-9596. Home of "The Diver," a gallon mixed drink that comes in a bucket. ✕♪ Overton Park Shell, Overton Park, 3 miles from downtown on Poplar Ave., 901) 274-6046. Live concerts in the park. The site of Elvis's first performance.

**Adventures and Attractions:** ✕◉ Graceland, 800) 238-2000. Make reservations for home tour, and on-premises museum. Write a note to Elvis on the "Wall of Love." ◉ Memphis Music Hall of Fame, 97 S. 2nd St., 901) 525-4007. The city's musical history from '40s to the '70s. ◉ Civil Rights Museum, Lorraine Motel, 450 Mulberry St., 901) 525-4611 ex. 104. Where Dr. Martin Luther King, Jr., was shot, history of African-American struggle. ◉ Music and Heritage Festival, 901) 525-3655. Third weekend in July. ✕◉ Underground Art Tattoo Studio, 2287 Young Ave., 901) 272-1864. Where Devin got inked. ◉ Sun Recording Studios, 706 Union Ave., 901) 521-0664. Tour the small studio that produced Elvis, U2, and Bonnie Raitt.

## TEXAS

**Nickname:** "The Lone Star State." **Capital:** Austin. Department of Transportation: P.O. Box 5064, Austin, 78763, 800) 452-9292. Texas Parks and Wildlife Dept.: 4200 Smith School Road. Austin, 78744, 800) 792-1112.

**AUSTIN:** Convention and Visitors' Bureau: 201 E. 2nd St. Austin, 78701, 512) 478-0098.

**Where to Stay:** ✕♠ Best Western Atrium North, 7928 Gessner Dr., 512) 339-7311. Rooms start at $60. Indoor pool, free continental breakfast, and free cable included. ♠ 21st St. Co-op, 707 W. 21st, 512) 476-1857. $10 for a bed and a meal. ♠ McKinney Falls State Park., 512) 243-1643, In an old ranch house at south edge of the city. Starting at $8.

**Where to Eat:** ✕◑ Ruby's BBQ, 512 W. 29th St., 512) 477-1651. Lively late night eatery. ◑ Chuy's, 1728 Barton Springs, 512) 474-4452. Soulful Mexican food in kitschy surroundings: Cadillac fenders grace the walls, thousands of fish hang from the ceiling, and there's even a shrine to the King. ◑ Tamale House #3, 5003 Airport Blvd., 512) 453-9842. A place with absolutely no attitude, just good, basic, cheap, Mexican eating that will fill you up for around $3. ✕◑ County Line Restaurant, 5204 F.M. 2222, 512) 346-3664. BBQ.

**Night Life:** ♪ Antone's, 2915 Guadalupe, 512) 474-5314. Austin's legendary blues bar. ✕♪ 311 Club, 311 Sixth St., 512) 477-1630. The 6th St. district offers excellent live music venues like jazz, rap, funk, and reggae. ♪ Emo's, 603 Red River St., 512) 477-EMOS. Free most nights if you are 21+. Hosts wide variety of college/underground/punk/noise music. Look for Kozic paintings in the pool room. Their motto is "This Place Sucks."

**Adventures and Attractions:** ◉ Zilker Park, city park west of downtown, 512) 476-9044. Popular recreation center has a huge pool at 2201 Barton Springs Rd., that is usable year-round. ◉ Austin Museum of Art at Laguna Gloria, 3809 W. 35th St., 512) 458-8191. American art from 1900 to present. ◉ Bat colony at the Congress Ave. Bridge from mid-March to November. Just before dusk, watch these night-fliers emerge from beneath the bridge to feed on the mosquitoes. ✕◉ South by Southwest Music Festival, third week in March, citywide, 512) 467-7979. This 3-day show features the best bands from Austin and around the world. ✕◉ Palmer Auditorium, 400 South 1st St., 512) 472-5111. All sorts of shows, antiques, symphony, live music. ◉ Stevie Ray Vaughan Memorial, on Town Lake, Riverside Dr., call the Visitors' Bureau for info.

**SULPHUR SPRINGS:** Chamber of Commerce: 1200 Houston St., Sulphur Springs, 75482, P.O. Box 347, 75483, 903) 885-6515.

**Where to Eat:** ◑ Mary Puddin' Hill Store, 201 E. I-30, 903) 455-6931. Yummy homemade soups and sandwiches in a country and western atmosphere.

**Adventures and Attractions:** ◉ Governor Hogg Shrine State Historical Park, 45 Park Rd., Quitman, 903) 683-4850. Three museums featuring Governor Hogg and his family. Also, you can go hiking and picnicking. ◉ Southwest Dairy Center and Museum, 1210 Houston St., 903) 439-6455. Antique milking machines, hands-on exhibits, and homemade ice cream. ◉ Hopkins County Dairy Festival, June, 1210 Houston St., Civic Center, and City Park, 903) 885-8071. Dairy Pageant and fresh ice cream. ◉ Fall Festival, Sept., 1210 Houston St., Civic Center, 903) 885-8071. Country crafts. ✕◉ Central Rodeo Association Finals Rodeo-mid Nov., 1210 Houston St., Civic Center, 903) 885-8071. Three-day event featuring the greatest cowboys around.

**Sidetrips:** ➜ Texas Ranger Hall of Fame, off I-35, Waco, 817) 750-8631. Weapons, wax statues, and saddles. The most famous law-enforcement agency of the Old West. ➜ Inner Space Caverns, exit 259 in Georgetown, off I-35 going N., 512) 863-5545. Sound and light show in caverns.

# UTAH

Nickname: "The Beehive State." Capital: Salt Lake City. Salt Lake Valley Convention and Visitors' Bureau: 180 S.W. Temple, 84101, 801) 521-2868.

## BOULDER

Where to Stay: ♠ Quiet Falls Motel, P.O. Box 279, 75 S. 100 W. Escalante, 801) 826-4250. Your basic motel, very clean and comfortable, complete with cable and kitchenettes. ♠ Escalante Petrified Forest State Park, 801) 826-4466. Toilets on premises, but basically you're on your own. Plus, you can go boating and swimming.

Where to Eat: ◐ Cowboy Blues Diner, 530 W. Main Escalante, 801) 826-4251. Open for breakfast, menu consists mostly of southwestern and Mexican fare.

Adventures and Attractions: ◉ Anasazi State Park, 460 N. Highway 12, 801) 335-7308. Scenic spot with cool replica of a Native American village. ✗◉ Boulder Outdoor Survival School, P.O. Box 1345, 84716, #2 School House Lane, 801) 335-7404. Register for an intense outdoor experience. Ask David Wescott for more info.

MOAB: Information Center, Center and Main St., 84532, 800) 635-MOAB.

Where to Stay: ♠ Lazy Lizard International Hostel, 1213 S. US-191, 801) 259-6057. Owners arrange rafting trips. Hot tub and VCR available. Stay in a cabin, tent, or teepee. ✗♠ Best Western, 16 S. Main St., Moab, 801) 259-2300. Rooms start at $89. Outdoor swimming pool and hot tub.

Where to Eat: ◐ Moab Diner, 189 S. Main St., 801) 259-4006. Burgers and great fries. ◐ Eddie McStiff's, 57 N. Main St., 801) 259-BEER. 12 homemade brews, salads, pizza, pasta. ◐ Honest Ozzie's Cafe and Desert Oasis, 60 N. 100 W., 801) 259-8442. Vegetarian food and fruity drinks. Great for breakfast.

Night Life: ♪ The Rio, 2nd S. 100 W., 801) 259-6666. The only place in town that serves mixed drinks sans food. It's a private club, so get sponsored by a member or buy a two-week pass for $5. ♪ Poplar Place, 100 N. Main St., 801) 259-6018. Perfect place for a cold brew after a day on the trails.

Adventures and Attractions: ◉ Hole 'n the Rock, 15 miles south of Moab on US-191, 801) 686-2250. 5,000-square foot, 14-room former home of Albert Christiansen, who spent 20 years carving it out of solid sandstone. ◉ Navtech Expeditions, 321 N. Main St., 801) 259-7983. Take a rafting trip down the Colorado River or a jeep tour in the canyons. ◉ Moab Fat Tire Festival, held during the last week in October, 800) 635-MOAB. The best-known mountain bike festival in the US. ✗◉ Slickrock Trail, off Mill Creek Rd., a couple miles east of Moab, 801) 259-6111. Fabulous hiking and biking.

Sidetrips: ➔ Nearby National Parks: Canyonlands, Arches, Capital Reef, Bryce Canyon, and Zion. ➔ Monument Valley Tribal Park, Navajo Indian Reservation, Goulding, 801) 727-3287. Towering mesas and rocks.

SALT LAKE CITY: Info Center: 180 S. West Temple, 84101, 801) 521-2822.

Where to Stay: ✗♠ Red Lion Inn, 255 S.W. Temple, 801) 328-2000. Heated indoor pool, exercise room, free cable, and an indoor whirlpool. ♠ Ute Hostel, 21 E. Kelsey Ave., 801) 595-1645. You'll meet tons of people. Perfect location, and they give you free coffee and tea. What more could you ask for? $15/room.

Where to Eat: ◐ Ruth's Diner, 2100 Emigration Canyon Rd., 801) 582-5807. You'll eat well in this high-mountain setting. Live music on certain nights. ◐ Bill and Nada's Cafe, 479 S. 6th East, 801) 359-6984. 24-hour diner with fab jukebox.

Night Life: ♪ The Bay, 404 S. West Temple Blvd. 801) 363-2623. There's no alcohol or smoking, but the dancing is wild. ♪ Squatter's Pub, 147 Broadway, 801) 363-2739. They brew their own beer here and they offer it until midnight. ♪ Bar X, 155 East 2nd S., 801) 532-9114. Neighborhood beer bar.

Adventures and Attractions: ◉ Museum of Church History and Art, 45 N. West Temple, 801) 240-3310. There is something for everyone. Mormon sites and descriptions of the 12 tribes of Israel. ◉ The Mormon Church Visitors' Center, Temple Square, 801) 240-3221. The world's headquarters for the Mormon faith. You can go see the Mormon Tabernacle Choir for free in this Salt Lake City skyscraper.

Sidetrip: ➔ Park City, 30 miles east of Salt Lake, 800) 222-PARK. Together with nearby Deer Valley, this is the largest ski resort in Utah. The place to ski

VERNAL: Chamber of Commerce: 134 W. Main, 84078, 801) 789-1352. Ashley National Forest Service: 355 N. Vernal Avenue, 84078, 801) 789-1181.

Where to Stay: ♠ Sage Motel, 54 W. Main St., 801) 789-1442. Big rooms and cable. ♠ Echo Campground in Dinosaur National Monument Quarry–Visitors' Center, 801) 789-2115. Not many campsites, but this one has a perfect area for looking at the night sky. Around $10/site. ♠ Campground Dina RV Park, 930 N. Vernal Ave., 801) 789-2148. Cheap. ✗♠ Dine-A-Ville Motel, 801 West US-40, 801) 789-9571. Look for the pink dinosaur out front.

Where to Eat: ◐ Ranch Restaurant, 77 E. Main St., 801) 789-1170. The prices here are unbelievable. You won't need to bring more than $5, and you'll leave full. ◐ Dine-A-Ville, 801 W. Main St., 801) 789-9571. Located on the west end of town. ◐ Open Hearth Donut Shop, 360 E. Main St., 801) 789-0274. Delicious donuts.

Adventures and attractions: ◉ Dinosaur National Monument Quarry, Visitors' Center, 7 miles from intersection of US-40 and Park Rd., 801) 789-2115. Enormous dinosaur bones that will blow you away. ◉ Utah Fieldhouse of Natural History and Dinosaur Garden, 235 E. Main St., 801) 789-3799. Life-size dinosaur models and cool fluorescent minerals. ◉ Dinosaur Roundup, 801) 789-1352. A July rodeo where dinosaurs once roamed.

Sidetrips: ➔ Ashley National Forest, north of Vernal on US-191, 801) 885-3135. Great biking and hiking trails. Swim in the beautiful Flaming Gorge Reservoir.

# WEST VIRGINIA

Nickname: "The Mountain State." Capital: Charleston. West Virginia Division of Parks and Tourism, 1900 Kanawha Blvd., East Bldg. 17, Charleston, 25305, 800) CALL-WVA.

## HICO

Where to stay: ♠ Mountain River Tours Campgrounds, Sunday Rd., 304) 658-5266. Shaded campsites at affordable prices.

Where to eat: ◐ Chef Dan's High Country Cafe, Rte. 60, 304) 658-4000.

Night Life: ♪ Rosie's Hideaway, off Rte. 19, on Smales Branch Road, 304) 658-5034. Small bar that's big on character.

Adventures and Attractions: ✗◉ Mountain River Tours, Sunday Rd., 304) 658-5266. Great rafting trips. Ask Mary to set you up on the ride of your life.

Sidetrips: ✗➔ Quantico, Virginia. Marine Corps. ➔ Air Ground Museum, 2014 Anderson Ave., in front of OCS, Quantico, 703) 784-2606. Hangars, airplanes, tanks, and other cool military stuff.

# WASHINGTON, D.C.

Washington, D.C., Convention and Visitors' Association: 1212 New York Ave. N.W., Suite 600, 20005, 202) 789-7000.

Where to Stay: ♠ Washington International Youth Hostel, 1009 11 St. NW, 202) 737-2333. Located right in the middle of the city. Rooms with several beds apiece, air-conditioning available. $18-$21/night. ♠ Allen Lee Hotel, 2224 F St. N.W., 202) 331-1224. Not known for its cushy ambiance, the Allen Lee is a great, cheap stay in a convenient location. Inexpensive. ✗♠ Holiday Inn, 10,000 Baltimore Blvd., College Park, MD, 301) 345-6700.

Where to Eat: ◐ Raku, 19th St. and Q, 202) 265-7258. Asian Diner. Most meals are under $10. Very hip decor, they play Godzilla movies while you eat. ◐ AV Ristorante, 607 New York Ave N.W., 202) 737-0550. Super-cheap, super-popular Italian place with size to match its popularity. ◐ Sarinah, 1338 Wisconsin Ave. N.W., 202) 337-2955. Delicious Indonesian food in a tropical atmosphere. ◐ Polly's, 1342 U St., 202) 265-8385. Veggie plates and burgers, mostly under $10.

Night Life: ♪ The great thing about going out in this city is that it's busiest right after the workday, so going out late is without hassle. ♪ Capital Ballroom, 1015 Half St. S.E., 703) 549-7625. The place to see alternative shows and popular local bands. Call ahead to see about

purchasing tickets. ✗♪ State of the Union, 1357 U St. N.W., 202) 588-8810. Dancing. ♪ 18th Street Lounge, 1212 18th St., 202) 466-3922. Top floor features live jazz band, the middle floor, acid jazz. Shorts are not allowed, cover varies. ♪ The 930 Club, 815 V St. N.W., 202) 265-0930. Concert venue for up-and-coming alternative bands. Minor Threat, Fugazi, and the Slicky Boys all started here. Usually has a low cover.

Adventures and Attractions: ◉ National Air and Space Museum, 601 Independence St. N.W., 202) 357-1300. This museum has lots of interactive displays that put APOLLO 13 (the movie) to shame. ◉ The Pentagon, 703) 695-1776. Hosts several guided tours a day. This mammoth building won't let you down–its square footage is three times that of the Empire State Building. ◉ Georgetown. If you love to shop, this is the place to go. ◉ The Mall, the mile-long stretch from the Capitol to the Potomac River. A great place to enjoy a picnic under the beautiful cherry trees–frequent live concerts.

Sidetrip: ➔ Great Falls, VA., 45 minutes outside the city on the Potomac. Bring your kayak. Rock climbing.

# WYOMING

Nickname: "The Cowboy State." Capital: Cheyenne. Division of Tourism: I-25 at College Dr., Cheyenne, 82002, 800) 225-5996.

Department of Commerce, State Parks, and Historical Sites Division: 6101 Yellowstone Rd., Cheyenne, 82002, 307) 777-6323.

GILLETTE: Chamber of Commerce: 314 S. Gillette Avenue, 82716, 307) 682-3673.

Where to Stay: ♠ Best Western Tower Lodge, 109 N. US-14-16, 307) 686-2210. Laundry room, bar, and weight room on premises. ♠ Green Tree Crazy Woman Campground, 1001 W. 2nd St., 307) 682-3665. Shaded campsites.

Where to Eat: ◐ Countryside Cafe, 10698 S. Highway 59, 307) 686-2358. Delicious home cooking. ◐ Humphrey's Bar and Grill, 408 W. Juniper, 307) 682-0100. Satisfies all appetites.

Night life: ♪ Boot Hill Night Club, 910 N. Gurley, 307) 686-6404. Live country music. ♪ Ghostwriters, in the National Nine Inn, 1020 East Hwy. 14-16, 307) 682-5111. New saloon with live country music.

Adventures and Attractions: ◉ Campbell County Recreation Center, 1000 Douglas Hwy., 307) 682-5470. Fly down the water slide or just relax in the pool.

Sidetrips: ✗➔ Devil's Tower National Monument, 60 miles east of Gillette, 307) 467-5283. It's worth it to see this giant mass formed by molten rock. CLOSE ENCOUNTERS OF THE THIRD KIND made this monument more popular than ever. ◉ Keyhole State Park, 50 miles east of Gillette, 307) 756-3596. On a clear day, you can see Devil's Tower. There's a huge reservoir for water sports, and camping is available. ➔ Hulett: Loggers & Ranchers Days, Sept., horse shows & cookouts. ♪ Rodeo Bar, 101 North Hwy. 24, Hulett, 307) 467-5959. Have a drink with the local cowboys, bikers, ranchers, and farmers. ♪ Ponderosa Bar, 115 Main St., Hulett, 307) 467-5335. Local hangout.

# Happy trails.

**THINK**

Drinking and Driving: From a bartender's perspective it is a very serious issue. I have seen the repercussions and they are scary. As a bartender, 90 percent of the time you can't stop it. I'll bet that only 50 percent of the people driving home from bars on a Saturday night are sober. Take it upon yourself to be the designated driver. It can be more fun to sit back and watch your friends make fools of themselves than to drink yourself, and you're guaranteed a sober and safe ride home.  **–TIMMY**

Drinking and driving: I don't do it, I don't believe in it. In Flora they call it Road Trippin' and they go out and drink and drive. One night I went out drinking and I came home and I had a dent in my car, but I had no idea what happened. That was the last time I ever drove tipsy—ever. It could have been much worse.  **–EMILY**

I think that all of us know someone, whether it be a friend or a friend of a friend, who has been killed in a drunk driving accident. That's the ultimate reality-check, and it's amazing to me that it still continues to happen when so many have been lost. I'm the biggest partier of all, but that's something I don't touch. I think, when you're young, it's not always easy to promote sober driving to your friends, and it can be hard to say, "No, I won't get in your car," or "I better sleep this one off before I drive," but it's the easiest thing in the world—if you listen to your common sense.  **–KIT**

# MEET THE ONLY ARMCHAIR TRAVEL GUIDE EQUIPPED WITH AN EJECT BUTTON.

BUY THIS VIDEO AND GET DISCOUNT COUPONS TO SKI TELLURIDE AND WHISTLER!

Ice climb a frozen waterfall in Colorado. Glide high above treetops in a Costa Rican cloud forest. Hurtle out of a helicopter and ski British Columbia. See it all—then get off the couch and do it yourself!

Journey to the edge of adventurous vacationing with Road Rules cast members Kit Hoover and Mark Long, who'll take you to four of the hottest and coolest spots in the Americas. And use the handy resource listings at the end to learn the secrets of planning your own outdoor odyssey.

©1996 MTV Networks/MTV: Music Television, its titles and logos are trademarks of Viacom International Inc. / MTV and Sony Music Video are trademarks.

This book was produced by Melcher Media
170 Fifth Avenue, New York, NY, 10010, 212) 727-2322

EDITORIAL DIRECTOR........................**Charles Melcher**
EDITOR.........................................**Genevieve Field**
DESIGNED BY.............................**Number Seventeen**
(ESPECIALLY BY)....................................**David Israel**
PHOTOGRAPHY EDITOR.........................**Russell Cohen**
MANAGER OF DEVELOPMENT, BUNIM/MURRAY...**Scott Freeman**
EDITORIAL ASSISTANT.....................**John-Ryan Hevron**
RESEARCH ASSISTANTS.......**Joy Cohen and Dina Richter**
MAP AND ICON ART....................................**Eric Zim**

SPECIAL THANKS TO: LORI Allred, LISA Berger, ERIN Bohensky, MARY-ELLIS
Bunim, LYNDA Castillo, GINA Centrello, ANITA Chinkes, OSCAR Creech, AMY
Einhorn, CHRISTINE Friebely, LISA Hackett, LISA Haskins, ANGELA Holcombe,
BRIAN Hueben, MAUREEN Jay, SHERYL Jones, GREER Kessel, OLIVER
Kurlander, MARK Kirschner, STEVEN Lichtenstein, ANDREA LaBate, SARAH
Malarkey, CLAIRE McCabe, JONATHAN Murray, DONNA O'Neill, CLAY Newbill,
ED Paparo, RENÉE Presser, DONNA Ruvituso, TAMBI Saffran-Stollman, MAGGIE
Shearman, LAURA Scheck, ROBIN Silverman, DONALD Silvey, LIATE Stehlik,
DAVID Terrien, VAN Toffler, STACEY Toyoaki, ELIZABETH Ward, KARA Welsh,
IRENE Yuss, ALLISON, CHRISTIAN, DEVIN, EFFIE, EMILY, KIT, LOS, MARK,
SHELLY, and TIMMY.

An Original publication of MTV Books / Pocket Books / Melcher Media

# Made in the USA

Pocket Books, a division of Simon & Schuster Inc.
1230 Avenue of the Americas, New York, NY 10020

Copyright © 1996 by MTV Networks. All rights reserved. MTV Music,
Road Rules, and all related titles, logos, and characters are trademarks of MTV Networks, a division of Viacom International Inc.

All rights reserved, including the right to reproduce this book or
portions thereof in any form whatsoever. For information address
Pocket Books, 1230 Avenue of the Americas, New York, NY 10020

ISBN: 0-671-00374-7

First MTV Books / Pocket Books / Melcher Media trade paperback
printing November 1996

**10    9    8    7    6    5    4    3    2    1**

Pocket and colophon are registered trademarks of Simon & Schuster Inc.